THE SCROLL OF SEDUCTION

TRANSLATED FROM THE SPANISH BY Lisa Dillman

rayo *An Imprint of* HarperCollins*Publishers*

THE
SCROLL
OF
SEDUCTION

A Novel

GIOCONDA BELLI

TO Lucía AND Lavinia,
MY SISTERS.

❉·❉·❉·❉·❉·❉·❉·❉

HarperCollins books may be purchased for educational, business, or sales pro-
motional use. For information, please write: Special Markets Department,
HarperCollins Publishers, 10 East 53rd Street, New York, NY 10022.

FIRST EDITION

Book design by Shubhani Sarkar

Library of Congress Cataloging-in-Publication Data has been applied for.

ISBN-13: 978-0-06-083312-1   ISBN-10: 0-06-083312-2

06 07 08 09 10 DIX/RRD 10 9 8 7 6 5 4 3 2 1

ACKNOWLEDGMENTS

Historical research for a novel like this owes a lot to others' work. I would like to express my gratitude for certain books that were absolutely essential in my reconstruction of the period and of Juana's life: Bethany Aram's extraordinary book, *La reina Juana* (Marcial Pons, Ediciones de Historia, S. A., 2001); Miguel Ángel Zalama's exhaustive, intellectual study, *Vida cotidiana y arte en el palacio de la reina Juana I en Tordesillas* (Universidad de Valladolid, 2003); Michael Pradwin's *Juana la Loca* (Editorial Juventud, 1953); Manuel Fernández Álvarez's *Juana la Loca, la cautiva de Tordesillas* (Espasa, 2000); and José Luis Olaizola's *Juana la Loca* (Editorial Planeta, 2002). I would also like to mention, of the many other books I consulted, Nancy Rubin's *Isabella of Castile* (St. Martin's Press, 1991), William Manchester's *A World Lit Only by Fire* (Little, Brown & Co., 1992), José Antonio Vallejo-Nájera's *Locos egregios;* Julia Kristeva's *Black Sun, Depression and Melancholia* (Columbia University Press, 1989); Michel Foucault's *Madness and Civilization* (Vintage Books, 1988); John Adamson's (ed.) *The Princely Courts of Europe* 1500–1750 (Weidenfeld & Nicolson, 1999); and Thomas Kren and Scott McKencrick's *Illuminating the Renaissance* (Getty Publications, 2003).

I would also like to sing the praises of the Internet, that fabulous source of data we now have at our disposal and which was invaluable to me for any number of diverse consultations. I want to thank Professor Teófilo Ruiz at UCLA for personal conversations as well as his The

Teaching Company lectures on the Catholic Monarchs of Spain; thanks also to Doctor Charles Hoge, Doctor Toni Bernay, and Doctor Iván Arango, for their contributions on Juana's illness.

I want to express very special thanks to my sister Lucía, who lent me not only her name for the protagonist of the novel, but also helped compile books and information from Madrid, where she lives. I thank her and my niece Teresa for their company on visits to different places where Juana lived in Spain, especially Tordesillas. I thank my sister Lavinia, my daughter Melissa, the tireless and indispensable Sergio Ramírez, Claribel Alegría, Anacristina Rossi, and my editors, Elena Ramírez, in Spain, and Rene Alegría at Rayo, HarperCollins, for their time, their advice, and their encouragement. To Bonnie Nadell and Guillermo Schavelzon, my agents in the United States and Spain, thank you for your support and enthusiasm for my work.

"... any woman born with a great gift in
the sixteenth century would certainly
have gone crazed, shot herself, or ended
her days in some lonely cottage outside
the village, half witch, half wizard,
feared and mocked at."

—VIRGINIA WOOLF,
A Room of One's Own

Manuel said he would tell me the story of the Spanish queen, Juana of Castile, and her mad love for her husband, Philippe the Handsome, but only if I agreed to certain conditions.

He was a professor at Complutense University. His specialty was the Spanish Renaissance. I was seventeen years old, a high school student, and from the age of thirteen, since the death of my parents in a plane crash, I had been at a Catholic boarding school run by nuns in Madrid, far from my small Latin American country.

Manuel's voice rose densely within me, like a surging tide on which floated faces, furnishings, curtains, the adornments and rituals from forgotten times.

"What conditions?" I asked.

"I want you to imagine the scenes I describe for you in your mind's eye, to see them and see yourself in them, to feel like Juana for a few hours. It won't be easy for you at first, but a world created with words can become as real as the shaft of light that at this moment illuminates your hands. It's been scientifically proven that whether we see a lit candle with our eyes open or imagine it with our eyes closed, the brain has an almost identical reaction. We can *see* with our minds and not just our senses. In the world I'll conjure up, if you accept my proposal, you will become Juana. I know the facts, the dates. I can place you in that world, in its smells and colors; I can make you feel its atmosphere. But my narration—because I'm a man and, what's worse, a rational, meticulous historian—can never capture—*I* can never capture—what's inside. No matter how I try, I can't imagine what Juana felt when she set off, at sixteen, on the armada's flagship, accompanied by one hundred and thirty-two vessels, to marry Philippe the Handsome."

"You said she didn't even know him."

"She'd never laid eyes on him. She disembarked in Flanders, escorted by five thousand men and two thousand ladies-in-waiting, to find that her fiancé was not at the port to meet her. I can't imagine how she felt, just as I can't begin to conceive of her innermost thoughts when she finally met Philippe at the monastery in Lierre and they fell so suddenly, so thoroughly, so violently in love that they asked to be married that very night, so anxious were they to consummate a marriage that had actually been arranged for reasons of State."

HOW OFTEN HAD MANUEL MADE REFERENCE TO THAT INITIAL meeting? Perhaps he enjoyed seeing me blush. I smiled to dissimulate. Although I had spent the last several years in a convent, surrounded by nuns, I could picture the scene. I had no trouble at all imagining what Juana must have felt.

"I see that you understand." Manuel smiled. "I just can't stop picturing that young woman—one of the most educated princesses in all of the Renaissance—who, after succeeding to the throne of Spain, was locked up in a palace at the age of twenty-nine and forced to remain there until she died, forty-seven years later. During her formative years she was tutored by one of the most brilliant female philosophers of the day, Beatriz Galindo, known as 'La Latina.' Did you know that?"

"It's sad to think that jealousy drove her insane."

"Well, that's what they said. And that's one of the mysteries you can help me unravel."

"I don't see how."

"By thinking like her, putting yourself in her place. I want you to let her story flood your consciousness. You're almost the same age. And, like her, you also had to leave your country and be on your own since you were very young."

✳ MY GRANDPARENTS DROPPED ME OFF AT THE BOARDING SCHOOL ONE September day in 1963. Although the stone building was austere and gloomy—high-walled, windowless, an imposing front door with an old coat of arms on the lintel—its solemnity perfectly suited my frame of mind. I walked down the tiled hallway and into the stillness of the reception area feeling that I was leaving behind a noisy world that in no way acknowledged the catastrophe that had cut short my childhood. Neither day nor night, countryside nor city, managed to register my sadness the way the silence of that convent did, with its one lone pine shading the tiny central garden that no one ever visited. Four years I had lived there resigned and uncomplaining. And though the other girls were pleasant toward me, they also kept a prudent distance, influenced, I think, by the tragedy that had thrust me in their midst. The nuns' good intentions surely contributed to my isolation. They must have told the other girls to be compassionate and sensitive toward me, to avoid doing anything to reopen my wounds or to further sadden me. They even refrained from talking about their family vacations and their home life in my presence, thinking, I imagine, that talking about their parents would make me miss mine. Their restraint coupled with my rather introverted nature and my initial unwillingness to discuss the issue of having suddenly become an orphan, dramatically reduced my possibilities of forging new and close friendships. What's more, I got good grades, and the nuns held me up as an example of the triumph of will against adversity, inadvertently widening the chasm that separated me from the others.

✳ "TO BE HONEST, I DON'T EXACTLY UNDERSTAND WHAT YOU EXPECT me to do. Of course I can speculate about what Juana might have felt, but she and I are centuries apart. We're the product of two different times. I don't see how you'll be able to deduce anything about her by my reactions."

"When it comes to feelings, what difference does time make?" he asked. I could read Shakespeare and Lope de Vega, the poetry of Góngora and Garcilaso, tales of chivalry, and still be moved by them. Time passed, settings changed, but the essence of passion, of emotions, of human relations, was surprisingly consistent.

"Think of this as making art, a piece of historical theater. After all, it won't be any different from what novelists do. They do their research and then try to inhabit the spirit of whoever lived through this or that historical event. The works of literature, painting, even music are but attempts of the human imagination to recapture emotions, bygone eras. And sometimes the result, the intensity and correspondence that is achieved, cannot be explained rationally. One reads descriptions of the creative process written by the authors themselves and inevitably there will be the passage where they talk about the mystery of being "possessed" by their characters, or by something inexplicable. There are those who compare inspiration to a trance and swear that when they write they feel as if they were taking dictation, or experiencing visions that all they had to do was put down on paper. Classical works are still current because essentially we're caught up in the same dramas, reliving the same stories. You might think more openly about love because you'll never be forced to marry anyone for reasons of State, but when you fall in love, the way you will experience that attraction won't be so different from Juana's. Let's just say, if you like, that you'll be closer to feeling what she felt than I can ever hope to be."

"You're very persuasive." I smiled. "But you talk as if you were trying to convince me to board a time machine. You're just going to tell me a story, after all. If you do it well, I won't have any trouble imagining it. I have an active fantasy life. So at least I can try."

"It's not just about me, you know . . . there are those mysteries that concern you too, that you would like to see revealed . . . the issue of jealousy, for example. It could give you a better understanding of it."

IN A FEW SHORT MONTHS, MANUEL HAD GOTTEN TO KNOW ME QUITE well. I had met him in the spring, on my grandparents' last trip to Madrid. I remember I was wearing an English woolen suit and an Hermès scarf—a present from my grandmother. I first saw him in the hotel's lobby as I paced up and down, waiting for my grandparents to come down from their room. He looked like a character from another time. His hair was completely white. His skin was also so light it was almost transparent, and he had dark, thick eyebrows and blue eyes that seemed to contrast with his full, pink lips. He was sitting with his legs crossed in one of the damask armchairs under the lobby's art nouveau dome, smoking with relish. His peculiar coloring, and the way he inhaled smoke from his cigarette, caught my attention. Later he told me that he had noticed me too. It was unusual in Madrid, he said, to see a young woman who combined a tropical café aut lait complexion with a tall, Nordic build. It wasn't the first time I'd heard that. I knew that at five eight I was striking, though I considered myself rather ungraceful, giraffelike. I even thought my eyes—large and melancholic—resembled those of that animal. When I sat down in one of the easy chairs in the lobby, he smiled at me with the knowing look of people who wait impatiently at train stations or airports. Finally, my grandmother emerged from the elevator and behind her, my grandfather. He was a handsome man in his seventies who seemed protected by an impenetrable self-assurance. He walked slightly hunched over, as if trying to make up for the difference in height between him and his wife. My grandmother was short, and she always walked very erect, with a learned elegance that appeared forced and struck those who didn't know her as arrogance. She wore a beige suit and she'd had her hair done at a salon. Her face softened when she saw me. My grandfather took me by the shoulders and looked me over before giving me a kiss. It was a typical gesture of his, but I couldn't help thinking he was trying to ascertain whether the time had come for them to stop worrying about me. After my grandparents and I embraced, Manuel walked up and introduced himself. He was the person that the agency had sent to take us on a private tour of El Escorial. He wore a navy blue, Burberry raincoat and a plaid scarf, and I remember noticing he smoked Ducados. He escorted us to his car, a polished, black Seat. During the trip he and my grandparents made comparisons between General Francisco Franco's dictatorship and the one we'd endured in our country. While my grandparents took in the sights from the back seat, he turned to ask me about my favorite subjects at school, my impression of Madrid, if I had many friends. It was during that conversation when I found out he was a university professor and that his research was on Juana the Mad and Philippe the Handsome. He asked me if I had any knowledge of those historical figures. Not much, I replied.

Wasn't Juana the queen that went mad with love? So says the legend, he said, sighing in resignation. The real story lent itself to other interpretations, but few were willing to delve into it. Juana was the mother of Emperor Charles I of Spain and V of Germany, on whose empire it was said the sun never set. Therefore, she was also the grandmother of Philippe II, the king who ordered the construction of El Escorial, which we were on our way to visit.

To be honest with him, I said, keeping track of so many queens and kings was confusing for me. He laughed. But Juana was very special, he said, very special indeed.

"You look like her. She was a brunette too, with black hair, like you," he said. "I have never seen such an uncanny resemblance before."

I guessed that Manuel was probably about forty. He said he'd been orphaned when he was young too. His mother's sister, Águeda, was the only family he had left. And although he was there to give my grandparents and me a private tour (during which I caught a glimpse of his erudition), it turned out he was no tourist guide. The man who was supposed to accompany us was a friend of his. Something had come up, he explained, so he was doing him a favor by standing in.

I HAD BEEN TO EL ESCORIAL SHORTLY AFTER I ARRIVED IN SPAIN, with a guide who hurried us through all the salons. It was a totally different experience this time, seeing the palace with a history professor who not only knew all about Philippe II and the period he and his ancestors lived in, but who also seemed somehow to feel transported back to that period, sweeping us along with the fervor of his gestures, the deep, mellifluous tone of his voice. I even found Manuel's erudition moving. He seemed to regret not living in the fifteenth and sixteenth centuries and being limited to having to conjure that period with his imagination. As I watched him, standing in front of the portrait of Philippe the Handsome, in the shaft of light falling from the window, I had the disturbing sensation that there was a physical resemblance between the two. It was there, next to that painting, that he told us about Juana and Philippe's first meeting. And the way he spoke, it was as if he had borne witness to the instantaneous, irrepressible love that drove them to consummate their marriage that very night. My grandmother must have noticed his intensity, because she interrupted him to ask about the sedan chair on display near the portrait. He explained that it was the same chair in which Philippe II made his last journey from Madrid to the palace, after he had fallen ill. Then Manuel told us about Philippe II's diseases, his gout, his religious devotions, his four wives, who all died one after the other. The king practiced self-flagellation, he said, and wore a crown of thorns. He made love to his wives through a sheet that had one crucial hole cut in it, to insure procreation. He made his wives recite the rosary while they had intercourse. He begged for the Almighty's forgiveness for any pleasure that might slip in between the linen and the darkness. (My grandmother stared at the floor, my grandfather at me, as if to apologize for the guide not censoring his language in front of a young lady such as myself, but the professor was oblivious, lost in his own world, swept away by the passion of his own tale.)

Before she left for London, my grandmother gave me a stack of old papers I had asked for, which had come from my mother's desk. When my parents died, I went with Mariíta, our old housekeeper, to clear out the house. Even though she had begged me," child, let me take care of all this, there's no need for you to go through all that pain," I insisted on being there, along with the housekeepers temporarily on loan for the occasion from my aunts and uncles. I was there when they cleared out the closets, emptied the bookshelves, kitchen cabinets, desk drawers, and nightstands. People's lives are full of papers, and I insisted on keeping the ones we found scattered around the house. "Your grandfather already has the insurance policies and the deeds. No one told me what to do with the other papers. Who am I to say no, if you want to save them for when you're older," Mariíta said. I had no trouble going through the clothes, shoes, belts, and scarves and sorting out the things I thought I might want one day, and putting the rest in boxes to take to the Sisters of Charity, but I could not force myself to look at my mother's precise calligraphy or my father's handwriting without bursting into tears and feeling overcome by sorrow. Now, almost five years later, I felt prepared to do it. I read through those papers at boarding school, in the silent dormitory where I had a small bedroom with an iron bed, an armoire, a sink, a chair, and a high window overlooking the trees in the garden, their new leaves resplendent in the fresh, spring air. My first years there I had slept in a large dormitory with a hallway separating the cubicles on either side, which were closed by starched white curtains. A nun woke us up every day at seven o'clock, clapping loudly. After a few minutes, she would rush from cubicle to cubicle, jerking back the curtains to make sure we had gotten out of bed and were standing before our sinks. It was a routine more suited to military barracks and it never ceased to unsettle me. Luckily, the previous year, I had been moved to a room of my own. It was like going from a boardinghouse to a five-star hotel. Because I suffered from insomnia, and in light of my tragic circumstances, Mother Luisa Magdalena, who was in charge of the dormitory as well as the infirmary, had given me permission to leave my light on at night until I was able to fall asleep.

My hands were cold when I opened the bundle of documents while sitting on the bed in my pajamas, the bedspread pulled up over my legs. I could hardly contain the anxiety I felt about revisiting the gulf that separated my life into a before and after. I pulled out five manila envelopes and a few books. I smiled when I saw Dr. Stella Cerruti's *Human Sexuality* among them. These were books my mother had kept under lock and key so they didn't fall into my hands. I could almost hear her: "Your time will come; right now you're still too young." I wondered if she ever knew I had learned how to open her desk drawer by slipping a knife behind the bolt. That was how I read Aldous Huxley's *Brave New World* as well as that book on sexuality, full of black-and-white cross-section illustrations of male and female genitalia. For fear of being caught, especially with that book—which seemed like a bigger transgression than Huxley at the time—I only managed to read the section on coitus. Back then, I was dying to know what it was that people did on the famous "wedding night;" my friends and I used to speculate all the time. From the feelings that were beginning to awaken in my own body, I was sure it had something to do with the body part that my mother called *down there.* "Don't touch yourself *down there,*" "Make sure to wash *down there.*" I was sure that the secret goings-on between men and women that were never named but were implied by "sleeping with a man" had to do with couples somehow joining up at the crotch. What I couldn't figure out, though, was how they managed to pull off the intricate stunt required in order for the whole operation to work. I knew nothing about erections, so the only way I could imagine it happening was if either the man or woman lay down on his or her side and slid down, legs spread at an angle, until locking into the genital embrace which—by virtue of its position—would make it impossible for their faces to be anywhere near each other. All in all, it seemed like an excruciating, uncomfortable, as well as unpleasant phenomenon devoid of all romance, although I tried desperately to make sense of it, sketching countless naked men and women in my notebook. Once I learned that blood rushes to the penis, causing it to inflate like a tire so that it can penetrate the vagina, I wondered what pleasure could possibly be found in *that*. It did, though, seem more practical, and it explained the horizontal position one most often saw in drawings of naked couples. I laughed when I pulled out that book, recalling my childish naïveté.

One by one I emptied the manila envelopes onto the bed and sifted through the contents, separating the remnants of everyday life (receipts from the laundry and other services) from things like letters, notes, and annotations. In among the subscription receipts, invitations to birthday parties from my friends, telephone numbers jotted on blank cards, and snapshots of me as a little girl, I saw a postcard that my mother's Colombian friend Isis, who lived in New York, had sent from Italy. I was struck by her tone. "You should have come with me. It would have done you good." At my parents' funeral, Isis stuck right by my side the whole time. She cried more than anyone in my family. Her head just kept convulsing, and she kept apologizing for having insisted that my mother come visit her in New York. "I had no idea the plane would crash, Lucía, I'm so sorry." Isis wanted me to come live with her. She only had one daughter. She said I could go to a girls' school in New York and then to college at Columbia. She would try to raise me the way my mother would have wanted. I loved Isis. I had always called her "*tía*"—auntie—and I was used to seeing her around the house; she'd come for weeks and stay in the guest room. But my grandparents had other plans. They thanked her politely for the offer but did not accept. The two of them had already discussed it and decided to send me to Spain. They didn't think the United States was the best environment for an adolescent. American society was too liberal, and they didn't approve of its values, which they considered excessively materialistic. Isis realized there was no point arguing. When I said good-bye to her at the airport, she told me to call her whenever I wanted. Maybe my grandparents would at least let me come spend the holidays with her. And when I turned eighteen and finished high school, then I could make my own decisions, she said. By that time, my grandparents probably wouldn't object if I decided to go to college in New York. When I felt nostalgic and homesick, I toyed with her offer, but I wasn't free-spirited enough to disobey my grandparents. To do that I would have needed more of a motive than the desire to feel at home again, to feel like someone's daughter again; after all, it would have been just an illusion. I found a thick stack of letters from Isis, others from my maternal grandfather, index cards with dates and captions that made no sense to me, and two spiral notebooks full of scribbles. The papers from the first group, though they were insignificant, had a sort of archaeological value: they allowed me to reconstruct my mother's daily life and gave me insights into what was involved in running the house. Looking through them, I could picture her sitting at her writing desk after I had gone to school, paying bills, making shopping lists, figuring out what to eat that week, what had to be taken to the dry cleaner's. Those documents, more than anything, seemed to bear witness to the way her life was suddenly cut short, to all that remained undone, those errands and chores that were undertaken mechanically but with a sense of continuity that could be seen in her innocent notes: tell gardener to spray ferns, take Ernesto's suit to the tailor. Tears rolled silently down my cheeks as I read through them. But it was no longer the disconsolate, desperate sobbing it had once been. Now I cried sad tears, old tears. My mother's writing took on the strange, disembodied aspect of an old manuscript or a work of art in a museum, when the artist's life seems so remote it's hard to imagine that person holding the brush in a distant past.

NEXT I READ ISIS'S LETTERS AND THE OBSERVATIONS IN THE spiral-bound notebooks. As soon as I came across the first sentence alluding to the problems tormenting my mother, my mouth went dry. I was tempted to stop, but my curiosity won out. And I plunged headfirst into the drama that the letters and endless index cards allowed me to reconstruct. Isis was skeptical at first; incredulous at the letter my mother must have written her in which she told about a series of anonymous phone calls—a woman's voice—she had received detailing my father's infidelity. Why would he waste his time with that sort of thing? Isis wanted to know. But in subsequent letters, she consoled her, because apparently my mother was certain, and Isis talked about "the proof" and begged my mother to make sure it was incontrovertible, because things could be falsified, jealousy could make people turn remarkably cruel. Then there were letters, all dated close together, in which Isis begged my mother not to act rashly, to keep her cool, and to realize that she was an extraordinary woman, not to fall prey to insecurity, to confront my father. Next Isis commented on my mother's obsessive detective work, the results of which I now had before me: dates, places, things she had found in his pockets, words he had said to her and that were jotted down in the notebook, jumbled together with painful comments my mother made to herself: halfway down the page, the question "My God, what is wrong with me?" or "I'm going mad." The words *mad* and *crazy* scribbled repeatedly in the margins, beside the name "Ernesto," with the *o* retraced again and again in graphite pencil. Isis insisting that she forget about it. It was just a passing phase, it wouldn't last. It happened to plenty of men. It didn't mean that Ernesto didn't love her. She had to relax, let it pass. Then came the idea of a little getaway, taking him to another city, seducing him, making him fall in love all over again. My mother had seen the other woman. Young. Pretty. You're pretty too, Isis said, you're gorgeous and you always have been. And more notes: "E. came home at 11 P.M. He reached for me. I couldn't do it. I couldn't. I hate him. How could he?" Isis insisting on the trip. The letters becoming less frequent. Complaints about my mother not writing back. "Celia, please, I am so worried. If you don't come see me, I'm coming to see you. Write to me. *Please.*"

I didn't sleep at all that night. Mother Luisa Magdalena knocked on my door early the next morning. She found me in such a state that she left and came back with a cup of thick hot chocolate that she made me drink as she sat beside me, rearranging her purple habit and glancing down curiously at the piles of papers stacked up on the floor. "They're letters and things from my mother." "Ah," she replied. She asked if I didn't think it was better to let my mother rest in peace rather than rummaging through things she wouldn't have wanted me to see. "She is in peace," I said. "There's nothing I can do to disturb her now, and it's been a revelation for me. It's unbelievable, the way you can live with a man and woman your whole life, love them and be loved by them, and not know anything about them. Anything at all," I said. She said it was natural. I was so young when they died.

Mother Luisa Magdalena was tall and thin, and she had long features that made her look harsh and stern. She hardly ever smiled, and the girls respected her because she had a way of imposing her authority categorically, but without saying a word, just a glance was enough. When I was new at the school, I was afraid of her. One morning I woke up with a fever and she came to take my temperature. Before she left, she bent over me, stroked my head, and smoothed the sheets. Her affectionate touch unlocked the place where I stored dusty memories of hugs and kisses, terms of endearment. After she left, I was wracked by an overwhelming nostalgia and sobbed disconsolately. It occurred to me that behind her stern facade, Mother Luisa Magdalena was in need of love too. I ended up crying for both of us. I stopped being afraid of her that day. I became affectionate toward her. It changed our relationship. We became friends.

"It must be so hard for you, growing up without your parents," she said, "and yet you never talk about it. I sometimes wonder how you do it. You must be very strong. I lost my mother when I was seventeen and my religious vocation was like a refuge to me, my only consolation. I entered the convent when I was nineteen; now I'm fifty-four."

I remember how she reacted when I asked her if she regretted it. She smiled. She said that at first she'd thought she wouldn't make it. She missed music, and the hustle and bustle of the streets. She said that reading Santa Teresa of Ávila had been her salvation. She was a passionate woman who had found her beloved in Jesus Christ.

✳ THE WOMAN WHO I GLIMPSED BENEATH MOTHER LUISA MAGDALEna's habit persuaded me to tell her about my discovery and even show her some of my mother's index cards. I couldn't keep it closed up, couldn't contain the anger and the confusion I felt. I didn't understand why my mother would have chosen to live with the anguish and anxiety that her notes and letters betrayed rather than leave my father. It would have been less painful, and then she wouldn't have taken that trip to rekindle the flame in her marriage. And if they hadn't taken the trip, I would still have my parents, divorced but alive.

"Loving Christ must be very safe," I said. "There's no jealousy, no risk of being disillusioned. I can't believe my father did that to my mother. My dad was so sweet to me, but obviously he made my mother suffer endlessly. She was insanely jealous. I can't believe something like that happened between them. I always thought they loved each other so much."

"Well, I'm not the one to tell you about jealousy, my child," Mother Luisa Magdalena said, smiling sadly, "but in Spain we once had a queen who was so jealous she lost her mind. . . ."

I must have started. What a coincidence: even the nun was thinking about her!

"Juana the Mad," I said.

"Do you know her story?"

"A little. But I know someone who knows all the details."

"Well, you'd like the story. I don't know any specifics and I think a lot of what people say is more invention than anything else, but that was a very sad time in our history. Juana was supposed to be queen when her mother, Isabella of Castile died, but instead they locked her up in a town called Tordesillas, near Valladolid. They say her husband's love affairs drove her mad. When I was a little girl, my parents took me to the Santa Clara Monastery, where Philippe the Handsome's coffin was kept for some years. It made a big impact on me, hearing about that queen, locked up in a castle for so many years, and about her daughter Catalina, who grew up there. She slept in a tiny, dark room next to her mother's. At some point they opened a window for her so she could watch the children play below."

"Was Juana's husband unfaithful or did she imagine it?"

"They say he was unfaithful, but they also say that the two of them fell madly in love at first sight, and that they loved each other passionately. They had six children. Catalina was born after her father's death. There's a book by Michael Pradwin about her in the library here. I could get it for you if you like."

EVENTUALLY I SHARED WITH MANUEL WHAT I HAD LEARNED ABOUT my parents and how my whole life's memories changed because of what had happened between them. Queen Juana's plight became a reference point for me. I gravitated to her story, seduced by her anguish and the consequences her tragedy had for Spain. According to Manuel, the country's destiny changed forever because of her.

"SO HOW ARE WE GOING TO CONJURE UP JUANA'S SPIRIT? WITH A Ouija board?" I asked, in jest.

He didn't smile back. Sitting opposite me, he leaned forward, elbows on his knees, staring insistently. I straightened up in my chair and glanced back over at the closed window.

"I don't know if you know anything about dream catchers, little nets that are woven and used by Native Americans to trap dreams. Well, I suggest we make one. I have a dress made in the style of the time. I want you to dress like Juana. I want you to imagine yourself in her place as I tell you the story, identify with her passion, her confusion. Some people make intricate time machines in order to travel to other times. What I'm proposing is a trip that requires nothing more complicated than silk and velvet. And through my words, she'll come to you and we'll both get to know her. I don't know why, but ever since I first saw you, I was sure that you'd be able to understand her. Not a moment goes by when I'm with you that I don't feel her presence near me."

I STARED AT HIM, NOT KNOWING WHAT TO SAY. THE IDEA BOTH attracted and scared me. I already knew for sure that Manuel's voice would be able to transport me to another reality. It was like a current, and time swam in it, untroubled. He talked about the past the way people talk about the present. My maternal grandfather had been like that: a fabulous storyteller who had fanned the flames of my imagination since I was a little girl. I thought about Scheherazade and the caliph and how she saved her life by spinning tales. I wondered what Manuel thought he would get out of it. I was well aware of the power of words; after all, words were what had led me there, to that strange proposal, that afternoon.

LESS THAN A WEEK AFTER OUR VISIT TO EL ESCORIAL, I GOT A LETter from Manuel. It was late afternoon when Mother Cristina handed me a letter postmarked from within Spain. I didn't recognize the writing. Through the flimsy, white envelope I could see the colors of a photograph. In the afternoons, the nuns passed out squares of chocolate with slices of baguette. I had never tried bread and chocolate together before coming to Spain, but ever since that first day when I followed the other girls' example, placing the chocolate between two pieces of bread like a sandwich and biting into it, I fell in love with the combination. It was delicious, and I usually ate mine sitting on a bench behind some bushes, next to the niche with the Virgin Fatima statuette. Rather than play basketball with the rest of the girls, I liked to spend that time of the afternoon reading. And that afternoon in particular I put the envelope in my pocket and took several pieces of bread and chocolate to my little spot. When I ripped open the envelope, I found a postcard. It was a reproduction of a fifteenth-century painting of a young woman with delicate features, her hair parted down the middle. It was Juana of Castille as painted by Juan de Flandes in 1497. Disconcerted, I read the back of the card.

"*Lucía, Juana of Castille was sixteen years old when she married Philippe the Handsome. She felt lonely in Flanders, like you do. She was far from her family. Let me know if you need anything in Madrid. Feel free to write to me at this address: calle San Bernardo, 28, 4°, Madrid, 00267. Warm regards, Manuel de Sandoval y Rojas.*"

✳ I ANSWERED HIS LETTER THE VERY SAME DAY. I WROTE DURING study period that night. After nine o'clock, the nuns had what they called their "great silence," they only spoke if it was strictly necessary. We were supposed to keep quiet too while we sat in the big hall at tables lining the rectangular, high-ceilinged room with its tall windows. Mother Sonia, who was in charge of supervising us, sat behind a desk on a dais in front of the blackboard. At regular intervals, perhaps marked by the time it took her to recite the rosary, counting the polished, olive-pit beads that hung from her waist, the nun would get up and wander slowly up and down the rows of girls. Her footsteps were almost silent, as if she were levitating, but the coarse material of her habit as she moved, her rosary beads clicking against one another, and the overpowering smell of wool that trailed behind her were like the wake of a huge ship gliding stealthily through the sound of turning pages and pencils scratching on paper.

I did my homework, finished my reading, and then began my letter. I wrote carefully, taking care to make sure my handwriting was neat and well rounded. I used a piece of lined cardboard under the onionskin paper to keep my lines straight. The whole process gave me great pleasure. I don't know how I ended up writing so much just to thank Manuel for his postcard. I filled page after page, telling him about myself, taking great delight in creating a text. In spite of my age, I felt mature, as if my suffering and orphanage had granted me a higher level of understanding than one might surmise from my biography. I wanted to know more about Juana, I said. I was captivated by the idea that the queen in the portrait and I were almost the same age and that, despite all our differences, we both might have felt the same loneliness. Mine, as an only child, was always strewn with characters out of books, or the ones I'd invent to keep me company from a very early age, I said. Even though I'd had to adapt to another culture, in my case, leaving home—where my parents' absence would have been palpable and unbearable—was a form of salvation. I was also interested in Juana's tragedy, the love she felt for Philippe the Handsome, and her jealousy, I added toward the end.

By ten thirty, when Mother Sonia clapped her hands to let us know it was time to go to bed, I had written seven pages. Back in my room, I spent a long time staring into my mother's silver mirror, imagining that she could see me in the reflection of my eyes. Maybe through Juana I could come to understand what she had gone through. It struck me as providential that Manuel had written to me just then, when thoughts of my parents were hounding me night and day.

❋ THE NEXT DAY I SIGNED OFF, SEALED THE ENVELOPE, STAMPED IT, and took it to Rosario, the doorwoman and caretaker who was in charge of posting our letters. That was the beginning of a correspondence that introduced me to a life of risk and adventure, one that I embraced with a passion even I myself didn't comprehend. I supposed it was because no man had ever shown any interest in me before, and at my age I was just beginning to imagine what it must feel like, or maybe because it was the first chance I'd ever had to express myself to anyone who knew nothing about my family situation, whose opinion of me would be based solely on me and whatever I did or didn't say. As I wrote, I imagined the impact my words would have on my correspondent: I pictured him outside, in the hustle and bustle of the metro, going about his daily business, reading my letters as he had a cup of coffee or a glass of wine in some local bar. I felt like a castaway, sending messages in colored bottles and tossing them out to sea.

I realized as I walked down the hall on my way back to the room that few things in the last few years had given me as much pleasure as writing to him. I liked the way my neat, round calligraphy looked on the paper; I liked trying to imagine the person my words would conjure up in Manuel's mind. When I stepped back and disassociated myself from the letter, I had to admit I liked the girl portrayed in my digressions.

I imagined Rosario carrying the mail to the box on the corner, my letter slipping through the slot and dropping onto a dark pile of envelopes at the bottom.

Manuel wrote back immediately, charmed and impressed by my maturity.

But he didn't just write.

✳ "WAS THAT WHY YOU SENT THAT POSTCARD TO ME AT SCHOOL?" I asked apprehensively. "Because you thought I could help you get to know Juana?"

"I don't know what I thought, Lucía," he said kindly, softly, taking my hand. "I liked how smart you were, your interest in history. I suspected you'd have a lot in common with Juana." He smiled. "I teach the Renaissance at college, but I don't often meet girls of your age who show much curiosity in what they're studying. Besides, I have to cover Juana's entire life in one class. Even though I'd love to dedicate more time to her the syllabus does not allow it. I thought instead that you might share my interest."

"You know, it's funny, after you mentioned her, her name came up in a conversation I had with Mother Luisa Magdalena about my mother's jealousy."

"That's not surprising, Lucía. Ask anyone. Ideas have magnetic properties, thoughts attract other thoughts, they lead to sudden revelations and inexplicable coincidences. To some extent, we've all had that sort of experience, those apparent coincidences."

Manuel got up to make coffee. I watched him maneuver around in his tiny kitchen. It felt so natural to me, now, to be there with him. But if it hadn't been for a whole series of events, we might never have met and there might not have been another chance for us to become friends. There was no doubt that he was the one who had orchestrated our encounter. The Sunday after our trip to El Escorial I bumped into him down the street from my school.

✳ THAT DAY I HAD WOKEN UP WITH A MIGRAINE. MOTHER LUISA Magdalena found me doubled up in bed. She tucked me in, gave me a few drops of Cafergot. She had been nice to me all week, considerate and attentive. It was her way of trying to console me for something that neither of us could do anything about. In the early afternoon she brought me lunch and stayed, sitting with me for a while. The hot soup and medicine started to have an effect. They were soothing, and I began to feel better. She suggested that I take a bath and then go for a short walk before it got dark. The bakery would still be open, she said, winking. She was very observant. She knew I always came back on Sundays with a selection of pastries.

I took a long shower. On weekends there was never any fear of running out of hot water after everyone had bathed, since so many girls went home then. So I used that time to wash my hair, scrub my hands and feet with a pumice stone, shave my legs, and just wallow in the pleasure of water running down my naked body. Over the four years I'd been there my body had undergone tremendous changes, and I had watched the process, startled and thrilled at the same time. My breasts began to take shape almost overnight, two raised mounds crowned with large, light pink nipples. From a size 32A at thirteen, I had gone to a 36C. My pubis, which had been smooth and hairless when I arrived in Spain, was now entirely covered with curly, wiry, black hair. My waist had become slightly more defined, though not much. I would never be one of those women with dramatic, voluptuous curves. My hips were narrow and my legs were skinny, though I did have a nice, round bottom. I didn't know if I'd grow any more before I turned eighteen, but I prayed to God I wouldn't; I already felt like a giant. The thing I liked most about my body was my flat stomach; my belly button was so deep and tiny that the only way I could clean it—as part of my weekly ritual—was by using a cotton swab that went almost halfway in before hitting the end. And for some inexplicable reason, whenever I did that, I felt a tickling sensation in my rectum.

After the shower, I felt less dazed and sluggish. I powdered my face and put on some eyeliner. On my way out, I crossed paths with Margarita, one of the other boarders. She was just coming in, walking through the foyer—which was decorated with Talavera ceramic tiles—wearing a plaid, pleated skirt and carrying a few packages. Margarita was a tall, childlike girl from Guatemala; she had a big heart and we got along well.

She was also good at telling jokes and knew how to make me laugh. She seemed surprised to see me. That morning, Mother Luisa Magdalena had told her I was sick.

"I see you're feeling better." She smiled.

"It didn't last long. I had a headache, a migraine. But it's almost gone now. I'm just going to the bakery and coming right back."

To get there I had to walk up the narrow steep street that intersected with Atocha, by the Antón Martín metro stop. The school was in one of Madrid's oldest neighborhoods, close to the train station, the botanical gardens, and the Lavapiés district. It was almost the end of May and the days were getting longer. But at that time of the afternoon—a little after five—there weren't many people wandering about. In Spain people ate lunch at two or three, so most of them were either finishing up their extended Sunday lunches or having a siesta. The cool wind blew in my face. I walked past Castilian-style buildings in the bright afternoon air, looking up at the wrought iron balconies that stuck out at regular intervals. The street level of what had once been stately homes were now shops, businesses, and bars. Regardless of whether it was sunny or overcast, there was always a sorrowful air on that street. Probably because just in the stretch next to the school there was a convent of cloistered nuns, cut off from the rest of the world for life, a hospital with high walls and gloomy architecture, and the municipal morgue. I had stopped absent-mindedly to look at a pair of shoes in the window of a small store when I heard a voice beside me.

"I can't believe it! What a marvelous coincidence."

When I looked up I saw Manuel. He was wearing the same clothes as the last time I'd seen him, and he was carrying a portfolio. I remember I stood there looking at him, not knowing what to say, not daring to think he might have been hanging around hoping to see me, though it was hard to believe he was actually there by chance. His friend Genaro lived nearby, he said by way of explanation. He was the man who was supposed to have been our guide at El Escorial, the reason why we had met in the first place. Manuel said he was returning some papers to him. Then he asked me which direction I was headed. As soon as I recovered from my shock I told him I was just going to the bakery and then back to school. He offered to escort me, and we started up the street. He was smoking with relish and looking around as if he'd never taken a Sunday stroll in his life. He told me he spent most weekends reading in his aunt's library or assembling models of some sort. He was a big fan of models and jigsaw puzzles. He did not enjoy the multitudes wandering aimlessly like robots summoned by an invisible command to have fun. Instead, I loved going out on Sundays, I said. The school was like a fortress, and being locked up in there made it hard to remember the city even existed. That day, though, my headache had kept me in bed. "Poor thing," he said gently, placing his right hand lightly on my back for just a second. "Wouldn't you be better off staying away from pastries?" I smiled. On the contrary, I said, the sugar would do me good. The way I saw it, just walking into the bakery was a delight. After all, the nun who was taking care of me had been the one to suggest it. Desserts, chocolates, sweets, were my weakness. What I missed most from my country was a thick guava jelly that we used to eat at breakfast. My grandparents had a guava tree in their garden, and it smelled incredible. "You'll have to teach me about tropical fruits. I'm sorry to say I've never even seen a guava." When we crossed the street, Manuel put his hand on my back again, near the shoulder. "I really enjoyed your letter," he said. "You write very well. I forget how young you are when I hear you talk, and I forgot it even more when I read your letter. Your observations are very wise."

We had reached the bakery. Old women in mourning, wearing thick black stockings and clunky black shoes, were clustered around the counter. The owner greeted me as I walked in. The smell of honey and cookies was wafting in from the oven. I chose my standard treats. Manuel was looking up at a stack of guava paste boxes and asked the baker to get one down. (Those are very expensive, Manuel, I said, getting close to him.) He made the owner open a box so he could see the block of cellophane-wrapped guava paste inside. He raised it to his face and sniffed, and then held it to my nose. I breathed in and then sighed. The smell of the fruit reached my lungs despite all the packaging. I couldn't persuade him not to buy it, even after I told him that in my country it was never prepared in a thick, densely flavored bar. "That's how they eat it in Cuba, with pieces of cheese," the owner said. "It's exquisite. Come on, sweetheart, you'll love it. Let him treat you if he wants to. You deserve it." Manuel wouldn't let me pay for anything. After all, didn't I realize that fate, by placing him on my street that day, demanded that he celebrate our fortuitous, unexpected encounter?

Besides the surprise of meeting him by chance, the memory of that day brought back to me the way he took my arm as we left the bakery. He leaned so close to me that I got chills down my neck. He seemed not to be particularly aware of personal space, and I didn't feel like he was doing it to provoke a reaction but more like a clumsy child, unaware of the effect of his earnest gestures.

When we got to the entrance of my school he made me promise to write to him again and then kissed me good-bye on the cheek. I stood there for a little while after he'd left, waving as I watched him walk down the street.

✳ "HE MUST HAVE BEEN HANGING AROUND ALL DAY WAITING TO SEE you," said Margarita, smiling maliciously. We were the only ones at dinner on Sundays. "It's hard to believe in 'coincidences' like that. You're so lucky: you hardly ever leave this place and yet you've managed to find yourself a boyfriend."

"Boyfriend? You've got quite an imagination, Margarita."

"Hey, let me try that guava paste. In Guatemala we eat it with cheese or cream, like in Cuba."

We didn't have any cheese or cream, but we spread it on our bread. And we savored it, as if little pieces of our childhoods, our distant countries, were dissolving on our tongues.

✳ "NOW THAT WE KNOW EACH OTHER BETTER, MANUEL, TELL ME. That day we met on the street by the school, was that merely chance or were you lurking around, waiting for me to appear?"

"Well, I *did* go there thinking of you. But I never thought I'd see you. I have to admit, though, that when I bumped into you I felt like there was more than just a coincidence behind it."

"Do you believe in telepathy?"

"Telepathy? Everything in the world is related, it all interacts. Telepathy is just a manifestation of that interaction, of the interconnect-edness of the world. Reality is both more complex and more malleable than it seems. And so is time. Which is why I think you'll be able to intuit Juana's innermost thoughts and feelings as soon as I immerse you in her atmosphere, her era, her personal circumstances. Believe me. It's not just some crazy plan so I can cast a spell on you. It will work. You'll see."

"Alright, Manuel. It's true that Poe, Borges, and Lovecraft are my favorite writers—I just never thought I'd end up in one of their stories." I smiled, slightly embarrassed at my own mistrust. "I'll do it, but where's that dress you were talking about?"

"Follow me," he said, standing up, holding out his hand. "We'll go to my room."

"If it makes me uncomfortable to wear it, you'll just have to tell me the story without ceremony. Agreed?"

"Agreed," he said.

CHAPTER 2

The nuns would never approve of what I was doing. Not even Mother Luisa Magdalena, my friend and protector, would understand my friendship with Manuel. That Sunday was not the first I had spent with him. I had seen him two or three times before the end of the previous school year and then several more after my summer vacation. We usually met at the Prado Museum, which I was used to visiting every Sunday. He would wait for me at the entrance, smoking and reading the paper next to the statue of Velázquez.

I had told him about my Sunday visits to the museum when I wrote to him after our chance encounter. "Most Sundays I go to the Prado around eleven o'clock," I wrote, perfectly aware of what I was insinuating.

The first time I saw him there I was wearing a new, plum-colored wool cape. On my way to the museum, I wavered between being sure he'd be there and fearing he might not have taken my veiled hint; I felt different—more mature, more womanly. I know I was giving off a different air because of the way men looked and smiled at me. Some didn't hold back even if they were in the company of a woman. Instead, the surreptitious exchanges seemed to add to their excitement. They flirted with me while they continued talking or hugging the women they were with. I was shocked by how experienced they seemed in their duplicity. I thought about my father. All week I had been distressed by the revelation of his infidelity. His ghost and the ghost of my mother had taken new life in my mind, as if every conversation and gesture of theirs stored in my memory were suddenly infused with new meaning. I was so mortified to have gained this knowledge now, when it could do no good, that I kept imagining I was living those memories anew, except that now I was scolding them, warning them of the price we would all have to pay for their marital crisis. And even though to a certain extent it helped me to appease the impotence I felt for having been an ignorant spectator to the drama, my effort to relive the past was choking me with all the words I wished I could have said to avert the tragedy. I felt hurt, tense. Perhaps that's why I told Manuel about it.

When I saw him, waiting for me by the Velázquez statue, I felt flushed. He walked over to greet me as if it were the most natural thing in the world. We had a long talk while we strolled through the gardens on Paseo del Prado. Queen Juana's jealousy must have been like my mother's, I said. He looked at me. He would have to tell me the whole story, he said. It was long and complex, it would last through many Sundays. After the summer vacation, I said. Once the school year started again, there would be no lack of Sundays.

I FOLLOWED HIM DOWNSTAIRS. HIS APARTMENT WAS LOCATED IN Malasaña, one of Madrid's older neighborhoods. San Bernardo was one of the only wide streets in the area. Farther ahead it gave out to the Gran Vía. To get to his apartment one had to go up a narrow set of stairs, past a wrought iron entryway. Manuel had told me that the buildings on either side had once been part of a palace that belonged to one of his ancestors. He said he divided his time between that apartment and his aunt's house. She needed his company as much as he needed his solitude.

THE BUILDING'S AGE EXPLAINED THE BIZARRE PARTITIONS THAT its current inhabitants had installed to make better use of the high ceilings. Manuel's apartment, for instance, must have once been a huge salon with very high ceilings, but now it was a split-level. The door, entryway, bedroom, and bathroom were on the lower level, which was so dark it needed artificial light even in the daytime. From there, going up another short staircase and a trapdoor one came out onto a bright, well-ventilated room that functioned as living-dining and study room with a tiny well-stocked kitchen. The French windows opened out onto a balcony where pots of hanging geraniums sat atop a row of phone books stacked one on top of the other. It was a very pleasant surprise after the gloomy downstairs area. The room smelled of tobacco. There were many books stored in antique bookshelves, a comfortable-looking sofa against the wall, a work table with a typewriter, and on the walls, beautiful old maps and manuscripts. Models of delicate sailboats were set up in different places, and there were also odd-looking mobiles made of scrap metal. Pushed to one side of the dining table there was always an unfinished jigsaw puzzle.

I had never been to Manuel's bedroom until that day. It was clean and tidy. He had a beautiful, mirrored armoire with volutes and rosettes carved into the wooden doors. His bed had a silk bedspread with orange and black diamonds, the night table, the lamps were tasteful and exquisite, most likely objects inhereted from his ancestors. He went to the armoire and took out a dress, which he laid delicately on the bed. As if it were a task requiring all of his concentration, he carefully pulled it from its protective case and frowned, examining it, before smoothing out the slightly wrinkled skirt. Where on earth did he get it? I wondered, gaping. It was sumptuous: alternating red and gold silk panels, a narrow waistline trimmed in delicate velvet ribbon, and a wider version of the same trim on the rectangular neckline. A row of tiny black buttons ran down the front of the bodice.

Manuel lifted the hanger up and turned toward me. Like a couturier with his mannequin, he held it up to me, squinting for the full effect.

"This was worn with hoops called *verdugos*, to accentuate the hips," he said, apparently satisfied with his visual inspection, "but we won't bother with those, partly because I couldn't make them and partly because you wouldn't be able to sit down in them."

"Are they like a corset?"

"Not exactly. *Verdugos* were bell-shaped extensions, worn around the waist and tied through the legs, so that when the dress fell it created the illusion of very wide hips. I'll help you get changed, if that's all right."

He means I should take my clothes off, I thought, staring at him, not saying a word. In my late childhood I had gone through a phase filled with elaborate, strange fantasies where, either imagining myself to be an Egyptian slave or an Aztec princess, always these rough, violent men would force me to get undressed. I would kick frenetically, fighting and struggling against them, but in the end, when my captors took me out to a plaza and exhibited my naked body before a frenzied crowd, I would get inexplicably aroused. Whether I was dragged by huge, fierce guards or tied to a post like Christ on the cross, as soon as I pictured myself naked I would feel tremendously powerful, despite being the victim. I would imagine those scenes as I showered, before I went to school. Sometimes I envisioned lecherous hands grabbing at me while I squirmed and protested, at others I would glare at them, proud and haughty. Unable to imagine the sexual act, my fantasies would climax when the hero rescued me, pulling me to his chest and covering me up with his cape. I got the same sort of thrill playing hide-and-seek with my cousins in the empty rooms of my grandparents' house. They would catch the oldest two or three of us girls and push us under the beds and touch us *down there*. For years I was convinced that *down there* hid the precise spot that connected all the fibers of my being, the magnet that kept me grounded, the place that was pulled down by the force of gravity like an invisible beam of light shining from inside me down onto the ground. I understood why my mother was so worried that something might obstruct it. Maybe it was the fear of us being catapulted into space, having lost our bearings, that made my cousins act so fast and snatch their hands away so quickly, as if the soft smoothness between our legs might burn them.

"Let's try it on," Manuel said, his back to me now as he unbuttoned the dress from its hanger, which was hooked over the armoire. "It's going to fit perfectly. Let me help you."

Manuel carried on with the determination of a robot programmed to perform a task. Possessed and obsessed, he seemed already to have been transported to another reality. Maybe that was why I was finally able to submit to the game without too much bother. I felt like I was with a scientist attempting to enter a parallel time; like a character out of some fantastic, far-fetched tale.

"You can leave your underwear on, but take off everything else. I'll slip the dress over your head. There's no zipper, logically."

Facing me, standing at the foot of the bed, he stared at me without malice. I was looking at him too, my back turned to the mirror where just a minute ago I'd seen my face, my cheeks blushing slightly. I was planning to tell him to look away while I got undressed, but instead I started to unbutton my top. I unzipped the suit pants I was wearing. The silk lining slipped down my legs, rustling softly. I pulled down my stockings and slipped them off. I could feel my heart pounding in my belly. I proceeded to stand up and take off my white blouse. When I took off my bra, he was still staring at me with that guileless expression.

"Ready." I smiled, cupping my hands over my breasts. "Hurry up so I don't catch a cold. It's freezing in here."

It took a second for him to react. He took down the dress as if he'd had to complete a thought before he could do anything else.

He walked over to me.

"Raise your arms," he said.

I stuck my head through the neck hole. Manuel was standing very close to me. His cold hands brushed against me. For a few seconds all you could hear was the sound of the material slipping over my body. I felt myself starting to get wet between the legs. It was such a luxurious feeling, to abandon myself to this game, and each touch of the dress against my skin was like a pebble falling into a pond, sparking off countless shudders. I thought it was funny, the way my childhood fantasies were coming to life. I hadn't felt vulnerable when I was nude. It seemed more like my skin was a magnetic field, charged with fluid energy. Even though it was a new feeling, my instincts recognized it.

Manuel leaned over me and said that now he'd have to button up the corset. I thought he would be clumsy, but I made no effort to help him. "Let's see," he said, "one, two, three, four, five, six, seven, eight, nine, ten." His long, slender fingers turned out to be very nimble, ably slipping each button into the piping buttonholes. The dress had wide sleeves, and the narrow bodice fit me perfectly. He stood back to look me over, head to toe.

"I won't go overboard and try to make you wear the steeple headdress. But we'll have to put your hair up. Do you happen to have a barrette in your purse?"

I said I did and he ran to get it. I heard him bound up the steps two by two. I looked at myself in the mirror.

I had become a character from another time. A Spanish princess from the days of the reconquest of Granada, the discovery of America. As girls we always played make-believe and pretended to be princesses. This is a game, I told myself. It's just that this one is about one princess in particular. I pulled my hair into two sections and held it back behind me to see the effect. Better. Long hair hanging down over my shoulders lowered my status. I looked more like a lover than Philippe the Handsome's wife. He came back with my purse, and I pulled out a brush and barrette.

"Let me do it," he said quickly. "Tell me if I hurt you." And he started to brush my hair, straightening it, and then slowly, gently pulling it back. Touching my ears and neck every once in a while, he slowly braided my hair and then secured it with the tortoiseshell clip.

Instantaneously, I looked completely different. Dignified. Elegant. Finally Manuel looked at me, and we smiled into the mirror. His eyes came back to the present. He took my hand and twirled me around and then went to the far side of the room to look at me from afar and get the whole effect.

"Extraordinary," he said. "Welcome to the Renaissance."

CHAPTER 3

In the Madrid early afternoon, with the mezzanine windows half-opened to a partly cloudy day, dressed like a princess, I sit on the sofa that Manuel places in the middle of the room. He sits behind me. And tells me to close my eyes. He speaks in a low voice, slowly, deliberately. He susurrates. I let the voice take me with it. I sink into it and emerge someplace else. I am Juana.

AND IT IS TOLEDO. NOVEMBER 6, 1479, THE DAY OF MY BIRTH. Beatriz Galindo, an olive-skinned woman with Castilian features, black hair pulled back into a low bun, and small, sparkly eyes, is there when her friend, Queen Isabella, my mother, delivers me. Finally, my head pokes out, and amid relieved cries and a solemn silence, the midwives wrench me from my original vortex and present me to the uncertain world I am about to join. I can feel slender hands, calluses on palms. No longer protected, enshrouded, my exposed skin registers the weave of the fabric swaddling me. I feel myself transported, from precipice to precipice, from one set of arms to another. The world is deafening and the brightness unforgiving. I want to go back to the warm, wet depths of the womb. I am hungry and distressed and I want to cry. A breast appears before me. Soon I will recognize it as belonging to my nurse, María de Santiesteban. My mother will not feed me; she has to feed the kingdom, and I am but her third child.

"I want my daughter to learn Latin, Beatriz," I hear my mother say. "I want her to enjoy the pleasures of the intellect. Given that she will never be queen, she ought to be a princess with a brain."

"Yes, Isabel. Now you rest. She'll be beautiful," says Beatriz. "Look how delicate her features are. She's a Trastámara."

"I shall call her Juana. Juan was named after John the Baptist. She will be commended to John the Evangelist."

In a little while, Ferdinand, my father, will come in to greet my mother and to meet me. He'll glance at me indifferently. I am not the son he had hoped for, and he casts his cold eyes over my tiny body, swathed in wool, startling me from my sleep and making me wail and holler. My mother comforts me. She rocks me for the first time, in front of my father. I recognize her warmth and her heartbeat; I recognize the body I used to inhabit, the castle where I was once my own cloistered room. Her proximity makes me feel whole again, makes me feel intact. My nose nestles her breast, searching for that familiar scent, that part of me that has been taken away. Lying in her arms, I no longer feel my father glower or notice the cold.

Manuel's voice, so close to my ear, whisks me through time, and my first few years blur into a series of shadowy images.

WE'RE A FAMILY OF NOMADS. MY ROYAL PARENTS ARE WAGING A WAR, and their itinerant court moves from castle to castle. First they battled the supporters of Juana *la Beltraneja* in the War of Succession. After their victory in 1485 they continued to consolidate their power and moved to end the domination of the Moors by conquering their last stronghold: Granada. They set up court wherever it is militarily convenient. My sister, María, was born, and now my wet nurse breast-feeds her, and a woman named Teresa de Manrique becomes my governess. I have hardly any time to play, because my mother has demanded that her children be raised as worthy princes and princesses of Castile and Aragon, which implies a number of duties. I learn to play the clavichord, to dance, to knit. If I behave well, Teresa takes me to the kitchen and prepares rose sugar sweets for me. If I am rowdy or laugh too loud, I get a smack because experience shows that physical punishment cures recklesness in girls and that pain is a healthy way of disciplining our bodies. I have started classes with my tutor, the Dominican Andrés de la Miranda. He left his monastery in Burgos in order to become our private instructor. In Latin class, my younger sister María puts her head down on the table and sleeps. I can't sleep because Father Andrés is very strict and admonishes me, describing the torments of hell. He burned the tip of my ring finger with a charred stick to help my imagination visualize the sensation of the burning flames that will consume me if I don't learn to be a good Christian. I kicked and screamed, but my mother, who came when she heard me calling to her, smiled at the monk and approved of his barbaric methods. Don Andrés talks about the large numbers of infidels who roam free in our kingdom and worship other gods. Beatriz Galindo contradicts him and extols the benefits of living alongside Jews and Moors. Secretly, she shares poems and stories of courtly love with me. I devour them on the nights my parents are busy with court festivities. I dream of becoming an adult and no longer having to live through wars, persecutions, and fear.

I, Lucía, remember the nun at the Catholic school in my country who, when I was a small child, also invited me to hold my finger over a lit match, to demonstrate the torments of hell. And then there is Mother Aurora, a fair-skinned nun with a glass eye, who often supervises us in the dormitory, and who told me that taking a shower for more than half an hour is tempting the devil.

Those are vestiges of the mentality that led to the Inquisition, Manuel says. Your parents were the ones who chose Torquemada as the Great Inquisitor, he adds. In securing an austere and intolerant court they seeked to debilitate the alliance between the traditional nobility and the corrupt, licentious priests, as well as raise their own status in the eyes of Rome. Their strategy worked. Those were the years when they abolished the classic, white mourning attire, and substituted it for all-black apparel. They cultivated a severe, penitent mind-set, which suspected color, the pleasure of the eyes, or the the delights of food. They shaped the "Castilian" spirit and made Castilian Spanish—with its harsh, guttural, masculine sounds, which only Latin American Spanish has managed to soften—into the official language of the land.

Poor Juana, growing up surrounded by punctilious governesses averse to fun and affection. Poor Juana, having a tutor like Miranda, who got his kicks by making note of the different types of heresy, from the common to the exotic, in dossiers that he always carried with him and that she read behind his back.

✳ I WOULD READ THE CONFESSIONS OF *CURANDERAS*, THE WOMEN FOLK healers who read the future in the bowels of rabbits. That sinister world seemed no darker to me than the corridors of our palaces, traversed night and day by whispering clerics who stared at me, even as a child, with obsequious compassion and thinly veiled concupiscence. Few were the joys I found among the men entrusted with my education and care. Perhaps my father's rejection was contagious and the three princesses born after Juan reminded them of the vagaries of a womb that seemed only to give birth to one female after another. María, Catalina, and I would always be reminders to my father that his virility had produced only one male heir to the throne: our weak, scrawny brother Juan, who I surpassed both on horseback and in archery skills; I never shot an arrow from my crossbow that wouldn't hit its target. If what happened to me when we were crossing the Tajo on our way to Toledo—when my mule lost its footing and fell into the strong river current—had happened to Juan, there would be no more crown prince. But I didn't lose my composure, nor was I paralyzed by fear when the icy water cut my breath and soaked my velvet dress, making it heavy as armor. I grabbed the mule by the ears and tugged her out of the deep water. Then I clung to her and dug my heels into her side to make her swim to shore. Though I was trembling, I was calm and triumphant, especially when I saw the faces of all those ladies and gentlemen and all those servants, staring at me, pale and dumbfounded, incredulous, relieved and full of admiration at my bravery. I was only ten years old, but I was my mother's daughter. So often I had seen her from my bedroom window at dawn, leading the cavalry on her way to battle the enemy.

To reward my courage I was taken to see my parents as soon as we reached the palace. My father embraced me and tugged on my braid affectionately. I think it was then that I recognized the part of him that lived in me, and he saw his own reflection in my eyes. He was proud of me. My mother held me tight. I didn't mind the rancid smell that clung to her, ever since she vowed not to bathe until Granada was taken back from the Moors.

Juan and Isabel were brought up to rule as king and queen. The same was not true for the rest of us. Only the two oldest accompanied my parents and saw them often. I applied myself to my studies of Latin and romance languages, and mastered the clavichord, in hopes that news of my progress would make my parents notice me, send for me to read aloud to them, or play for them one night. I was probably twelve when Beatriz Galindo, La Latina, gave me a book for my birthday that mesmerized me. It was called *Delectable Vision of Philosophy and Liberal Arts,* by Alfonso de la Torre. Until I read it, I had never thought about how extraordinary it was that our species had managed to deduce the existence of the soul, of internal and external realities, nor had I noticed the unrelenting insatiability of our thirst for knowledge. I had never wondered where the artistic impulse came from, never questioned the need for beauty, never considered that, as a woman, I could play a more active role in my household. Though I would never be queen, given the line of succession, I could propose to leave my mark, take more conscious control of my destiny, flatter my intellect over my vanity. Because I *was* vain. Why not admit it? Ever since my mother let me exchange my black dresses for crimson ones, even though the material cost twice as much, I had begun to take great delight in ordering new clothes. The mirror did not lie when it reflected my beauty as superior to that of my sisters. I was the spitting image of my Aragonese grandmother. The resemblance was so striking that my mother teased me, calling me "mother-in-law." But people also said I looked like Isabel of Portugal, my mother's mother, who lived in Arévalo in a fortified castle on the Adaja River. I was flattered to hear that I had inherited her dark-skinned beauty, so different from my mother and older sister's fair complexions. Nevertheless I didn't like being compared to her, because I often heard the ladies at court whisper that she was mad. They said she had a guilty conscience because she had forced her husband Juan I to execute his faithful but malevolent servant Don Álvaro de Luna, and it had driven her insane. Apparently, my grandfather never got over having obeyed her and died thirteen months later, in a deep state of depression, claiming that he hated being king and would have been happier as the son of a farmworker. They say that my poor grandmother, mortified, saw Don Álvaro's ghost everywhere, and insisted that the river that passed under her window whispered the dead man's name. My mother, however, had more lyrical memories of her childhood in Arévalo. Her eyes would water when she spoke of her childhood independence, the freedom she had to roam the Castilian countryside at will, until she felt that its tenderness had made its way into her very soul. When she was upset, she said, all she had to do was close her eyes and imagine the plains and the hills of Castile, the paths beside the rivers, to regain her inner peace. I think that from that experience my mother assumed that her own children would not miss her, not suffer when she was gone, and that we would learn to value ourselves and not be dependent on the family for affection. And though it might have worked well for her, I felt empty when she was gone, as if my heart had also left. As I grew, that longing for affection turned into physical pain. I would dream of affection and cuddling.

I OPENED MY EYES. I SUPPOSE THE BEST WAY TO DESCRIBE THE STATE I was in while Manuel spoke is to call it an interlude. The outside world faded into another reality, projected from inside me onto my retina. I don't know if it was the dress, his soft, gentle voice calling me Juana, or my lively, adolescent imagination, but I was completely swept away by his narration. A voice within me spoke out, completing Manuel's story, making comments and observations; I felt seduced and captivated by the same sort of fascination that makes us follow the complicated thread of convoluted dreams. I felt like my mind, wide as the sea, had been storing those images for years, just waiting to let them emerge, ready to project them the moment they were summoned. I felt what it was like to be born (sort of like being naked in front of a man for the first time), and to have a life determined by decisions that others made on my behalf. (I think the weight of that dress contributed to the latter, confining me in a silken suit of armor.)

"Manuel, what time is it?"

"Four o'clock."

"I have to go back to the convent in an hour."

"You will, but for now, close your eyes again."

IN ORDER TO COMPREHEND MY MOTHER'S COLDNESS, I NEEDED TO understand what her succession to the throne had entailed. It hadn't been easy. People at court had been talking about it my whole life, but it wasn't until I reached adolescence that I managed to put two and two together and reconstruct the past that had turned my mother into the formidable woman whose presence I longed for, but who also inspired in me the silent devotion others felt in temples in the presence of God.

My mother had truly loved her half-brother Enrique, the son of her father King Juan from his first marriage. When King Juan died, the crown was passed to Enrique, and he became King Enrique IV. Six feet tall and blond, this was a brother who liked to laugh at courtly ceremonies and received nobility on cushions on the floor, dressed as a Moor. He convinced my grandmother that it would be better for my mother and her brother Alfonso to go and live at court in Valladolid, far from the isolation of Arévalo.

Grandmother didn't want them to go, but she couldn't refuse. It was after her children left that she went mad. My mother was ten and Alfonso was nine. They spoke more Portuguese than Spanish. That was about when Princess Juana, the daughter of Enrique and Juana of Portugal, was born. My mother and uncle were there for her baptism and heard the king proclaim her future heiress of Castile. How could my mother have guessed that one day her succession to the throne would lead her to be at war with that child? King Enrique's licentious lifestyle, his fondness for boys, his disastrous affairs with courtly ladies, all contributed to the rumors that led to his nickname "the Impotent." Since impotent men cannot father children and since the handsome Beltrán de la Cueva was not only Enrique's favorite—the king had named him governor of his royal household and grandee of Castile—but was also on quite intimate terms with the queen, the noblemen began to insinuate that he had fathered the princess, calling her *"la Beltraneja."* But despite all that, rather than do away with Don Beltrán, the king bestowed on him more and more titles. He named him Count of Ledesma, arranged for him to marry a niece of Cardinal Mendoza, and to top it all off, named him alderman of the Order of Santiago, the largest landholder in the whole kingdom of Castile, with the exception of the king himself. This favoritism was too much for the nobles, especially the archbishop of Toledo, Alfonso de Carrillo. Carrillo, who commanded a great army, had been protector and tutor to both my mother and her brother since their arrival at court. Enrique's excesses and the question of his daughter's legitimacy led Carrillo and other noblemen to advocate that the crown be passed to my uncle Alfonso.

The heir apparent, however, died one night after eating trout—possibly poisoned, because after all, who dies of *that?*—so my mother became next in line for the throne. After several uprisings, military sieges, and increased pressure, the king accepted my mother as his successor and signed a treaty at Toros de Guisando to ratify the accord. But King Enrique went back on his word on more than one occasion. My mother lived through those years on edge. Several attempts were made to marry her to the king of Portugal, and to another noble suitor much older than herself, but finally Carrillo proposed that she marry my father, Ferdinand, in order to gain the support of the kingdom of Aragon in the War of Succession. My parents were married in Medina del Campo, in a secret ceremony. My father disguised himself as a mule driver in order to attend. Only after the formal solemn nuptials and the six days of celebrations that followed did they send a messenger to notify King Enrique of the event. His rage was such that he again proclaimed *La Beltraneja* his heir. Between my parents, it is told, love flourished since they first met. Both were young, handsome, and I suppose that the secretive nature of their wedding, the knowledge they were thereby uniting Castile and Aragon, the risks they took, fueled the attraction they felt for each other. They knew that they were the focal point of many expectations and much tension. Nothing like conspiracy to make the blood rush and ignite strong passions.

In order to prove that their marriage had been consummated and that gone were the days of Castilian impotence, my father came out of the conjugal bedroom on their wedding night to display the sheet stained with my mother's virginal blood.

My tutor, Andrés de la Miranda, and Beatriz Galindo recounted many stories that helped me form a picture of my mother as she must have been at that juncture of her life, when she gambled it all to possess (on not very transparent premises, according to my judgment) her right to the throne of Castile. But the most revealing thing about her temperament is the manner in which the day after Enrique died—having left no will—she had herself crowned de facto queen in Segovia, on December 13, 1474, by virtue of the Toros de Guisando Treaty, my father's absence notwithstanding. He had already accepted his role as king consort in a capitulation signed before Carrillo and approved by King Juan of Navarre, my paternal grandfather; but for Isabel to throw it in his face so bluntly clearly wounded his pride. So she devised a way to tend to his wound. When he reached Segovia on January 2, Cardinal Mendoza and Archbishop Carrillo were waiting in the outskirts of town to receive him, beneath a royal canopy made of the finest brocade. His mourning attire was exchanged for a cape embroidered with gold and ermine. On his way into the city he rode through suburbs decorated with standards, and all the people came out to give him a joyous ovation while music filled the streets. The finest minstrels were singing on the corners, conjurers threw pins and scarves into the air, and there were men breathing fire and balancing objects on their heads. It was a triumphal reception that lasted well into the evening, when he crossed the gates of San Martín, amid noblemen who knelt as he passed and held flaming torches aloft. My mother waited for the procession to reach the square before she appeared at the top of the Alcázar stairs, a vision of gold and fire, bedecked with her crown and a ruby necklace. Young and beautiful at twenty-three, she slowly descended the stairs amid her subjects' cries to meet her husband and accompany him to the cathedral, where he swore his allegiance to the city and promised to defend and enforce the laws of Castile.

A few days later, my parents chose their royal emblem and insignia: *Tanto monta, monta tanto, Isabel como Fernando.* Isabella and Ferdinand, equal rulers, ruling equally.

"Not bad for a fifteenth-century queen," I said to Manuel, turning around to look at him. I watched the afternoon light fade, reflected in the closed window of the building across the street. "I really do have to go back now, Manuel. It's almost five thirty."

I undid the low bun that my braid was pinned up into. My head hurt. More than pain, it was a sort of electrical buzzing that seemed to radiate from my skull. Visions of medieval palaces—the intensity of history being revealed to me like an old memory—gave the present a faded, unreal veneer, but I had to return to it, to go back to school, if I didn't want Mother Luisa Magdalena to become openly suspicious and interrogate me about my Sunday expeditions.

Without a word, Manuel took my head in his hands, placing his thumbs over my temples.

"Just relax for a few seconds."

I breathed deeply, my eyes closed, once, twice, three times. Then my hands began to unbutton the bodice.

"Let me, I'll do it." .

We went back to Manuel's room. He helped me get the gown off and then left so I could get dressed alone. It was all very quick and professional, with none of the hesitation that had been there a few hours ago. He assisted me as if he were the eunuch from one of the harems in *A Thousand and One Nights*, or the valet of a queen much older than myself.

My contemporary clothes did not immediately strip away the sensation I had of inhabiting another time. It was hard to adjust, go back to rushing, to the bustle of the street. I insisted Manuel let me go back to school on my own. I wanted to have a little time to myself, without feeling his presence, his attention. I didn't tell him that, but he must have intuited it. The street seemed to be taking a siesta along with its residents. The only people out were a few groups of boys, sneakily smoking on corners here and there. I had never smoked in my life. Up until that time, I'd never felt the urge to do adult things without telling anyone. But I was starting to see that neither the convent nor my academic education were going to teach me what I really needed to know about life. Adults had a knack for making one doubt one's own judgment. According to them, it was bound to be immature, juvenile. But what else did I have besides my own judgment? How was I supposed to learn to live? How?

Manuel fascinated me. His milieu, his obsession with Juana and Philippe, were more seductive than the cautious inner voices I heard, whispering the nuns' warnings. He could well be eccentric, strange, but I was flattered he had made me his accomplice. I could learn much more about history and human nature from him than from anyone my age. I wanted to know more about the intimate truth of men and women. What pulled them together and pushed them apart? What made them forego reason in favor of passion regardless of the suffering it could involve? I wondered why it was that the mystics the nuns presented as role models to us—people like Saint Teresa and Fray Luis de León—had to punish themselves, wear hair shirts, and choose to renounce the world for a life of solitude in order to find God and sanctity. I questioned whether my father's adultery couldn't just be a result of his human nature rather than an aberration. I could not be sure whether the negation of the flesh and all that masochism and self-denial was a trait of the Spanish character, if it was somehow related to the arid landscape, the desolate reddish plains of Castile.

As far as mysticism was concerned, I preferred Father Vidal's vision. He was a beautiful, broad-shouldered priest who had taken us on a spiritual retreat the year before. "God is vast, an all-encompassing presence, who is nevertheless aware of each and every one of us. God knows every one of us by name." The idea of God calling me by my name, thinking of me as Lucía, had made me weep. It was during that retreat when I first knew the notion of a loving, gentle God. God is love, the priest told us. That seemed much more acceptable to me than the idea of a white-bearded lord tallying up everyone's sins in a book he'd dust off on Judgment Day. That seemed like such a petty, narrow conception for a being whose intelligence was supposed to be limitless, who was all-powerful and all-knowing. Thanks to Father Vidal, God had become much more tolerant and compassionate to me.

When I left the metro station, I hastened my pace to arrive at the bakery in time to return to school with my habitual selection of pastries. I made it to dinner promptly, and Mother Luisa Magdalena came up to me at the dining hall to inquire about my day.

"I looked at Flemish paintings from the fifteenth and sixteenth century," I said. "Bosch and Van Eyck. And then I stopped for a snack on calle Goya."

She glanced down at my pastries on the table and smiled.

CHAPTER 4

On Monday night, I felt compelled to write to Isis during study period to tell her that I had come across her letters and my mother's papers. I started to cry as I wrote. Unlike Mother Luisa Magdalena, who, listening to my words, could only visualize opaque images, Isis and I both shared the precision of our memories. If I evoked my mother, she would know exactly what I was remembering. She would be able to picture the curve of the perfect lips my mother was so proud of. She lavished on them lip liners and lipstick in colors ranging from brown to red to purple. To enhance them she barely wore any other makeup. She purposely let her skin look pale and applied just a bit of mascara on those black eyes of hers I had inherited. The result was dramatic, because my mother's skin was soft and glistened like a pearl, so her bold mouth stood out suggestively, insinuating something ripe, edible.

To know that for Isis my mother's memory was filled with color and perfume and her unique gestures (like when she was nervous and wound her hair around her index finger, curling it again and again) released me from the necessity of explanations and freed my emotions. I didn't want to get sentimental, but I found myself drowning in my feelings. If writing to Manuel had made me feel mature and perceptive, writing to Isis I experienced myself as a desolate, infantile girl deeply in need of compassion. I wrote to her from a scarred childhood, an orphan's profound sense of abandonment I hadn't even realized I was so torn up with until it took shape on the page. My chest became stiff as canvas, and when I finished my letter, I left the study hall so I could go and cry like a child in my bedroom. It was as if it were the first time I had wholly internalized the definitive nature of my parents' absence, the fact that they would never, ever come pick me up from school; they would never, ever be sitting waiting for me in the parlor, sipping coffee and nibbling on cookies, like the other girls' parents. At no point would they come to take me home. I had no home. I was like a helium balloon that had no hand holding on to its colored string; a balloon that had drifted away, the wind charting its course. Being at a boarding school with other girls who were also not living with their parents had allowed me to play tricks on myself, to pretend that after all my years there, on any given day, if I did everything right and was a good student, I too would receive a visit from my parents, and would walk out the tiled foyer with them. But that was not to be. No one would come for me. I pictured graduation day. The celebration after the ceremony in the auditorium and the mass in the chapel. And I knew exactly what I would feel behind the smile I would display to share the joy of my peers, behind the expression I would wear as I wished them luck and said good-bye to them, and the emptiness I would feel when I trudged back to my bedroom to pack my things, Mother Luisa Magdalena by my side, chatting away to try to console me.

This realization shattered the illusions I'd been hiding behind. At one point my sadness scared me and I told myself that I had to stop crying. I hugged and rocked myself and started to console myself the same way my father used to: speaking softly, sweetly, saying it's okay, it's okay, it's all over now.

I sank into a deep sleep, and when I woke I felt like I was drowning. When I opened my eyes, I floated to the surface and gulped in air. It took me a minute to recognize my tiny room, the trees silhouetted in the window. Slowly the alarms ringing in my body quieted down as I saw the silent furniture, the walls (I never realized how immobile the world is until I confronted tragedy; that was when I began to see the soullessness of everyday objects). I hadn't stirred up the memories of those first days after my parents died, hadn't recalled the conversations I overheard describing the hangar where my grandparents identified the bodies. They didn't realize I was listening when they told my aunts and uncles the sickening details of black bags, tray tables, and the mystery of my father's right arm, which mysteriously remained intact, the only recognizable part of his body. The airline psychologist had explained this was relatively common: a random extremity would often manage to escape, uncharred. The fuselage would rip and the fire would miss it. At least they were lucky enough to be able to positively identify their loved one. Most people would just have to wait for the dental records. In my dream, I had taken my father's arm from the stretcher and thrown it over my shoulder, begging him to hug me one last time. In my nightmare, I saw the charred remains of his cadaver struggle to stand up, not just to hug me but to lean on me, silently begging me in a voice that just my heart could hear to get him out of there. But my stealthy attempt to reach the door unnoticed had failed because my father's movements were accompanied by loud, metallic noises, as if he were pulling a string of tin cans tied to him. When I had turned around to reproach him, I had seen that the noise was coming from my mother's blackened skeleton, which he was dragging behind him, pulling it by the hand. In the hangar, the other mourners had turned to stare at me disapprovingly. Suddenly I had heard my grandfather's voice. He and my grandmother had caught up with me and had pushed me toward the table where the corpses I was trying to take with me had been just moments before. Gesturing angrily, they had insisted that I put them back. I had not wanted to obey, but an overpowering will had forced me to please them. My father's forearm, his strong hand, had clung to me in a desperate grip. While my grandfather struggled, I had begun to scream, only to have my grandmother cover my mouth with her hand. Unable to breathe, I had woken up. It had been very cold the night before and I was covered with every one of my winter blankets.

IN THE ART HISTORY CLASS TAUGHT BY MARISA—THIN, WIRY, ATH-letic arms, librarian's face—we studied the Roman obsession with rites. She read us part of Thornton Wilder's *The Ides of March:* Caesar sends a letter to a wise friend expressing his irritation at the fact that due to evil omens and fortune-telling, the Senate session has been canceled. Marisa talked at length about the importance of rites at a time when the world was seen as inscrutable and science had not yet managed to explain natural phenomena or the psyche. It occurred to me, while I was doodling absently, that perhaps I was carrying out my own rites of passage and bidding my innocence farewell. I instinctively felt that my life was about to enter a new cycle, that the girl who still bore hopes of bringing the dead back to life and that believed tragedies could miraculously have happy endings was being left behind forever.

That night, I took the Pradwin book that Mother Luisa Magdalena had loaned me out of my armoire. On the back cover, I read that the author was Ukrainian, a historian, and that his biography of Queen Juana was the product of an interest in her that had arisen after one of his visits to Spain. I glanced at the engravings and reproductions of paintings from the period. I looked hard and long at Juana's face. Our resemblance *was* remarkable. It wasn't that we had the same features; it was something less obvious, a familiar air we had about us. Juana had delicate features. I was struck by the perfect curve of the thin eyebrows that arched across her high forehead. Were they natural, or did people already pluck them back then? Her eyes looked like they had no eyelashes. (The painter had simply traced a black line above her lids.) They were her most remarkable feature, dark and almond-shaped. Her nose was thin and straight, very aristocratic, and she had a small, well-defined mouth, with a sensual, full lower lip. It crossed my mind that one really had to be beautiful to look good wearing those headdresses, which hid the hair underneath a monastical velvet coif. Philippe the Handsome looked very delicate. Although the reproductions were black-and-white, one could guess his very fair complexion and the light brown, almost blond, hair. He had Manuel's coloring, though Manuel's hair was white. Would I have fallen in love with Philippe? In my fantasies, my heroes always had strong arms and broad chests rather than beautiful faces. I liked to imagine the strength of a man's body under my fingertips, the musculature of the legs, the coarseness of the beard, the firmness of the whole. But I also liked to imagine the eyes and the sound of the voice.

From what seemed a long way off, I heard the call for lights-out.

For the past few weeks I had surprised myself at the ease I had developed in escaping reality. Lost in my thoughts I could entirely forget time and space. I got up and placed the book among my school texts. I was not going to read it, I told myself. Were I to do it I would know too much and would not be as attentive with Manuel. I preferred to listen to his version of the story, at the apartment. There I would be wearing the same silk-and-velvet dress that Juana wore in the engraving I had just seen.

Maybe it was because I was experiencing new feelings, but that week I spent more time than usual with my classmates: Piluca, who was delicate and perfect and diligent; Marina, who was sweet and childlike; Cristina, the practical one; and, of course, Margarita with her jokes. I was curious to find out how they dealt with the problems of growing up and forging their way through the *terra incognita* of real life, which was confronting us all. I paid attention at recess and on breaks to their stories of domestic conflict. Piluca and Marina were day pupils, so they went back home every night, argued with their siblings, played and studied with neighbors. Marina was obsessed with a boy who lived in the apartment above her and who every afternoon, when he figured she was sitting by her window doing her homework, lowered a can tied to a string with messages to her. "He sends me stupid poems, they're ridiculous!" She'd laugh, blushing. "Or he copies passages from the 'Song of Songs,' the fool." She said she couldn't stand him, but it was obvious that they had developed a sort of curious intimacy—his bedroom being directly on top of hers—if only by knowing they were in such close proximity. She listened to his music. She knew when he got into bed, when he turned out the light. He'd even say good night to her by tapping gently on the floor. Piluca, on the other hand, lived in the shadow of her older sister, who was a singer and was starting to become known. Boys were constantly calling her house, and Piluca spent every second of her free time spying on her sister. I joined their talk, telling them about the games I used to play with my cousins, while I couldn't help picturing the expressions they would have on their faces were they to know that just the week before I had taken my clothes off in front of a man. It wouldn't be very long before I returned to Manuel's apartment. It wouldn't be very long before those conversations would ring even more naive and innocent to me. I already felt as if I had crossed the threshhold that took me past adolescence.

Lucía: you were given a most appropiate name, the Latin for light. Do you shine in the darkness, or is it that your memory shines within me during the day, when I close my eyes?

So long, Manuel.

It was Friday, and those were the words of his newly arrived letter. I went from anguish to a sort of sweet confusion. No one had ever addressed anything so poetic to me before. I slipped the letter into my skirt pocket and looked for excuses to be alone so I could keep rereading it. I spent all day in a near-beatific state of euphoria. I went to chapel in the afternoon. Kneeling in the dark, amid candles and the smell of incense, I saw Manuel's eyes burning in the flames of all the votives lined up before the altar.

CHAPTER 5

Before I left on Sunday, I dedicated some time to quiet Mother Luisa Magdalena's worries about me. In a motherly way she tended to be quite vigilant and aware of my moods. If she saw that I was pensive and silent, her instinct went on guard, and Christ's Amazon that she was, she set off against my melancholy, suggesting this or that distraction. I was surprised to see that rather than accept my customary visit to the Prado, she kept insisting I go with Margarita and a few other girls to the Puerta del Sol shopping district. I assured her that I wasn't sad or depressed, I just didn't feel like shopping. For the first time, I regretted having made her my confidante and protector, and letting her have an influence over me. Never before had she taken any part in deciding what I would or wouldn't do on Sundays.

I left the school with Margarita and the others, but said good-bye to them when we were out on the street. Intrigued, Margarita asked me if I was going to see my boyfriend. I denied it emphatically. That wasn't it, I said. I simply didn't feel like going shopping.

When I got to the Prado, I still hadn't shaken off the uneasiness I felt at being the center of attention just when I wanted to avoid questions and prying.

It had only been a year since I had been allowed to roam around the city by myself on weekends. Most of the time I would walk to the Prado, browse around department stores like Corte Inglés or Galerías Preciados, wander up and down the Gran Vía, or else go to the movies with Margarita. My routine had changed ever since Manuel appeared in my life. I had met with him every Sunday since the start of the school year in September. If I needed to go shopping or run errands, I went on Saturdays.

Manuel was waiting for me, cigarette in hand as usual. He was wearing a black wool coat, which made him look paler. His blue eyes were watery planets, floating in the pallor of his face. I let him whisk me through the museum halls. He wanted to show me a painting by Francisco Pradilla, *Doña Juana la Loca*. We stopped briefly before Bosch's *Garden of Earthly Delights*. I had spent hours staring at that triptych, I told him. There was always something new to discover, and it never ceased to excite my imagination. "All of Dalí can be found in that painting," he said. That was precisely what made it so fascinating to me, I said. One could imagine so many other painters dumbfounded before it. One could find later in those painters' works their attempts to go further, to unravel the past and future of those figures.

"Bosch is so unique, isn't he? He introduces a taste of hell in paradise, he plays on the duplicity of every possible reality," Manuel said. "You got a glimpse of that yourself, when you saw from your mother's letters what lay behind the apparent paradise you perceived. I thought a lot about that, and about you, this week. That's why I wanted you to see Pradilla's painting. He's not particularly well known, but he was a marvelous artist. When you see Juana's face, you'll be able to imagine your mother's innermost thoughts."

We spent a long time looking at that painting. The figure of Juana, wearing a nun's habit, was at the center of the canvas. The image was passive, dark, and for some reason I took her to be in motion. She seemed to want to stop anyone from glancing curiously at Philippe's coffin, keep anyone from approaching him. Manuel said that Juana had tried to take her husband's body to Granada to bury him beside Isabella the Catholic. From a historian's perspective, he thought her ulterior motives had been, on the one hand, to surround herself by the Andalusian nobility who favored her while ridding herself of the Flemish courtiers who had surrounded Philippe. On the other hand, by placing

Philippe's body next to Queen Isabella's, she sought to legitimize his royal claim, thus ensuring the succession of her son Charles. Legend had it, however, that her nocturnal journeys were a testament to the lovesickness of a queen who refused to leave her lover's side, and who claimed she could not travel by day, since her husband was a bright sun, and two suns could not shine at the same time in the world.

"They said she was so jealous that she wouldn't let any women near the body," Manuel added. "All fallacies, of course."

I wondered if maybe my mother had felt something similar to the proud impotence revealed by the woman in the painting on display. When she realized that she and my father would die together, she might have felt, amid the terror of the plane crash, relief at knowing that my father was now hers forever. Manuel kept looking at the painting and then back at me, as if he were trying to gauge each of my reactions.

We had a sandwich at a restaurant with tiled walls where, according to Manuel, they served the best sangria in Madrid. The sweetness of the fruit juice camouflaged the taste of alcohol and made my cheeks burn. Afterward, Manuel hailed a cab and gave the driver his address.

We sat very close to each other in the car. I could feel him tense his legs to keep his balance as the taxi took the corners. I didn't move away. When we got to Manuel's apartment, he lit a fire in the fireplace. It was the middle of September, but autumn had already taken on a winter chill. He spoke and smoked, his face shrouded in a rosy halo. He was saying something or other about some books he'd read that week. I was having a hard time paying attention. I was trying to calm down and not let on how flustered I was, not let on that his fantasies and mine were both having an effect on my mind and body. He asked about school. The life of a student at a convent boarding school was not an especially riveting topic, I said. But I had questions I wanted to ask him, I continued, things that had come up in the silence of morning mass, or the long, quiet hours of study hall.

"Why are you so interested in Juana the Mad? How did you first start studying her? What made you want to know so much about her, about that time period?"

"It's a family matter," Manuel said, blowing smoke and staring at me with a certain irony. "My ancestors were quite involved in Doña Juana's care. I grew up hearing stories about her, and in a certain way, as a historian, I wanted to discern reality from fiction. You must know that historians have a passion for the task of weeding out the fallacies that accumulate about a certain person or event over time."

"So your ancestors were historians too?"

"Not exactly. In fact, my ancestors' role in the queen's life was somewhat odious. Maybe that's why I feel I owe it to her to make amends, at least to her memory."

His father's name, Sandoval y Rojas, came from the line of the marquises of Denia. When King Ferdinand of Aragon died, Bernardo de Sandoval y Rojas—and later, his son, Luis—were commissioned by Juana's son Charles I of Spain—who was also Charles V of Germany—to govern her household in Tordesillas.

"But 'govern' is a euphemism," Manuel said. "They were actually commissioned to keep the queen isolated and not let her speak to or have contact with anyone. She was surrounded by servants who were loyal to the marquis, whose complicity was essential in the creation of a fictitious world for Juana. You already know, I'm sure, that she was locked up there for forty-seven years." Manuel stood up and brushed some ashes from his trousers, as if the task required all his concentration.

"I know that, but I still don't understand," I confessed, standing up to get a glass of water from the kitchen. "I mean, I really don't know much at all about Juana the Mad."

"You're not the only one. The truth is, we know very little about those who came before us. We inherit their anxieties, but not their experiences. I can assure you, though, that when I'm done telling you her story, you'll feel like you were part of her, that you and Juana are not so different from each other after all. If you'd been in her position, you would have felt the same sorts of passions, the same rage, the same desperation . . . maybe even the same devoted love. We'll bring the queen back to life. That's the only way we'll be able to understand her and judge her fairly. But you already know my conditions. I'll come downstairs to help you with the dress."

We went back down to the darkness of his room, and once again I took my clothes off, this time more slowly, feeling my embarrassment give way to pleasure, as if every part of me was being freed from obscurity and brought into the light for the first time, as if by being discovered by someone else my body was able to discover itself. Sitting on a bench with his legs open, elbows on his knees and chin in his hand, Manuel watched me, though we both avoided looking into each other's eyes.

Finally, he fastened the ribbons that crisscrossed my back and were tied into a knot at the waist. The donning of the dress and the entire ceremony had a curious effect on my psyche. It was as if my skin's contact with the voluminous skirt, the silk, the velvet, stirred up opaque memories of other times, and my will was overtaken by voices from history that flowed back and forth between Manuel and I like lost souls obliged to tell their secrets. I wondered if maybe in a previous life I had lived in that age, if the fact that Manuel and I had met was not a coincidence at all but rather something inevitable, the result of a chain of events that inescapably led to that afternoon, and to that apartment in Madrid.

Manuel sits behind me. He whispers. I am Juana.

IT IS 1485, AND THE KINGDOM OF ARAGON HAS RECAPTURED NAPLES from the French. Tensions persist, however. Border skirmishes break out regularly in Roussillon and Fuenterrabía. In order to seal a pact with the house of Hapsburg aimed at isolating the French King Louis XIII, my parents decide to arrange a double marriage. My brother Juan—the crown prince—and I will marry the children of Maximilian of Austria and Mary of Burgundy. Juan will wed Marguerite of Austria, and I will marry Archduke Philippe.

To banish the image of interminable conflicts, backwardness, and anarchy that reigned in Europe and in our country before my parents' ascent to power, they envisage our marriages as an occasion to display the magnificence of their kingdoms. Let it no longer be said that the Spanish court lacks the splendor and sumptuousness of its neighbors. My mother will personally oversee the formation and organization of the armada that—after accompanying me to Flanders—will return with Princess Marguerite, the future queen of Spain.

According to the terms of marriage, both brides will forego the traditional dowries. Each groom will provide for the upkeep of their respective houses and courts with rents allotted for this purpose. Later, this arrangement will prove disastrous for me, but at the time no one doubts the wisdom and goodwill behind such a disposition.

Ignorant of the details my parents discussed with the Burgundian ambassadors, I concerned myself only with impressing them. I wore a crimson dress made of heavy velvet, with a low neckline. I tied a black silk ribbon around my neck and hung from it a ruby pendant my mother had given me for my engagement. Attired thus, with my hair in a bun that pulled my skin so tight it made my eyes even more almond-shaped, I peeked over the balcony of the great hall just when I was sure I would not go unnoticed. The nobles did not take long to see me. It made me happy to note the approval revealed by their murmurings in French, their smiles and bows. Having achieved my aim, I withdrew once more. Not long after, Leonor—one of my mothers' ladies-in-waiting—appeared. Giggling, she told me that one of the ambassadors had asked permission to have Michel Sittow, the Flemish artist, paint my portrait. That way, the Burgundian court and my future husband would know before I arrived that those who described my beauty were telling the truth.

After my engagement, my life began to revolve entirely around preparations for the wedding. Unlike my sister Isabel, who had married Prince Alfonso of Portugal, in line to inherit the throne, I was not to marry a future king. However, preparations for my move to Flanders were the most ostentatious and expensive that had ever been seen in the Castilian court. Hardly four years had passed since the reconquest of Granada, the conquest of the Canary Islands, and the discovery of the Indies. During those four years, my parents' kingdom had been established as one of the most solid and prosperous in all of Europe. Paired with the news of enormous riches discovered in the New World, where it was rumored there were entire cities built of silver and gold—my parents' firm hand had imposed the crown's mandate throughout the peninsula, subjugating disobedient nobility and corrupt clergy. All of this heralded good fortune for the "Catholic Monarchs," as Pope Alexander VI had christened them.

I never saw my mother more spirited than when she devoted herself to assembling the lavish armada that would take me to Flanders. Preparations for the journey began in the summer of 1495, but since the spring, the royal court had moved to the Villa de Almazán. From there the king and queen would supervise the fleet's construction in the Cantabrian shipyards. It was a happy time for me. My father, who until then had scarcely acknowledged my existence, became a friend and accomplice. He would sit me on his lap or he would take me to the shipyards to show me the progress the artisans were making on the Genoese carracks that would transport my massive retinue. In addition to those, another fifteen biscayners and five caravels would transport the five thousand soldiers who were accompanying me in order to ensure our safe passage past the shores of a hostile France. I enjoyed watching the effect his presence had on the flocks of meticulous workers. My father wore power well. He had a natural flair for authority. His strong, athletic body seemed to take up far more space than he physically required. Even the most long-standing courtiers instinctively kept a prudent distance, as if he were a castle and they didn't dare cross the invisible moat. For him to let down the drawbridge when I approached made me feel extremely special and important. I proudly noted the characteristics of his personality that I saw in myself, and if I had once attempted to sweeten my character and behave as a complacent damsel, those months taught me the advantages of not tempering my opinions or sacrificing my visions in order to gain the devious, fleeting approval of obsequious courtiers.

My mother took pleasure in seeing how close my father and I were. Unfortunately, that happy filial period lasted only a few months. At the end of June, the French attacked Perpignan, and my father left for Catalonia in July. I remember when he bade me farewell. He called me "little queen." He said that, as per Juan de Arbolancha's suggestion, my mother had asked for the hundreds of ships transporting wool to Flanders to escort the wedding procession. One hundred and thirty-two boats would set sail simultaneously. You might not be marrying a king, my father said, smiling, but no one will doubt that you deserve to be a queen. I climbed up onto the battlement to watch him leave and stayed there until his entourage had disappeared from sight. I knew I would not see him for a long, long time and that when I did, things would be different. I had no idea just how different! It was my mother, then, who remained in charge of outfitting the ships. She rounded up the five thousand soldiers who would accompany me and taught more than two thousand members of my retinue about the particulars of the court of Flanders.

On August 20, preparations for my departure were complete. The seemingly endless process of loading and boarding the ships began at dawn. In the afternoon, an unexpected storm lashed down on the Bay of Biscay. I had already made myself comfortable in my cabin. It had a large, open area as well as a bedroom with a bed that was attached to the wall of the ship. A thick, vermilion velvet curtain separated one area from the other. The antechamber had chairs, a narrow desk, a divan, and a small armoire for my musical instruments. By my side, my mother was gazing out the holland-covered peepholes, staring at the dark horizon and the white-crested waves. If nothing else, the heat had subsided, and the two of us had a moment of peace and solitude after the hustle and bustle of boarding. We'd wait together until the storm passed, she said. Maybe the weather was a gift that God was giving us before we were separated.

"You will be far away, Juana. You are young and impressionable and I fear for you in the court of Flanders."

"WHAT DO YOU FEEL, AS A SIXTEEN-YEAR-OLD GIRL ABOUT TO LEAVE behind everything you've ever known and loved to embark on a one-way journey?" Manuel asked.

"Fear. And excitement. I think about the husband who's waiting for me, I wonder if I'll be happy, if he will really be 'handsome,' as they say he is."

"You play clavichord, though you also learned monochord and guitar. Of Isabel's daughters, you are the most educated. That night, after dinner, as the carrack rocks back and forth in the water, you laugh with the young ladies in your entourage while your mother thinks how beautiful you are and tries to restrain her heart, so used to misfortune and discord. You look at her out of the corner of your eye, because you can sense her apprehension and her sadness. Realizing that you can make her feel these sentiments fills you with a certain sinister glee. You mother has never been much given to affection, causing you to wonder whether she loves you as much as your nursemaid María de Santiesteban, whose old face broke out in sobs when she bid you farewell in Valladolid. So the sight of your mother looking upset amid all the merrymaking and revelry makes you feel loved and cared for, it lightens the weight of the many uncertainties of your journey. You are not intimidated by the voyage at sea because you have loved it ever since you were a child, you have imagined it to be a liquid magic carpet ready to take you far away. What worries you is the arrival, what will happen when you disembark.

FROM THE MOMENT I CROSSED THE GANGPLANK AND SET FOOT ON Captain Juan Pérez's carrack, amid all the cases and bundles, I became fully aware that the most valuable cargo was stowed inside of me: within me I carry my noble rank, the blood of my illustrious ancestors, my beloved Spain. After my mother says good-bye and leaves the ship, I will be the sole anchor and motor of this expedition. I will be the ruler of this retinue. Meanwhile, I rejoice in my unexpected intimacy with Isabella. I enjoy watching the way tenderness flutters across her face and makes her eyes shine in a way I have never seen before. Tears. Can it be? That night we sleep in the same bed. I have not seen my mother in a nightdress ever since I was very small. Stripped of her regalia, she is but a woman with a flowing mane of long, graying hair cascading down her back. A chiseled face resting on a pillow. I must force my lips into a melancholic expression, dim my eyes so that she cannot sense that the prospect of living in the Flemish court, as the wife of the Archduke of Burgundy, arouses more excitement than fear in me. For years I have heard stories about the luxury and dazzle of that court. I have admired the exquisite craftmanship of their goldsmiths and silversmiths, the unrivaled armor of their blacksmiths, the tapestries woven on their looms. The magnificence of their jousts and competitions is legendary, as is the splendor of their banquets and celebrations. I have also heard biting criticism of the licentious ways of the Flemish nobility. I have sensed envy in the comments of those who were most scandalized by the liberality and practices of a court that according to them is far removed from the austerity so proudly praised in our Castilian reign. It so happens that lately, even a trivial lack of modesty can turn into an inquiry before the stern Tribunal of the Holy Inquisition.

My mother locks her eyes on me and sees me as if I were her reflection in a mirror. She is with me, but she is also far away, her mind always looking beyond. I wonder if she might be recalling when she wed my father in secret and against the will of her brother, King Enrique IV. She has told me the tricks my father played to sneak into the castle at Medina del Campo, where the small, intimate ceremony took place. At that time she must have felt the same bewilderment and anxiety I feel, even more, I would think, since she couldn't be sure whether or not she would sit upon the throne of Castile.

"Do not forget your duties to Spain," she says. "Your father and I have bet our youth and our health to unify this country. Your marriage will give us important allies and strengthen our position regarding France. You must conduct yourself as the princess of Castile and Aragon that you are, you must not be seduced by games and excesses," she advises. "Your entourage is large, so you will be surrounded by your own. Seek support from the governor of your court, Admiral Don Fadrique Enríquez, a very noble man, and from young Beatriz de Bobadilla. She is young but wise.

Marriage might seem strange to you not knowing your husband, but your youth and his will be fertile ground for any seed you wish to plant. Let your wish be to love him, and love him you will. Do not be aloof and keep your temper under control. Men are afraid of fiery women, so be discreet and conceal your fire. Ward off the rainstorms that could extinguish your flames."

My mother keeps saying this and that. Her voice fades in and out, swayed by the rocking of the ship, and the gusts of wind blowing over the Bay of Biscay on that dark night, lit up intermittently by distant lightning.

☀ THE NEXT DAY, IT RAINS. I STAY IN MY CABIN WHILE MY MOTHER fights off her anxiety by going over the provisions for the journey with the ladies-in-waiting. That night, we dine with Beatriz Galindo. While we're having dessert, she takes from her bodice a small vial of liquid, made by the Moorish slaves. It is a love potion, she tells me, that I must take and give to my husband. She has been told it is a foolproof philter and will make us love each other till the end of our days.

Beatriz pours half of the liquid into my wineglass and I take it without saying a word, thinking of Isolde and the dangers of love.

Beatriz and my mother titter like naughty girls.

"Well, we shall see if it works. And do not tell your father about this; these are women's secrets."

We were still laughing when the armada's admiral, Don Sancho de Bazán, came to the door to tell us that the storm had passed and that favorable winds were blowing. With the queen's royal assent, we would set sail early the following morning.

My mother praised God and gave her consent for departure. With her habitual discretion, Beatriz took her leave and left us alone. We slept very little that night, thinking that perhaps we would never be together again.

"One day you'll see, Juana, how hard it is to let your children go. In the course of everyday life as they are growing up, you see your children and barely comprehend you once held that life in your womb. But all it takes is a farewell or a hazard to make your body riot and your blood dash in search of the creature you nurtured. But it is life's design that the greater love be the more giving, the one who leaves nothing for itself. I feel infinitely sad and infinitely happy. Sad because I am losing my daughter; happy because I am gaining a partner in the undertaking of making Spain greater and more prosperous."

The next day dawn had barely broken by the time everything was ready. Good-byes were prolonged by the procession: everyone kissed the hand of the queen, and then she gave her recommendations. Finally, it was my turn. I could hear my mother's heartbeat as I pressed myself to her chest. How it pounded! Neither of us wanted to cry, but nor did we want to let go of each other. We didn't utter a word. She made the sign of the cross on my forehead. I knelt and kissed her hand.

My mother stood on the pier and I on the ship's deck until there was no longer any coastline my eyes could see and I was left alone before the endless sea and the clear, blue sky of a shimmering day. I felt I was traveling on a long-tailed kite. As far as my eyes could see, there were brightly colored banderoles and plumes flapping in the wind, decorating the masts of the 131 ships that escorted me. It was a splendid sight. I felt like the character from a love song the minstrels would sing. Accompanied by Don Fadrique and other men and ladies of the court, I spent many hours on the carrack's deck those first days, admiring the calm seas and the schools of dolphins that swam along with us for long stretches of the journey, dipping and gliding effortlessly alongside the ships. Ships navigated in pairs. My Genoese carrack was in the center of the armada.

After three days of smooth, uneventful sailing, a furious storm lashed down, forcing us to anchor in the English port of Portsmouth. During the two days we were forced to stop there, the English nobility paid me homage. They arrived in haste as soon as news reached them of the floating city's unexpected arrival. I lodged in Portchester Castle, by the shore. It was an ancient building with poorly lit rooms and halls, but our hosts did what they could to ensure our comfort. After eight hours of tempestuous seas that tossed us back and forth with no mercy, most of my entourage was a wretched, pale lot. But since rough seas affected neither my stomach nor my equilibrium, the English found me singularly beautiful, and told me so repeatedly. It was only years later that I learned that King Henry VII himself had come, to see me from afar, since protocol would not allow for a king to leave the seat of his throne to receive a princess. Apparently my beauty had been exaggerated to such a degree that he could not resist the temptation to see me in person. I assumed he wanted to satisfy his curiosity. My sister Catalina—or Catherine, as the English called her—was about to be engaged to his son, and he must have felt the urge to see the stock that was about to join his own.

After that mishap we continued on our way with no additional setbacks until we hit a sandbank at our destination, the port of Arnemuiden, in Flanders, where I arrived on September 9, 1496. Still on the high seas, I was transferred to a biscayner, which transported me to the shore of the land that would become my adoptive country. Meanwhile, another Genoese carrack loaded with gifts for the Flemish court ran aground and was holed in the keel. Originally, my trousseau—consisting of fifty trunks—was to have made the journey on that ship. Fortunately, at the last moment, my mother had ordered all of my belongings moved to the flagship, so I had nothing to regret and dedicated myself to making sure that all biscayners available were used to save those who had been shipwrecked, so that all were rescued.

✳️ "LUCÍA, HOW DO YOU THINK JUANA FELT ON THAT JOURNEY?"

"Amazed, spellbound. She must have loved the English reception, the chance to shine her own light for once, without being overshadowed by her parents. I remember what it was like when I was a child, that feeling of not existing in your own right. Adults would search my face for traces of my parents, as if it were a question of ascertaining the quality of the copy. I wasn't the one they were interested in. What they wanted was to ingratiate themselves with my parents. It must have been the same for Juana. On the voyage, she must have realized that leaving her parents would mean she could be herself. Like the little chick that hatches from the egg one minute, and then a couple of hours later totters around on the grass with no hesitation. Maybe that's why she didn't get seasick even though the rough seas took their toll on everyone else; maybe it was a way to assert her character. People had always admired her bravery and her strength, right? As far as her beauty goes, I'm not sure how aware of that she was. I say that, based on my experience, though of course it's not the same thing. I mean, I like what I see in the mirror, I'm not going to lie, but it depends on the day and on my mood. I sense that beauty is full of contradictions. It is quite obvious, judging from the world we live in, that beauty is no small gift for a woman. I myself have prayed to God to spare me from being ugly, but I have also wondered if it's fair to say that someone is ugly, as if that mattered in the least. It certainly doesn't for men."

I had turned to look at Manuel, who was sitting behind me with his face forward, brushing against the arm I had thrown over the back of the chair. He seemed to be trying to detect signs of another time in me, although his eyes did not look into mine, nor were they focused within the confines of the room. Out of the blue, he laid his forehead on my arm, as if he were overwhelmingly exhausted. His sudden lapse made me uncomfortable, but he appeared to recover quickly and offered an apologetic smile.

I recalled the first time I had gone to his apartment. We had wine with lunch, and since it made me sleepy, he told me to feel free to lie down on his sofa and sleep for a while. It was almost four in the afternoon. I had to return to school two hours later, but the Noviciado metro stop was very nearby. I knew that if I could manage to drift off for even ten minutes, I would stop feeling so lethargic. I closed my eyes. I could hear him moving around, lighting a fire, filling the coffeepot with water. Typical Sunday noises filtered through the window: conversations on the street, cars passing sporadically, doors closing. Distant, muffled sounds that failed to intrude into the placid tranquility of siesta time; that remained trapped in the periphery of the motionless circle whose center was the sofa where I lay. Despite the fact that I knew the nuns would not approve of me visiting the apartment of a man I hardly knew, I liked the idea of being there. I felt comfortable, at ease, adult. The solitude that surrounded Manuel acted like an instantaneous link between us, a virtue we shared. It didn't cross my mind to wonder about the unusual interest of a grown man for the friendship and company of a young girl like me. I woke up to Manuel's long fingers stroking my head. When I opened my eyes, his face was very close to mine and he kissed me lightly on the lips. "Wake up, little one," he said, looking at me tenderly. I had thought of that kiss often over the summer, and it always made my mouth tingle.

"Let's go on," he said, interrupting my reverie. "I want to tell you about Juana and Philippe the Handsome's first encounter. You have arrived at Arnemuiden. The news that awaits you as soon as you disembark is that your future husband is not there to welcome you. You get this information from a Spanish noblewoman, María Manuela, the wife of Balduin of Burgundy. King Maximilian of Austria, Philippe's father, has assigned her and a small group of courtiers to receive you instead.

✻ TO GET FROM THE CARRACK TO THE BISCAYNER THAT WOULD TAKE me to dry land, I had insisted on wearing one of my best gold-colored dresses. Neither Don Fadrique nor Doña Beatriz nor any of the other ladies in my entourage were able to dissuade me. I wanted to show off my complexion, my black hair, draw the attention away from the gigantic clock I felt was beating in my chest. Getting me from one boat to the next on the high seas, considering the splendor of my attire, the flounces and hoops, was a harrowing task. I was lowered from the ship like a heavy, useless bundle. I bore the discomfort, imagining the expression on my fiancé's face when he finally saw me. But when only a small group of austere Spanish ladies came forward to greet me I was overwhelmed by a feeling of ridicule, which soured my mood. I felt utterly humiliated. I thought of my mother's efforts putting together such a magnificent armada to display the glories of Spain. From the shore the entire horizon looked like a great city all festooned and decked out for a day of festivities. Such a blunder confused me. Doña María and Don Balduin attempted to conceal their displeasure. They were dressed in the Burgundian manner: she wore a high hat and a fine brocade dress detailed with lace cuffs and collar; he wore knee-length baggy trousers and fine ocher stockings, suede shoes with little arabesques, and a shirtfront with diamonds embroidered in gold thread. The very loquacious Doña María was eager for news of the Castilian court, and she gave us all the details regarding the preparations under way for Marguerite's journey to Spain, where she was to wed my brother, Juan.

In the carriage on the way to our accommodations, no longer within earshot of gossipers, Doña María informed us that although my father-in-law, Emperor Maximilian, agreed with the Spanish crown on the need to isolate the French Valois, both the counselors surrounding Philippe since childhood and a great number of the Burgundian nobility were in favor of the French. They were full of misgivings about the powerful fleet, the number of soldiers and the large entourage I was bringing along. To them it was an unequivocal sign of the influence that my parents, the Catholic Monarchs, wished to exert over Flanders by virtue of my marriage. No doubt that the Flemish preferred to ignore Spanish power. The court of Flanders admired France. They considered the Spanish unsophisticated, rough, inflexible, arrogant, and prudish.

"You should know, Your Highness, that your fiancé the archduke is called not only Philippe the Handsome, but also *croit conseil,* the Easily Advisable, because he shows such blind faith in his counselors."

"The archduke has asked that you travel to Bruges, where he has prepared a reception for you," Don Balduin interrupted.

"But you might also elect to accompany us to Bergen-Op-Zoom. Seignior Jean de Berghes has asked me to extend a cordial invitation for you to attend the baptism of his daughter, and to be her godmother. Berghes is the archduke's principal chamberlain, but he is faithful to the crown of Castile and Aragon," Doña María said, a picaresque smile playing on her thin lips.

Her clear insinuation did not fall on deaf ears. At that moment nothing seemed more appropiate to me than spoiling my future husband's plans. I was still flustered from the fustration I had experienced at having to walk before the crowd at the port in my best golden dress without a handsome prince to welcome me.

"I love baptismal ceremonies," I responded. "I will visit Bruges another time."

✳ "LET'S STOP HERE. YOU MUST GO BACK TO SCHOOL"

I gently refused his offer to take me. We said good-bye at the entrance to the metro. All the way on the train I kept thinking of Juana's dissapointment. Driven to distraction, I missed my stop and arrived at school a few minutes past seven. Dinner had already begun. Mother Luisa Magdalena saw me come in from the podium where she watched over the refectory. On the way to study hall, she came up and asked what had kept me.

"I was on my way back when one of the old booksellers on Cuesta de

Moyano decided to tell me his life story," I said. "I just couldn't bear to interrupt him. Today I saw Pradilla's *Juana la Loca* at the Prado. Very impressive."

"It's beautiful indeed. I must say I was quite surprised to see you arrive without your share of pastries." She smiled.

I looked down to avoid meeting her eyes. I feared her acute intuition. I feared she would know I was lying, but I didn't feel like telling her the truth. Nuns had a tendency to issue warnings. Rather than trust your judgment, they preferred to ensure that you were never in a position where you would need to use it. Mother Luisa Magdalena's affection for me was no guarantee that she would approve of my actions. Above all else, she was a nun.

CHAPTER 6

A letter from Manuel arrived during the week:

On Sunday I spent some time analyzing the work of Francisco Pradilla, and his painting of Juana of Castile. I never cease to admire his ability to capture our poor queen's sadness and impotence at being ostracized and loveless at the peak of her youth. Juana's face makes me think of modern women who refuse to accept the asphyxiating conditions they are forced to endure by society. The more I look at these paintings the more convinced I am of both the painter and his subject's lucidity. It's interesting that Pradilla chose to portray his thoughts on Juana's state of mind for posterity. I could fill page after page with my thoughts on the topic, but just a look at his painting is enough to understand the magnitude of the queen's tragedy. Perhaps I bore you with my obsessions, but the history of Spain, and of that period in particular, is as vivid to me as the taste of the sangria I had with my Sunday lunch, as I watched people strolling down the street. I often ask myself how can this world produce a face as desolate as Juana's when in other faces one can still perceive the innocence of paradise.

In Spanish literature class I could hardly pay attention to the teacher, whose chin-length pageboy haircut looked like a stiff black helmet frozen into place with too much hair spray. I thought about

Manuel's words and tossed them around in my mind, trying to understand the emotions lurking behind them. Despite my love of reading and literature—or maybe because of it—Señorita Aguilar's lessons (we called all of the teachers "Señorita") invariably put me in a bad mood. She asked us to recite our lessons in class word by word. She forced us to remember dates and names, but showed little interest in expanding our knowledge of writers and their works. It was quite a shame to have someone like her teaching a subject that could lead to so much more than honing our memorization skills. Besides, whatever we learned with that system usually evaporated from our minds by the end of the semester—but Señorita Aguilar—not a very enlightened human being—apparently thought knowledge could be ascertained this way. Watching her in class I wavered between irritation and pity. Behind her desire to impose her authority, one could feel a sense of tedium and sadness. She was no longer young but pretended to look youthful, as if time could be defeated by makeup. Unfortunately she didn't apply it well, or just did it in a rush. The result was that her pale, violet lipstick always ran over her lower lip line, her eyeliner caked in the corners of her eyes, and the overall effect made her look like a tattered rag doll worthy of compassion.

THE FOLLOWING SUNDAY I WOKE UP BEFORE THE CRACK OF DAWN. IT was October and the cold had set in during the week, with icy winds blowing in from the sierra. Tucked up in bed, all I had to do was stretch out my legs and I could feel the cold plains at one end of the sheets. I thought about the coming winter. At night the nuns turned off the heat, and the thick walls soaked up the nocturnal chill like sponges, waiting until the dead of night to wring it out into our rooms. The luminous dial of the clock on my nightstand read 5:17 A.M. It would still be a few hours until daybreak, but I was wide awake, excited about meeting Manuel later at the Prado. In spite of myself, I had spent all week thinking about him, weaving absurd fantasies. Aside from feeling nervous and on edge, I felt a surge of energy, a clamoring in my chest that wouldn't let me be still. I would have gladly gotten up and begun to dress, but before I left I first had to attend mass, go to breakfast, feign the usual languorous pace of Sundays at boarding school.

✳ MANUEL WAS STANDING, WAITING FOR ME AT THE USUAL PLACE. This time he didn't even pretend to enter the museum. He started straight down the sidewalk, and when he got to the corner, he stopped a taxi and gave the driver his address. I just let myself be led along.

In his apartment, on the table by the sofa, he had set out little plates of appetizers, two glasses, and a bottle of wine. Conversation was always easy between us, although I often wondered why it was that Manuel puffed so eagerly on his cigarette. When we first arrived I had felt a bit uneasy, trying hard to seem relaxed and normal while I tried to calm an irrational fear: what if Manuel could see through me and read the romantic fantasies I had been entertaining? But his easygoing manner, the soft tone of his voice, and the way he picked up the thread of our conversation as if it had never been interrupted lessened my anxiety. The buzzing in my mind slowed down and my heartbeat regained its pace.

We had some wine along with the appetizers and then Manuel served the lunch he had prepared: baked trout, rice, and vegetables. I was telling him about my literature class, about Señorita Aguilar and her mania for having us learn the lesson by heart, when he asked me if I had ever been in love.

I knew I had blushed when I felt my cheeks get hot, but I burst out laughing.

"How could I? I've been locked up in a convent school since I was thirteen. . . ."

"But when you were twelve, eleven, wasn't there a boy who caught your fancy? I, for one, was given to platonic love. There was Amalia, my neighbor, for instance. I daydreamed about her, but I never dared tell her how I felt."

"I did like my cousin Alejandro. We were inseparable, and he would tell me that I was his girlfriend and that we'd get married one day. But the older cousins said we couldn't marry because we were related. Thinking that our love was impossible saddened me for some time. But we were kids. What about you? What happened with Amalia?"

"Amalia moved away one day, and I never saw her again. Then came Nieves. Does Alejandro write to you?"

"He had an accident about two years ago. He dove into a nearly dry swimming pool. He almost died. He was in a coma for a few months. Luckily he recovered, but he still has memory lapses, and one of the things he forgot was his love for me. He never writes. After Alejandro, I had a fleeting crush on an older man: the architect who built our house. He was really handsome, and he treated me very deferentially, as if I were an adult, but I think he was really taken with my mother. The minute she showed up he'd forget all about me."

"Were you jealous?"

"I suppose so. I hated being so young. I would hide in the room next to the studio, trying to catch something between them that I could tell my father about, but all they did was talk about construction. Still, I'm sure my mother liked the architect. She would get all dolled up to greet him, and her eyes sparkled when she looked at him. But why are you asking me all these questions?"

"Maybe because I've never talked about these things with anyone your age. I can hardly remember how I saw the world when I was a teenager, and when I think about Juana the Mad falling in love at sixteen with Philippe the Handsome, I wonder if such a young person can really fall in love."

"Why not? Besides, back then people got married at that age, right? So they must have felt something."

Manuel smiled as he poured me more wine and lit another cigarette.

"Whenever you're ready, you can get changed and we'll continue. I want to tell you about Juana and Philippe's first meeting. When we left off, she was on her way to the baptism of Jean de Berghes's daughter in Bergen-Op-Zoom."

ON THE TRIP TO BERGEN-OP-ZOOM, I WAS IMPRESSED BY THE NEAT and swarming Flemish cities; their rectangular, brick houses, lined up one after the other, topped with ornate triangular roofs reminded me of the illustrations in the book of hours María de Borgoña had given my mother. The farmhouse roofs were made of very dense thatch, the ends tidily chopped off into straight edges. Everywhere people were working in the fields or toiling away in bakeries and shops. There was an air of productivity very different from that of Castile, which seemed poor and pastoral by comparison. Jean de Berghes's family gave me a very warm welcome, making me and all my ladies very comfortable and putting us up in their chambers, which were exquisitely decorated with brightly colored tapestries. After having been at sea, those days provided me with the rest I so needed; I don't know how I would have survived the following month otherwise. At the baptism, I held the little girl, who they named Jeanne in my honor.

A few days later we left Bergen-Op-Zoom and headed to Antwerp, arriving on September 19. In each city along the way, the people received me with great celebrations to mark my joyous entry, and I returned their interest with smiles and salutations as I paraded down the principal streets with my entourage. My ladies and I rode sidesaddle, in the Spanish manner, on very fine, embossed saddles. We wore our traditional headdresses and mantillas over the gold and deep red of our most sumptuous gowns. We were accompanied by a retinue of trumpeters and standard bearers who made quite a commotion as we passed. These Castilian-style processions, which here also included fire breathers, jesters, and all sorts of entertainers, were aimed at presenting me to the public with a great display of ostentation and revelry, so as to mark the importance of my union with Philippe, particularly in light of my lineage and nobility. The simple inhabitants of these towns, with their rosy-cheeked faces and thin, fair skin, watched us pass in marked admiration. Their smiles and applause made up for what they couldn't express with their words. The Flemish seemed remarkably happy and bold to me. Men and women addressed one another with great familiarity, foregoing the modesty and formality of Castile. Women with tambourines lifted their skirts as they danced. And I saw more than one raise a stein of beer in greeting, from the windows of taverns. Don Luis de Osorio, my confessor, was so scandalized by these people's behavior that I couldn't help but laugh. He kept crossing himself discretely and glancing over at me in an attempt to ensure that I agreed that their conduct was licentious and reprehensible. But the truth is, the self-possessed spirit of the Flemish was so vibrant it was contagious. And even though the hospitality the nobility extended were commingled with clear indications that at times they wished to expose our lack of experience with Burgundian ceremony—as if they were making fun of our ignorance—I did not take it personally. It just seemed part of the jovial, animated, irreverent spirit that I was so pleased to discover in my future subjects. I felt lighthearted and happy. The compliments I received everywhere I turned, more than making me feel vain, made me grateful and also made me want to become a sovereign who they would come to truly love one day.

As days went by, and my understanding of Flemish or a phrase here and there in Latin allowed me to perceive that people envied my good fortune at marrying such a handsome, valiant prince, a good horseman with an admirable zest for life, my initial sadness and apprehension at being separated from my parents and everything I knew was replaced with a tremendous desire to make the most of my new life and become the charming foreign princess that would bring happiness to Archduke Philippe.

It was beginning to get cold. In Antwerp, despite the magnificent reception we were offered, fortune did not smile upon us. I came down with a high fever that made me delirious and left my entire body aching. I felt suddenly overpowered by the fear that my future husband's late arrival, as some had suggested, was meant to humiliate the Spanish crown. The real reason—which I was only just starting to glimpse— could be traced back to my fiancé's childhood. Since the death of his mother in a riding accident when he was four years old, his father had left him under the tutelage of Flemish and Belgian nobles who decidedly supported the French. While they governed the provinces, they kept him entertained with hunts, banquets, and celebrations. Now that he was a man, his father was attempting to free him from these influences and guide him toward the defense and administration of Germanic interests. That was why he had forced him to preside over the German parliament in Lindau, which prevented him from coming to meet me at the port. Nevertheless I found his absence unforgivable. When I fell ill and was in bed feverish after the initial days of joyful celebration, my delight at finding myself in this country that lacked the somber rigidity of Spain soon vanished. I fell into a state of depression that was only aggravated by the death of my confessor, Don Luis de Osorio, and the alarming news of the men and the fleet in Arnemuiden waiting to take Marguerite to Spain. Left to their own devices, thousands of soldiers and sailors were freezing, ill, and starving. Death had begun to decimate them. Impatient and cross, I dictated to Don Fadrique a letter for my fiancé, urging him to hurry to the monastery of Lier, where I was headed. Abbess Marie de Soissons had offered me her hospitality out of gratitude to María Manuela de Borgoña, who had not left my side.

Philippe arrived on the night of October 12, dirty and drenched after having traveled several days without rest, even resorting to taking horses from posthouses. The abbess set him up in a nice room with a fireplace so that he could dry his clothes and have something to eat and drink. The buzz of the archduke's arrival traveled quickly through the monastery eliciting whispers, comings and goings. The news of a masculine presence in their midst seemed to unleash who knows what memories or forbidden fantasies among the women confined there. Because she had been a widow when she entered the convent, the abbess knew of the ways of the world. Promptly after she finished attending to Philippe, she came to my chambers to make certain that my ladies-in-waiting were taking care of my apperance so that my fiancé would be impressed when he first saw me.

Fortunately, I had recovered from my brief illness. The excitement that permeated the air after the news of Philippe's arrival shook off the last vestiges of my melancholy. I intended to display before him the personality I had so often rehearsed when I daydreamed about our meeting. I wanted him to see me like a radiant creature. I chose a deep red dress with a square neckline and wide sleeves. I did not wish to flatter his ego by overdressing. Around my neck I wore the ruby my mother had given me for my engagement, and I let my hair down. I even refused to wear the whalebone stays to extend my skirts, choosing instead to let the velvet fall over my hips and lengthen my figure. Standing before the mirror I could not help but glimpse the fantasies reflected in the eyes of my ladies-in-waiting. Their eyes shone brighter than mine at the thought of what lay ahead. I, on the other hand, had trouble controlling the jumble of contradictory thoughts informing me that misery was as likely as bliss. God knew anything was possible. If Philippe did not captivate me, I would have to put up with years of suffering. Fervently, silently, I prayed for that man to find a way to touch my heart. Amused by my state of agitation, Beatriz de Bobadilla handed me the vial of love potion that Beatriz de Galindo had made me take the last night we dined with my mother. Now I had to find a way to get my future consort to take it, she said playfully. I slipped the vial into my bodice and, finally, accompanied by the abbess, Beatriz, Don Fadrique, and Doña María Manuel de Borgoña, I made my way to the hall where the archduke was waiting.

The moonlight shone through the stained-glass windows of the cold, dark monastery corridors, casting moving shadows of the pine trees in the garden lashed by the wind, and the incessant rain. With both hands I clutched my shawl to my chest, and thus, terrified and covered up, I lay eyes on Philippe for the first time.

Before my eyes could focus, I saw his, staring at me from the blue blur of his clothing, as if his gaze were an entity of its own, trapping me, encircling me, like a strange, delightful silk bow. Slowly, the gaze acquired hair and cheeks, neck and long fingers. He was taller than I, thin, blond, and handsome, but none of that mattered as much as the energy that flowed from him to me, the complicity with which he transmitted his initial doubts, and his present relief. I felt the abundance of warped, foreshadowed images we both had about our meeting. And though we would both have confronted our destinies regardless of our mutual impressions, gazing at each other and realizing that we both liked what we saw unleashed a strange, euphoric complicity. Conscious of how little each of us had intervened in the machinations of our lives, we wordlessly communicated to each other the conviction that together we would find new ways to use the freedom our marriage granted. So well did our silences speak that little doubt remained in our minds that we had fallen in love at first sight. I was about to curtsy, but he stopped me, taking my hand instead and leading me to the other side of the fireplace, motioning for me to sit, out of reach of our attendants. I admired the aplomb he showed before the others, a quality so hard to come upon us, women. We had hardly begun to converse when he asked the abbess, the members of his court and mine, to leave us. Given that we would be spending the rest of our lives together, he told them, we might as well start to know each other without delay. Once everyone had left, my determination to berate him for not having met me upon my arrival was totally dissipated, replaced by a warmth in my chest that rose all the way up to my eyes, producing a sort of dizziness that made me whimper and giggle with relief. Not knowing how to conceal these inappropriate emotions—so unfitting for the moment—I buried my face in my hands, fighting to regain composure. He knelt beside me, concerned, but I told him not to worry. I was tired after so many days on the road, and pleased to see that I would have no cause to curse my destiny, after all. He took out a handkerchief and dried my tears. I think not even five minutes had passed when he embraced me and kissed my lips. He lips were thin, but his tongue was like a sword darting into my mouth. I could taste beer, and I recall the tang of malt and the heat that his tongue produced on mine, which traveled down my throat like a flame, making me tremble and feel that within me lived a body I had not known I possessed.

I pulled away to take a breath. His blue eyes were so close that they seemed like a moon on his forehead. He touched my cheeks and I touched his, which were hot and flushed. Then suddenly, he took my hand and placed it between his legs, beneath his blue riding jacket. What I felt was like a bunch of grapes, and I moved my hand around in order to understand it, since in truth I had almost no knowledge of male anatomy. As I explored, Philippe kissed my collarbone, and his mouth, leaving a moist trail, bit into the edge of my breasts that peeked out over my décolletage. At that moment, I remembered the vial hidden in my bodice, and the thought of him discovering it made me suddenly recover my other body, the one that knew no passion. I took my hand from between his legs and placed it between us.

"I beg you to desist, my lord," I said. "We must be patient and wait until our union has been blessed," I added, making a face as I smoothed my skirt, ran my hands over my bodice, my hair, and then stood to step away from him.

"I am only doing what they have ordered us to do," he replied devilishly, flashing me a smile I could not help but return. He stood and went to the table to take a long drink of beer. Then he smiled again and added, "Now that I have seen you, I can see no reason why we should not be free to decide when and where we carry out our orders. Let me show you right now."

He strode to the door. As we had both suspected, members of both of our entourages were huddled just on the other side, trying to overhear our conversation. Philippe ordered his governor to call the abbess. When she arrived, minutes later, I was shocked beyond belief to hear him ask for authorization to carry out our wedding ceremony immediately.

"The princess and I have lost an entire month and we would like to spend the night together tonight," he said, adopting a solemn air, his expression making it perfectly clear that there was no room for argument.

I sat down, staring at the reflection the candles made on my velvet skirt. Despite the considerable embarrassment I felt at being so willing to take part in this game, despite my fear that Don Fadrique and Beatriz would think I had lost my wits, each time I glanced up at Philippe's back I was flooded with joy at the fact that fate had bestowed such a man upon me. I could not have hoped for anything more daring or chivalrous than the scene unfolding before me. Courtiers came and went. His governor exchanged hushed comments with mine, off in a corner. The abbess had gone to find Don Diego Ramírez de Villaescusa, my chaplain, who rushed in and then approached me, whispering in my ear, "Is this what Your Highness wishes?"

I lowered my eyes with false modesty, concealing the glee and the disquiet I felt in my chest.

"I am happy to abide by my future husband's decisions. And I concur; if I have come here to marry, there is no sense in postponing what

I came here to do," I whispered, meeting Philippe's eyes. Unlike me, he made no attempt to hide his amusement.

The memory of the improvised ceremony beside the fireplace where he first kissed me is still vivid. Candles were lit and brought in from other rooms, and before the crude table from the abbey entry hall, Don Diego married us, in the presence of the most cherished members of our entourages. The shadows of those present were elongated on the building's gray walls. I saw the silhouette of my hands in his (his fingers as long and slender as mine) projected like storks' beaks above the priest's head. Without having even used the vial that was still concealed in my bodice, my fiancé seemed to have fallen under my spell. He looked at me in joy and adoration, as if what was happening were the culmination of a long-standing desire. I felt the same, awed at his awe. We had fallen in love with the possibility of love. My mother had been correct in thinking that our youth was fertile ground. I thought of her as the priest gave us his blessing. She would not have approved of our urgency. And yet, her wedding had not been so very different.

"LUCÍA."

It was as if a wave had hurled me from the gentle sea to the hard surface of a rocky beach. I opened my eyes. It must have been four or five in the afternoon, judging by the light. Manuel was walking to the kitchen. He returned with two glasses of red wine.

"I think a little wine will help us return to reality," he said with a sad smile.

"You say that as if you'd rather not come back."

"I'd give anything if I could be inside their heads. Imagine. She was sixteen; he was eighteen. They'd just met. She was a virgin, beautiful and flustered. He was worked up after the cavalcade, excited by the power of his rank. His sexual desire intertwined with the wish to provoke the Spanish and defy convention. It was cold. Juana would have looked like you, rosy-cheeked, trembling. Come, let's get those clothes off. You look like you're under a spell."

On the stairs going down into the darkness of Manuel's room, my legs felt wobbly. I didn't want to leave behind the scenario my imagination was still projecting: undergarments strewn across the floor of an austere, monastic bedroom.

Manuel sat behind me and gently removed my pendant, and as he did so he bent over my neck and kissed it tenderly, running his tongue along my hairline. I was about to protest, but instead my skin rose up as if dancing, lifting itself against my reticence and my surprise. It felt as if the world had become all silk and gauzes. I closed my eyes and let myself drift into a time hundreds of years in the past. I was Juana all over again. Philippe and I were alone at last after the ceremony. He was tracing the contours of my shoulder blades with his lips while his hands undid the ribbons on the front of my dress, making it fall softly around me. I felt like a dove being let out from her cage. I inhaled deeply. His kisses, the wetness of his tongue went after every inch of my skin like short-frequency-rippling-lake waves tugging my clothes off little by little. My breasts were set free, emerging out into the open space. My nipples stiffened, contracting like round gourds. He embraced me from behind. His hands cupped my breasts, kneading them slowly and deliberately like dough, as if he had to make the yeast of my skin rise until it swelled up in pleasure.

When the dress fell down over my waist, Philippe pushed me lightly. He led me silently, wordlessly to the bed. I felt the silk of Manuel's bedspread on my back. He was breathing heavily as he slid the gown down my legs and over my feet. I was naked now, just with my panties on, and I didn't want to think or to open my eyes. All I wanted to do was give in, pretend I had no will of my own. I wanted to open my body, cast aside all warnings, let it happen. Manuel tugged at his clothes. I felt his masculine body, the plain skin enveloping his taut muscles, no round forms just solid, angular shapes, the scant hair on the chest, the pounding, racing heart at its center, brushing against my breasts. And Philippe leaned into me, rubbed himself against me, sank his mouth into my hair, into my ears, making a sound as if in pain, touching me all over, feeling his way along my ribs, my legs, tugging off my panties hurriedly, as if he feared I might suddenly disappear. I glimpsed a white body, his penis erect between his legs, coming out from the bush where it lived in hiding, like a large index finger in the act of offering an almost laughably stern reprimand. I stared at it, fascinated, as he lay beside me and began to kiss my navel, to run his fingers slowly down the entire length of my legs, like a command, making me want to spread them wider and wider, so that his hand would come and stroke my pubis. Then I heard my moans join his, while inside a warm sensation spread like honey pouring out of my entrails, honeycomb oozing a warm, viscous liquid. He plunged his hand between my legs, wetting himself with my juices, taking his fingers to his mouth and then wiping them over my lips, letting me taste myself. I writhed madly and instinctively took hold of Philippe's strong, erect member and brought it to my lips like a goblet of wine. Then I grabbed onto his back to help him mount me and I shivered at the exquisite sensation of the first approach, his hardness trying to cross the moat that guarded my innermost castle, but when my instincts encouraged him to enter, to come into my secret chambers, suddenly alarm bells began ringing and the pain of forbidden places, of doors intractably locked, interfered. I whimpered and whispered that I couldn't, that it wouldn't fit, but Philippe or Manuel, I don't know which and no longer cared, pinned my arms down on the pillows and despite my cries pushed himself inside me like a drill in search of water, and I felt the agony of penetration, his flesh losing itself in mine, and I cried out in pain and in relief, thinking it's done, it's all over now, feeling that it was what he had to do, forgiving him, crying, as we both rocked back and forth, our cries louder and louder until suddenly there he was pulling out of me, kneeling above me, and letting his hot, thick liquid spurt onto my stomach.

CHAPTER 7

"Kyrie eleison."

"Kyrie eleison."

FATHER JUSTO, THE SCHOOL CHAPLAIN, SWUNG the censer above the altar like a pendulum. Dense, fragrant smoke filled the chapel. I closed my eyes and let myself be carried off by the rhythmic clinking of the censer's chain. Beside me kneeling on the bench were Margarita and Pilar. I wondered if they noticed the smell coming from me; I felt as if my skin were producing its own sacred aroma. I had showered the night before, but when I woke up that morning I stuck my head under the covers and noticed a sort of ocean smell. I rubbed myself with a towel and then had to rush to make it to the second mass, for day pupils, trying not to aggravate the pain and burning I felt between my legs. Paradoxically, that aching made me feel absurdly superior to the other girls, to the eleven thousand virgins surrounding me. The image made me smile into my missal.

I couldn't believe it was so easy to hide such a transcendental event, that it wasn't written all over my face in great, big letters. The routine, the Mondays of the world, were going on as usual. But inside me, everything was changed. I felt like my parents' house on the day the movers came and put everything into storage: my corridors full of boxes, the lawn strewn with shredded paper, chairs and tables all out of place. My virginal girlhood was moving out of me. I couldn't help but wonder why innocence was considered such a valuable virtue. Now that I had lost mine, I certainly didn't miss it. Quite the contrary: childhood and puberty seemed like a long, dark period full of confusion and superstitions. All that fear of the body and its orifices. All that imagined pain and shame when sexuality seemed full of clarity: a revelation of the intimate bond between body and spirit. How could I not be awed to see my body instinctively act with such confidence? To see how in tune my skin and my brain were? It was like finding an old map hidden in my subconscious. Or coming upon Aladdin's lamp and having the genie pop out the first time I rubbed it, turning wishes and fantasies into reality. Even though, in the darkness of the chapel, kneeling between the virgins in my class, I wondered if I should feel ashamed. Inside all I felt was joy and celebration. I wanted to take communion when the priest raised the host before us and asked us to come up. I thought having made love allowed me to understand the idea of communion. Now I knew what it meant to cherish another being in the most intimate part of yourself. And yet I didn't dare go take the host. I was scared. I was sure that if I went to confession, Father Justo would scold me and might even deny me communion. Like the poor nuns, he would never know what it was to make love. The love of the flesh was impure according to them. They held, and would always hold, the absurd belief that sex was just a necessary evil, something required for procreation. The priests and nuns distorted one of the most crucial elements of life, turning it into some dark act. I felt a surge of anger when I thought about the constant admonitions warning us about the wailing and gnashing of teeth. Luckily, at my house, religion had always been more of a social formality, a convenient artifice, something that provided a sense of continuity and stability. Or, as my father used to say, it was a story, a morality tale we told ourselves in order to feel better about the inevitable end. It was soothing, he said, to imagine heavenly courts and intergalactic journeys after death, instead of just nothingness, which for him was a certainty. But everyone had to find their own truth, go through their own process, and it was I, after all, who would have to decide for myself once I could discern between science and mythology. My mother didn't contradict him, but she did maintain that neither of them was any worse off for having had a religious education. She liked to pray with me at night, but I got the distinct impression she did it for tradition's sake, like a sweet and harmless ritual. My parents' indifference to the principles of faith—which the nuns hammered into us as if making sure we felt guilty for our existence was the only path to becoming decent human beings—had restrained my devotion. I wasn't indifferent to the sermons on eternity and everlasting damnation, but the cruelty of the punishments described didn't seem to fit with the intelligence of a Supreme Being capable of creating a hummingbird or a wave. The idea of a gentle, loving God seemed much more consistent, as far as I could see. But it was hard to know if my father would see the absence of divine retribution as a good reason for allowing myself to be seduced by Manuel, for example. The idea of his watching over me made me very uncomfortable. I thought I'd better find someone outside the convent to take my confession, some adult, someone who could give me counsel. It couldn't be Father Justo, but if I avoided communion again, Mother Luisa Magdalena would notice. And even a skeptic like me didn't feel comfortable taking communion without having confessed.

That week more than ever I regretted not having a close friend, someone I could tell I was no longer a virgin. It seemed like such a transcendental occurrence that I was dying to tell someone, to share a secret that I was sure that neither Margarita nor Piluca nor Marina would be able to swallow without choking or gaping at me in incredulity. It wasn't the risk of their disapproval that stopped me but the fear that they would be unable to contain themselves and might tell others. News would spread throughout the school like wildfire, and that was a chance I couldn't take. But I wanted so badly to show off in front of them! The truth is I felt proud of my affair, even though I could hardly believe I had been so daring. How could I have let Manuel seduce me, just like that? Would he think I was some sort of shameless hussy? And where did my own uncontrollable sexual urge come from? Why instead of ebbing away, it kept coming back every time I thought about Manuel's hands, about the way he touched me, about the tender way he soothed me after it was over and I cried like a baby?

In the middle of the week I made up a reason why I had to call my grandparents so that I could use the pay phone and call Manuel. He seemed disconcerted by my phone call. He said he wasn't expecting it. I didn't talk for long because he felt so distant it made me uneasy. I hated being so susceptible, but I had been like that ever since I was a little girl. Sometimes I was overwhelmed by the fear that because of my sorrows no one would fall in love with me. I wondered if perhaps Manuel was regretting what had happened. Perhaps the guilt I lacked was all weighing on *his* conscience. Maybe he'd say we shouldn't see each other anymore. I was so worried I couldn't sleep. I hardly ate. But on Friday I received a postcard with a picture of a Flemish tapestry.

Lucía, I've had a lot of work this week. I would gladly exchange my desk for a green meadow where I could contemplate Juana's life in Flanders at my leisure. At midday on Sunday, could you have lunch with me?

Manuel.

In the Church of San Cipriano, not far from school, they took confession on Saturday afternoons. I walked in and genuflected as I tried to make out the confessionals in the dim light. They looked like huge wooden armoires on either side of the church's circular nave. I took a seat on the benches near one of them, where several old women were waiting their turn. I was immediately wrapped in the church's cavelike, silent atmosphere. No matter the times I had told myself I wouldn't be condemned for what I had done, first of all because hell probably didn't even exist, and secondly because God would understand me, being there made me feel like a sinner, an impure Mary Magdalene. The effigy of Christ on the cross above the high altar was like a higher authority, rebuking me with his agonized presence. I held my head in my hands. At that moment, my repentance was genuine. I wanted to believe that I was being honest when I told myself I wouldn't do it again, that I would return, like the prodigal daughter, to the path of righteousness. But my mind jumped from one thing to the next, preoccupied with figuring out how to tell the priest. "A man seduced me, Father, and I let him," or "Father, I confess to having lost my virginity." The first version seemed like it would be more palatable for the priest, less incriminating for me, but not altogether honest. That was as far as I had gotten when it came time for my turn. My hands were sweating as I knelt and repeated the set phrases of the Ave Maria. The confessional was very dark and smelled of old, rancid wood, of musty, spilled sins. The priest was hidden behind a short purple curtain, but I could see his shiny shoes through a crack.

"Come, child, tell me your sins," the deep, masculine voice said, after asking me how long it had been since my last confession.

"I made love with my boyfriend, Father."

There was a pause. The priest cleared his throat. I dug my fingernails into my arms, which were crossed over the wooden ledge below the little window.

"Did you do everything you could to resist temptation?"

"I don't know. I wasn't expecting it. This force just . . . came over me," I faltered, not knowing what else to say.

"Tell me all about it. Tell me what happened."

I couldn't do it. I ran out, flustered. It was ridiculous, to be expected to confess such intimate things. What right did priests have to hear one's most private affairs? In the end I went to the confessional in the school chapel. I confessed to Father Justo for having impure thoughts and desires, sure that God would be able to decipher my code.

Sunday, rather than hail a taxi, Manuel led me down the side streets near Paseo de la Castellana to a small, cozy restaurant with low ceilings and adobe arches. They served tapas. He ordered mussels, Spanish tortilla, Serrano ham, cheese, olives, mushrooms, and I don't know what else. To drink, he ordered the house red wine. He was acting normal, just like always, as if nothing had happened. I was a little disconcerted. But seeing him so unemotional I thought maybe that was the way adults acted, so I played my part.

I noticed he looked pale and had bags under his eyes.

"Is everything okay, Manuel? You look tired."

"I didn't tell you when you called, but I've had to take care of my Aunt Águeda all week. She's normally very healthy, but when she gets sick she becomes absolutely helpless and gets in a bad mood. I've hardly been at my apartment these past few days. Fortunately, the library where

I work is in my family's home. It's a beautiful house, a museum of the history, the shame, and the secrets of my family."

"And is your aunt better now?"

"Yes. She had an ear infection that ended up causing labyrinthitis. That's an inner-ear inflammation that makes you lose your sense of balance."

"Why didn't your Aunt Águeda ever get married?"

"Because of me, most likely," he said somberly. "She's always devoted herself to me. You'll have to meet her," he added in a lighter tone. "She's like a magpie hording her treasures. I suspect she has a few she hides even from me. Once, when I was a teenager, she told me about a trunk that belonged to Queen Juana that she'd seen as a child. I only recalled that recently when I came across references in some old documents to a trunk the queen kept hidden in her room that contained her most cherished objects. I asked Águeda if that might have been the one she'd seen, but she seemed not to remember anything and denied ever having mentioned it. I don't know what to think, but I'm intrigued by the possibility that she really does know where it is. If it exists, she'll have to tell me one day."

We were having coffee. Manuel stirred sugar into his espresso pensively.

"Just imagine if you find it. I wonder how it would feel, peeking at things she hid centuries ago," I said.

He put his hand on top of mine and squeezed so hard that I withdrew it.

"I'm sorry," he said, flicking back a lock of white hair that was always hanging down in his eyes. "You don't know how much it means to me to have you take part in this investigation with me. Some people live entirely in the present, they hurl themselves into the chaos of existence as if there were nothing beyond their senses. But others among us don't see time as linear, we see it as a constant state of becoming, with the only division between past, present, and future being artificially established by human emotional needs. For a historian, studying reality the way someone from a specific period of time perceives it is like exploring the unknown depths of the ocean for a marine biologist. As far as I'm concerned, there is nothing more exciting than uncovering the mysteries of human behavior. The Marquises of Denia deceived Juana for years, lying to her about what was going on outside the four walls of Tordesillas. Ferdinand the Catholic, her father, had been dead for four years before Juana heard the news. The marquis tried to convince her that her ill father had retired to a convent. He instructed her to write to him. He wanted to use her letters as proof of her insanity. Not only that, but in order to persuade her not to leave the palace, they told her the plague had spread throughout town and organized bogus funeral processions all day beneath her window. Did they take pleasure in being the architects of this farce? They must have felt *some* kind of pleasure. But what kind? Do you know that poor Catalina, the posthumous daughter of Juana and Philippe, who grew up imprisoned with her mother, used to spend all day at a palace window tossing coins down to the children below so that they would run over and she could at least watch them play? You'll learn the rest of the story soon enough. We've hardly even got past the passion of their first meeting. The body is so simple, Lucía. It's the purest thing we have. The mind, on the other hand, is full of twists and turns. The mind is the real labyrinth. And in real life there is no Ariadne, no silver thread to find your way back. It's just you and the Minotaur, panting. And he's always close by."

AT LUNCH AND ON THE WAY BACK TO HIS HOUSE, WE DIDN'T TALK about what happened last Sunday. Personally I thought it was rude— given that I'd lost my virginity—that he didn't even bother to ask me whether or not I had felt uncomfortable. But maybe men thought women's discomfort was something trivial, something that didn't merit comment. Or maybe he thought it was impolite to ask. The other disquieting possibility was that maybe he thought it had happened between Juana of Castile and Philippe the Handsome rather than the two of us.

CHAPTER 8

The clock turns back again. I don the gown. I take my seat. The Madrid afternoon fades away beneath the balcony.

✳ JUANA'S UNIVERSE WAS TURNED UPSIDE DOWN AFTER HER FIRST night with Philippe in that monastic cell turned makeshift wedding chamber.

✳ DISCOVERING THE PLEASURES OF MY BODY MADE ME QUESTION everything that so far I had considered certain in life. There was no place in the sensations I had experienced in bed for the guilt and damnation or the punishment associated with the Sixth and Ninth Commandments. If the nuns heard my cries there was no way of knowing what they must have thought, because Philippe encouraged me to groan and purr at will and he roared and cried out, and we both laughed out loud at our own shamelessness. It was hard for me to believe I was the same person I had been the day before. In just a few hours, all of the modesty and reserve I'd stored up in my lifetime had disappeared. I surrendered so willingly to pleasure and lost my inhibitions so thoroughly that people might have guessed me the daughter of a courtesan, not of the Catholic Queen.

In the morning, sitting naked on the bed with my legs crossed as I toyed with his soft, sleeping member—a distant cousin of the dragon who was quietly regaining his fire—Philippe told me about the life I would lead in Flanders. Beauty, he said, was power's greatest reward, and living in his country I would soon forget the narrow-minded Spanish mentality. "They sent you here surrounded by spies, priests, soldiers, and severe, ascetic handmaidens. But here, as you have seen, the terrain is smooth and flat, misty and green. I'm going to teach you to enjoy life, to savor wine and yourself. Next to me your strong body will know the pleasures of being alive and sated. Your sense of touch will learn about silk and the intricate patterns of Bruges lace. Your eyes will surrender to the light of our painters. They will make you see why we sing the praises of creation. You will see how the colored threads in a tapestry can be as alive as the life they portray. You will eat from sets of dishes whose every plate is a work of art. You will see, Juana, the life you will discover with me. It will make you forget the bonfires where your people burn the poor devils accused of heresy. You will forget the intolerance of your lineage, but you will have to consent to being surrounded by our nobles, to being separated from the court you brought from Spain, the court that cannot comprehend our splendor, that is even suspicious of it." He had placed his hand on my stomach and his index finger traced circles around my navel like a horseman circling a castle's moat. I so much wanted then to hand over to him—whom after all I was supposed to submit to—the reins of my life so that he would show me what lay beneath the obscurity attributed to pleasure at the Castilian court. We spent all day in bed. He rolled around in my hair, fed me his seed, he knew me like I could never get to know myself. At night he called for wine, bread, and fruit. He used my sex like a dish. We bit and tasted each other. He refused to let me sleep because he said he wanted to see the light of the rising sun shine on my skin, and so it was that we watched the dawn of a new day nude, exhausted, and insanely happy.

Manuel too brought me something to eat in bed. Unfortunately, he said, I would have to see the new day dawn from my room, but we could play at making a night of the afternoon.

I was naked, lying on my stomach, still panting, when Juana left the convent and said good-bye to Marie de Soissons.

I LET MY EYES EMBRACE THE SILHOUTTE OF THE ABBEY IN THE FIRST morning light. Its gray walls appeared to be a liquid substance blending in the mist with the subdued color of the atmosphere. The nuns in their dark habits, standing in the doorway, lifted their arms, waving good-bye. Philippe's and my horses headed the procession at a trot. Shortly before Antwerp, we would separate so that Philippe could accompany his sister Marguerite to Arnemuiden, where she would board a ship to Spain. Marguerite had come to Lier to make my acquaintance. When she met me I was dressed only in a loose, white nightshirt, because my husband didn't lose time asking me whether I minded if she came into our bedchamber. I thought she would make Juan happy because, like her brother, Marguerite was full of vitality and contagious energy. All my fragile brother had to do was to allow himself to be loved. I could imagine how amazing it would be for him to be faced with the exhuberance of the Austrias and my sister-in-law's golden splendor. The letters I received from Spain, after the wedding, confirmed my intuition. Juan, who was only two years older than me, had surrendered himself passionately to her love.

Philippe admired my riding skills on the cavalcade to Antwerp, and he had the woman who had been his governess—Jeanne de Commines, Madame de Hallewin—ride beside me. He told me he thought she should be in charge of the ladies in my court and be at my side to instruct me in the protocol and dealings within the Burgundian court. No one could do it better than her, he said. Madame de Hallewin wore a pointy hat with a delicate veil hanging from the tip. The hat—like all of her attire—was done in the latest French fashion, something that inspired in me an instant prejudice, which I tried to dismiss so as not to offend her or displease Philippe. Notwithstanding her French-style wardrobe, Madame de Hallewin had to her advantage the fact that she spoke Spanish perfectly. She was a middle-aged woman, with very fair skin, an angular face and kind, earthy green eyes. Her wide, well-defined mouth diminished somewhat the overall impression she gave of being a sexless angel. I told myself I had to get to know her better and not be guided just by my instinct. Given that she had been Philippe's governess and considering how charming he was, there was no reason to think she wasn't worthy of my friendship and trust. As she began to speak about the festivities that were organized in Brussels, Ghent, and other cities to celebrate my wedding, I caught Beatriz de Bobadilla on my right, glancing over distrustfully. I took the first opportunity, during a stop to rest, to go to her and tell her about Philippe's provisions.

"I will have two first ladies," I said, "because I am certainly not planning to renounce your company. You must not think that this madame can take your place, in my confidence or my heart."

"Be careful, Juana," she said. "I have the impression that your husband wishes to surround you with Flemish nobles and cast aside the Spaniards. It seems rather underhanded to me. Do not allow yourself to be blinded by love."

It wasn't only love that blinded me. In the following months, the inhabitants of the Low Countries received Philippe and I in a series of joyous entries to the principal cities. The colors, the revelry, the joyfulness of those festivities—despite the gray skies and light rain falling like a veil over the Flemish landscape—filled me with an eager desire to take into my heart a country that was now mine. The bliss my flesh experienced every night incited me to rebel against the remnants of Castilian rigidity that prevailed in the retinue that accompanied me who continued to be loyal to my mother. I did not object when Philippe began to substitute them for noblemen and ladies he held in his confidence, people whose customs were better suited to our lifestyle. I even neglected my duties to some of those who, having risked their lives and served me faithfully, had accompanied me on the dangerous crossing from Laredo to Flanders. Some say soldiers in the thousands froze to death that winter, awaiting fair weather to set sail with Marguerite of Austria. I take that to be an exaggeration. But that is what they said. Beatriz reproached me. My confessor Diego Ramírez de Villaescusa reproached me and also complained about my lack of interest in religious devotions. He tried my patience, with his straitlaced prudishness and his severity, his discourses claiming that my subjects showed more interest in drinking well than in living the "good life," as if food and drink were forbidden pleasures, as if they were sinful. After only one year, my royal household had been restructured in line with Burgundian protocol, and only eighteen of the initial ninety-eight members of my Spanish entourage remained. With no income of my own, I could do little to retain them. The terms of my marriage stipulated that Philippe would maintain my servants and provide me with whatever I needed. And he did. But given that he was paying their wages, he also decided who they were. Beatriz complained. She said she could not understand how my parents could have agreed to such an arrangement. The nobles who returned to Spain must have brought my royal parents this news, because they sent an ambassador, Fray Tomás de Matienzo, to the Low Countries. His words made clear that they blamed me for the exodus of my Spanish courtiers, that they condemned my actions, and disapproved of my behavior. Independence had gone to my head like liquor. I still had not realized that my destiny had simply changed hands, from my parents to my husband. In Philippe's hands, all I saw were instruments that stroked and strummed me, making music emanate from within me. He was quite skilled at making me think his decisions were made in accordance with the same principles as mine. So when I obeyed his wishes I felt I was affirming my own and proving the existence of my own criteria. I had no doubt that I owed Spain my loyalty, but I thought that it would better serve the aims of my country to have the Flemish accept me as their sovereign, to have them see me as living proof of our respective countries' common interests. To think I could set up a Spanish island in Flanders was outlandish and utterly unrealistic. But for my parents not to understand that and to send Fray Tomás to scold me both hurt and infuriated me.

My husband was no malingerer, but his advisors would have been more than happy to join forces with the Valois and not the Spanish if it weren't for King Maximilian. The Flemish nobility was much more influential than ours, and it did not take long for me to see that these men knew that with my parents so far away, they would eventually be able to increase their sway over me simply because they were constantly by my side.

As soon as Philippe and I had settled in Brussels, the Flemish took on all of the most important positions in my royal household, or shared them with my aides and attendants, so that I could rarely be alone with those I knew and trusted. I protested, but Philippe used the burning passions of our intimacy to appease my discontent. He pampered me with endearments and fabulous gifts. Almost every afternoon, we would go riding through the forest close to the palace and make a game of galloping off at top speed to lose the nobles who'd accompanied us. Once we were alone, we would dismount in the nearby villages, stroll through the streets and visit the markets like two well-dressed commoners. Philippe liked to corner me someplace and kiss me passionately in full view of the passers-by. More than once, holding hands, we visited artisans' workshops where they made jousting swords or beautiful tapestries. The master craftsmen would invite us in for a glass of wine and tell us about their simple lives. And then, after our antics, we'd return to the intrigues of the palace, the jealousies between Philippe's courtiers and mine, the latent power struggles surging up around us that—when we were alone— we managed to elude. Then just our eyes making contact was enough to create a sheltered space protected from all else but the immense love we felt and that kept our blood rushing through our bodies like an impetuous river. Alas, our love was besieged by interests of State, and my naive infatuation suffered its first real disenchantment the afternoon I received the dreadful news of my brother Juan's death.

My sister-in-law Marguerite and the nobles at court had relayed the details of their lavish wedding ceremonies and celebrations. Like Philippe and I, Juan and Marguerite had fallen in love as soon as they set eyes on each other. But Juan did not possess my hearty constitution and he melted like a wax taper in the legendary passion of the Austrias. Or at least that is what people said: that he had given himself to Marguerite, and by the time he rose from the nuptial bed he'd already grown pale; that his body was unable to protect him when he came down with a high fever in Salamanca while visiting the city with his new wife. Barely seven months after his wedding, poor Juan died in my father's arms on October 6, 1497.

I never could have guessed anything like that would happen, especially because Marguerite had recently written to me to say that she was with child. Juan's death unsettled my bones. I received the news on an opaque, listless autumn day in Brussels, and I was suddenly hit by the realization that Philippe had separated me from everything I loved. I had let my husband dismiss nearly all of my Spanish courtiers. I couldn't even share my sorrow with my own kind. Aside from Beatriz and Ana de Viamonte, no one in that room cared about Juan's death. In fact, sitting in an armchair by the fire, I could hear them chattering away animatedly. Crying for Juan, I regretted not having written to my mother, refusing to be influenced by her, as per Philippe's counsel. I don't know exactly when, but at some point I stood up and began to shout, banishing the Flemish attendants from my chamber because I could no longer stand the hideous sound of their guttural language nor bear to see their insincere expressions of condolence. They must have called Philippe, for he appeared almost instantly and, taking no notice of my sorrow, began raving like a madman, insisting we had to call the envoy—Señor Manrique—and tell him that since Juan was dead, we wanted the titles of Prince and Princess of Asturias bestowed upon us immediately. We had to avow our right to the crown. I told him he was mad. Not only was my sister Isabel alive, but his own sister Marguerite was pregnant. He in turn claimed that I was the mad one, for not seeing that this was the chance we needed to be considered heirs to the throne of Castile and Aragon. I can't recall all of the other things he said. At a certain point his words blurred into an indistinct drone and his face—which I never thought I could find objectionable—looked like that of a bird of prey perched on my brother's shoulder, waiting to disembowel his corpse. I covered my ears and ran from the room, telling him to do whatever he pleased. I didn't care. He would have my mother and father to contend with, after all.

And that was what happened. My mother and father reacted angrily to his audacity and confirmed Isabel as their heir. After the death of Prince Alfonso, she had married King Manuel of Portugal, and since Marguerite and Juan's son was stillborn, there was no other option. I had to remain levelheaded in my husband's presence, because the truth is that my parents' pronouncement, though understandable, still affronted me. Philippe had been clumsy and aggressive in his pretensions, true, but by casting him aside they left me alone, bleeding, and swimming in shark-infested waters.

A year passed from the time we married. I was beginning to worry that all of our lovemaking seemed to bear no fruit when, finally, I realized that I was with child. Philippe was delighted, and I could not contain my joy. My body began to grow. The skin on my belly became a taut drum, crisscrossed with delicate blue subterranean rivers. Lying in bed with my hands resting on the round moon that wriggled of its own volition, I could spend hours imagining how that bouncy baby residing within me might turn out. But despite how I lost myself in my fantasies, I was not oblivious to certain unexplained absences on Philippe's part. Aware of my terrible moods, Madame de Hallewin and Beatriz tried to console me, assuring me that it was an old custom for a husband not to threaten his child's welfare by expecting his wife to fulfill his needs in the latter months of pregnancy.

"Your own mother, Juana, endured the same. That was when your father's bastard children were conceived, and you know that they were brought up at court, because Queen Isabel is magnanimous and sympathetic and she deigned that it be so."

"You must understand, child," admonished Fray Tomás de Matienzo, the envoy my parents had sent who now lived in my court.

"Well, I don't," I replied, glaring at him, feeling my cheeks burn with the feverish rage coursing through me. "Men excuse everything. I would have no trouble accepting this if Philippe—like my uncle King Enrique with his wife—were to consent to me finding my own lover and conceiving my own bastard children."

I repeated this remark that night at dinner, in public, in front of Philippe. If Fray Tomás had been shocked at my words, Philippe gave so much credit to my threats that from then on he spent every night with me and we found many creative ways to surmount the hill of my belly. I told him that not during that or any future pregnancies, so long as God granted me life and good health, he would need to seek others when it was I who best knew how to satisfy his hunger.

My first daughter, Leonor, was born on November 15, 1498, in Lovaina. Ysabeau Hoen, a midwife from Lier, assisted in the delivery. I was extraordinarily nervous. Only two months earlier, on August 23, my sister Isabel had died in childbirth. My desolate mother had written to me. Isabel had died in her arms, an hour after giving birth. I knew how much my mother loved her. In under a year her two eldest children were no more. How could that be? And poor Marguerite. Her pregnancy had ended in a pool of blood. Her womb had not sheltered a child but a shapeless mass. Miguel, my sister's Isabel newborn, was named then heir to the throne of Castile and Aragon. It had already been confirmed by the Cortes.

In the throes of my labor pains, I kept seeing Juan's and Isabel's faces floating over my bed. Fortunately, Ysabeau not only had soft, skilled hands, but the presence of mind and fierceness required to take me by the shoulders and shake me from the panic that overcame me just when I should have begun to push the baby out.

"Never! Do you understand? You will never die in childbirth," she shouted in Flemish, shaking me so hard that I was forced to stop covering my face with my hands.

It was an order, a spell, I don't know, but from that moment on I never again doubted myself or my health when it came time to deliver. My body unclenched, and Leonor was born with no mishaps. I cried when Ysabeau placed the little girl in my arms. I fully understood the terrible sorrow of my mother's recent loss, and fervently wished her to be there with me. If she had been there, I was sure she would have felt it as a rebirth, for Leonor was a Trastámara.

As is the Burgundian fashion, Philippe did not arrive until I had been comfortably settled into the chamber of honor, and lay waiting to receive the court's congratulations in a green canopied bed with an ermine-fringed gold blanket. He too was overcome when he took Leonor in his arms, but he glanced at me indifferently, as if the baby had transformed me into some other Juana. The moment my milk began to flow, though, he became a curious little boy, fascinated by my swollen breasts and by the sight of me suckling our baby. He would spend his mornings with Leonor and me in bed. Philippe and I were spellbound, gazing at her like two idiots. And Leonor wasted no time. She attached herself to my nipples with relish, and while she fed, I felt as if her gums were biting into my womb. It was a very odd sensation. Perhaps the vast love I felt for my delicate little girl made my insides crave to protect her once more.

I told Philippe I didn't want my children to have wet nurses. I would feed them myself, regardless of whether that was how things were done at court. He made no attempt to dissuade me. In fact, he came to love being around me when I breast-fed. He loved to see his noblemen's expressions when I pulled down my dress. Afterward we'd laugh, discussing their reactions, and he'd encourage me to flaunt my breasts.

"They're so beautiful, Juana. I want everyone to be jealous. I want to watch my courtiers as they lust for you and have to hide their desires. It's very entertaining."

When Leonor was one month old, he appeared very gallantly in my chamber and gave me a pearl-encrusted pendant. Not long after, he organized a joust in my honor and wore yellow, which was my color. The proof of my fertility had magical effects on the Flemish nobles and ladies in my court. Although my economic dependence restricted my ability to govern my own household, I still felt happy and well loved. My body matured with motherhood, and our nights of passion became luxurious and indulgent. Often dawn would be upon us as we were still entangled in our lovemaking, our thirst unquenchable no matter how we drank. And thus I conceived again.

Toward the end of my pregnancy, Ghent generously offered five thousand florins to be chosen as the city of our child's birth, and Philippe accepted. My husband considered it a way to strengthen his ties to the city. He commissioned two new luxurious, velvet-upholstered carriages to transport me there shortly before I gave birth and even asked the Anchin Abbey nuns to loan me their most distinguished relic: a ring that the Virgin Mary was said to have been wearing when she gave birth to Jesus. Philippe was so attentive that my initial unease at what had seemed a commercial transaction at my expense evaporated.

Once we had settled into the castle in Ghent, Philippe invited several of his friends to come and celebrate at the palace on February 24, Saint Matthew's Eve. Once the guests had all arrived, I was caught up in the festive atmosphere. Though my belly was huge and I felt heavy, I was still agile and in high spirits. I played the clavichord for everyone and then began to teach the guests a Spanish dance. Suddenly, I felt a sharp pain in my lower abdomen. I ran to my chamber with Beatriz, excusing myself and leaving the guests in the salon. Thinking I needed the lavatory, I went to the toilet and had hardly begun contracting my muscles when I felt my waters break and run down my legs. I called for Beatriz, who ran out like a madwoman in search of help. I got into bed, trying desperately not to push out the child, whose head I could already feel between my legs. But by the time Beatriz returned, the baby was already on the bed, having been expelled from within me. Madame de Hallewin, María Manuela, and Ana de Viamonte rushed in. Then Philippe arrived, pale and shaken. The midwife arrived next to cut the cord, clean the baby, and lend a hand. And the news that it was a male child was sent out in all directions as if carried by flocks of courier pigeons. Shortly thereafter we heard fireworks being launched from the bell tower of Saint Nicholas's Church, and bells ringing out all across the city. I lay back on the pillows. I had worried about this birth, that it might not be as easy as the first one, that I might disappoint Philippe with another girl. And yet there had been no cause for alarm, and I had hardly felt a thing. I sent for Leonor and showed her the stern, wrinkled face of her little brother. She didn't understand what was happening, but I wanted her by my side. I needed to make sure that she didn't feel scorned. How differently did the world celebrate the arrival of a boy!

"Charles," Philippe said, holding his son proudly. "He will be named Charles, after my grandfather."

I had just given birth to Charles I of Spain, Charles V of Germany, the king in whose kingdoms the sun would never set, the one who was to be Europe's most powerful monarch. My son, the one who knew no mercy toward me.

I CAME OUT OF MY REVERIE. MANUEL HAD THROWN ME A BLANKET.

"You ought to cover up," he said.

CHAPTER 9

When I returned to the boarding school I said I had already eaten dinner and went up to my room. I walked down the narrow aisle and its small, wooden bedroom doors, lined up one after the other on either side. I could hear sounds coming out from behind several of them. Going into others' rooms was strictly forbidden by the nuns. I knocked on Margarita's door, but she wasn't in, so I went to mine, thinking I'd take a shower. I got my things and went to the bathroom. The hot water from the showers had steamed up the mirrors. The girls there were laughing and talking about a movie they'd seen that afternoon. I got undressed and went to the farthest cubicle so I didn't have to listen to them. Standing under the stream of water, I closed my eyes. It would have to be a quick shower because the hot water wouldn't last long. I rubbed the rough, frayed washcloth over my arms, my neck, my breasts. "You're very uninhibited for a virgin, especially such a young one," Manuel had said. When I told him that I liked being naked he said that, as a man, he tended to think of women as being more reserved. It struck me as a ridiculous comment and I teased him for it. Both my parents were nudists, I told him. They had never hidden their bodies from me. I assumed that was why I had no hang-ups about being nude. Nudity is beautiful, I said, suddenly noticing the towel he'd tied around his waist. I thought you agreed. He had been raised in a very different sort of environment,

101

he said by way of excuse, refusing to look at me, acting like a teenager who'd suddenly gone all shy.

I washed between my legs, scrubbing so hard with the washcloth that it actually started to burn. I was determined to try to understand why Manuel's comment had made me so uncomfortable. I hated to admit it, but suddenly and inexplicably, when he had tossed me the blanket, I got embarrassed. I had assumed that since women were nicer to look at, we would be expected to cover up less than men in bed. In all honesty, seeing him naked didn't excite me. But there was no doubt that my nudity had an effect on him. Was I just acting overconfident? Manuel must have thought I was being distant when we said good-bye, because he tried to dismiss the incident, saying that my attitude was surely healthier than his, but the damage was already done. I got out of the shower and dried off. Back in my room, I put on my nightgown and climbed into bed, laying my head at the foot of the bed. That way I could look out the window that was halfway up the wall above my headboard and watch the golden tree outside slowly succumb to winter.

If I tried to imagine that I was someone else, to look at myself objectively, I had to admit that the seventeen-year-old girl lying in that bed had spent the past several weekends way over her head. I was no longer a virgin. I'd made love to a man some twenty years older than me, a man who was obsessed with a fifteenth-century queen. He might well be imagining, when he touched me, that he was with her, a woman whose passion and temper were legendary. He claimed he wanted to understand her, but when he saw a reflection of Juana's attitudes in me, he was afraid and tried to control and criticize the passion he had set free. There was no other way to explain the hostile, almost offensive tone he'd used when he asked me to cover up. And it made even less sense for him to blame me for feeling natural with no clothes on when he was the one who, the week before, had gone on about nudity being a symbol of innocence. It made me think of my mother and her contradictions. She tried to impart to me the notion that every natural function of my body was harmonious and wise, nothing wicked about them. But at the same time, she would warn me: don't touch yourself *down there*, never talk to strangers. And it had been impossible for her to tell me about the birds and bees without blushing. In truth, I had learned about sex on my own, surreptitiously reading the books she kept under lock and key.

My father's image became superimposed over Manuel's in my thoughts. That my father cheated on my mother should have been enough to prove to me that I had a very limited understanding of men's minds. Maybe I should cover myself with a sheet next time. It seemed ridiculous, though. What could I do?

I fell asleep unable to come to a conclusion.

DURING THOSE WEEKS AFTER THE WALL CAME DOWN THAT SEPA-rated me from the adult world, what I found most extraordinary was to understand what it meant to be an individual entity. I had a new awareness of the freedom I enjoyed within the boundaries of my mind and body. I was queen and sovereign of that realm. Until then, freedom—to me—had been an intangible concept, because other people had always made decisions on my behalf. Now, though, I was discovering it in all its splendor. Others might have thought that I was still a schoolgirl trudging from class to class with books under my arm, but inside of me every point of reference had changed. For the first time, I was beginning to see just how wide my horizons were, and this new awareness had a physical side too. I felt like I was breathing deeper, like I took up more space on earth. I loved the idea of being impenetrable, the idea that no one had access to my private world. I was amazed at how much information and insight, how many opinions, ideas, and projects I had without anyone suspecting what was going on behind my habitual demeanor. The loneliness I had to endure in order to keep my secrets seemed a trivial price to pay for the privacy and inviolability of my intimacy. My biggest challenge was in study hall, returning Mother Luisa Magdalena's quizzical look innocently, without getting ruffled. For a nun she was very intuitive, and although she might not have admitted it even to herself, she had a fine-tuned radar that seemed to pick up any disturbance around me. But she had no reason to sound the alarm as long as I kept getting good grades and did everything I was supposed to do, offering her no evidence to justify her concern. And I *had* managed to get back on track, after having stumbled through my first weeks of the semester. I felt sorry for Mother Luisa Magdalena; she was clearly upset at the way we were drifting apart, but I didn't know how else to protect myself from the power she had over me by virtue of her affection. I worried that she might interrogate me about my Sunday activities at any moment despite the number of lies I had spun to make her believe I was visiting every historical site Madrid had to offer. Weeknights, when she was on study hall duty, I made sure she saw me consult city guides to plan my Sunday excursions. Then I'd spend Saturday afternoons, when I said I was going shopping, visiting the places I had researched so I could answer her inevitable questions. Margarita lent a hand too. When I confessed to her that the man she shrewdly suspected had set up a "casual" encounter with me on the school's street was my boyfriend now, she was thrilled to be in on it and only too happy to help keep the nun's suspicions in check. We'd leave together and arrange a time to return together. Margarita said I would have to introduce her to my mysterious beau one day, and I promised that I would, that we'd arrange a date so she could meet him.

I received a letter from Isis. She said that although she hadn't wanted me to find out the real reason my parents took that final, fatal trip, at least my discovery meant she no longer had to keep it a secret from me. One day, when I was older, I'd understand how fragile love was, and see the pain and suffering people in love had to endure. She said that her invitation still stood, that I was welcome to stay with her in New York if I decided to go to college there, as she'd once suggested. She wanted to know what my plans were, and to make sure I knew that she loved me and I could count on her. Her letter arrived at a good time. It made me feel less lonely. Isis was a modern woman. Maybe in the future I would even dare to ask her for advice.

TO RECONCILE WITH THE NEW SENSATIONS IN MY BODY ONCE I WAS alone in bed was a challenge. My skin was so sensitive that I wondered whether the end of virginity released a signal that activated previously dormant nerve endings in the female body. Even the sheet brushing against me was arousing, and it sparked off a desire I couldn't shake no matter how hard I tried. Insomnia would have me tossing and turning

until I gave in to my instincts. Then I'd take off my nightgown and panties and let my naked body, the contact of my skin with the night air,
stimulate my imagination the way oxygen fans a flame. My cheeks would
flush, and with my eyes closed, I would fantasize about other places,
other circumstances. My hands became ardent lovers. Playing the role
skillfully, they caressed my breasts, my stomach, my sex. Unfaltering,
knowing the exact coordinates of my pleasure, they delved into foun-
tains, unearthing warm, flowing water. Slowly, very slowly, like someone caramelizing fruit, they rubbed the wetness over the bud of my sex,
flicking it, releasing it, making it blossom, turning it into a tiny bloom
ready to explode and scatter its pollen. Possessed by my moaning and my
urgency, my lover-hands became hummingbirds, hovering and fluttering vertiginously over the fleshy flower that grew at the center of my
body until my head was filled with its aroma. Finally, the enormous
flower would melt, disintegrate, ululate and pulse and contract, releasing delicate golden clouds while I, like a wet petal floating over the narrow cot, slowly returned to my young woman's existence.

Some nights I repeated this ceremony again and again. I'd challenge
myself to push the limits of my desire and my endurance, thinking it
would be a perfect way to die. But in the end, neither my spirit nor my
death wish was strong enough, and I would simply fall asleep.

I REALIZED SOMETHING REMARKABLE: I DIDN'T KNOW IF I WAS IN
love with Manuel or not. When I thought about him, I would end up
wondering about myself. It was as if his gaze were a spotlight shining
down to pinpoint the exact spot where I stood on the stage of life. If I
used to think of myself as a flat, naive painting, now I saw myself as a
three-dimensional being with depth and shadows. Up until that point
I'd been just an empty jug, a vessel that adults felt they had to fill with
instructions, rules, and vague notions; Manuel instead had no charge
over me, no predetermined goals. I had no idea where all of this was
leading. I didn't know where he ended and Philippe began, or if when I
was with him it was Juana who loved her husband through me, or if it
was just Manuel and I making love. Whatever we had didn't exist without Juana and Philippe. Inside Manuel's apartment it was always the

Renaissance. His voice was so evocative that I could hear the sound of silk dresses sliding down Flemish palace steps clearly, or smell melting wax dripping from the candelabras. When Manuel was Philippe and I was Juana, I was overwhelmed with love. But after I got dressed and left, when I tried to separate myself from Juana, I would stop and wonder where was my relationship with Manuel leading to. At some point, we would have to disconnect ourselves from them. After all, time would continue passing for us, the live ones, once Manuel had finished telling me the story of Juana and Philippe. We'd just have to see. I couldn't begin to imagine the future, as caught up as I was in re-creating the past. After all, the future was like the notes my mother jotted down, instructions for the gardener for when she came back from vacation. How long had it taken her to write all that down? She had three whole pages of notes. She'd even made a sketch showing which type of flowers she wanted to plant where. And what for? What good had it done her?

I LONGED FOR SUNDAYS. I WAS LIKE A SPLIT PERSONALITY, AND I would force myself to be Lucía during the week.

The story had imposed its own tone, its own routines. I'd get to Manuel's apartment, go downstairs, and put on the dress.

ON JULY 20, 1500, JUANA, YOUR FORTUNE CHANGED DRAMATICALLY. After just twenty-three months, Prince Miguel, your sister Isabel's son —heir to the throne of Castile and Aragon—died. So many deaths, Juana. And your parents have no choice but to name you and Philippe the Princes of Asturias. You went from being third in line as successor to being the future queen of Spain.

I never thought I would be queen, nor did I wish for it. When I fell in love with Philippe I thought that I had been blessed by finding happiness while also fulfilling the destiny my parents had chosen for me. I thought I could just be Archduchess of Burgundy. My plan was to take pleasure in my role as a minor player—the only girl in my family not to marry a king—without any monumental obligations or concerns. Ironically, I thought that by sending me off to marry Philippe, my parents were somehow permitting me to be a freer spirit than any of their other children would ever be. And I took advantage of that freedom, perhaps excessively. I wanted to prove that I didn't need them, to prove that lovely, shameless Flanders suited my personality just fine. I thought I was escaping the religious zealotry that had descended upon Spain like a gray shield, imposing its rigid intolerance. I could not forget the sight of the anguished, weeping Jews forming a never-ending, heartbreaking procession; even if they had nowhere to go to, when their expulsion was decreed they were forced to leave. I never understood how my parents could consider themselves righteous when they severed the roots of an entire population, forcing them to seek another land to call their own. My sister Isabel inherited their fanaticism and refused to marry Manuel of Portugal until he promised to expel the Jews from his kingdom as well. But in the Low Countries people are naturally tolerant and religion does not cloud their understanding or compel them to waste their entire earthly lives in the pursuit of a favorable position in the afterlife.

I wanted to show my parents, who had sent me off into uncertainty, that I could find my way in those realms whose beauty and extravagance had earned them ridicule, better than I could in an atmosphere of religious piety. I was relieved to be far from the prayers and devotions that my compatriots had so arrogantly entrenched themselves in. I decided not to write to my mother, because I didn't want to have to explain myself or to be submissive. So instead, I used my anger to distance my soul from my country and my family. Perhaps it wasn't the right thing to do. Sometimes I feel haughty and become convinced I can do anything—or everything—on my own. I become vengeful and arrogant. Rage bubbles up from deep down inside me and then it boils over; I don't know where it comes from. I revolt against obedience and against the idea that other people can decide what happens in my life. Then I act rashly and end up regretting what I do. And yet, I cannot play the meek role I've been assigned without it turning my stomach. I am a Renaissance princess. I've read the classics and discussed philosophy with Erasmus of Rotterdam, who according to my brother's tutor, Pietro Martire d'Anghiera, was astonished by my intelligence. I speak Latin, French, Italian, and English fluently. I love Mallory and Matteo Boiardo's *chansons de geste*. Von Strassburg's *Tristan und Isolde* is one of my favorite books. Durero, the engraver, comes to show me his vivid images and to talk about the genius of Bosch. I feel lucky to be alive at a time when new lands and routes are being discovered and at the same time, Europe is rediscovering its love of form and of philosophy, and everywhere you go people are talking about the artists changing the shape of Rome: Michelangelo, Raphael, Bottticelli. Here in Flanders, I admire the determination and desire to beautify everyday objects: stunning plates and utensils are made by silversmiths for our meals, fabrics we wear for warmth are extraordinarily soft and delicate, prayer books have exquisite, colorful illustrations. The way I see it, the fact that I wear a skirt detracts nothing from my talents. My mother taught me that women have no cause to be humble. She even had her royal standard embroidered with "*tanto monta, monta tanto,*" to proclaim herself and my father as equal rulers, ruling equally. But it seems her view of women as much more than just life-givers was not applicable to others. She extended traditionally male powers to herself and no one else. Her daughters she saw fit to use as currency, which she could use to buy power and loyalty. She acted as if she were the only woman on earth exempt from servitude to her husband. While all my brothers had respectable dowries, I had none and was left at the mercy of Philippe's miserly advisors, who hate me for being Spanish. Of all the princesses, I am the poorest; I cannot even keep my loyal courtiers, since I have no maravedis with which to pay them. One by one, they've taken their leave. Even my parents' envoys were shown no hospitality. When Philippe refused to offer them a single meal in our home, all I could do was pout and cry.

I think my mother also gives her confessors too much credit, which makes her suspicious of my passion for Philippe. No one tells me the rumors, but I can sense it in the air. I know that Torquemada, Cardinal Cisneros, and the prelates who surround my mother like a flock of crows are worried about my joie de vivre, my vitality, and what they call the "detrimental influence of Flanders." The fact that I am comfortable with my body strikes them as dangerous, as a weakness. Hypocrites. On the one hand, they distrust me for taking pleasure in what is perfectly legal within marriage; on the other, they overlook the scandals in their own church and advise my oh-so-very Catholic parents to come to the defense of Pope Alexander VI in order to create a united front against France. Have they not heard the stories about the Borgia? Do they not know that Giulia Farnese, the pope's lover, lives a stone's throw away from the supreme pontiff himself? And what about their three illegitimate children, whom he insisted on naming bishops? My cousin Juana of Aragon, married to the Duke of Amalfi, writes from Naples to tell me of Cesare Borgia's orgies. He tosses chestnuts onto the floor and makes women get down on all fours to pick them up, naked. And not just any women, but ladies of noble birth. No one says a thing. And yet my love for my lawful husband scandalizes them. There is no doubt that the Flemish do not look favorably upon the Spanish. There is no doubt that they feel more loyalty to France, more love for the French. But who can blame them? The stories my sister-in-law Marguerite tells of what she saw during her two-year stay in Spain only add to the opinion that we Spaniards have "barbarous" ways. Marguerite was in Granada visiting the Nazarí Palace of the Alhambra the day Archbishop Cisneros—my mother's ascetic, fanatical confessor—went into a zealous rage and ordered that every Arab book in the city's libraries be burned. Books on agriculture, mathematics, sciences: eight hundred years of Moorish culture were reduced to ashes in Spain that evening. The prelate saved a total of only three hundred books. Marguerite said people hid what manuscripts they could (and I remembered well how many there were when I went with Beatriz Galindo to the Alhambra library after Granada was reconquered), but the rest were destroyed.

As a result of those winter nights we spent around the fire, listening to Marguerite tell of the atrocities committed during the autos-da-fé and of Torquemada's fanatical cruelty, Philippe began to punish me, indirectly taking revenge on my parents for their complicity in those crimes against humanity.

My marriage has become a two-headed dragon. Some days Philippe is overflowing with love and tenderness for me, and others he seems to despise himself for loving me. After a night of passion and giggling, he might get up in the morning and refuse to speak to me. He is haughty and humiliates me in front of others, as if I were just a nuisance to him. Sometimes I still smell of him when I find out he has gone to Lovaina to hunt for several days without so much as letting me know or saying good-bye. Madame de Hallewin is usually the one to tell me. She whispers in my ear when she sees me wandering the palace, searching for him like a dog for its master. On those days, I lose my sense of self, my confidence, everything; I become obsessed, wondering what my courtiers or I might have done to irritate him. I make an effort to regain control, to calm myself, and I long for the bliss we shared just a week ago. Not even my children's laughter can shake me from my anguish and insecurity when I feel him drifting away from me. If today the distance between us is like a crack, I fear tomorrow it will be wide as a gulf.

Under these circumstances, the news that we will be queen and king has made me more nauseated than either of my first two pregnancies, or the third, which I now bear. My parents have called us to Spain. Philippe and I must be officially named so that the Cortes can ratify our succession. The Archbishop of Besançon, François de Busleyden— whom Philippe has never so much as blinked without consulting— has convinced my husband that before he goes to Spain he must quell French fears and strengthen Flanders' relationship with France. He and Philibert de Veyre, another inveterate French defender, have convinced Philippe to secure this alliance by arranging a marriage between my son Charles and Claudia, the only daughter of Louis XII. For Philippe—on the verge of being named heir to the throne of Castile and Aragon—to choose *this* as the time to approach Spain's historic rivals and offer them our daughter is such a hostile act that I am overcome with rage—rage that I have struggled so hard to contain, especially now that I live in fear of him deciding, one fine day, that he no longer loves me. When he appeared before me, like a wolf in sheep's clothing, to ask me to sign the document that would help ingratiate him to Louis XII, I flew into a frenzy. I ripped the parchment in half and then continued to shred it into tiny pieces, deaf to the insults he began to hurl at me as he grabbed me by the hair. He forced me down violently into the chair beside the desk next to the fireplace.

What right did I have? Who did I think I was? he shouted, again and again, unable to proffer any but those two, trite insults.

"I've never denied you anything, Philippe. Let go of me this instant."

He let go. He begged me to forgive him. He knelt and wrapped himself around my legs. He would never mistreat his son's mother, he told me. He had no idea what had come over him. But I had to understand that it was his responsibility to defend Flanders. Good relations with France might be of no concern to Spain, but they were vital to Burgundy.

"Your adoptive country is tiny, Juana, and regardless of how Spanish you may feel—especially now that you'll one day be queen—you must be prudent and understand my position. Marrying Charles to a French princess is not condemning him to a life of indignities and affronts. Quite the opposite. Think about it. He will rule an empire far greater than anything we can hope to imagine: Spain, France, Flanders, Germany, Sicily, Naples."

"Perhaps later, Philippe, but now is not the time. Louis de Valois has only just begun to govern. When we understand what is best for Spain, when we assume responsibility as future sovereigns of Castile and Aragon before the Cortes, then we can make these decisions. But until that time, I refuse to consider it; I will not sign any such pact."

I didn't sign. After that scene, Philippe saw the light. I even felt he admired my courage in standing up to him, and for weeks he was as sweet to me as he had ever been.

What was Philippe afraid of? I had only to listen to him to realize that few things terrified him as much as the idea of facing my parents. When he was far away, it was easy to pretend he would know just how to behave. I am always astonished by how readily people fool themselves. They make great claims about what they are going to do or say. Their spirited intentions make it easy to feel bold. Why, I myself have rehearsed speeches to Philippe that I never deliver. He walks in the door, and the carefully crafted arguments that had until that moment risen from the dust of my rage like a strong, solid edifice suddenly crumble and collapse in a heap of rubble. My courage turns tail, my body becomes filled with the thick sludge of dread, and suddenly I fear that whatever I say might be the last straw, the thing that finally kills his love for me. I am terrified that Philippe will stop loving me, even though I know that in the end my fear is exactly what will lead to my downfall. He fell in love with my self-assurance and my bravery, not with the submissive, whimpering Juana I have become. I am sure of it, and yet I am unable to change my behavior, to go back to the way I was. Other forces that I cannot grasp exert more power over me than the light that shines on my reason, to no avail. I have always heard that love is not rational, but never did I guess it could make me act against my own interests. And yet I do, much to my regret. I denigrate myself, I lose my head. Perhaps being loveless is like being dead, and so one clings to love at any price. Being so desperate for love that you will make do with scraps, like someone who is starving to death, seems such a tragic fate. I do not wish to appear before Philippe like a beggar, but that is what I am. Lamentably, that is how I feel. When I am rational, I can see my husband's weaknesses: his fear, for example, of going to Spain. He was so anxious to be Prince of Asturias, had so many plans for us and for our children, and yet with each passing day he finds new excuses to postpone the voyage. Unintentionally, I have become his best one. My pregnancy is advancing. My belly has grown mercilessly. Traveling under these circumstances would be risky as well as uncomfortable. Yet my parents insist, they despair. They send messages asking me to intervene and offer to send an armada to the port of Zeeland for us. They want us to make the voyage by sea. By land we would have to cross France.

Fortunately, Philippe has rejected this idea. Knowing how stormy the Cantabrian Sea is, it seems inconceivable that my parents could believe their plan takes my safety into consideration. It is not my welfare but their priorities which concern them. And this stark reality, this doggedness that my parents exhibit, is what scares Philippe— though he may also be worried that I will confess how restricted he has me in Flanders and how anxious I feel. I don't know. I feel like a wood chip tossed into a nest of termites. I am wracked by doubts. I hate myself, and my hatred either erodes my foundations or boils over, seeking revenge. On more than one occasion, my hands have reached out and tried to wound him while we were making love. I have sunk my nails into his arms and back, I have had orgasms imagining his lifeless face. But just when I want to give in to my homicidal fantasies, he puts his tongue to my sex and I forget my rancor and my futile plans, as my mind is lapped by Pentecostal flames. With just one thrust, Eros conquers my hatred and I give in like a gentle dove awakening after having dreamed itself a hawk.

"It's bizarre, isn't it? Why would Philippe refuse to go to Spain to be named official heir to the throne?"

"Philippe was no fool. And his advisors were shrewd indeed. They knew that the Catholic Monarchs would find a way to compromise his loyalty, that they'd pressure him into giving up his flirtation with France in the interest of strengthening his role as Spanish heir. Philippe suspected the Catholic Monarchs would try to keep Charles there, so they could educate him as they saw fit. And in order to offset his in-laws' ambitions and their influence, the archduke hatched his own plan. He left the children with his father in Austria, and made sure that on the way to Spain, he stopped for a visit—with all the pomp and ceremony imaginable—in France. That way he could go to Spain, but en route he could also calm his friend Louis XII's concerns, reaffirming Flemish loyalty to France. You have to realize that in just a few years, Spain had become a great empire, and like all empires, it had expansionist pretensions that its neighbors were well aware of. And the Flemish boasted that they were more civilized and learned than Spaniards. When Juana got to Coudenberg Palace in Brussels, she couldn't believe the magnificence and beauty of the chambers. Spanish palaces were more like fortresses built for monarch warriors. Until they conquered Granada, Fernando and Isabel's itinerant court slept in tents if they had to. Whatever the Reconquest required."

"So when did Juana and Philippe finally travel to Spain?"

"A year later. Juana's third child, Isabel, was born on July 16, 1501, and in January 1502, after a short stay in France, they arrived in Spain."

"Juana didn't waste any time getting pregnant." I smiled.

"She was an extraordinarily strong, healthy woman for her time. Are you tired? If you like, we can leave it here for today."

Manuel scooted closer and looked at me tenderly, brushing the hair out of my eyes.

"I just feel sad for Juana. Not knowing whether or not someone loves you is something that makes me think of my mother's letters to Isis, where you can feel the desperation and insecurity in her tone. It's strange, isn't it? I have the impression that it was uncertainty that made both my mother and Juana feel so weak. If either of them had known for certain that their husbands didn't love them, I think they probably would have been stronger. But that element of doubt—the idea that whether or not their men loved them depended on how they acted—was deadly for them. Maybe their love was too passionate, too devoted."

"That's pretty common," Manuel said. "Don't you think it could ever happen to you?"

"With you?"

"Maybe," he said, exhaling a cloud of smoke.

"I doubt it. To begin with, you're already in love with another woman." I smiled maliciously.

"And who would that be?" he asked, smiling too.

"Juana, obviously," I said calmly. "I know you're in love with her."

"What if I were? You'd have nothing to fear. She's a ghost; she no longer exists." He grinned.

"Ghosts do live, in a way. I have proof of that now. Anyway, she protects me, I think, makes sure I don't fall head over heels."

"That's a shame," he said, blowing smoke rings at the ceiling.

"Why, would you want me to be madly in love too?"

"Juana was not mad and my question was hypothetical. Anyway, I can tell you're tired. Let's go visit my aunt Águeda; you'll like her."

CHAPTER 10

Aunt Águeda was a tall, big-boned woman in her seventies with bleach-blond bouffant hair. She had the same blue eyes and pale skin as Manuel, though she hid her pallor under a layer of pinkish makeup. She must have been pretty when she was young. She still was, actually. She was wearing blue slip-on shoes and a gray knit outfit: matching knee-length skirt and cardigan. A gold chain with a cross hung from her neck, and she wore earrings and a thick, gold bracelet with coins dangling from it—Roman coins, she told me, when she noticed I was staring at them.

To get to the house you had to go through a gate on calle Cid—a tiny, shady lane between Serrano and Paseo de Recoletos, close to the National Library—and then walk through a garden. It was a beautiful Castilian-style corner mansion that had about it the air of a shipwrecked boat. The patina of time, humidity, and moss had stained the lower edges of the outside walls. A huge chestnut tree stood on one side of the house, and the stairway that had at one time led up to the main entrance was now blocked off by huge pots of half-dead plants. I thought the house was like an ancient lady clinging to a world where she no longer had a place.

Manuel led me down a stone path, and we went in through what once would have been the service entrance. After the bright, midday light outside, it was like venturing into a chilly cave. At first I couldn't see anything, but when my eyes adjusted to the darkness I noticed a pair of high-backed chairs and a round, marble-top table with baluster-turned legs. The walls were ocher colored, and off to the right there was a coat-rack with three or four coats, several pairs of winter boots, and an umbrella holder. Manuel walked up a staircase against the wall of a large kitchen with shelves full of utensils. There was a window that looked out over the garden with sunlight filtering in through the branches of the chestnut tree, and beside it sat a solid wooden table with a few chairs. We walked from there into a magnificent salon decorated with crystal chandeliers and furnished with Castilian-style leather chairs, beautiful tables with elaborately carved legs, braziers, and other chairs with bronze appliqués. The air of decay visible on the outside of the house was nowhere to be found in here. It was obvious that its furnishings dated from long ago but had been lovingly preserved. Everything was clean, the wood and bronze were polished and sunlight was kept at bay, the rooms were dim, the muted light inside the house came from a skylight over the central vestibule and a couple of open windows I could see on the top floor. A portrait of an austere-looking man wearing a fifteenth-century ruff hung above the fireplace in another room which, judging by the books and sewing basket, must have been where Manuel's aunt spent most of her time.

"One of your ancestors?" I asked Manuel.

"None other than Bernardo de Sandoval y Rojas, grandee of Spain and first Marquis of Denia. Remember I told you that the Denias were the ones who guarded Juana? This is the father."

In the portrait, Don Bernardo looked serene, so calm and sure of himself it bordered on arrogance, as if he thought misfortune were somehow beneath him. Dressed all in black—like almost everyone back then—he had the same white, translucent skin as Manuel. His lips were so thin you could hardly see them, and his expression proclaimed that he was proud to have tamed the temptations of the flesh. He looked very comfortable with the spiritual rigor of his times. I imagined him as the type who would condemn others' weaknesses without one iota of charity or compassion. You could see it by the way his chin—partially hidden by a carefully trimmed goatee—jutted slightly upward. Like Manuel, his hair was white too.

"People from the other side of the Atlantic, from the Americas, like you, don't have to worry so much about history."

That was the first thing the aunt said when she walked into the living room and saw me staring at the portrait.

"Just its consequences," I replied.

Without moving, Manuel glanced over, satisfied with my comeback. I felt like he wanted to protect me, trace a dividing line between his aunt and I, form some sort of nonaggression pact.

"We have to deal with the consequences as well, believe you me. But I was referring to these familial reminders. I don't think you in America care as much as we do about family trees," she said as she planted a kiss on each of Manuel's cheeks and then approached me and offered her hand.

"Lucía," I said, feeling the cold of her rings against my skin.

"How old are you, child? You look very young. Manuel only told me that you were from Latin America," she said, glancing back and forth between us.

"Seventeen."

"Oh!" she exclaimed, in a tone that was open to several possible interpretations. "Let's have a little something to eat, shall we?"

We went into the kitchen, and she made us sit down as she got out cookies, juice, and other things that she set on the table. Through the window I could see a stone path leading from the door to a fountain, out beyond the chestnut tree. It was still, and all overgrown with moss and ivy. Vines that climbed freely up the walls also ran over onto the ground, giving the whole place a cloistered feel.

"Don't even look at the garden," Águeda said. "It's in ruins. It's hard enough just to keep up the inside of the house."

"My aunt has little interest in anything that takes place outside these four walls." Manuel smiled.

"Well, nor do you, child. And at least I live in the twentieth century," she retorted.

I watched her, curious. It was clear they liked teasing each other about their eccentricities.

Obviously at ease, Águeda moved confidently around the kitchen.

She grabbed milk from the refrigerator, put the teakettle on the stove, and passed Manuel plates and cups so that we could set the table.

While we ate, Águeda talked about her education, which she'd received from private tutors. Her father had refused to send her to school, she said. He hated nuns. She had always been devout, but she had to pray in secret. She asked me about boarding school and about my family in that typically Spanish way: expansive, direct, and lively. I found it simultaneously charming and overwhelming. She had a huge range of expressions and gestures, and seemed to walk a fine line between her friendly tone and stern judgments, as if she were constantly on the lookout for the traces of hardness of character that she disliked in herself. But she was nice. Quirky. Then out of the blue, she lost interest in our conversation. She seemed tired and absent. Manuel had told me that she was becoming increasingly withdrawn. She had two or three friends she'd talk to on the phone who Manuel referred to as the Captives' Club. This reclusive lifestyle must have run in the family, I thought. I only knew of one friend of Manuel's, and that was Genaro, another historian, the tour guide.

The shadows in the garden stretched through the branches of the chestnut tree. It had been so rare for me to have the chance to be with a family, to experience that intimacy. The quiet and the dim light reminded me of rainy days when I was a girl. I felt happy, relaxed, no longer tense at the prospect of this family visit. I found Manuel's relationship with his aunt very intriguing. As we spoke, he had taken some papers from his backpack and begun reading and making notes. From time to time he'd glance up and look surprised that his aunt and I had anything to talk about. Águeda looked at him often too. But the second he returned her glance, the tenderness in her expression would disappear. They both pretended they were just putting up with each other, but it was clear to me that they loved each other more than either of them was willing to admit.

Before we left, Manuel took me to the main vestibule of the house, which was an open atrium with a staircase leading up to the two upper floors, where he said only a few of the rooms were in use. He admitted that having his own apartment was a gratuitous luxury, but he said he needed to be alone sometimes. He wanted me to take a look at the stones embedded in a circular pattern in the floor.

"They're all precious stones," he said. "Rubies, emeralds, aquamarine, lapis lazuli, topaz. They say they're from Juana's treasure, which Charles V surreptitiously snuck out of Tordesillas. The queen kept them locked up in chests in her room. Purportedly, these stones are the price that Charles paid for the Denias' job of keeping Juana from having any contact with the outside world. There were so many gems that the Denia grandson, who built this house, decided there was no better place to keep them. When I was a kid, I tried using a knife to get an emerald out, but I got caught." He laughed, pointing out the spot on the floor where one could see a minuscule white mark in the marble beside an enormous emerald.

There were lots of valuable objects on display around the atrium, on tables, shelves, and in niches in the wall: porcelain plates balancing on delicate wrought iron tripods, a collection of silver liturgical objects in a glass-doored cabinet, antique boxes, keys. The walls were hung with tapestries that were in better condition that many of those in the Prado. Manuel showed me a collection of Toledo swords, a helmet, and canes with intricately carved handles dating back to the Reconquest. I could imagine his aunt Águeda with her duster bustling around all day, busying herself with chores she thought her ancestors' ghosts were watching her perform.

I wondered if that kind of obsession afflicted all nobles whose worth in modern times depended on the merits and pedigree of their past.

"WHEN WAS JUANA TAKEN TO TORDESILLAS?" I ASKED MANUEL AS WE walked back toward the boarding school late that afternoon.

"It won't be long before we get to that part of the story," he said, walking quickly, his hands thrust into the pockets of his jacket. "Maybe you could come up with an excuse to spend a whole weekend away from school. That way we could move ahead faster and your curiousity wouldn't torment you. There must be girls who leave for the weekend, right?"

"Of course. But it's not that easy. You have to have a family agree to take responsibility for you; usually it's friends of the girls' parents. Or in my case, grandparents."

"My God! You're not a baby. Couldn't you just say you were spending the night at a friend's house?"

"I don't think so. But let me find out. You'd better let me go the rest of the way alone; I don't want any of the girls to see me with you."

❊ MANUEL'S IDEA WAS VERY ENTICING. I WAS TEMPTED TO SEE IF I could push the limits of my very restricted freedom. He was right. I wasn't a little girl anymore. It had never occurred to me to solicit privileges more suitable to my age. Maybe the nuns would be flexible. It wasn't fair for them to just keep applying the same rules I'd had to follow when I was thirteen years old. But I couldn't just lie, and I didn't have any easy alibis. Maybe the best thing would be for him to come and meet Mother Luisa Magdalena; after all, he *could* just be a professor friend of my grandparents. Manuel's face would fit the picture she had of academics, and they'd never be suspicious. I wouldn't even look at him, so it would be impossible for her to pick up on anything. Although that wouldn't even be necessary. What Manuel and I did in private didn't translate into the conspiratorial glances exchanged between lovers. We were nothing like the couples who made out on benches on Paseo del Prado and La Castellana. Our passion was solely mediated through Juana and Philippe. Only when I became her—wearing her clothes or lying naked like her—was my silky skin stirred by the desire that normally lay dormant under my school uniform.

❊ AFTER MULLING IT OVER FOR SEVERAL DAYS, I DECIDED TO CALL MY grandparents. As I'd suspected, Margarita confirmed that I had to have their authorization in order to get the nuns' consent. It wasn't hard to convince them to send a telegram to the mother superior, granting permission for my weekend getaways. As soon as they heard that Manuel and his aunt came from a long line of Spanish nobility, they assumed they had nothing to worry about.

Manuel and his aunt came to school the following Thursday afternoon. Mother Luisa Magdalena wanted to meet them. It was protocol, in cases like mine. I was called to the parlor, the elegant room with polished parquet floors and heavy wood furniture where formal visitors were received. It was the same room where I'd said good-bye to my grandparents, tearlessly, when I first arrived. When I got there, Águeda and Manuel stood and greeted me politely, paternally. They both played their roles perfectly. With the information he'd gleaned through our conversations, Manuel pretended to be a close friend of my grandparents, whom he said he'd gotten to know on their trips to Spain over the past few years. He said he had offered to give me Spanish history lessons some time ago, but that several things had come up and, unfortunately, he'd forgotten all about it. Luckily, one day he bumped into me on the street, and when I'd told him my interest in learning more about the city and its historic monuments, he'd recalled his promise and realized how far away my family was. At any rate, he and his aunt would be happy to have me stay with them on weekends, so I could experience a different environment and have someplace to go. It was a shame that I'd had no surrogate family until this point, but it was never too late. There was still time, even though this was my last year of high school, for me to leave Madrid having had other experiences and made new friends.

Mother Luisa was surprised that I had never mentioned our bumping into each other before. I contradicted her. Didn't she remember me telling her about that historian who was studying Juana of Castile? Her expression acknowledged that she did, and I made the most of it, stating that I'd only just realized that being seventeen warranted a degree of freedom that I might not have been ready for at thirteen. And when I had run into Manuel and his aunt and they had invited me, I was motivated to ask my grandparents for permission. She seemed satisfied with this explanation.

With her habitual shrewdness and intelligence, the nun prolonged the conversation a little longer. While aunt and nephew were engaged in gaining her favor, she weighed them up with her eyes. Finally, the combination of pedigree, kindness, and the Rojases' solidarity—along with my grandparents' telegram, of course—produced the desired effect. After all, Mother Luisa Magdalena was a kindhearted, modern woman; and besides, she liked me.

"See them out, Lucía," Mother Luisa said. "I have to get back to the infirmary."

I led them down the tiled hallway.

"Águeda, thank you so much for coming along," I gushed.

"It's the least I could do." She smiled. "Manuel was right when he said my presence would help calm the nuns and make your request seem more respectable. Even with your grandparents' permission and all the rest of it, I'm not sure if they would have let you go just with him. And with you in the house, it means I'll get to have Manuel back on weekends. Lately he spends them all in his apartment. I'll make up a room for you. It's a big house, as you know. We don't use a third of the space we have. It will be like a breath of fresh air, having a young person there. Plus, Manuel can carry on with his story of the queen's life," she concluded, obviously pleased with herself.

"You see, Lucía? By broadening the horizons of what you believed possible, your reality has changed. It all turned out perfectly," Manuel said.

✳ SATURDAY, I THREW A FEW CLOTHES, MY PAJAMAS, AND A TOOTH-brush into my backpack and left school with Manuel and Águeda, who had come to pick me up.

Walking down the street between the two of them on the way to the car that first time, I experienced some trepidation as I left the convent behind. I was going to spend the night at the Denia mansion surrounded by objects that had belonged to Juana, in the care of her jailers' descendents.

Águeda led me to a large bedroom with a balcony overlooking the garden. I helped her draw back the heavy, damask curtains to let the soft midday light filter in between the branches of the chestnut tree. The room had high ceilings, and the tapestry on the walls was in excellent condition, though it must have been very old. It was somewhere between mustard and ocher in color, silky soft, its panels framed in maroon molding. The bed was a bronze four-poster, and the room also had a delicate-looking divan upholstered in the same bloodred damask as the curtains, and two small, blue sofas. It was a feminine room, with a beautiful Oriental rug on the floor and a fireplace. I walked over to the window, which overlooked the motionless fountain below.

"This is a beautiful room, Águeda, thank you."

"This is where my sister used to sleep," she said.

"Manuel's mother?"

She nodded, caught up in her memories momentarily. Then she recovered.

"I left you some clean towels and other things in the bathroom."

"Thank you so much," I said. "You are so very kind."

"It's nothing, child," she replied, pausing for a moment to look around once more, not bustling as she had been since the moment we arrived. She smoothed her hair down. "Why don't you lie down and rest for a while? If you need anything, just give me a call."

Manuel had gone out to meet Genaro, so I stretched out on the bed and looked around the room. I decided to spend half an hour not thinking about anything. I'd just pretend I was in a four-star hotel and forget about Juana and the Denias for a while.

✳ I MUST HAVE FALLEN ASLEEP. MANUEL KNOCKED ON MY DOOR AT about two o'clock. I was so used to my tiny cell at the convent that it startled me to wake up in what felt like a cathedral. I was cold and shivering.

Águeda had prepared lunch for us, Manuel said, poking his head in the doorway. They'd be waiting for me in the kitchen; I could come down as soon as I was awake enough.

"After lunch I'll tell you about Juana and Philippe's first trip to Spain."

I washed my face in the immaculate bathroom, which had a porcelain and bronze claw-foot bathtub. The edges of the mirror above the sink were dappled, and there were patches where time had worn away the mercury. I looked at my sleepy face and felt comforted by my reflection. I was the person I knew best in that house.

Lunch was short and frugal: Serrano ham, olives, Manchego cheese, and bread. Águeda asked a few questions about my family and my time at boarding school. I usually found it easier, with older people, to talk about my parents, grandparents, or other relatives. Águeda, however, managed to steer the conversation so that I found myself discussing my intellectual concerns, my love of reading and writing, my trips to the Prado, and my opinion of Mother Luisa Magdalena. I was grateful for it.

When it came time for coffee after the meal, I could tell Manuel was growing impatient.

"If you'll excuse us, Aunt Águeda, Lucía and I will have coffee in the library."

"Whatever you like. Don't worry about me."

She wouldn't let us help clear the table and sent us off with the coffee tray to the magnificent library, which I had never seen before.

It was a rectangular room, with a small reading nook beside the fireplace where a fire was burning. The far wall had built-in, floor-to-ceiling bookshelves, and the side walls had bookcases running from one end to the other. There must have been hundreds and hundreds of volumes, and some, judging by their appearance, were probably ancient and priceless. Two well-worn, green leather sofas sat before the fireplace, and the rest of the furniture was comprised of a few tables stacked with art books, a desk and typewriter, and several long, tube-shaped antique cane holders. The slight messiness of all those books and objects piled up all over the place, compared to the orderliness of the rest of the house, made me want to take off my shoes and curl up in a chair.

"Welcome to the inner sanctum, Lucía. A bona fide library: the best thing this family has."

"You must love studying in here." I smiled, looking around the stunning room. There were several sixteenth or seventeenth century portraits hanging by the fireplace: three men and four women.

"I do." He sighed. "It's such an ideal place for reflection that the voices in these books come to life. I can almost hear Plato and Kant giving speeches from their respective shelves. Paraphrasing the Bible, the spirit of knowledge floats in this air. I can feel it."

He motioned to me to come sit by him on the leather sofa. His cheeks were flushed from the wine we'd had at lunch. Cheerful and relaxed, he looked younger and more handsome.

I sat down, and he put his arm around me. I wanted to feel at ease, to pretend this was my house, but the scenario was so new that I was a little awestruck. Suddenly I was particularly aware of the fact that I hardly knew Manuel.

"I know you don't know much about me," he said, surprising me with his intuition. "I know I just sort of burst in on your life. You're so young. I realized that just now, while we were having lunch. It made me think about my own adolescence and how insecure I was. You remind me of me at your age: lonely. We were both orphaned at a young age. Maybe that's why our minds are so in tune, you know?"

"It's only natural for me to feel lonely in the convent, I think. But why are you so alone? How come you never got married?"

"I know myself. I am married: to my books, to history, to this house. That's all I need. I've chosen a solitary life. It's just a reality I accept. It doesn't bother me."

"Being alone doesn't bother me either," I said, uncomfortable with the way the conversation was going. "So did you bring Juana's dress from your apartment?"

"Of course."

He smiled sadly, as if wishing I weren't in such a rush. But after all, he said, the whole idea of spending the weekend together was to make headway with Juana's story. He got up and took the dress from a small closet beside the shelves at the far end of the library. "You should probably just put it on here," he said. "You won't get cold if you change in front of the fire."

We were starting our little game all over again. I felt a warmth that started in my belly and began to spread through me.

"Are you sure Águeda won't walk in?"

"Positive."

I took off my clothes and draped them over the sofa by Manuel. He sat watching me, and he took his time before getting the dress and slipping it over my head, as was our routine.

"It seems a shame for you to wear clothes at all. You look so beautiful in the firelight."

I sat on the sofa. Manuel pulled over one of the high-backed chairs and sat behind me, scooting closer until his lips were right beside my ear, and then he began to whisper.

✳ YOUR DAUGHTER ISABEL WAS BORN ON JULY 16, 1501. THERE IS NO longer any reason for you and Philippe to delay your trip to Spain. Before leaving, your father-in-law convinced you to agree to the engagement between Charles and Claudia, Louis XII's daughter. The arranged marriage will ratify the treaty signed in Lyon by Maximilian I, Philippe, and Louis XII, strengthening ties between Austria, the Low Countries, and France. You agreed on the condition that Philippe would find no further obstacles to delay your trip to Spain.

IN ORDER TO HELP PREPARE ME FOR THE VOYAGE, MY MOTHER finally sent an advisor, Juan Rodríguez de Fonseca, the bishop of Córdoba; he is shrewd and intelligent. The bishop has made me feel less alone and helped me figure out the complexity of the interests at stake, which I already suspected but until now had not understood. My decisions have not been unwise. Bishop Fonseca assures me that my prudence and strength of character in the Flemish court have been well praised in my parents' court. He says that even the Spanish ambassador, Gutierre Gómez de Fuensalida, when he returned from Flanders, told the king and queen that I was an honorable daughter to them, and that given my age I was without equal. I was greatly pleased by this news. Both the bishop and Fuensalida are of the opinion that Philippe's advisors are gluttons, drunkards, and loudmouths who are given to slander. These weaknesses—in addition to their fear of losing their influence over Philippe once he is in Spain—are what led to the repeated deferral of our trip. The bishop blames them for having convinced Philippe to abandon the idea of making the voyage by sea and opting, instead, to travel overland and thus through France. These Flemish courtiers cannot resist the idea of being received by the court of Louis XII with all of the French pomp and ceremony. So fond are they of delightful banquets, exciting jousts and hunts, and the splendor of courtly ceremonies that the opportunity could not be passed up. And, of course, I cannot entirely condemn Philippe's ambition, as he will supposedly soon become sovereign of a kingdom that will combine his father's empire with the realms of my throne, as well as his Burgundian possessions. It is not unreasonable for him to aspire to good relations with France given the circumstances. Even I have come to wonder if, once Philippe and I rule Spain, the tensions with France might cease and we might find some lasting peace for all concerned. I would be proud to put an end to old quarrels without resorting to new wars.

Bishop Fonseca, however, says that his greatest worry is that Philippe might decide to rule Spain from Brussels as if it were a province, that he might not even be willing to move to Valladolid. If this were the case, I would have to be prepared to confront my husband and forbid such an absurdity. My parents trust that I will tip the balance in favor of Spain. They have no idea how arrogant and hardheaded my husband is, or to what degree his advisors have effectively stripped me of influence and cast me aside.

But I must not fill my heart with grave predictions. I pray my country will seduce Philippe. We will see who wins this round. Suddenly the palace is in upheaval with the preparations for our departure. Philippe's mood has improved, and he once again holds my court and me in his favor. My retinue has received gifts and favors and has grown to include seven Spanish ladies and thirty-four Burgundians. The Viscount of Ghent, Hughes de Melun, will be my gentleman of honor on the journey. To celebrate the birth of Isabel, my husband has showered me with jewels and clothes. He takes pleasure in the idea of my beauty outshining the pale French ladies and, as if excited by the prospect, has once again begun to scavenge my body like an insatiable bull in search of love and kisses. At times I think happiness is beginning to creep back into my household, but after making love I have nightmares filled with lonely, silent labyrinths. I should be happy, I tell Beatriz, my faithful Beatriz. My children are beautiful, my womb is fertile, but the floors of these palaces full of light and tapestries are riddled with scorpions, and there are daggers and treachery hiding in the cracks of the Burgundian walls. I am not the same innocent girl who once believed in happiness and knew nothing of trickery. My heart has aged quickly and, if it were up to me, I would run far away with Philippe and lick off his horrid ogre's skin, that dragon's crust that bears no resemblance to the noble, joyful man I know. His malicious, calculating courtiers are the ones who goad him into raging against me, who cause his irritation. But I know the naked Philippe that they can't perceive. I know the little boy who curls up against me and seeks in my breasts the smell of the mother he lost. I know the man who navigates through my body and my soul with his sails spread out. And that is who I see beneath his crimson rage. It is for him I submit and keep my silence, because love can see beyond tears.

My parents wanted us to bring Charles to Spain, but Philippe refused outright, so my three children left for Malines, where they will stay with their great-grandmother and their Aunt Marguerite. I won't see them again for months. I had to wean Isabel at just three months and hand her over to a wet nurse. My darling blond baby! When I look at her it's like looking at my older sister. Charles was eighteen months old, and he clung to my skirts and wailed up a storm when the Prince of Chimay lifted him from my arms to put him in the carriage. Only Leonor managed to remain calm, though I saw her lip begin to tremble as she tried to hold back the tears when I hugged her good-bye.

I would go insane in this palace without my children if it weren't for the tailors and seamstresses, coiffeurs and silversmiths running in and out at every minute, bringing me velvets, silks, and brocades, shoes and wigs to select for the journey. There will be more than a hundred wagons to transport our luggage. Bishop Fonseca, God bless him, gives me advice constantly. He warns me to be watchful and make certain I do not allow myself to be pushed around by the Valois with their clever games and deceits. As the son of a French woman and a Burgundian archduke, Philippe will undoubtedly be received as a French peer—a noble, but also one of the king's vassals. I, on the other hand, am heir to the realms of Castile and Aragon and a future queen, and cannot accept that vassalage; I must act wisely so as not to hinder either my husband's interests or my own.

IT WAS AS IF ALL OF BRUSSELS CAME OUT TO BID US FAREWELL. OUR entourage was magnificent as we began our journey to Valenciennes on the way to Bayonne beneath autumnal, overcast skies. Riding beside my carriage, Philippe lights up the day with his radiant beauty. He shines like the sun, so what need have I of the one in the sky? We wave to the people crowding the streets as we pass. The villagers and settlers admire us reverentially; they are in awe of our beauty, our youth, and the smiles we exchange, in which any man or woman can see a bond more essential and human than that of crowned heads. The archbishop of Besançon, François de Busleyden, is in the carriage ahead of mine. Philippe, when not riding beside me, trots along with him, and they immerse themselves in long conversations that make me as wary as mine with Philippe must make the archbishop. No one in the entire Flemish court hates me as much as that old man. Nor do I hate another as much as him. In the entire kingdom, we are the two who love Philippe the most, which is why we fight to possess him and would like nothing better than for the other to fall out of favor. Besançon's hand peeks out from between the curtains and he points to someplace off in the distance. His fingers are long and delicate, feminine, as is a part of his soul. Regrettably, he possesses all of the vices and none of the virtues of my sex, but Philippe is blind to his warped mind. The man has been by his side since he was a child. Philippe regards him through the veil of filial love and does not possess the distance required to see him for what he is.

Beatriz de Bobadilla and Madame de Hallewin doze beside me. We have traveled all day and the light on the road is beginning to fade. I pull a blanket over my shoulders. Soon we will reach Valenciennes, and there will be celebrations and royal welcomes in our honor. I have never been to the south of the country and look forward to resting and basking in the love of my subjects. There are still several days before we reach France.

"IMAGINE, LUCÍA, WHAT THOSE TWO MONTHS PHILIPPE AND JUANA spent traveling from Valenciennes to Bayonne must have been like. The French monarchs had planned lavish displays of hospitality and all sorts of honors all along the way. Wherever they went, they were treated like kings. In each city, they were welcomed by the premier nobles. Church bells rang incessantly. Streets were decked out and crowds cheered, anxious to catch a glimpse of the royal couple so famed for their beauty, for the elegance of their retinue. Philippe was granted the honor of pardoning condemned men and presiding over the courts of justice. At night there were banquets and balls, and during the day they held tournaments and jousts. Juana impressed her hosts with her distinguished deportment and especially with her fluent Latin, which she used in speeches to thank and to greet people. But following the bishop's advice, she discretely withdrew from the festivities in honor of the king of France.

"Philippe must have loved all that flattery."

"He was almost entirely unaware of how delicate the situation was for Juana. And she forgave him, because his happiness put him in the mood for love."

※ IN PARIS BOTH THE CITY AND THE WOMEN WENT TO PHILIPPE'S head.

I watched him laugh, his head buried in courtesans' ringlets. And it was only Beatriz, tugging on my skirts, who managed to stop me from reprimanding him and insisting that he behave decorously, at the very least while in my presence.

The praises that were sung about that city! I had dreamed of seeing the river, the bridges, Notre Dame, but Paris was cold, and it drizzled for days on end. No matter the candelabras that shone in sumptuous palaces, no matter the brightly colored frescoes and the gold; I just wanted to leave as soon as possible. Philippe would be out all day hunting, and then return filthy and stinking of wine and horses. He climbed onto me with such gusto and resolve that I could guess the fantasies of other women that he was entertaining. I convinced him to let me go on to Blois before him. I would take the entourage, and then he could catch up, riding post-horses. I left him in Paris, fearing that if I were forced to witness any more of his conceit, the claws and teeth I so wanted to bare would become uncontainable and my desire to scratch and bite would win. I don't know where my wrath and frenzy come from, but when I see him enthralled by another's cheek my emotions run wild. He cannot even see the deceitfulness of those women who admire him and falls into their traps without realizing how puerile and ludicrous he looks to others. But of course, all those around him give in to his every whim, humoring him and chortling away at every little thing he does. And if I am upset, then I am the witch, the evil one who comes along and spoils his fun, keeps him from making the most of his youth and beauty. "Pretend you don't notice," is Beatriz's advice. "Men end up hating women who go into raptures over them," declares Bishop Fonseca. I think my idea of leaving Paris, of not letting my eyes see and thus my heart feel, was a wise one, despite the emptiness and anguish that I feel in my heart.

We awaited Philippe at the gates of Blois. He appeared that morning, riding majestically atop a shimmering, black charger. He knelt before me in an exaggerated show of respect, wearing a large, black felt hat adorned with a copper-colored feather. He was cheerful when he embraced me, in a good mood. As soon as he arrived, the procession grew lively; we were happy and joyful as we entered Blois Castle beneath clear, auspicious skies. In the throne room, a large crowd of splendidly clad nobles awaited us. When the chamberlain announced Philippe, proclaiming, *"Voilà, sire, Monsieur le Archiduc,"* King Louis, dressed in a white jacket embroidered with gold fleurs-de-lis, responded, *"Voilà, un beau prince."* My husband bowed three times before the king, but I entered after him and curtsied only once. The king stepped forward then, offering me his arm, and kissed my head tenderly. A little while later, implying that I must be bored of their men's talk, he sent me off to the queen's chambers with the other women.

My ladies and I withdrew. Queen Anne offered us tea and fruit juice in an exquisite salon with enormous windows overlooking a perfectly manicured garden with trimmed hedges and topiary trees. The queen was an affected woman, with a long face and big, gray eyes. Like her ladies, she looked me up and down quite openly. I decided to return the gesture. It was immediately apparent that we were not destined to be the best of friends.

The following day during mass, when it was time for the offerings, she sent one of her ladies over with a silver tray of coins for me to tithe on her behalf. Doing so would mean pledging vassalage to her royal authority. I declined the offer. I did not care that Philippe had stooped to accept the coins the king had sent to him. For my part, I said that I would make my own offering. When mass was over, the queen did not invite me to join her entourage as she left church. I stayed where I was, pretending to kneel in prayer, and left when I was ready. That night at dinner I elected not to wear my Burgundian attire and instead chose a Spanish-style dress, ordering my ladies to do the same.

While I was busy drawing boundaries with the king and queen, Philippe accepted a falcon and falconry lessons from His Highness Louis XII. He went riding and hunting with the king daily. He was in love with the man's customs and courtesy, and Louis XII very cleverly bestowed upon Philippe the title "Prince of Peace."

"King Louis is of the opinion that even if your mother dies, your father will not cede power or agree to retire to Aragon. Any other king consort would, but not Ferdinand of Aragon," he told me one night, inspired by wine and the comfort of our feather bed. "We will need allies to claim the throne, Juana. And who better than the king of France?"

"*You* will need allies," I said. "I have no plans to confront my father. His love is worth more to me than any kingdom."

At the time I could not have dreamed how prophetic his words would turn out to be, or how much I would suffer for my loyalty.

My refusal to show respect to the king and queen of France led to such tension that Philippe decided to avoid the whole matter by drawing short our visit and continuing our journey to Spain. He had managed to consolidate his ties and his friendship with King Louis and was afraid I would jeopardize his hard work if we stayed any longer.

LEAVING BLOIS EARLY MEANT THAT WE HAD TO CROSS THE PYRENEES and the Cantabrian sierra in the dead of winter. Amid snow and ice, on January 26, 1502, we reached Fuenterrabía. The commander of Leon, Don Gutierre de Cárdenas, and the Count of Miranda, Don Francisco de Zúñiga, received us there with great splendor. They provided us with accommodations for several days in a palace overlooking the sea and gave us a pack of strong Vizcaya mules to cart our goods for the remainder of the journey. Our train was too heavy and encumbered to cross the mountains, so we had to send our carriages back to Flanders and continue on horseback and mule. We were utterly exposed to the cold and snowstorms as we crossed the narrow Saint Adrian mountain pass. It was five hours of sheer torture as we advanced at a snail's pace, with both the animals and the attendants on foot slipping and falling at every turn. I buried myself in a bearskin, shivering under the hood as I licked my cracked lips, trying not to think about the Flemish in the retinue who would surely be cursing this utterly inhospitable welcome to Spain.

Fortunately we were able to rest in Segura, although not before the nobles, settlers, and inhabitants paid us homage, many of them having come from miles around for the celebrations and royal audience that left Philippe and me exhausted.

A FEW DAYS LATER IN THE EBRO VALLEY, ON OUR WAY TO CASTILE, high spirits returned. For me, returning to Spain, hearing the sweet sounds of my mother tongue, seeing the striking features of my people, the familiar colors, was like coming out of hibernation. My blood coursed and my heart raced. Commander Gutierre de Cárdenas told me that in preparation for our arrival several months ago, my parents had given permission for the black mourning outfits made compulsory after my siblings' deaths to be replaced by fine materials and bright colors. So everywhere we went, dignitaries dressed in new, magnificent attire came out to receive us. Philippe was obviously pleased and surprised by the nobility's wealth and prosperity and by the number of striking, fortified castles we came across on our way. At the gates of Burgos, a group of soldiers mistook us for an invading army and closed the city gates upon our arrival. We found it very amusing, because no sooner had the misunderstanding been cleared up than the city launched into the sumptuous reception they had planned for us. Eighteen horsemen clad all in red raised a golden canopy over our heads. As a symbol of his sovereignty, Philippe's principal squire raised the official sword pertaining to the heir to Castile that my parents had sent. The crowd cheered and applauded madly. Later, Don Íñigo de Velasco, constable of Castile, entertained us with bullfights and an exquisite banquet.

We were treated to the same lavish receptions in Valladolid, Medina del Campo, Segovia, and Madrid. While it's true that in Valladolid Philippe became furious when one of his trunks went missing—it had been filled with valuable gold pieces—I was too happy to be back in my country to get upset. I was touched to be reunited with Don Fadrique Enríquez, admiral of Castile, who had accompanied me to Flanders on my sea voyage when I first left Spain to be married; he was still a noble spirit and wished me every happiness.

We reached Madrid on March 25, Good Friday, and rested there until April 28. On several nights, Philippe and I escaped the palace dressed as commoners and mingled with the men and women at the town fair; no one recognized us. Philippe also came along with me to sponsor the baptisms of Moors and Jews. My confessor, Diego Ramírez de Villaescusa, felt that witnessing the beautiful, solemn liturgy would diminish the prince's unease at our practice of converting infidels. After long days of tiring activity, rather than collapse in exhaustion, Philippe would return at night with his energy redoubled. Mollified by good Spanish wine and appeased by the admiration and hospitality all around him, he celebrated our love with great displays of creativity and passion in which I was decidedly both complicit as well as enthusiastic. He made love to me squeezing grapes over my skin, or stroking me with feathers. Our disagreements could not encumber the smooth syntax of our bodies which, like exquisitely calibrated mechanisms, engaged each other in a perfect harmony we could neither understand nor resist. We both felt an overpowering urge to become one, to melt together. I had only to stroke his arm or his neck, he had only to do the same, for our hatred to temporarily stop in its tracks, like an image trapped in the reflection of distant lights. The more heated our arguments, the more passionately we clung to each other when we made up. "This is mad, Juana; it's mad," Philippe would whisper. Sometimes I would think about Beatriz and the phial she gave me before I set sail for Flanders. I wondered if Philippe had drunk from it too, if I had somehow slipped him the love potion and simply could not recall.

I was extremely thankful to my parents for those days of happiness in Madrid. I especially appreciated their staying quietly in Andalusia and allowing Philippe and I to enjoy the honors and celebrations that nobility and settlers held in our honor. Otherwise, I knew, Philippe's mood would have been tarnished by his fear of my parents, formidable sovereigns who had the respect and admiration of the entire world. By traveling through Spain we had borne witness to the grandeur, to the order of the kingdom. The commoners sung praises about their rulers and constantly compared the present to the anarchy, abuses, and skirmishes that had continuously beset the country before the Catholic Monarchs came to power. On the other hand, a good part of the nobility resented the control and vassalage they had imposed and took every opportunity to warn Philippe of my parents' ambition, offering him their support if he would defend their interests. Philippe told me about these conversations—with men whose names he refused to reveal—as a means of justifying his fears and his advisors' suspicions about the cunning and manipulation of my forbearers and their supposed plotting.

{✳} FINALLY WE EMBARKED ON THE JOURNEY TO TOLEDO, THE CITY where I was born and where the Cortes would grant us the royal mandate and officially recognize us as heirs to the throne. As bad fortune would have it, Philippe fell ill with measles in Olías along the way. My father made the journey up to inquire about his health.

I was certainly not expecting any such show of affection. I recall how pleased and surprised I was when I got up from my feverish husband's bedside to look out the window after hearing the commotion on the patio of the villa where we were staying, only to see my father dismounting from his horse. I raced down to meet him, and he gave me such a hug it nearly took my breath away. I pulled back to look at his cherished face, his round features now tanned and hardened by the sun and the years gone by. His dark eyes bore into me and then looked again, simultaneously recognizing me and not. Dressed all in black, his clothes smelling of dust and wool, his prickly beard now speckled with gray, my father hugged me over and over again. I remember the hilt of his sword digging into my ribs. As he gave me news of my mother and kept repeating how much I had grown over these years, he asked me to take him to my husband's bedside right away, as he was extremely worried for his health. I realized that beneath his hidden concern lay the ghosts of my siblings, whose sudden deaths were the reason Philippe and I had journeyed to Toledo to begin with.

My father said that the news of his son-in-law's poor health had come just as the procession of bishops and dignitaries that were to accompany my parents to the city gates had been about to leave. When they canceled the ceremony, fears spread.

"I wanted to come myself," he said, "to make certain you are well provided for."

We went upstairs to the bedroom. My father removed his felt hat as he entered. The court physician had just confirmed his diagnosis. Philippe's face was flushed with fever and illness. On seeing the king, he attempted to get up, but my father refused to allow it and motioned for him not to even rise to kiss his hand.

"Please forget all formalities and reverences, son."

I translated his words into French. My father was very friendly and good-natured, and he praised Philippe for the good impression he had made on those he'd met in Spain thus far. His only concern should be his own convalescence, he said. It made no difference if the ceremony before the Cortes were postponed a few days. His wife, the queen, was planning to come visit him the following day, he added, despite being unwell herself.

Philippe made a supreme effort and in a display of true gallantry insisted that the queen not wear herself out, especially at risk of catching his fever. If he found that she were preparing a visit to Olías, he would certainly go out to receive her at the gates of the city, regardless of his state of health.

His determination pleased my father. I smiled in silence at the contrast I observed between these two men in my life. Compared to the king of France, to my father-in-law, or even to Flemish nobles, my father lacked sophistication. His plain black clothes were not to be compared to the elaborate Burgundian outfits. And yet his simple attire underscored his gallantry, the natural way he communicated his authority. Philippe, on the other hand—fine-looking and sophisticated—more resembled a timid mouse forced to converse with the cat he knew full well could behead him with a swift movement of his claws. He was tensely gripping the sheets he held up to his chest, the tendons in his neck muscles revealing the effort he was making to keep his head high on the pillow. My father, meanwhile, sat beside him on a chair, legs splayed, body leaning forward. He explained briefly what would happen during the ceremony in Toledo, and after half an hour he rose and said that he would leave so that my husband could rest and recover.

After years of feeling alone and vulnerable in Flanders, the presence of my lord the king made me feel more aware of my royal stature than any of my confessors' or advisors' speeches had ever done. After bidding him farewell in the patio and watching him ride off with his party of attendants, I returned to Philippe's side. The visit had revived him. He recovered a few weeks later.

ON MAY 7, WE MADE OUR TRIUMPHAL ENTRY INTO TOLEDO. DIGNI-taries and grandees lined the streets for what seemed miles, and they joined our entourage as we made our way toward the city gates. There were judicial envoys, aristocrats, clergy, French ambassadors, Venetians, Cardinal Mendoza, six thousand nobles from the kingdom, and, finally, my father, riding a beautiful chestnut-colored stallion. Philippe and I, on our mounts, rode beside him. The three of us were the crowning glory of the enormous procession. It was a splendid spring day: the brilliant blue sky offset the red earth beautifully, and the eager faces of the town's inhabitants and farmers lining the streets were wide-eyed and smiling at the joyous display of colors and royal standards. I wished my children could have been there to see it all. At one point I stopped, struck by a farm worker's daughter sitting on her father's shoulders amid the crowd, so much did she resemble my little Isabel. When I looked back to the procession once more, my father and Philippe were still riding together under a golden canopy that several pages held above them; they had forgotten all about me and left me behind, I was greatly pained that they had not waited. Without even turning around, my father continued to ride toward the nearby cathedral accompanied solely by Philippe. A few feet farther on, I saw Cardinal Cisneros and my mother emerge to receive them.

For them to have reached the cathedral without me was a blunder that neither my mother nor I could disregard. But I refused to let myself be overcome with rage. I forgave their conceit, their male need to mark territory and punish the fleeting nostalgia of a woman who misses her child, because at that moment I laid eyes upon my mother. Dressed in black from head to toe, she had not granted herself or my father permission to come out of mourning, as she had her courtiers. My siblings' deaths were clearly inscribed on her face, which I'd recalled as smooth and fair. Now the dark circles beneath her eyes denounced her grief, as did the deep lines curved from her nostrils to her mouth. But as soon as she saw me, her eyes shone from within their deeply shadowed sockets, and as she embraced Philippe, she looked at me sidelong and I understood the message in her eyes: don't fret, daughter, I will put things right. Finally it was my turn to receive her embrace. I closed my eyes as she hugged me, taking in a scent so different from the rancid stench she'd had when I left. Now she smelled of lavender and wool. She ran her hands over the braids wrapped around my head, unable to contain a rare gesture of love. Six years had passed, and her happiness swelled that day under the arch of the Cathedral of Toledo, which we then entered to be sworn in as future sovereigns. Then came the Te Deum, hymns, and incense. We walked out into the ecstatic roar of the crowd.

My father didn't leave Philippe's side who, feeling he was already king, cast his eyes around with the arrogance of a supreme ruler. We walked to the palace, where the four of us were to remain alone until the celebratory banquet began later that evening. Once in private, Philippe gave my parents the tragic news we had received in Orleans: Arthur, the fifteen-year-old Prince of Wales and husband of my sister Catalina had died. A widow at seventeen, she was fast losing her hopes of becoming queen of England. Once again, the issue of Spain's future alliances was to remain unresolved. My mother could not but let out a dreadful wail, a death rattle she held in by clamping her hand over her mouth. My father got up and put another log in the fireplace with an angry gesture. *"Porca miseria,"* I heard him utter between clenched teeth, in the Italian of his beloved Naples.

TWENTY-FIVE YEARS OF FORGING ALLIANCES AND ARRANGING MAR-riages to consolidate Spain's power, and the only thing they knew for sure was that a Fleming who didn't even speak their language would sit on the throne of Castile and Aragon. That is what they must have been thinking. Even I thought it. Philippe tried to feign anguish, but he could not have understood the utter desolation of the man and woman who sat in painful silence in the gray room of the palace at Toledo. My joyful reunion with my parents had been short-lived indeed. Tomorrow every-one would go into nine days of mourning. I would receive the Cortes of Castile mandate to become heir to the crown of those death-wracked kingdoms from men dressed as crows. I wondered what was going through my mother's mind as her soul was stabbed by jagged daggers: would she be feeling regret, or thinking that so much misery was divine retribution for having usurped the crown from *la Beltraneja* and locking her up in a convent? I shuddered to think that now the accursed king-dom would be my lot. Mine, Philippe's, and our descendants. The words of Jesus Christ came to mind. "Father, let me not drink from this chalice."

※ MANUEL RESTED HIS HAND ON MY HEAD. I OPENED MY EYES AND sighed deeply, expelling all the air from my lungs.

"Back then, that many deaths so soon after one another must have been seen as some kind of sign from the heavens, don't you think?"

"Absolutely. Scientific thought didn't come into play until the seventeenth century. Before that, people interpreted events through superstition or religion, which is essentially the same thing."

"Wouldn't you say that Juana's lack of interest in power came from a superstitious belief that misfortune was at her heels and could afflict her offspring? I would have feared that."

"That's an interesting hypothesis. It's definitely true that Juana was not ambitious; she had no interest in power, and in fact seemed to try to avoid it, as you'll see later on. That was one of the arguments used to theorize on her madness. Incidentally, until this trip to Spain, the only criticisms of her behavior were based on her lack of religiosity and her scant correspondence with her parents. It wasn't until after 1508, according to the scholars who have studied her alleged insanity, that she started to show signs of mental instability. But I want to hear what you have to say about her defiance, whether you would attribute it to madness. It's late, though. Let's stop for today."

※ WE'D BEEN IN THE LIBRARY THAT AFTERNOON AND THEN AGAIN after supper. It was ten thirty and I wasn't sleepy, but Manuel seemed tired. He stood up and poked the logs in the fireplace. The embers had almost gone out. He said he'd walk me up to my room and then come back down to turn out the lights and smoke his last cigarette of the night. That way he could make sure the fire had burned out all the way. If that old house ever caught fire, he told me, it would go up like a tinderbox.

"You may as well leave the dress on. Águeda will have gone to bed by now."

CHAPTER 12

Manuel walked into my room and closed the door softly. He undid the bows on the dress and handed me a white robe so I could cover up, moving silently so his aunt wouldn't get suspicious. She probably wouldn't hear anything, but it was better to be safe than sorry. Draping the dress over his arm, he whispered good night. His room was the last one before the staircase, he said. If I needed him, that's where he'd be. Águeda's room was across the hall.

I BRUSHED MY TEETH AND PUT ON MY PAJAMAS. ÁGUEDA HAD DRAWN the curtains, but I opened them slightly to let the moon cast its soft light into the room. I took the Pradwin book on Juana that Mother Luisa Magdalena had given me out of my backpack. I'd decided to read up on the Denias and see if what I found coincided with what Manuel and his aunt told me. The lamp on my nightstand was made of delicate glass, with a pale, yellow satin lampshade. I put my mother's mirror on the little table like a lucky charm and got into bed. It smelled of mothballs and clean sheets. There was no way Manuel would dare get into bed with me at his aunt's house, I thought, still feeling the contact of his fingers on my back. Curled up underneath the light down comforter, I wished he would. My body responded to him when he was near, recognizing him as the source of the fantasies and ruminations I weaved in the quiet atmosphere of the boarding school. Without even bothering to open the book, I thought instead how I would have liked to spend the night with him.

Over dinner, I hadn't had the usual feeling of him being a man trapped in the past. And afterward, I had liked seeing him look comfortable and peaceful among his books in the library, his cheeks red from the fire. He seemed sweet and accessible, and it wasn't Philippe I thought about, but him, Manuel. Understandably, being in his family's house imposed certain limitations, though. His aunt, having taken responsibility for me, would surely not stand for any behavior other than that which was appropriate between a man of his age and a young lady like me. But maybe tomorrow, before going back to school, we could stop by his apartment.

I lay there, staring at the ceiling light, seeing the room reflected in its crystal teardrops. My Siamese cat print pajamas made the chandelier twinkle in black and white. It seemed quieter there than at the convent. Every little while, the house would creak. I closed my eyes to quiet my apprehensiveness.

JUST WHEN I'D STARTED TO DRIFT OFF AND FEEL THE WAVES OF sleep slowly wash over me, I heard a metallic sound echo throughout the entire house, jolting it to life in a jarring, inexplicable way. It sounded like sluice gates or hatches, latches clicking and echoing everywhere, including my room. I sat up in bed, startled and scared. Though I was unable to figure out where the noise had actually come from, I associated it with Juana's imprisonment, a castle drawbridge suddenly being raised ominously. I thought I must have imagined it. Frozen, the book in my hands, I sat and waited. Then I got up and went to the door. I stuck my ear to the wood. Everything was still. I quietly opened it and went out into the hall, barefoot, tiptoeing down the hall to Manuel's door. I could see a sliver of light underneath. There was a light on in his room.

As quietly as possible, I scratched the door two or three times with my fingernail.

Manuel opened. He was barefoot, dressed in sweatpants and a white T-shirt. As soon as he saw me, he put his finger to his lips and pulled me into the room by my wrist.

"Manuel, what was that noise? It frightened me," I whispered.

"What noise?"

"I don't know, it was a metallic sound, like latches or traps being set or something."

"Oh, that." He smiled, lighting a cigarette. "Don't worry. There's an alarm system that activates locks throughout the house. My aunt sets it to go on every night at eleven. It's one of the insurance company's stipulations. There are so many valuable objects here; this house should be a museum."

He hugged me awkwardly with his free hand and kissed the top of my head. I leaned into him.

"Cute cat pajamas." He smiled, leading me to his bed. They were my favorite ones. The silky, white fabric was smooth against my skin. I looked around. There were two high shelves crammed with model ships, sailboats, castles, and—just like at his apartment—fragile-looking mobiles and complex constructions stacked up in a neat pile of boxes of jigsaw puzzles.

"What are you doing? What if your aunt hears us?" I asked.

We were whispering.

"She locks the doors just before she falls asleep, and besides, she's a little deaf. We'll have to be quiet, but I missed you. I'm glad you came."

"I missed you too. Not Philippe. You."

"All women are potentially adulterous," he said, mockingly.

His movements went from tender to rough in seconds, and I had the distinct impression that he was angry, that he wanted to hurt me somehow. I tried to pull away, but he wouldn't let me and unbuttoned my top. The last button popped off when he yanked impatiently at my pajamas.

"Wait, Manuel. Stop it. Don't rip my pajamas off," I said, holding my top closed over my chest with my hands as I looked at him, scared and confused.

"I'm sorry," he said, letting his arms fall and staring down at the floor. "I don't know what came over me."

"I thought you might be interested to know that I don't always think about Philippe," I said, venturing a grin as I straightened my top.

He smirked.

"The great thing about being your age is that you dare to tell the truth. I never knew you thought about Philippe *at all* when you were with me."

"Well, I always assume you're thinking about Juana," I said honestly. "More than that, I feel like we *are* them, like they possess us, and come back to life to make love to each other through us."

"You do? That's what you feel?"

"Well. I mean, I also feel you."

"That makes four of us, then."

I smiled.

"But today you were the only one I missed. Just you," I said, hoping he believed me. "I wanted to be with you. I wasn't planning on coming to your room when I opened the door to try to figure out where that noise came from. My feet just brought me. Suddenly I was at your door. So I knocked."

He stood and pulled me up from the bed, buttoning my pajama top.

"Come on. I'll take you back to your room."

We tiptoed out. Suddenly I wanted to cry, ashamed at my own naïveté, horrified that I might have hurt his feelings and unsure I could fix things. When we reached my door, I turned. He saw how upset I was.

"I'm sorry, Manuel," I managed to blurt, my voice trembling as I tried not to cry. I felt pathetic, but my tears were also the result of my fear, and of realizing that I felt more for this man that I had realized or accepted.

He pushed me into the room. He held me in his arms, he kissed me, he was suddenly all over me, as if he'd become several men at once. And that sudden change, having thought I had ruined things and now seeing I had not, persuaded me not to stop him, to let him kiss my chest, shoulders, neck, mouth. I pushed up against his body, rubbing up against him like a cat, hardly able to breathe, unable to keep from moaning. I let out a low purring, which mixed with my saliva and my runny nose. My face was burning up. We tore our clothes off and made love on the bathroom floor, on a towel. Manuel passed me another one to hold to my mouth and stifle my cries, because either out of anguish or relief I came again and again. My body was like a spring that just kept uncoiling. It writhed in pleasure, and one orgasm would lead to another, and another, as if each time Manuel plunged into me, the tip of his penis struck a bell, a gong that set off waves of pleasure that began between my legs and then swelled out throughout my body. Manuel kept his eyes closed as he held me; he never opened them when we made love.

I don't know when he left. I woke up in the middle of the night, cold and naked, alone on the bathroom floor.

I dragged myself to bed and slept until ten in the morning.

The sun streamed in through the partly drawn curtains.

WHEN I WENT DOWNSTAIRS, MANUEL AND ÁGUEDA WERE SITTING at the kitchen table, talking. He had a big stack of papers beside him. She was knitting. There were plates, bread and butter on the table, but it was obvious that they'd already had breakfast. As soon as I walked in, Águeda set down her knitting needles and asked me if I wanted eggs, or cereal. I didn't want her to go to any trouble, so I said I'd have bread and coffee.

"Lucía got scared last night when the alarm system set the locks," Manuel said, moving his files to make room for me beside him.

Águeda looked at me and raised her hand to her forehead.

"I should have warned you; I don't know what I was thinking. This house is like a modern-day fortress. It's a nuisance, but Manuel probably told you that the insurance company requires it."

"Yes, he told me."

"Next time you come, I'll show you some of the objects we have here. There are some amazing treasures, antiques. Fascinating things."

"Stolen," said Manuel.

"Don't say that, Manuel." It was obvious she'd heard that remark more than once and kept pouring coffee.

"All part of the Denia family's plunder of Queen Juana's possessions."

"Don't pay him any mind, Lucía. When the queen died, Charles I rewarded the Denias for their services, paying off the queen's debt with jewels and works of art."

"Here we go again, the same old story," Manuel said, finishing the last of his small cup of espresso.

"I've never accepted your theories, Manuelito. The queen was mad, and taking care of her was no walk in the park; it was a difficult task, and one that left its mark on our family. They deserved what they got. *More* than they got, I'd venture."

"The queen was not mad. She was a prisoner."

"You tell me, Lucía, if she was mad or not. Every night, after Philippe the Handsome died, she ordered them to open the coffin and she kissed his feet. And what about the funeral cortege to Granada? Who in their right mind would travel all over Spain with a coffin?"

"I don't know why you insist on saying that; we've been through this before. She had them open the coffin *twice*, and that was to make sure the body was still there. The first time she thought that the Flemish had removed not only his heart but his whole body."

"The Flemish took his heart out?" I asked.

"Yes, to bury it in the Low Countries."

"Well, that's how Pradwin justifies her behavior, but plenty of scholars disagree," Águeda interrupted. "Who knows who's right? As far as I'm concerned, madness is the only explanation for Juana's behavior."

"You refuse to let go of the idea that Ferdinand the Catholic was a good man, but he was unscrupulous. Ferdinand was the man Machiavelli based *The Prince* on! What do you think, Lucía? Do you think love makes people go crazy?"

I looked at the pair of them. Águeda had gone back to her knitting, but she glanced up now, waiting for me to answer.

"Um . . . I don't know."

"What kind of a question is that, Manuel? How would she know? She's probably never been in love!"

"Is that true, Lucía? Have you never been in love?"

I think I must have blushed. I couldn't understand why Manuel was doing this. How could he have asked me a question like that in front of his aunt? And he seemed so intense. His eyes were boring into me.

"Leave her alone, Manuel."

"You stay out of this, Auntie. She can answer for herself."

"The nuns say that girls my age are in love with the idea of love." I smiled.

"That's right, you tell him, child."

"But Juana was your age when she fell in love with Philippe. *You* could feel that kind of love. Intense passion. Most people on the planet experience love in their adolescence; that's why women's bodies are programmed to conceive while they're young. Besides, as the saying goes, love is neither young nor old."

"Good Lord, Manuel, that's just something dirty old men say to justify getting involved with young girls," his aunt said. "Anyway, what do *you* think? Can love make people lose their minds?"

"I think it can lead to behavior that might be confused with madness, to blind rage, for example. Why else would there be so many crimes of passion?" he asked.

"But you claim that Juana wasn't mad," she insisted.

"Exactly. She might have been worked up, but she wasn't crazy. They cornered her, and she reacted the same way any modern woman would have. She had no other options. She could resort to rage, or she could go on strike, as she so often did: refuse to bathe, to eat, make people fear for her life. Who knows? Maybe she had so little freedom that she doubted she was in her right mind herself."

"What do you think, Lucía?" Águeda asked me.

"I don't think I know enough about it to have an opinion," I said. "But I would like to know if you've ever fallen madly in love, Manuel."

"Once," he said, drawing on his cigarette. "See? At least I admit it." He smiled, looking at me.

"You did?" Águeda asked, amazed. "I hope it wasn't one of those silly students of yours who call you up and never want to leave a message."

"Good God, Águeda, those are students!" Manuel exclaimed.

"They're young girls. The sort you claim fall madly in love."

"I think it's time to change the subject," Manuel said, looking at his watch as he stood up. "Lucía and I have to get on with our history of Queen Juana."

"Go on, off to the library. I'll make lunch."

I helped Manuel light a fire. We hardly spoke. Hand me this; light that. Pass me the dress. I asked him why he insisted on my wearing it. I didn't need it to feel like Juana anymore. That was what I thought, he said. There was no dissuading him. Naked, my arms crossed over my chest as I waited for him to slip it over my head, I felt more vulnerable than before, as if last night had changed things. Maybe Manuel was right and today I did need the damned dress. Maybe, I thought, having breached the circle where we played Juana and Philippe would affect my ability to inhabit that timeless space Manuel conjured up with his words, that space where Juana's inner thoughts came to me so clearly that I found it hard to distinguish between the words he spoke and the conversations, thoughts, and feelings I imagined as his voice reached me.

Águeda's comment about Manuel's students had upset me. I found myself wondering if he gave this sort of "lesson" to other girls too. Was it just a way to seduce girls?

WHERE WERE WE? WE LEFT OFF IN TOLEDO, RIGHT? ARTHUR OF Wales died and Philippe is the one who gave the Catholic Monarchs the news. The next day, the city went into mourning. As you feared, Juana, you are surrounded by courtiers dressed in black for nine days. Philippe takes refuge in your rosy skin, and it's all you can do to force him out of bed to accompany you to mass and to say prayers for the dead. How can you stand all that prudishness, all those priests and prayers? he asks. What is it about your countrymen that makes them so terrified of hellfire?

Worried about your husband's state of mind, you speak to your parents and agree that while you and Philippe wait for the Cortes of Aragon to anoint you, a group of nobles will take the prince under their tutelage and ensure that his spirits do not flag, showing him the splendors and the potential of his new kingdom. Your father cannot help but comment sarcastically that it would be far easier for Spain to seduce Philippe with amusements and pleasures than with reasons of State. While you and your mother preside over masses and mourning, your husband goes off to Aranjuez to play pelota and doesn't return until his daily routine has dissolved the sorrow. When he does come back, he goes on hunting trips with his father-in-law in the forests of the sierra. He practices his falconry and takes part in Spanish-style jousts. He learns about bull-fighting. He is pampered by the court, where everyone makes an effort to keep him entertained. So attentive is the court to Philippe that in the end he feels obliged to repay their generosity. With his characteristic charm, he convinces you to help him secretly organize a banquet in your parents' honor: a Flemish banquet. Dressed in a golden dress with a wide, Burgundian ermine neckline, choker, canary diamond earrings, and a high-crowned hat with a very fine, gold-thread veil hanging from the tip, you stand beside him to receive the delighted guests of honor. During the banquet you exchange complicit glances with your parents and your old friend the bishop of Cambray, and Jean's brother, Henry de Berghes, leader of the pro-Spanish faction in Flanders. Meanwhile, the archbishop of Besançon, François de Busleyden, and Philippe's pro-French advisors hardly eat a bite and stare at you with ill-concealed hostility.

THE BOAR, PIG, AND DEER WERE BOUNTIFUL AT THAT BANQUET where, under candelabras burning with the light of hundreds of aromatic candles, we drank the best Burgundian wine, and I imagined my future realms as an amalgamation of the best that Flanders and Spain could offer. One day I would preside over a court that would be the epitome of tolerance and culture, the best in Europe. I saw myself ruling Spain with my children and Philippe by my side. We would be a fortunate, loving couple whose throne would bring together not only ancient pedigrees but also the new colonies of the vast Americas that would be ours to explore and govern. My naive dreams spread to rugs, curtains, faces, dishes, and I thought that all of that grace and beauty would protect me and keep me safe from plots, intrigues, and misfortune. Later, when Philippe and I were alone, I played clavichord for him and danced the dances my Moorish slaves had taught me. But after we made love, as we were lying in bed commenting on the details of the feast, he suddenly burst out laughing and began to make fun of my compatriots, of the crude manners of this duke or that marquis, the smell of the priests' beards, and the greasy, "unimaginative" cooking. He'd never appreciated Flanders as much as now, being in Spain, he said. It was taking all of his patience to keep waiting for the Cortes of Aragon to receive us so that we could finally be declared heirs. He thought the delay was just a ruse, so that we'd be forced to postpone our departure. He claimed my father was hoping to hold the ceremony in the midst of the French conflict with the Aragonese crown, so that Philippe would be forced to take sides against his friend, the king of France. The bishop of Besançon had told him that tensions over the division of Naples were on the verge of provoking another war between the kingdom of Aragon and France.

"Your father wants to force me to make enemies with Louis at all costs. He does not realize that my loyalties are not at Spain's disposal."

"Besançon advises you poorly, Philippe," I said, pretending his words had no effect on me. "You're speaking against your own interests. You will one day be king of Spain and you must embrace the Spanish cause now."

"It is *I* who shall decide the Spanish cause when the time comes. I have no reason to inherit petty rows that will serve only to isolate Flanders from her historic allies; I have no reason to continue your parents' politics. You shall see. When we return to Flanders I will get rid of Henry de Berghes. I cannot stand his complacency, his servility to all things Spanish. You are the only agent of Castile and Aragon that I need. You smell divine," he said, burying his head between my breasts. "You are my Castilian flower; you have given me the most beautiful children; you are my Spain."

Philippe knew just how to put out the fire before the flame reached the powder keg and caused an explosion. How could I defy him when he spoke such beautiful words? I didn't want to. It was important for him to feel that he was the one in power. He couldn't fully accept the idea that I would be queen and he, my consort. That meant that I had to be on guard to ensure I didn't offend him by insinuating that my words held more weight than his. He was of the opinion, for example, that the Aragonese could easily avoid amending Salic law by simply ruling him heir to the kingdom. It wounded his pride to see them take so long debating how to brush him aside. He did not possess my father's wisdom, or his ability to amass real authority and forego the formality of titles. And I, lacking my mother's fortitude, found myself unable to confront him. I feared his fits of rage, dreaded the arrogance he displayed whenever he felt insecure. His sudden mood swings kept me on edge at all times. It took all my energy to mollify him, to make sure his pride was intact so that he would at least be willing to keep playing his hand in the game life had seen fit to deal us.

Before we got up the next day, I resorted to love and passion in an attempt to convince him not to get rid of Berghes and to insist that my father, more than anyone, was the one trying to speed things up in Aragon. I asked him not to listen to anyone telling him differently. I reminded him how worried and courteous his father-in-law had been when he visited him in his sickbed in Olías. I extolled de Berghes's kindness, how well he treated me, and begged him not to be so rash. And for a few months, my efforts were successful and he gave up his plans. But hardly had summer arrived when the hot sun penetrated my husband's body, desiccating him and requiring vast stores of water to refresh and cool him. He treated me like a despot, ridiculing my intelligence and then, hours later, cornering me in my chambers and telling me he never tired of my beauty. The oppressive, dry summer felled the Flemish like a plague. There was no dancing or laughter to be found in the torpor of those stifling afternoons. It must have been August when Emperor Maximilian of Austria wrote to Philippe, exhorting him to collaborate with my parents. Rather than have the desired effect, however, the letter sent him into a state of extreme agitation. Philippe detested his father's interference in his affairs, although nothing pleased him more than his approval. He accused my parents of spreading false rumors and intrigue to turn his father against him. And since he did not dare indict them directly, he took it out on me, denigrating Spain and hurling epithets. Despite my remonstrations, he kept his word and ordered Henry de Berghes and the pro-Spanish members of the court to return to Flanders immediately.

My mother, who thought that women's wiles held magic powers, begged me to intervene. I told her that it was my intervention that had led to his decision being postponed for several months, but she insisted that if Philippe refused to listen to me now, it was because I had not been sufficiently convincing and would have to make a stronger case. The sexual spell I was said to have cast was the talk of the palace in Toledo; it had become legendary. Who could deny the passion between my husband and I, they said, after having heard me moan in pleasure, the sound carrying through the silent corridors at night? Besides, my body could not lie. I was pregnant again. For my husband to keep frolicking with me when I was already five months gone was proof enough of insatiable appetites that broke even the most basic tenets of Christian moderation. All of which made my mother think that my powers were the oldest weapon women possessed and capable of achieving absolutely anything.

Aggrieved at my inability to make her see what a difficult position I was in, I finally decided to reveal to her the flip side of my nocturnal paradise, telling her about my husband's moods. I don't know how much she believed, but finally, seeming unconvinced and displeased, she stopped reproaching me and resolved to speak to him herself. To no avail. Not only did she butt up against his Flemish hardheadedness, as I had, but the conversation actually made her fear and despair for the future she had so carefully been forging for Spain. It was a great setback for her to realize that after all of her efforts, her son-in-law's loyalties still lay outside the borders of Castile and Aragon. Neither she nor I knew how to gauge the hidden rage that led Philippe to contradict his father. I think that was when my mother hatched the plan to confront him and force him to clearly and openly commit to the mandate he would inherit. She was calculating, and she knew that such an action would force Philippe to weigh up his love for me, and vice versa. Of course, in that stratagem I was to be the propitiatory victim, like Abraham's Isaac, or Agamemnon's daughter Iphigenia.

The heat wreaked havoc on the Fleming's health and conspired with destiny to aggravate the tense situation. Early one morning toward the end of summer, the archbishop of Besançon, François de Busleyden, was taken ill. In the wee hours, they came and knocked on our door, requiring Philippe's presence, and he got dressed immediately and rushed out. He returned a few hours later, distraught, and tore off his clothes. The smell of death was all about him, he said. He looked like a disconsolate little boy, crying mournfully. Busleyden, more than his father, had raised him. He'd been his tutor and advisor from a very tender age. And yet Philippe's love had proved unable to keep him alive. He was overcome with sorrow and rage, emitting horrible, guttural sounds as he attempted to speak, his choked words repeating spitefully that Busleyden had been poisoned. My people, he objected, were responsible for this. My people had assassinated the wisest and most loyal of all his advisors. Pacing frantically, he shouted that my father was to blame, that if he thought this would make him abandon his alliance with France, he was wrong. The more I attempted to calm him, the more hysterical he became. He called for majordomos and chamberlains, ordering them to prepare for our departure. He didn't plan to wait for them to kill *him*, he cried. He would not stay on in Toledo. We would go to Zaragoza, and whether the Cortes of Aragon anointed us or not, we'd head to France as soon as possible.

I took advantage of the reigning chaos to send word to my mother in Madrid, through one of my best horsemen, so she could be apprised of the situation. When I returned to Philippe, he was shouting orders, insisting that the Castilian guards leave the palace so that Flemish soldiers could take their place. Next he ran like a madman to the kitchen and fired all the cooks. It would take a few days to embalm Busleyden's body and prepare for our departure, and in the meantime he wasn't taking any chances. I, of course, could not feign the same sorrow at the archbishop's death, nor did I commit the blunder of insisting that there was no way my father had been involved. I kept quiet. Philippe could interpret my silence as he saw fit.

My mother responded to my message with one of her own, addressed to Philippe. She was terribly sorry to hear of the archbishop's sudden death, but she commanded Philippe to remain in Spain and forsake his idea of returning to Flanders via France. Hostilities had intensified, and we could all end up as Louis XII's hostages. My father, in turn, sent an emissary with the news that the Cortes of Aragon were finally ready to carry out the ceremony and swear us in as heirs to the throne.

Before leaving for Zaragoza, Philippe wrote to the king of France to keep him abreast of the situation, request a private meeting, and ask for his assurance that we would not be taken hostage while traveling through France. Louis sent a friendly reply. We had nothing to fear, and in order to prove it he was sending ten nobles to Brussels as a guarantee of his pledge; they would remain there until we had returned safe and sound.

"You see, Juana? Instead of taking advantage of His Highness's respect for me and delegating me to agree to a truce with the French, your parents want me to cut my ties. *That* is what worries them; they are well aware that we are at no risk traveling through France. The only place I am in danger is *here;* that is why no one will change my mind about this. I promised my dear mentor when he was on his deathbed."

ZARAGOZA RECEIVED US WITH AS MUCH SPLENDOR AS TOLEDO HAD. Crowds cheered. The royal standards of Aragon, Valencia, Sicily, Mallorca, Sardinia, and the county of Barcelona fluttered in the wind above thousands of people clad in red who lined up to kiss our hands as an expression of respect and subjugation. Bells rang, doves were set free, colored ribbons hung from every balcony. The Cortes of Aragon, however, had imposed a condition. I was to be named queen, but if I died, Philippe would not be king. What is more, if my father remarried after my mother's death and had an heir, the crown of Aragon would go to his child.

Shortly after the ceremony, my father left to return to Madrid, concerned about my mother, who was confined to bed with fever. Before leaving he asked a very sullen Philippe to preside over the remaining formal sessions of the Cortes. My vain prince interpreted this deference as a conciliatory gesture that recognized his status as future king. We were both naive. When the session opened, seated beside him under the canopy of the chapter house, I gazed at Philippe, his chin held high, his chest stiff, his eyes taking in the crowds, and I felt a mixture of pride and tenderness. Like me, he was maturing, trying to fill the mold of the statues that would be erected in his honor.

The secretary stood to read the order of the day. Then we realized the trap my father had set: the session Philippe was to preside over was intended to approve the subsidy needed to finance the war with France. Outrage spread throughout the Flemish party present there. I felt the cacophonous grumbling and comments being directed at me as the crowd turned my way, like wild horses in a nightmare. They must have thought I was complicit in the ploy. Philippe defended me gallantly. He stood and turned to me, as calm and majestic as any sovereign, bowing to me and asking my permission to open the session. Then, as a Spanish sovereign would have done, he proceeded to address the agenda.

Relief, fear. I don't know what my overriding feeling was; but I was perfectly aware of the fact that at any moment the tides might turn against me. My clothes were suddenly too tight; I felt tangled up and couldn't breathe. I remember that was the first time I forced my mind to take flight. While the meeting was in session, I pictured the first clavichord I'd had as a child, with orange and amber details painted on the wood; I imagined its marble keys, the Josquin des Pres sheet music with its black notes, and though my eyes were open and my hands still, I once again became an eight-year-old girl reading music. In my mind, my fingers played the melody note by note. My body found its harmony, and I left the chapter house tension behind.

Once the vote was approved, Philippe closed the session. The movement of bodies getting up to leave broke the spell I had been under. I breathed deeply, peacefully. My blood flowed easily and I was calm as we left the premises.

After that incident, I had no doubt as to how I should react. The pendulum of my loyalties stopped swinging. I decided it was time to place marital love above filial love. Whatever the disagreements between my husband and I, our marriage required that we both wear a coat of mail to protect ourselves. Beyond the moat that was our hostility lay the fortress where our children lived. I too wished to return to Flanders. I missed my son and daughters. I pictured their days and nights, and I ached to caress them so badly my fingertips hurt. Why deny that Philippe could negotiate peace with His Majesty Louis XII? He did not feel the rancor of Spain, and his mind would be clear, his resolve more stable.

My father's dirty trick reminded me that in my family, the role of power always outranked that of parent.

⁂ THAT NIGHT I OFFERED MY HUSBAND MY LOYALTY. I PROMISED TO make common cause with him, to support his desire to return to Flanders via France. All of the rage that had kept him distant and haughty with me, his face tense, his hands stuffed into his pockets, collapsed like a windless sail. His sarcastic, scathing look melted into the sensual, complicit embrace that had first seduced me. That was all he had hoped for, to have me on his side, he said. I would not regret my decision, I'd see. He wouldn't let me down, and in the end my parents would be forced to realize that their authoritarianism did not always bring the results they hoped for.

I threw all my energy into preparing for our departure. I ordered new saddles as gifts for my children. I ordered mantillas for my sister-in-law Marguerite and other ladies in Brussels. I ordered new, wide dresses for my time in the French court, where Philippe and I would settle the issue of Charles and Claudia's wedding, which I had finally agreed to. The comforts that were to be provided for me on our return journey demanded great care, given that I was now in my seventh month of pregnancy. As a rule I cared little for that sort of luxury, but this time I had to ensure that nothing caused me to go into labor prematurely, to avoid the gauche possibility of giving birth to a Frenchman.

One night before we left, I dreamed about a fire I had seen when I was little and my parents' court was camped near Granada. Years later I still recalled the tents in the sierra burning in the night, the fire branding the sky with its ephemeral signs, the sentinels who'd become human torches, attempting to flee and leaving behind the sickening stench of burned flesh. In the dream, I was searching for my children in the flames, to no avail. I could hear their distant cries, but when I got nearer, their wailing turned into the piercing howls of those burned at the stake in the autos-da-fé. I woke up distraught, terrified, and jumped out of bed as if the devil himself were after me. In the corridor I bumped into Philippe, who'd come to tell me that my mother had sent a messenger, requiring his presence in Madrid. The queen wished to see him before we left, and he could not decline, especially given her delicate health. He would ride post, night and day, so as not to waste time, and be back as soon as he could. Tenderly, he kissed my round belly, then my forehead, and my lips, and he was off.

I stayed in bed all day. Each time I closed my eyes, I heard my children cry.

❋ "ISN'T IT WEIRD THAT ISABEL CALLED FOR PHILIPPE AND NOT FOR Juana?" I asked Manuel.

"When Ferdinand got to Madrid and told the queen about the terms that the Cortes of Aragon had imposed, Isabella feared for the unity of Spain, which was what she'd dedicated her life to. She wasn't happy to learn that once she died, if Ferdinand remarried and had a son, Juana would be stripped of the crown of Aragon. She knew the Aragonese would make her daughter pay dearly for her husband's fondness for the French. And she felt it was unacceptable that, having accepted Ferdinand's infidelity for the sake of her children's inheritance, the whims of a foreign prince could now come along and put her legacy at risk. If Philippe loved Juana, he should renounce his friendship with Louis and stay in Spain. She summoned him because she wanted to be frank with him and tell him how much he was risking by letting his urges dictate his actions."

"Did she convince him?"

"Ha! Not at all. Philippe kept insisting that he could stop the war and thus gain favor with Aragon. He told the queen about his responsibilities to his subjects, who threatened to rise up in arms if he did not return, and added that his father needed him in Germania. No. The queen did not convince him, nor did the king. Philippe spent three days in Madrid insisting that his decision was irreversible, arguing with your mother and father, who were unable to dissuade him. Then Isabel pulled the ace from her sleeve: you, Juana.

"Given that he wouldn't listen to reason, she said, there was nothing she could do to stop him. But she would not allow your life and that of your unborn child to run the risk of being victims of his obstinacy. She would not permit you to travel through the Pyrenees in the dead of winter. If he decided to leave without you, he'd have to wait until your health, the war, and the climate permitted you to return to Flanders. You mother tried, as a last resort, to insinuate that Philippe might lose you, to make him believe that not only the crown, but his marriage too was at stake."

"How did he react?"

"Well, the queen did make him vacillate for the first time. But in the end, he didn't change his plans."

TWELVE DAYS AFTER PHILIPPE LEFT FOR MADRID, THE PALACE LOOK-out sighted a party of men on horseback. I was flooded with relief, but when I looked out the window to see the group of new arrivals, there was no sign of Philippe. It was the Marquis of Villena, come to bring me a message. The marquis appeared before me, looking very handsome and gallant. His brown eyes, peeking out from underneath perfectly arched brows, looked me up and down, making no attempt to conceal their admiration. Dressed in leather breeches and a woolen cape, he took his hat off respectfully. I, however, was in no mood for courtesy. I immediately ordered him to tell me the reason Philippe was still in Madrid.

"Your Highness, your husband awaits you in Alcalá de Henares. He has sent me here to escort you. I have instructions to make the journey in stages, so you are not worn out, but as far as what he wishes to tell you, only he knows that."

"I beg you, tell me if the queen is in good health," I asked hesitantly, suspecting she was gravely ill or in her death throes. But the Marquis of Villena calmed my fears at once.

"Your Highness, the queen has recovered. Fear not for her health."

We prepared to depart in just a few hours. Though I dared not feel optimistic, I wondered if the queen had persuaded Philippe to remain in Spain. Beatriz de Bobadilla, my loyal first lady, was of the same opinion, and even Madame de Hallewin seemed to feel it could be so. In fact, she sulked and seemed withered on the way to Alcalá, so unappealing was the idea of staying to her. Beatriz and I, on the other hand, started imagining the implications of such a decision and spent the whole trip discussing the best way of moving the children, which palace would be the best suited residence for Philippe and I, and who should be in our entourage.

MY SPIRITS COULD NOT HAVE BEEN LESS CONDUCIVE TO HEARING the news Philippe gave me. The moment I saw him, I noticed his shifty look and the stiff way he held himself. In just a few days, his face had grown sharper, more angular. After welcoming me and asking for us to be left alone, there was hardly any vestige of the tendernes he'd shown when bidding me farewell. Though I was sitting beside the fire, I felt cold. I sat listening to him beat around the bush for what seemed ages as he attempted to explain his decision to return to Flanders. And little by little, as his words dashed my hopes, I felt the fury within me take on the force of a whirlwind. When I spoke, the words shot out of my mouth like daggers. Spite ruled my speech. *This* was how he repaid my loyalty, he who felt so committed to his? Was *I* not the person who best knew what my body could or could not handle, how strong I was? Why this sudden concern for my health, when these considerations had not hampered our plans to leave until this point? If he thought my parents were so sensible, their reasoning so sound, why not wait himself until our child was born in Spain? There were only two months left. If we parted now, who knew when we would be reunited? Had *I* not been patient when month after month, for over a year, he put off our journey to Spain to be recognized by the Cortes? Why this sudden urgency that made him unconcerned about leaving me behind, far from him, from my children, and under my parents' rule? Did he have no idea how much I missed my children? What if I died in childbirth?

I paced back and forth like a crazed pendulum, unable to calm myself or keep quiet. I went from questions he left unanswered to insults aimed at provoking any sort of reaction at all. I called him shiftless, weak, dim-witted, incapable of ruling a kingdom. What were his stupid Low Countries compared to the power of Spain? He was an arrogant fool, I spat. He was unable to put aside his pettiness to take the reins that destiny held out to him.

Speechless, Philippe stared at me from his seat beside the fire. His silence made me even more furious, enraged at my desperation and my impotence. I wanted to bang my head against the wall, to kick and scream, to destroy. I could not accept the idea of staying in Spain without Philippe by my side. And beneath my rage spread fear, like a lake whose waters were rising, threatening to drown me. I was sure that as soon as he left, my parents would take control, moving me this way and that like a pawn on a chessboard. I would have less freedom than the most wretched of my slaves. My eyes bulged in unbridled fear, and believing all was lost, I knelt before Philippe and clung to his legs, imploring.

When he realized I had lost my composure and my arrogance, it was his turn to be livid. He pushed me aside, saying that he detested everything I represented, my dark, parched country full of bloodthirsty monks and fatuous, twisted nobles, my country of ignorant fools, of murderers. Who was I to talk if the throne I was to inherit had been usurped, the kingdom built on deceit, blessed by lascivious popes, if my parents governed by authority alone? Was it possible that I did not see that the very nobility that surrounded them also abhorred them? He had never seen a court so full of intrigue and deceit, so quick to betray and stab others in the back. Nothing but a band of murderers, and he would not allow them to kill another of his friends, much less him. My father was ready to get rid of anyone who stood in his way. I was the only one who couldn't see how twisted his mind was.

He would not return to Spain like some sacrificial lamb. He would make allies with those who would protect him. Could I really not see that my father would willingly sacrifice both of us even if tears blinded him?

He was no fool, my Philippe. A long while later I would recall those words, again and again, but that day they sounded so terribly unfair. Sprawled on the floor, I covered my ears and told him to get out, told him I didn't want to see his face for another second, told him to go hunt and drink with his French friends, those idlers who did nothing but stand around in salons and dance basse danse and pavanes. That is how my love and I took our leave. Philippe departed, and I stayed on to rot in Castile, like carrion for the vultures.

CHAPTER 13

H ave a chocolate, Lucía."

While Philippe left for France, and poor Juana bore her pregnancy under her mother's watchful eye; while the events of the early sixteenth century left a trail of sadness and dismay among the books in the library, Manuel and I took a lunch break. Águeda served lasagna on a silver platter. For dessert, we had little cakes and the chocolates she was now holding out to me in a beautiful gold box. Gazing at the pair of them, aunt and nephew, seated side by side, I was astonished by how much they resembled each other: light eyes, arched brows, small, narrow noses, and wide lips. There was a majestic aura about them that came more from their limited interest in the present than it did their ancestry. The only discordant note, in Águeda's case, was her excessively made-up look and her bulky bracelet.

"You look so much alike," I said.

"My sister and I were twins."

"Really?" I was surprised.

"Yes, but my mother was the black sheep of the family. The 'mad woman in the house,' and I don't mean that in the sense Saint Teresa did when she discussed the imagination," Manuel said.

"She *was* imaginative, though. A lot more than me. I was always the practical one. She was the dreamer, the one who believed in art, the bohemian. And she was not mad, Manuel, though she may have shown poor judgment. She was born in the wrong time and thought my father would understand her need to rebel. She was wrong. From then on, no one in this house dared to question his parental authority. My mother and I couldn't help her. This means nothing to either of you, I know; you have no idea how strict our father was." Águeda sat stirring sugar into her coffee, staring off into space.

"Good God, Aunt Águeda, here we are in the late sixties and the police still ban making out in public," Manuel interrupted jokingly. "Things haven't changed *that* much."

"Oh yes, they have. Believe me," she said, looking up, emerging from her reverie. "People are rebelling all over the world. All you have to do is turn on the news and see those girls in Washington burning their brassieres. Young people today know time is on their side. You're not so scared anymore, not as tortured by scruples as we were."

"But Manuel's mother married very young, didn't she?" I asked.

"She never married," Manuel said, tearing off a chunk of bread. "I was born out of wedlock. My father was a high school teacher who decided to disappear without a trace rather than face his would-be in-laws. And my grandparents disinherited my mother, just in case he decided to turn up. They took everything from her. Even her son."

"Believe me, Manuel, it was better that way, better for you to just forget about your father. And I didn't mind at all, not since the first time I saw you, so tiny, so sweet. Aurora never came back. I raised Manuel," Águeda said, smiling beatifically as she gazed over at him.

"Until I was sent to boarding school . . ."

"I would never have sent you to boarding school, Manuel, you know that, although I did think, later, that it was best for you to be away from your grandparents."

"Don't remind me of what I went through. They wanted to make such a proper Castilian of me, they almost finished me off," he said, turning to face me.

"Well, you can't say I didn't save you from getting your behind whipped a good many times!" Águeda added, suddenly playful, as she tossed Manuel a chocolate.

"Oh yes, Auntie. You were my guardian angel." He laughed, catching it.

"Well, it was the least I could do for poor Aurora."

"What did your mother die of, Manuel?"

They looked at each other.

"An overdose. Tranquilizers. She committed suicide in a hotel in Portofino," he replied.

"Poor Aurora never recovered after father kicked her out."

"That's terrible!" I said.

"Yes, child, sometimes parents do terrible things. And the worst part is that they think they're doing them out of love." She sighed.

"Do you know how long Isabel and Ferdinand forced Juana to stay in Spain after they refused to let her go back to Flanders with Philippe?"

"Oh, Manuel, come on, you're going to bore her to death."

"How long?" I asked, curious. Besides, royalty seemed like a safer topic.

"A whole year. After Juana returned to Flanders, her relationship with Philippe was never the same again."

"That year in Spain marked the beginning of her madness, didn't it, Manuel? She insisted they let her go back. She shouted at her mother, hit the people who took care of her," Águeda said.

"I'm not surprised," I said. "It must have been infuriating for a woman with four children of her own to be told she has no free will and can't even go home."

"You see, Auntie? It's a question of perspective. A modern woman cannot see how the rebellion Juana was accused of is anything but fully justified."

"I'm not saying history treated her well. But, my God! She was a princess! She should have controlled herself. Worse things happen and women learn not to lose their cool. What kind of world would this be if every woman lashed out against anyone who treated her unfairly?"

"Maybe it would be a better place than the one we live in now," I said, thinking of my mother and feeling a burning sensation in my chest.

Águeda's only response was to stand up and start clearing the table. I tried to get her to let me help, but she absolutely refused.

"Go on, you two. Off to the library."

"We'll have coffee there," Manuel said. "In a few hours I must take you back to school."

✳ I WENT TO THE BATHROOM AND THEN TO THE LIBRARY. AS I WENT in, I saw a black dress lying on the sofa. A bitter, vaguely chocolaty, taste filled my mouth.

"Oh no, Manuel, please don't make me put that on," I said, touching the cloth (quality wool, tightly woven, soft and lustrous to the touch). It had a high neckline, with white lace pleats down the front, and puffy angel sleeves that tapered out at the forearm.

"You'll be very comfortable. Don't forget: you accepted my conditions. Go on. For me. Please. Be a good girl."

No point in arguing. I got undressed. Manuel, slightly nervous, hurriedly tied the ribbons at the back. It was so strange his insistence with this gown ritual. I pulled my hair back. The smell of wool reminded me of the nuns. It wasn't a new dress. You could smell the mothballs.

Once I had it on, I had to admit that Manuel wasn't entirely wrong. Something happened to me that allowed me to distance myself from my everyday persona and imagine I was somewhere else. Around me, the light of the fireplace cast a golden reflection on the bookshelves, furniture, and papers. The room seemed to be levitating inside a bubble. I closed my eyes, letting the unreality of it all wash over me.

✳ YOU WISHED THE RAGE YOU FELT WHEN YOU BID PHILIPPE FARE-well had lasted a little longer, Juana. That way your first night without him would have been less painful, lying there on the cold sheets of the royal bedroom in the Archbishop's Palace in Alcalá de Henares. You thought of the high hopes you'd had on your way there: the court and palace that your imagination filled with faces and furniture and where you caught a glimpse of yourself living with your husband and children on Spanish soil; you recalled how anxious you were, how badly you longed for that reunion. Desolate now, you regret each and every one of your spiteful words.

ONE BY ONE, I WEIGHED THEM, REPEATED THEM. I IMAGINED THE disastrous effect they would have had, piercing their way into Philippe's consciousness with their spiked barbs. He hates me now, I thought, and he shall never forgive me. Lying distraught in the darkness, I recited out loud each sentence I recalled having pronounced. I wanted to trap the sound of my voice and wring it out, crush it, stamp on it, like a child trapping bugs and then squashing them. I could see Philippe riding through the arid Castilian sierra, lashed by the wind, which would carry the echo of my insults to him once more. I did not sleep until I had taken a vow of silence as penitence for my impulsiveness. I intended to keep quiet for a good, long time.

My mother could not comprehend my silence. She sat with me, trying to have a conversation, asking me questions. She would demand I have some soup, some stew. I was dying of hunger, and thirst, but I had promised myself I would keep my mouth shut. For two or three days I did nothing but cry.

Finally, Beatriz convinced me that I had to eat. For my child. For that bird who was pecking his way toward life from within me. My child demanded that I live, he was digging his heels into my ribs. Priests paid call, nuns paid call. Cardinal Jiménez de Cisneros stopped by every morning to inquire as to my health, before leaving for the university he had founded. I listened to him, because he brought news of Philippe. It was through him that I learned of the trials that my husband had endured during the two months it took him to reach the French border, thanks to my father's attempts to waylay his progress, ordering that he be denied horses and even lodging in castles along the way, under the pretext of the imminent war with France. I thought that perhaps so many obstacles would have made Philippe desist and took up hope, thinking he might turn back, but of course he did not. Finally, my father realized that his stubborn son-in-law would not give up, and he opted to give in himself, by entrusting Philippe to represent Spain in the negotiations with the king of France over the dispute for Naples.

It was clear to me that my husband would not retrace his steps.

✳ ON MARCH 10, 1503, I GAVE BIRTH TO FERDINAND WITH A MINIMUM of pain and no complications. The palace bells rang in celebration announcing through Alcalá de Henares the good news that my second son had been born in Spain. My baby was healthy and handsome. He took more after my side of the family, escaping the protruding Hapsburg chin that my little Charles inherited. I thought I could finally return to Flanders, to Philippe and my children. There would be nothing stopping me now. Tremendously relieved, I slept for two days straight.

A few days later, a horseman from Lyon arrived with a gift from Philippe: a beautiful gold choker with seven enormous pearls symbolizing the Virgin Mary's seven joyful mysteries.

Though black had been reintroduced as the official court color, I refused to dress in mourning on the day Ferdinand was baptized. I wore a dark red dress with golden embroidery and a plunging neckline designed to call attention to my necklace. As we entered the church, I insisted on carrying the baby myself. During the ceremony in the cathedral, the bishop of Málaga, Diego Ramírez de Villaescusa, the same one who had performed our wedding ceremony, praised me to the high heavens during the homily. He said that God had rewarded me with healthy children and that, just like the Virgin herself, I laughed and smiled while giving birth. Fifty days and fifty nights, he said, would not suffice to count my virtues. Though his flattery was quite exaggerated, my gratitude to him was heartfelt, because not only were my mother and father present, but all the grandees in the kingdom had come for the dedication. And clearly I could use some champions now that everything I did or didn't do was interpreted capriciously. Many attributed my melancholy and displeasure at being so far from my loved ones—even my lack of appetite—to a feeble mind and a lack of wits. This widespread disposition to portray me unfavorably and present Philippe and I as a threat to the stability and interests of the crown led my husband to command that no one be allowed to enter in my service without his permission.

But when Ferdinand was born, my parents sent seventy Spanish nobles to work in my retinue, taking no notice whatsoever of Philippe's wishes.

I was at the center of a power struggle whose objectives became clear to me over time. The weeks went by and no one seemed to listen to my insistent demands that I be allowed to return to Flanders. When I grew impatient and proposed journeying to Lyon to meet up with my husband, they forced me to desist, brandishing the same reasons they'd given Philippe: I couldn't risk being held captive by the French, used for ransom to obtain advantages in the war over Naples. When I asked to make the voyage by sea, they said it would be impossible until after spring, since the Biscayan sailors were predicting squalls throughout the season. Between my parents' stance, the snippets of conversation I over-heard, and the constant rumors, it slowly dawned on me that my mother planned to keep me in Spain indefinitely. She was convinced that time would wash away my regrets and that eventually I would realize that be-coming the queen to whom she would bestow her legacy was well worth the sacrifice of living apart from Philippe. She trusted that I would place the duties of my station above my duties as wife and mother and that I would choose political power over domestic bliss and love.

The more aware I became of my mother's wishes, the more incensed my heart became. Defying her turned into an obsession. I set out to de-stroy her peace and harmony, and to ensure that each day she forced me to wander the halls of that palace were bitter pills for her. I wanted her to long desperately for my departure. We would see who gave in first. It was not difficult to put my plan into action; I was wracked by rage, an-guish, and desperation. I gave little Ferdinand to a wet nurse and, for want of allies, armies, or other weapons, turned to my last resort: my body and my willpower.

"ISABEL NEVER EXPECTED SUCH SUSTAINED RESISTANCE," MANUEL said, getting up to poke the fire. "But Juana had a queen's mettle. She could go for days without eating, sitting motionless in bed, staring off into space, snubbing everyone, refusing everything. Her mother ordered the Cortes to be moved to Alcalá de Henares and, day and night, between running the State and taking care of business, she visited her daughter and berated her, insisting she give up this silent treatment. Juana would only repeat her demands: that they let her go to Flanders to rejoin Philippe and her children. It was obvious at first glance that the princess was losing weight. She was pale, unkempt, her vanity absent, as if she could care less about anything related to her person.

I WANT MY MOTHER TO BE ASHAMED BY THE CHORUS OF COURTIERS in the palace worrying about my demise. I want her to fear for my life, for my health. I want her to evoke the ghost of my grandmother. No doubt she remembers her mother wandering aimlessly with a forlorn look through the rooms in the Palace of Arevalo. Those memories are a private hell for her, and I fan the flames with no shame or regret, because what I now feel for my mother is something akin to hatred. As soon as I hear her footsteps echoing in the hallway and the sounds of whoever accompanies her on her daily visits, I feel my blood begin to bubble up like water boiling in the cauldron of my belly. I have no qualms in defying her when we are alone. If as a child I found her presence often overpowering, now I wait for her unmoved. Sometimes I simply refuse to respond, I don't react at all when, fearfully, she takes my hands in hers. Totally absent from the room where we both sit, I use my clavichord trick and imagine my sheet music until she finally leaves, depressed and impotent. Other times, I cry or talk about my children.

"Mother, is it possible that you do not miss Isabel and Juan, my dead siblings? Do you not remember when they were babies and their little bodies fit into the crook of your arm? Do you not remember their smiles, their squeals as they played together? Do you never think of wrenching them from their graves and bringing them back to childhood? Because I think about my children in Brussels, I think about them all the time. I think I can hear them, hear what they think of the mother, who has abandoned them. I do not know, my lady, how you who have suffered so many deaths and absences can do this to me. Or did we never matter to you, Mother? Did you never feel anything for us, and that is why you cannot understand how I can be so sad now?

Or I remind her of how she was tormented by jealousy.

"Do you remember, Mother, when you found out that father had gotten another woman with child? Did you picture him stroking and caressing another body with the same hands that touched you at night? Did you not perhaps feel, as I do, a mouthful of sharp teeth biting you from within? Philippe is young. He cannot survive for long without love, and when he seeks out another, what will happen if her kisses are sweeter, if forbidden love is more exciting for its sheer novelty? You shall be solely responsible for my misfortune; you and only you. How do you make a stone feel, make it have a heart? I never ever want to be queen if it means becoming as hard and as heartless as you."

The queen asked me to be patient. She deceived me, saying that as soon as the weather improved I could leave. Then she recriminated me, insisting I remember that the destiny of Spain was so much greater than that of any of us. Her pale face, blue eyes, and the golden curls peeking out from her cap made her look like a candle wax virgin, remote and unlit. When I was angry, I turned red. She, however, grew pale. Often our conversations ended with hostile barbs. I spoke from my heart and said what I felt, without fear or favor. I showed my mother no respect or consideration. Why should I submit to her? I was suffering as her victim, and I refused to turn the other cheek.

Beatriz reproached me. Upsetting my mother would only worsen her illness, she was sure, and my attitude only fueled the rumors that I had gone mad.

Let them speak! Those who are born submissive and obedient like serfs have no will of their own and know not how to affirm their independence. I, instead, had been born a princess, was going to be queen, and my demands only extended to what was rightfully mine. It would please me to see how those who dared call me mad would act if they were in my place! For the life of me I could not understand my mother's pretense that I gave precedence to my loyalty to her at the expense of the obligations to my own family. It was only her and my father's ill will toward Philippe that made her demand such a thing. They could not forgive that he was loyal to his own dominions, nor his determination to decide by himself what was best for our future and that of our children.

Philippe, in fact, had managed to negotiate a truce with Louis of France, by agreeing to divide Naples between France and Spain until our children, Charles and Claudia, were married, at which time it would become part of the unified crown that combined both of their realms. Philippe would act as regent for the Spanish, and Louis would name a French regent until they came of age.

However, of this truce, which favored my return to Philippe's side, I was not informed, on my mother's explicit instructions. Had Beatriz de Bobadilla not contravened royal prohibition by telling me, I would never have known it had been signed.

My mother and I had left Alcalá de Henares and gone to Segovia. I was led to believe that, in addition to escaping from the heat, by traveling north we were beginning the journey that would eventually take me to the port of Laredo, and from there to Flanders.

Just as before, though, a week followed another and there was no sign of my trip getting under way. The disputes between my mother and I reached such an extreme, both of us were so distraught and convulsed, that the royal physicians Soto and De Juan finally convinced my mother that the two of us should not share the same space. It was decided that I would go to Medina del Campo, to La Mota Castle, farther north.

Within this castle, with its high battlements and enormous walls rising up from the arid, red earth, I watched the summer I should have embarked to Flanders get to its end. A year had passed since I had seen Philippe and my three oldest children.

The desperation caused by my impotence was wreaking havoc on my stomach. I was eating so little that I had no energy and no want other than sleep. I thought obsessively of Philippe and imagined his passions channeled into carefree lascivious pleasures. I pictured his lips traveling down the voluptuous and curved backs of seductive women in an orgy of naked bodies. Sometimes these fantasies aroused me uncontrollably, taking me to the peak of pleasure. At other times they left me in a morose heap on the floor, wailing and sweating profusely. I stopped bathing, stopped grooming myself. What did I care if I was filthy and unkempt? After all, I was a wretched prisoner locked up in those austere corridors, nothing more. How could I be expected to show even a scrap of dignity when my freedom was so utterly trampled? As the sun set each day, I thought I could sense my children's growing oblivion: each day taking from their memories another feature of my face, making it fade just as the dying day faded away over the fields of Castile. I could feel the red liquid substance of Philippe's love growing fainter too, dwindling, becoming a trickle that soon would dry altogether. My bitter thoughts were strangling my will to live. I refused to taste even a bite of food, determined to bring death to myself once and for all.

IT WAS EARLY NOVEMBER. DAY OF THE DEAD HYMNS WERE STILL floating in the air when, one afternoon when the whole world seemed to have sunk in the mist, a rider appeared with a letter from Philippe. Beatriz came in and handed it to me. She remained by my side, waiting anxiously for my reaction with trembling hands, for she feared the force of my desolation. I read the letter by the window while the governess held little Ferdinand back, impeding his attempts to stand up by grabbing onto my skirts. From the first lines, I could tell it was a love letter. He couldn't stand to be without me any longer, he said. I had to find a way to return to Flanders. And he sent me the name of the captain of a wool trading merchant ship who was ready to make the journey whenever I commanded.

Just like a bear who comes out of hibernation after the coldest of winters, so did my heart awake in my chest, warmed and bursting with the desire to dash swiftly and hungrily into my husband's arms.

I called for a bath to be prepared for me and sent for some food. I called my most trusted ladies-in-waiting and told them of my plan to leave for Bilbao as soon as possible. No one else must know, I told them. Stealthily, we would prepare our trunks and leave in two days' time.

BUT—ALAS!—WHILE WE BUZZED AROUND LIKE BEES PREPARING TO leave the hive, Captain Hugo de Urríes, betrayed Philippe's and my desires and wrote to my father denouncing our plans.

THE MULES WERE READY AND WAITING. WITH LITTLE FERDINAND IN my arms, I was out on the castle courtyard, ensuring that the trunks of clothes, books, and provisions were well secured when suddenly we heard the sound of horses approaching. Riding across the drawbridge, they galloped through the castle's open gate, led by Juan de Fonseca, the bishop of Córdoba, who had once been my friend and advisor. The moment I saw him at the head of a party of soldiers, my legs went weak and quivery. This could only mean more obstacles in my way. The bishop dismounted, bowed reverently before me, and asked me to explain what was behind all of this bustling around.

"I am leaving," I said. "My husband awaits me in Flanders and I must join him."

"Forgive me, madam, but how is it that your mother the queen has no news of your departure, nor has she given her consent? How is it that you plan to take your leave without bidding her farewell?"

"That is a matter between my mother and I. Neither she nor anyone else can oblige me to stay here so far from my family any longer."

"And where will you go? Captain Urríes, at your father's urging, has desisted from his mission. There is no longer any boat awaiting you in Bilbao."

Beatriz and Madame de Hallewin came up on either side of me, taking my arms, encircling me and offering me their protection. I was blinded by rage. My body was a sea of lava, and a boiling, shrieking fury spilled out from my heart.

"I don't care if that wretched captain has decided to betray me," I hollered. "I will journey through France."

"Do you not know, perchance, that France is at war with Spain?"

"With Spain, yes, but not with me. Let's go," I cried, wrenching myself free of those who were trying to protect me, rushing to the middle of the courtyard to instruct the servants, who were waiting on edge. "Continue with the preparations."

"In the name of Her Majesty, Queen Isabella, I command you to stop," the bishop shouted, contradicting me. Before I could prevent it, he motioned to the soldiers in his party to seal the castle gates.

"I forbid you," I screamed. "No gates will be sealed here until I have departed."

"Juana, Juana, I am only obeying the orders I have received from our lady, the queen, your mother. Please, I beg you, calm yourself," the bishop said lowering his voice.

At the mention of my mother's name all my efforts to impose my authority went unheeded. Deaf to my frenzied orders, the soldiers went ahead to raise the drawbridge and close the gates. Intimidated, my ladies began to retreat. Slowly, the servants started to untie the bundles and unload the trunks from the mules and carts. I ran from one to the next, upbraiding them for their submissiveness, but all I got in return were looks of fear and compassion. I was overcome with despair. The bishop had ridden out just before the drawbridge was raised. I deposited Ferdinand in Beatriz's arms and charged up the parapet behind the walls. I could see him on the other side of the moat, and I shouted to him, insisting that if he did not let me out he would pay dearly when I was queen. I would have them all hung, each and every one, I screeched, frantic. I could not see any reason that could justify the shame and humiliaton I had been made to suffer at the eyes of everyone in my court. I believe at one point I charged against the soldiers posted at the gates. The poor men put up with me hurling abuse until Beatriz intervened.

Bile rose up in my throat, I could taste it in my parched mouth. For quite some time all I could see were faces, spinning and twisting like snakes slithering up to strangle me; they were the faces of those I had confronted as I ran, crazed, back and forth across the palace courtyard. When I was back in my right mind, I sent a messenger to intercept the priest and try to convince him graciously to allow me to leave, as well as beg forgiveness for my sharp tongue. But he who had once been an ally sent back my envoy, Miguel de Ferrara, with the message that his patience was not to be tried with insults and disrespect, and that he would inform the queen of my behavior that very night. His reply wounded my pride. I sent Ferrara once again, to ask Fonseca to tell my mother that neither rain nor sun nor wind would force me back inside the fortress of La Mota. I would remain in the courtyard, waiting for the gates to be opened so that I might take my leave.

And there I stayed. I leaned up against the guard's sentry box and closed my eyes. Gradually the wild pounding of my heart slowed and the fire that lit my cheeks and burned my hands and thighs began to die down. The guards and servants retired respectfully. Only two of my mother's soldiers, Beatriz, and I remained in the courtyard. From the corner of my eye I could see Beatriz, seated at a prudent distance behind me.

I kept my word. I did not reenter the castle I had been so joyful and lighthearted to exit just a few hours earlier. I would have gone deaf inside, listening to the echo of my plans and hopeful visions rebounding off the dark, hulking walls, before they crumbled like a tower of worm-eaten wood. The very idea made me nauseated. I cursed my destiny, forced to submit to the will of those who were determined to tame me like a wild beast! I tried to think clearly, but all I could see was the image of an endless corridor filled with thick, white smoke, its narrow walls closing in on me. I was smothered, stifled, by my name, by closed doors, by my utter dependence on others. My royal body was divided, each half tied to wild horses that raced each other madly, not mindful that they tore me apart. When night fell it grew cold. Beatriz brought me some blankets, but I told her to leave me in peace. Inside the sentry box, a remorseful-looking soldier who hardly dared glance at me discretely lit a fire. Had it not been for him, I might have died. His thoughtfulness moved me, and I cried silently for a long time. I passed the time counting my tears, thinking how strange it was, the act of crying, the idea of pain and sorrow pouring out of our eyes.

The next day and night were worse than the first. My sadness overflowed and every part of me plunged into its depth. With no strength left, I crumbled like an empty shell against the wall. I would have died perhaps—and in good time—had it not begun to rain, forcing me to accept the shelter the soldier offered me in his box. His name was Sebastián and he was from Andalusia. On the morning of the third day, I heard the far-off sound of trampling hooves, and I knew that before long, my mother would be standing before me.

THAT WAS MY LAST ENCOUNTER WITH ISABELLA, MY MOTHER, AND she would later grieve, accusing me of having said unthinkable things to her, when in truth I said what any bereft daughter would dare say to her mother. I did not insult her, but I did bemoan her lack of love for me to her face, I denounced her willingness to sacrifice me for reasons of State, her inability to love anything or anyone but her realms. I told her she was dry and arid like a moor and that she had used every one of her children as coinage to trade for power and territory. I cursed life for making her my mother. My only real mother, I said, had been my wet nurse, María de Santiesteban. I wished her a lonely, painful death so that she might atone for all of the pain and suffering she had so cruelly prescribed for me.

It gave me great pleasure to watch her bewilderment as I railed on and on, rushing to get out all the words that had been corroding my insides. Little remained of the girl she had left in Laredo, the girl who she'd rocked in her arms as the storm blew. She herself had destroyed me.

But in our duel, my mother reserved for herself the last stroke: she would consent to my journey, she said, if I agreed to leave my little son Fernando behind, in Spain, to be raised by my father and her as a Spanish prince. That was her requisite to allow my departure. If I accepted and left my son, I could set sail for Flanders as soon as spring arrived.

CHAPTER 14

December drew near and with it, midterm exams. Fortunately, my student life continued to unfold without major variations. I had begun to think of myself as two different people: the one who lived in and the one who lived out. The girl inside the boarding school and the other out in the city streets. The good girl and the woman. When I returned from my first weekend with the Denias, Mother Luisa Magdalena called me to the infirmary. She began by asking if I was still constipated, but it didn't take her long to work her way around to asking about the house where my friends lived. I told her about the alarm system and the automatic locks. I thought the best way to calm her fears would be to chatter and be bubbly, like an enthusiastic girl recounting all the details of a field trip to her mother. Mother Luisa Magdalena's maternal instincts had found in me an ideal target. By contrast, given what had been going on with me, I had no desire to have a mother as a confidante. I didn't want her to realize this, though. She still clung to the short-lived intimacy we'd shared at the beginning of the school year. I had the impression that she thought our relationship had not deepened further out of some personal fault of her own, so she was constantly seeking a way to reestablish the lost connection between us. The infirmary was a small, white-tiled room with metal cabinets—also white—against the walls, and a desk and chair. It looked out on the shady side of the interior garden. Through the window, one could see the pine tree at the center of the courtyard. It was a cold room, and inevitably my teeth chattered after I had been there for a while. The nun went out to get me a cup of hot chocolate.

"So, that is really great," she said, setting it down on the table beside a plate with a slice of bread and a square of chocolate. "I think you're very lucky to have met a family in Spain that is so well versed in history. I imagine it must be fascinating for you to learn more about Queen Isabella and her children."

"Oh, it's mesmerizing," I quipped. I tried to hide my irony by taking a big gulp of the thick, hot chocolate. "You have no idea how much they know about Juana. Especially Manuel, the nephew." I smiled with feigned naïveté. "I think he's obsessed, actually, with trying to reconstruct her life. The aunt, well, she's more concerned with the family estate and whatnot. They're both a little weird, there's no doubt about that. Very solitary characters," I added, compelled by a smidgen of honesty.

"That's very Spanish," she said. She always sat up very straight. The convent chairs—uncomfortable and high-backed—had left her permanently looking like a soldier awaiting inspection.

"Really? I thought Spaniards were supposed to be sociable and boisterous. Not that I mind; I'm introverted myself, so it's fine with me."

"Well, all that business about Spaniards being gregarious is a generalization, a stereotype. We like to talk, sure, but there's a part of our character—especially the Castilian character—that's very mystic, very austere. It's something you have to take into account. Even though you're from the tropics, you seem more Castilian in your personality. At your age, you should be out making friends, spending more time with your classmates," she said sweetly, maternally. "I hardly ever see you talking to them. Piluca and Marina are very fond of you, you know. And I used to see you together all the time."

"I don't like hearing them talk about their families and their summer plans. It depresses me," I said, taking refuge in my own black legend.

"But you have family, Lucía. Oh, and by the way, you should write to your grandparents to see what they want to do about Christmas. Do you think you'll go back to Málaga? Or to London? When is your cousin's wedding again?"

My routine was going to change over Christmas. I would have to think of an excuse not to leave Madrid. I had already written to my grandparents, excusing myself from the wedding on account of a heavy load of schoolwork in my last semester of high school.

"I'm not going to the wedding. It's too long a trip. And to be honest, I don't want to go. I might just stay in Madrid," I said, tentatively.

"Oh, child, the walls will close in on you if you do that. It's very lonely around here at Christmastime."

"Well, I bet I could spend the holidays with Manuel and his aunt. They'd probably love to have me. They don't have many friends, you know. Like me." I smiled, still testing her.

"The aunt is very sweet, if eccentric, I think, but are you sure her nephew isn't a little taken with you?"

"Mother Luisa!" I cried. "Manuel is much, much older than me."

"That's never stopped men before. Quite the opposite, in fact. Men *do* fall for younger women, you know; it happens all the time."

"Well, not this time. Manuel just sees me as another student. I think the fact that I'm so enthralled by the way he recounts history probably boosts his ego, but that's it. You're imagining things."

"Well, you might be surprised, you never know."

I wondered if she suspected the truth, if God maybe had some secret contact with people like her who dedicated their lives to his service. As worried as I was about being discovered, and as ashamed as I was of my duplicity, I was also amazed that a nun who had no real life experience could pick up on what Manuel and I thought was so well concealed.

"Are you trying to say I shouldn't spend the holidays with them?"

"Just that you need to think about whether you would enjoy spending Christmas with people you hardly know."

"I know them better than I do the nuns in Málaga."

"Yes, I suppose you're right. And I'm not saying you won't be able to do as you like."

I kept quiet, staring at the rays of sunlight that fell on the pine tree, giving it a fairy-tale look. Then I made as if to go.

"Wait, Lucía. Look, I must admit it's a little embarassing for me to broach this subject with you, but I've been thinking that there are some facts of life you should know at your age and that, for lack of your mother, I should tell you." She had leaned over to pat my hand, and she was blushing. I looked back at her intrigued.

"I'm talking about your sexual education," she said. "I know that here at school we don't deal with that and basically leave it up to the parents, but in your case . . ."

I was agape, not knowing how to respond. I almost wanted to laugh at the irony of it all, thinking that at this rate I could probably teach a class on the subject to all the students at the convent, if indeed they hadn't already learned those lessons themselves.

"Women's bodies start to mature after their first period, and I'm sure that your anatomy classes have given you an idea of how your sexual organs function, but those textbooks and illustrations are very schematic, and as far as I'm concerned, young women these days should at least have some basic information about the dangers of exposing themselves to certain experiences before the time comes."

"What kinds of dangers, Mother Luisa?"

"Well, unwanted pregnancies, sexually transmitted diseases, that sort of thing. The flesh is weak and instincts are a force of nature that we can't always anticipate. Like a hurricane, or an earthquake. Boys don't pay as high a price as girls do. Believe me, I've known more than one who has ruined her life through ignorance. It's not school policy to instruct girls on these sorts of things. I am doing this because of my own personal conclusions on this matter. So it's just between you and me, all right?"

The shaft of light had disappeared. The pine tree was fading in the golden, dusky light. I could hear doors closing, footsteps on the corridors; the school was preparing for supper. I was trapped like a deer in headlights. The nun's eyes were on me, and I didn't dare move. I'd have to let her finish her speech. I could think of no delicate way to get out of it, to get up and go. Maybe I would learn some anatomy. My mother's sex-education book was at least fifteen or twenty years old. The illustrations had the same style as the black-and-white engravings of old art books. I had trusted Manuel to know what he was doing. He had drawn a diagram of my menstrual cycle, marking my "safe" days and my fertile days, because he thought that condoms were unnatural and awkward. When I told him I'd never seen a condom, he showed me one. At first I couldn't figure out how that flat rubber ring topped with gelatin and sealed in its little aluminum packet was supposed to work. I couldn't see the gelatin but I felt it when I pulled out the ring, which resembled a foil-wrapped chocolate coin. He told me it went over the penis and had to be rolled down with thumb and forefinger. I got the giggles when I saw the rubber on him but I also felt sorry. It looked like it must hurt, although he said it didn't. I tried to keep tugging it downward so that it would fit snugly, covering his member from top to bottom, but he stopped me. You had to leave a little room at the tip, he said, for the semen. Once it was on, the hood looked eerie and a little ridiculous. How could they not have invented anything better than that, at least aesthetically? I agreed that we'd be better off going with the rhythm method, which, he said, had been used since time immemorial. He asked me if my periods were regular, and when I said yes, he took note of my dates on a sheet of graph paper, numbering squares from one to twenty-eight. He blocked off certain days when we'd abstain and others when, if we made love, he would make sure to withdraw and not to ejaculate inside me.

And that's how we had done it. And I had felt safe.

I lowered my eyes, staring at my school uniform skirt. I had to have it washed. Lately I forgot about things like that. It wasn't so stained, but I could see a few dark patches between the pleats.

"Am I making you feel uncomfortable by talking about this?" Mother Luisa Magdalena asked me.

I said she wasn't. Why should I feel uncomfortable? If she, who had never even touched a man's body, thought she could teach me "the mysteries of life," as our science teacher called it, then why shouldn't she? I was touched. Mother Luisa was a very unusual woman. That's what I liked about her.

We stayed in the infirmary until dinnertime. Mother Luisa Magdalena took out some anatomy books and drew diagrams, explaining what each part of the female genitalia was called and what it was for. She told me that in some parts of Africa, girls under ten years old had their genitals mutilated. Their clitorises were cut off so they would never be tempted by the pleasures of the flesh. It was barbaric, she said. She explained that the clitoris was like a minute penis, hypersensitive. She wasn't blushing anymore. She took on the tone of a professor, but you could tell that the whole system fascinated her. Amazing, isn't it? she said at one point. I kept wondering how it was that she'd ended up a nun. Hearing her speak so passionately, so poetically, about sexuality made me want to cry, but I hid my eyes so she couldn't see them welling up. I didn't want her to feel bad.

It was a very useful conversation in the end; it cleared up a lot of things that until then I'd only intuited about bodily functions and sexual relations. Yet I was anxious when I left. Mother Luisa Magdalena did not put as much faith as Manuel did in the rhythm method. According to her, it was very unreliable, since the hormonal balance that controlled women's—and especially young women's—menstrual cycles could be thrown out of whack by lots of things, things as trivial as getting upset, and then all those calculations went down the drain. I consoled myself by thinking that my chances of getting pregnant were probably very slim, given how infrequently Manuel and I saw each other.

The idea of my body as an oven that could produce other humans made me think of the silica used by glassblowers to make jugs and decanters. I too could blow up, I thought apprehensively, recalling the image of pregnant women's bellies, like taut balloons. I fell asleep with my hands crossed over my stomach.

That week I felt less alone at school. Having a place to go on the weekends, adults besides the nuns who would look after me without being paid to do it, made me feel like a normal girl. Piluca and Marina wanted to know what the Denias' house was like. I described it with great exaggeration, which seemed to earn their respect and admiration.

In civics class I gleefully took part in playing a trick on the teacher, who was a young, awkward, very self-conscious man. "Okay, everybody in the front row, stare at his shoes the whole time and see how nervous he gets," said Florencia, a girl from Cádiz with very straight, blond hair and wide, doll-like eyes. We walked in giggling. The teacher was sitting on a dais in front of the chalkboard. We took our seats at our desks and, the moment he began to speak, started staring at his shoes. They had been polished. Brown brogues with ornamental foxing and perforations around the tongue and laces. After a few minutes, the poor man didn't know what to do with his feet. He crossed and uncrossed his legs, put one foot behind him and then the other, and reached down furtively to pull up his socks. We were nearly hysterical but managed not to laugh. Mother Blanca, who sat in the last row knitting, theoretically keeping an eye on us, hissed to get us to be quiet. "Girls!" she cautioned. As soon as class ended, he rushed out the door and we burst out laughing. "We didn't do anything, Mother Blanca. We were just looking at his shoes." The nun shook her head slowly from side to side, smiling, infected by our hilarity. "You little devils. The poor man. Don't do it again."

CHAPTER 15

W hat did Juana leave behind in that fortress at La Mota, in her mad rush to reach Laredo and board ship before her mother had a chance to rethink and change her mind?

She left her son, who had just started to walk. She tried to capture his image and engrave it in her mind as the carriage pulled away from the fortress, poking her head out to stare at the crowd waving her off until they faded into a little brown stain in the distance. She left Beatriz de Bobadilla, who had fallen in love and asked to stay on in Castile so she could marry. And she left her mother, with a pithy, frosty farewell.

MY SOUL WEIGHED LIKE LEAD IN MY CHEST BUT I TRUSTED THAT the winds of my voyage would blow and scatter my sadness away. The word Laredo was music to my ears. I dried my tears and smiled at Madame de Hallewin. She too had grown thin. We looked as if we'd been through a war. I was craving all that I had missed, my palace at Coudenberg, even the gray rain of Brussels. Would Charles recognize me? Would Leonor, and Isabel? Would I recognize them? They would have grown quite a lot. We made our way along slowly, and at dusk the dark, heavy skies erupted in white lightning, and a March storm showered a deluge down upon us. Not a good forecast. When we reached Laredo, Captain Colindres appeared at the house where we were lodging, his boots muddy, and told me that we were in for a few days of bad weather.

It was not a few days but two entire months that I was forced to wait. My initial agitation gave way to calm acceptance. I realized that I was exhausted. I could not tell night from day, sleep from wakefulness. I decided to rest and recover, let myself be pampered. The Moorish slaves I had brought with me initiated me in their secret ways. They gave me massages with aromatic oils. They washed and braided my hair. They decorated my hands and feet with henna. And I let them; I surrendered myself to them and accepted all of their indulgences gladly. I rested, I read, and I ate until May arrived and the storms on the Cantabrian Coast abated.

PHILIPPE AND HIS RETINUE AWAITED ME IN BLANKENBURG. AS WE entered the harbor, the surging gray waves lost their force and the boat swayed gently once more. It was one of those rare, radiant Flanders days. Anyone would have thought that our ship had brought the Spanish sun with it. From the deck, I could see the skyline of the Flemish city: its pointy roofs, the triangular facades of its houses, their uneven outlines dotted with gargoyles, the familiar profile of the church and castles lining the water's edge. Tiny figures crowded around the fortress and on the pier where we would dock. I was overcome with joy at the idea of seeing Philippe and my children, but also anxious and worried that during our long separation an insurmountable distance might have arisen between us. It had been such a long time; I could not assume everything would be the same. I knew already that for me, things had changed. I gathered my blue skirts around me. While we'd sailed, my spirits had soared free and light; now that the voyage was nearly over, doubts crept in, and I recalled my first years in the Low Countries, lonely and beleaguered. Gradually, I was able to make out the rubicund faces of pages and courtiers, their sumptuous attire, their decorated horses and the royal insignia of the Hapsburg standard. My spirits flagged and I felt as if my feet had turned to lead, rooting me to the spot like a statue. I realized I would no longer speak Spanish. I glanced at Madame de Hallewin, her eyes sparkling and alert as she made out the faces of her friends and the personages who had come to meet us. Until a few hours ago she had been my confidante and loyal servant, but now the Flemish air was blowing on her, sweeping her off.

Philippe's eyes were like a bridge laid down for me. I smiled and sunk into his look and then his arms, as the court applauded and trumpets sounded. I closed my eyes and breathed him in. My Philippe, if possible, was even more handsome. Time had defined his features, and his body was strong and mature. He returned my affection discretely, begging me with his eyes to wait until we were alone. His complicit look was like a key that slipped into my lock in an instant, awakening a desire that time had sent to sleep. My children were there: Leonor, with her golden curls, dressed like a little woman, and smiling from cheek to cheek; Isabel, who hardly recognized me and gazed on with more curiosity than anything; and Charles, wearing formal dress with a ruff and hiding in his fathers cape, his suspicious eyes doubtful that I could have anything to do with his childhood.

I was happy to see Jean de Berghes, Gustave de Chamois, Ana de Viamonte, and the palace attendants once more. After greetings and salutations we boarded the carriages and began our journey to Brussels. Along the way, we stopped in several cities and small towns where banquets and tournaments were held in my honor, and everyone came to pay us homage. But even amid the celebratory atmosphere, I perceived a new distrustfulness. Would they have to submit to Spain? Would they be orphaned when it came time for us to ascend to the Spanish throne?

When I was alone with Philippe I bemoaned feeling more foreign now than I had before. I deplored the fact that the nobility slyly insinuated that I showed more interest in the realms I would inherit than in Flanders. Philippe glowered unsympathetically and criticized what he claimed was my tendency to speculate. "You're imagining things," he'd say. That phrase became a litany on our trip to Brussels.

In the bedroom I noticed his lovemaking had taken on a new ferocity that at first I attributed to the pent-up desire he'd accumulated during our separation, and that I reciprocated in kind. For the first time, though, no matter how we groped and bit and kneaded each other's bodies, carnal love did not sate us and instead left us irritable and bad-tempered.

In spite of Philippe's assurances to the contrary, I felt that the gulf that separated me from his court and his country had never been so wide or so deep. After my first days back in Coudenberg Palace, once the relief of being back in a routine I feared lost had subsided, I began to have the distinct feeling that I was treading among upturned knives. The moment I left a room, the atmosphere transformed behind me. My words, shuffled and redealt like cards, were attributed new meanings. I trusted no one, and no one trusted me.

The tension in my head was like a vise around my skull. I awoke with my jaw and temples sore. My headaches would blind me for hours, or force me into bed, nauseated. Concerned about my health, the governor of my household appeared one day with Theodore Leyden, an eminent physician of Turkish origin who had come to treat me.

If I had told Philippe, surely he would have dismissed my opinion as the result of a vivid imagination, but I am certain that the moment that man walked into my chambers the air turned clear, as if rather than a human being, a brisk, country morning had come in. Leyden was a man of medium height and slender, delicate build, with beautiful, deep eyes. His face was framed by the dark fuzz of a very well groomed beard, a fine mustache, and a perfectly brushed and cut curly head of hair. At first his slender hands and long fingernails seemed distasteful to me. He wore a gold earring in one ear and spoke in a soft, hypnotic voice. He treated me with respect, but without distance. And it seemed that, just by gazing into my eyes, he could discern everything that was going on in my heart. There was nothing lustful or self-interested in his look, rather it seemed he possesed the rare ability to forget himself. Perhaps that is why his visits and cures not only eased my physical aches and pains but also had a calming effect on the turbulent waters that often flooded my thoughts.

Many a night I heard little Ferdinand crying out to me in my sleep. I would awaken and search for him beside me. Unable to go back to sleep I would lie in bed, imagining him in any of my parents' castles, left to the care of indulgent servants. I had pretended to Philippe that it had seemed a good idea to me to leave my son in Spain. I did not want to fodder the discord by relating to him the circumstances under which I'd departed. This, however, earned me his reproach for having "abandoned" our son. In response I told him that *he* had been the one who'd abandoned both of us there. And anyway, I argued, his sister Marguerite was raising our older children. At least Ferdinand would learn Castilian Spanish.

THE ABSENCE OF MY YOUNGEST SON, THE FROSTINESS OF THE FLEM-ish court, the glances and giggles that preceded and followed me throughout the palace, Philippe's violent, harsh passion free of tender words, the memory of my mother's hard, affronted eyes, the want of Beatriz and her loyalty, were all like the bars of a prison, locking me up in dark solitude without even a tiny glimmer of light. The only thing that saved me was Theodore and the teas he prepared for me from long, fluted flowers and other fragrant herbs. Under the spell of his magic potions, my sorrows lost their sharp edges, and happy memories seemed closer, within reach. I saw my brother Juan, played with my mule Sarita in the palace stables, smelled the sweet, milky scent of my wet nurse's breast. My children returned to their early childhood, when they still looked at me as a continuation of themselves, not like now, when they refused me their love for fear I would leave them once more.

After these fantasies, which would sometimes last all day long, I would get up for dinner in the palace salons, calm and unconcerned as I received the court, indifferent to their attitudes, the sole denizen of a mist-enshrouded island who looks on from the distance at an inconsequential theater filled with trivial players. How I would have liked to stay there forever, like a bird soaring above the crows! But the crows would not stop their squawking, and one day Pietro Martire d'Anghiera came to see me, to give me some writings from my friend Erasmus of Rotterdam, and to whisper in my ear that it was time I heard what was being said at court: Philippe, who until that time had been discrete in satisfying his needs with the occasional, harmless courtesan, had now made the grave mistake of becoming emotionally involved with one of the ladies who was now in my service. Anghiera felt this was unacceptable. Had Busleyden been alive, these things would never have happened, he said; *he* had known how to curb Philippe's rash impulses. Now I would have to be the one to put an end to it, to avoid having his infidelity strip me of any remaining vestige of the respect my subjects still had for me. It was up to me to teach the Flemish that Spaniards would not put up with their insidious vulgarity.

I have never been stung by a scorpion, but I had no doubt that its poison would feel like those words as they sunk into my body. Rather than tears, I felt shards of glass well up in my eyes, and my head throbbed like an enormous heart trapped in a tiny wooden box. I lost all notion of my physicality. I became a knot of rage, an idea, with no arms or legs. I stood rooted to the spot, unable to move for quite some time. And then it began to come clear, the strange atmosphere I'd been feeling ever since I'd returned. I knew who the woman Anghiera was talking about was. A redhead with milky, white skin and freckles on her face and breasts and back, and a lovely face, feline yet pixie. What did Philippe see in her? What did she have that I did not have more of? Was I not rounder, fuller? How could my husband betray me with someone like her? I thought of my father's children, which my mother had allowed to be looked after in the palace, my half-brothers and sisters whose origin was one of the mysteries of my childhood. It sickened me, to think of some redheaded child having any of the same features as my children.

Pietro Martire left after counseling that I exhibit maturity and restraint. I called for Theodore and hid nothing from him. I was convinced this had happened because of my absence, I said. When I was in Spain, my intuition had warned me that anything flammable would go up in flames regardless of the presence or absence of love, and that insisting on Philippe's chastity would be like asking wood not to burn when it was set alight. Of course I would have wanted his passion to burn only for me, but for men, the memory of love does not warm cold, winter nights.

A wise interpretation, he told me. And therefore I must not be afraid. While I restlessly paced the antechamber of my bedroom, Theodore had the look of someone who is all-understanding and the knowing smile of one who accepted evil as an inevitable part of existence. In my mind's eye, I could just see the woman beneath the pointed ogival window, comfortably arranged on the orange cushions of the bench that ran the circumference of the tower wall. In that very room she sat among the ladies of the court, including me, to sew, tell stories, and gossip in the afternoons. Theodore suggested I exhibit the maturity and benevolence of a queen. I should speak to Philippe, be understanding, and tell him that I would forgive him if he promised to end his dallying.

And that is precisely what I did, that very night. I do not know how I found the strength to display such self-control, given that I felt I was floating above the floor rather than held up by it, and the walls and furniture wobbled before me like melting wax. Philippe denied nothing. He watched me pace before the bed and stared calmly, arms crossed behind his head with his fingers interlaced. I was petrified and intimidated, and I babbled uncontrollably, so much so that as I railed on and left him no room to explain himself, I justified his behavior and offered reconciliation. By the time I climbed into bed, all he had to do was concur with my rationale, praise my intuition, and be amazed at how well I knew him. He insisted that he loved me no end, that he could not stand being alone. We'd never be apart again, he said. I was the only woman he wanted. His desire for me was like a disease, consuming him from the inside out.

AT THE DENIAS' MANSION IN THE SALAMANCA DISTRICT OF MADRID that night, Manuel talked about jealousy. I lay naked, facedown on the bed, and he ran his fingers lightly up and down my back, provoking earth-like tremors on my skin. I imagined Juana's anguish had been similar to my mother's: a sense of failure, of frailty, of ineptitude, a powerlessness that, according to Manuel, made jealousy resemble death. Love blurs the boundaries of one's identity, he said. A person in love allows the lover to enter not only his or her physical being but also the sheltered inner space of the psyche. The enclosure of the self opens up, and through that aperture destruction can also find its way. Love is like a Trojan horse, a thing of beauty; but if there is betrayal, one can wake up any day with the enemy already inside the city gates.

"WHEN HER FEARS ABOUT PHILIPPE'S INFIDELITY WERE PROVEN AND she was faced with the certainty of it, all Juana's good intentions flew out the window. She couldn't keep her cool. She had to go out into the night to prowl, to stalk her love; she had to stab holes in the wooden horse's belly over and over again, to ensure that there were no soldiers hiding there. Your mother did the same.

"Don't put on any clothes. There's no need for the gown. For this part of the story, you're better off nude. Vulnerable. Like Juana."

SINCE CONFESSING HIS GUILT, PHILIPPE MADE AN EFFORT TO BE- have like a loving husband and gave me beautiful gifts: an exquisite, red velvet-covered Grimaldi breviary, illustrated by the Master of the David Scenes. The miniatures were beautiful. I appeared in several of them, and others illustrated figures holding our coats of arms. Philippe's read "Who will dare?" and mine responded "I will dare." We had thought of that motto when we got married, that he and I would dare as much to love each other as to take on anything fate dealt us.

Fate might have dealt me another life if I had forgotten my husband's infidelity the way my mother had forgotten my father's dalli- ances. But I had no desire to be queen, and at that moment I loved the freedom of not having to be one, thinking that my mother still had a long life ahead of her. Theodore still tried to calm me with his aromatic teas, but I hardly stopped to taste them now. I had no idea whether or not Philippe was keeping his promise of not dwelling on the redhead, but *I* did nothing but think of her. I reinitiated the evening sewing ses- sions with my ladies solely to watch her, to denude her with my eyes. She was very fair and had light, downy peach fuzz covering her skin; caught in the sun, it shone like a radiant halo. She favored brown and blue gowns. Her hair was truly beautiful, thick, curly, and shiny as burnished copper as it spilled down her back. I learned through gossip and breaches of confidence that it was this fiery mane that had first driven Philippe wild. I could not bear to look at her without burning with the desire to rip it from her head, lock by lock, imagining the lurid details of my tor- ture as I sat primly and embroidered cross-stitch. She avoided my eyes, concentrating on her needles, and when she thought I was distracted, she'd laugh with the others, leaving me distraught at her irreverence. She would have no cause to laugh that way—nor my ladies any cause to treat her with deference—I thought, if she felt defeated or had truly learned her lesson. I pricked my fingers trying to interpret her glances and gestures, keeping watch over her and not my knitting. One afternoon while we were embroidering and I, concentrated on my work, eavesdropped on their conversation about the never-ending battle for control of Naples, I caught a glimpse of the redhead out of the corner of my eye, a wicked smile playing on her lips as she showed the others something concealed in her bodice. Their excitement might have gone overlooked by anyone who was not waiting for it, but it did not slip me by.

Without giving myself even a moment to contemplate my actions rationally, I sat up straight as a board and then leaped out of my chair. I dove onto Philippe's lover amid the crash of furniture and swishing silk. She jumped back, attempting to cover her chest with her hands, but she was no contest for me. Like a hawk swooping down on its prey, claws extended, I threw her to the ground, my knees on her rib cage. The sound of ripping cloth could be heard over the other ladies' cries. I shoved my hand into her bodice and wrenched out the letter she'd tucked in there. The redhead whimpered and covered her face as I tried to scratch her. Madame de Hallewin grabbed hold of me by the shoulders and pulled me away, with the help of Ana de Viamonte and a few other women. Brandishing the note in my hand, I regained enough control to order them all to leave me be. I threw them all out, even my poor Madame de Hallewin and the Spanish ladies, shrieking as loud as I could in order to scare them.

Slamming and locking the door, I leaned up against the wood and then slid down to the floor, closing my eyes and trying to stop panting. I held the note to my face, in search of Philippe's scent, praying to God that it not be so. Please, God, no. Please. But then I began to cry, because my intuition knew better what I was about to confirm.

I read. "Madame: Nothing has changed. After the vespers bells, in the library. Yours. Philippe."

"Who will dare? I will dare." My mind was set on pronouncing the ensign of my marriage over and over again. My thoughts could only repeat those words.

After a short while I stood. I made my way to the woven sewing basket, took out three pairs of Toledan steel scissors and lay them on the table. Then I walked into my sleeping chambers. I splashed water on my face, fixed my hair and looked in the mirror. I was beautiful too. My cheeks were flushed. I gulped down several glasses of wine from Philippe's decanter. Then I waited a prudent time before unlocking the door and ordering my guards to call all the ladies in my court immediately. All of them.

They walked in one by one with their heads bowed, the redhead hiding at the center of the group. They gathered very close together beside the table in the middle of the room where I awaited them. Madame de Hallewin approached me with the clear intention of exchanging a few words out of earshot of the others. Raising a hand, I stopped her in her tracks. My compatriots gazed at me in fear and solidarity both. I smiled at them, calm, intuiting the curiosity and fear that overwhelmed them. I bade Blanca and María, my Spanish attendants, to sit the redhead in the chair beside the table. They exchanged glances, and I repeated my order, louder. The redhead began to cry. Madame de Hallewin interrupted. "What will you do, my lady?" But they sat her down. I approached and tied her hands behind her back with some colored ribbon I had left atop the table. The women held their breath, fascinated, as if they were about to bear witness to an execution and could not, would not, do anything to stop it. Slowly, parsimoniously, I unclipped the redhead's hair, letting it fall loosely around her shoulders. I stroked it. It was soft, silky. I thought of Philippe's hands. Then I took the scissors and slowly, deliberately, began to cut it, possessed by the snipping noise the scissors made, hearing it ring louder than the women's exclamations, the victim's sobs. I couldn't stop. I cut and cut, faster and faster. Who will dare? I will dare. And the locks fluttered to the floor. Who will dare? I will dare. And there was more snipping, more sobbing, until I saw her translucent scalp and then stood back to see what she had become: an ugly boy, her face all red, her swollen nose dripping snot onto her skirt.

I sat down on a chair afterward, the scissors on my lap. Madame de Hallewin untied my victim. All the ladies rushed out. Who will dare? I will dare. Then I gathered up the curls from the floor and scattered them all over Philippe's pillow.

WHEN PHILIPPE ARRIVED I WAS CALM, EMPTY. HE CHARGED AS IF he were riding a furious steed, rushing to defeat his opponent in a tournament. He grabbed me by the hair and began to slap and hit me, insulting me and calling me names. He would never make love to me again. He detested me. How dare I? People were right to say I'd lost my wits, I was mad. The redhead (he said her name, I can't recall it) deserved nothing but love; the love he gave her and would keep giving her, regardless of how I tried to stop him. Who will dare? I will dare, I shouted. Oh, do you? he asked, raising his hand once more. This time I turned, but his hand still glanced the edge of my right cheek. I lost my balance and fell to the floor, but he dragged me up by my gown, forcing me to stand once more. His eyes were wild with fury, his hands brutal. In the end, I became frightened. I had the presence of mind to realize that, as with wild animals, the most prudent thing was to keep perfectly still. I stood motionless in the middle of the room, my hands crossed over my skirt, my head bowed. Whatever he did, he could not touch my soul. At least that was what I thought at the time. My tranquility infuriated him. He shook me by the shoulders, but I was as limp as a lifeless doll, having gone to a space he could not touch with his hands. I think he realized, because finally he ceased his attack and left, slamming the door. When I tried to leave my rooms, I found that the door was locked from the outside. I spent all night banging on it, hurling objects against it, anything that would crash and then fall to the floor and break into a thousand pieces, anything I could lay my hands on. Philippe would be made to hear my riot. Whenever he didn't spend the night with me, he slept in the chambers just below mine. I wanted to make noise to communicate my fury, the degree of my inconformity and rage. Wrapped in my ire, my body aching from his blows, I stayed awake all night. The following day, Philippe sent Theodore de Leyden to my rooms. Still stinging from the events of the day before, I was pacing back and forth, contemplating the detritus left behind from my indignation. When Theodore walked in, I dropped into a chair, relieved that it was he who had arrived. I could not allow Philippe to lock me up and just keep quiet, without protest, I said by way of justification. It was indefensible that he should lock me in my rooms. That was why I had determined not to let him get any sleep. Theodore looked at me as he picked up pieces of jugs and mirrors, placing them delicately on the round table in the corner, as if he'd decided to make a mosaic. When I stopped speaking, he came up and smiled softly, paternally. He sat down beside me, arranging his baggy trousers. He had the habit of playing with his rings while he thought.

"WHAT WOULD YOU HAVE DONE, LUCÍA?"

"I don't understand Philippe. His cruelty is beyond my comprehension. I mean, I don't understand my father either, but at least my mother had the option of divorcing him. I admire Juana. She had no options, but she decided to rebel, to confront the situation and not keep her mouth shut. That must have been almost unheard of back then, so good for her, that's what I think."

"Well, Theodore de Leyden suggested more subtle tactics. Perhaps more along the lines of what Isis recommended to your mother. You couldn't fight desire with rage, he said. You had to fight it with more desire. Philippe was not indifferent to Juana's feminine charms. So rather than behave boorishly and give him more reason to justify his infidelity, she should brandish the most intimate weapons of her sex. Theodore was of the opinion that if she cast the nets of her seduction, if she caught his attention with perfumes and used love to heal the wounds of their separation, her husband would be unable to resist. And what better revenge than regaining his love so that all and sundry could see that Philippe still loved her? Thanks to Theodore, the Moorish slaves Juana had brought on her voyage from Laredo came back on the scene, the same women who had consoled her during those two months she spent waiting for the stormy seas to subside.

THE MOORISH WOMEN KNEW ALL ABOUT LOVE POTIONS AND SPELLS. They wouldn't betray or scorn me. I put Fatima in charge of the group. Born in Algeciras, she was tall and brawny. She had strong hands and few qualms about speaking her mind. I liked her Andalusian accent, and I found the traits of her character comforting, for she had lived fully and seen enough not to be scandalized by anything. Besides, Philippe would take no interest in her because she had a manly build. Contrary to what one might guess from her personality, Fatima was very delicate in everything she did, whether washing my hair or giving me massages with citrus-scented oils. She called for a copper tub to be brought to my room so that I could soak in long baths. But no matter how moist and silky my skin became, inside I was a cracked, parched desert. I am dried up and dried out, I thought, and when I closed my eyes I could see my mother's musty skin and imagined her as Beatriz described her in her letters, prostrate with fevers and thirsty day and night. "The queen is very ill. You should prepare yourself, and think that soon you shall inherit these realms." With my eyes closed, I tried to picture myself ruling not just Castile and Aragon but the new territories discovered by Admiral Christopher Columbus. I could recall the admiral on his visit to my parents after his first journey. He had returned to Spain on January 4, 1493, but he did not arrive in Barcelona until April. In the plaza before Santa Clara Church, he approached the golden canopy where we stood, accompanied by six half-naked savages he'd brought from the New World, their bodies painted in red-black designs, their hair adorned with bones and feathers. Others in their procession carried cages with colorful birds that looked more like flowers than animals. I recalled the tray of gold pieces shaped like monkeys and lizards that he offered my parents, the scent of the tobacco leaves and the never-before-seen cocoa beans, which we now used to make chocolate. Perhaps during my reign I would organize an expedition so that Philippe and I could travel to see the crystal-clear seas they had called the Caribbean and the jungles full of unfamiliar animals. The idea of those lands, surrounded by water, inhabited by primitive peoples, noble savages who possess an innocence we have lost, is so seductive. The descriptions of those who have been in the Indies have let my dreams and fantasies run wild.

The baths and perfumes, combined with my endearments, had the desired effect. Philippe and I made up. The passion we shared together before that cursed year I spent alone in Spain was the memory I clung to with my eyes squinted shut when we made love. But often I felt we were not alone in bed. Other bodies, like specters, slipped in between the sheets. Copper curls, feminine faces, peeked out like ghosts from behind the curtains. I caught the whiff of unknown smells and imagined that Philippe, his hands on my breasts, was dreaming of other contours, and that he fed his pleasure by evoking what he did on the nights I was absent. As we panted in unison, without his noticing, I scrutinized his face in search of memories he kept concealed behind closed eyes. At those moments, I yearned to stab my fingers into his eyeballs, to wrench the visions from his sockets. I pretended to moan in pleasure, but I was consumed by jealousy and whimpered, instead, from rage and impotence. My love had turned into an anguished need to possess him, to ensure that, whatever the price, my lover was mine and mine alone.

Good God, what shall I do? What shall I do with all the anguish I hold inside, the unremitting pain that this love brings me? I am constantly suspicious of Philippe. I want to maintain my dignity, but all I do is berate and interrogate, denigrating myself before him. But I have to know. There is nothing so pathetic, so pitiful, or so painful as being the deceived wife. It is not just the love I profess but my pride that leads me to stalk him. I cannot allow him to betray me, nor what is worse, to successfully deceive me. Ever since I returned I have had the strange feeling that Philippe has a double. I cannot accept that the man I love and the one who abuses his authority, lies to me, laughs in my face, and makes me out to be a lunatic are the same person. When the false Philippe approaches, I shiver. I fear his harsh words and eyes, which would drill through my heart with impunity if they could.

I was quite taken with Fatima's ablutions. So much so that I convinced Philippe too to let himself be perfumed and rubbed with oils. But before long, my pleasure began to make him uncomfortable. He was jealous that I could find my slaves hands so sweet, their touch so restful. In truth they pleasured me with more than just baths and massages. Those women had silky soft hands and knew all the secrets of the body. Several of them were quite beautiful, and seeing them naked and feeling their breasts brush against me as they washed my hair excited every sort of devilish temptation I held inside. They were not content just to massage and oil my body nor rub sugar to slough away my rough skin; they used their tongues to wash it away. The first time Almudena licked my sex, I was dozing lightly. I pretended not to awaken and to dreamily enjoy the softness of her tongue. She was a woman, so she knew exactly how much pressure to exert in order to make me melt from the inside out, to exhaust me and bring me to the sweetest, most exquisite pleasure that humans have ever known. Those slave women working above me made me float in fabulous, prolonged ecstasy, which I would later recount to Philippe when we got into bed together. He would be aroused by my descriptions of Melina's kisses, of the way Fatima licked my nipples, fingers, and toes. And what I told him as a harmless game, to feed our passion, was also my form of revenge, my way of showing him that I too found pleasure in other places. I provoked his jealousy, which was my aim, but it was a pyrrhic victory. He began to berate me, to call me perverse and say I acted against nature. I was committing the sin of the island of Lesbos. I must not carry on with those practices, he said, and he forbade it. Theodore and my slaves would be forced to leave the palace.

When I refused to dismiss Fatima, Almudena, and particularly Theodore, Philippe sent Pedro de Rada, my chamber quartermaster, to warn me that until they were sent away, my husband would not visit me again. It was an ultimatum: him or them. My choice. He got my unwavering response: I had his messenger thrown out of my rooms. In retaliation, Philippe ordered that I be kept behind locked doors once more.

Months later I found out that because my parents were worried about rumors that I was mistreated, Philippe had ordered Martín de Moxica to keep a record of everything he reported about my behavior, to compile a logbook. Among other things, Moxica had jotted down— as if it were a crime—that I bathed several times a day, often washed my hair, and that my rooms smelled so strongly of musk it was hard to breathe. Finally, Philippe sent this dossier to my parents, intending to prove that I was losing not only my wits but also my ability to discern good from evil.

It was Philippe's evil twin who thought nothing of getting rid of Theodore as well as twelve of my servants, my Moorish slaves among them. He would not even allow Madame de Hallewin to stay by my side. In her stead, he sent a pro-French lady who detests me, the Viscountess of Furnes, Alienor de Poitiers. He sent my confessor back to Spain and outright refuses to give me any money for my expenses as he ought, claiming that he has not received the incomes due him as prince of Asturias. Perhaps, indeed, I am mad, but Philippe and this horrid man cannot be the same person. No one else realizes that there is deceit underfoot, because no one else knows the real Philippe as I do. And that is why I have elected to stay in bed. Alienor de Poitiers shall not be the one to make me eat, or dress. If I am to be denied my attendants, then no one shall lay a hand on me. I will die of hunger if this is my only means of getting the Philippe I love to come back and take charge of our household.

"IN LATIN AMERICA WE SAY: A SAINT ABROAD AND A DEVIL AT HOME. Juana saw the play of light and shadows in Philippe's behavior.

"But Philippe was just behaving normally for a man of his time. It was Juana, on the other hand, whose jealousy and torment and inability to feign indifference—her total transparency, which was so unusual for a woman of her station back then—turned her into the weakest link," Manuel said. "It was easier for her contemporaries to write her off than to try to understand her, not only because it was simpler but also because there was political gain to be had from it."

"Her husband's contrariety was probably reason enough to confound her and make her doubt her sanity. And if you add to that the uncertainty and disquiet Juana had been experiencing, what with her parents trying to separate her from her spouse, plus Philippe's infidelity, plus the isolation forced on her . . . Poor thing. It's no wonder she thought Philippe had a double."

"He didn't want her to have any contact with people who made her feel like herself; making her think she was losing her mind was all part of the plan, and there were times when she probably preferred to believe that it wasn't reality that was so cruel but her own mind playing tricks on her, though to me that seems even worse. Tragically, the idea that she was mad was politically useful both to Philippe and to Ferdinand, as a means of justifying their ambitions. On November 23, 1504, three days before Queen Isabella died—and no doubt using Martín de Moxica's dossier as proof, since by that time Philippe had sent it to him—Ferdinand played another one of his ruses. He convinced Isabella to add a last-minute clause to her will. It goes without saying that since she was already on her deathbed, she was in no condition to put up a fight. And this clause stated that if Juana were absent from Castile, or if she were incapacitated to rule, then King Ferdinand would govern on her behalf. So, really, he took the documents Philippe had sent him in the hopes of being granted greater command when *he* ascended to the throne and used them for his own ends: checkmate."

WHEN THEY FOUND OUT, PHILIPPE AND PARTICULARLY GUTIERRE Gómez de Fuensalida, the Spanish ambassador, realized they'd fallen into a trap. Gómez de Fuensalida had switched camps and was now supporting the man he assumed would be the future king when Isabella died. He had become Philippe's most faithful advisor, standing in for François de Busleyden, the archbishop of Besançon. Forced to change strategies to ensure that Ferdinand had no way to strip Philippe of power, the prince and his counselor then decided to claim that Juana was, after all, sane so as to make light of the rumors they themselves had made sure to spread. But it was too late. After the queen died, Ferdinand convened the Cortes of Castile in January 1505 and read out Martín de Moxica's lengthy account of Juana's behavior. Immediately, the Cortes declared him governor of all her kingdoms. So Philippe realized that only by taking Juana to Spain and presenting her as a queen that was fit to rule could he oppose Ferdinand effectively.

"WHEN DID ISABELLA DIE?"

"On November 26, 1504, but Philippe and Juana didn't get to Spain until April 27, 1506. Philippe couldn't leave the Low Countries until he put down a rebellion in Guelders, and Juana was pregnant again, giving birth to her third daughter, Mary, on September 15, 1505. If you do the math, she must have gotten pregnant in December 1504. Philippe came back to her the moment Isabella died. He'd refused to see her ever since the incident with the Moorish slaves."

"The *real* Philippe would have consoled her." I grinned.

"Maybe Juana was right. Philippe oscillated between his passion and his ambition. Historians debate whether Philippe's behavior was controlled largely by his advisors. He was very easily influenced. Personally, I think they both swayed between love and hate."

CHAPTER 16

On my way back to school I dozed off on the metro. I didn't know whether to blame my lethargy on the arrival of winter's grayness or on the fact that it was so hard for me to return to reality and leave behind the sixteenth century world in which Juana threw fits of jealousy, attempted reconciliation, and ended up ever more isolated.

I remembered that when I was a girl, and the lights came on at the end of a movie, it was almost impossible for me to leave behind the protagonist's borrowed identity. And it was that person who was transformed into an adolescent leaving the matinee for the tropical sun, who saw the world through my eyes.

And that was how I felt with Juana. Manuel was right when he guessed that I'd be able to penetrate her inner world with no trouble. She wandered the avenues of my mind with her passions and her turmoils, and I knew that when our paths crossed, I would embrace her, anxious to transcend the centuries that separated us like folds in the cloth of time. I did not doubt her sanity. In fact, I thought it was her very lucidity that had betrayed her. Juana believed she was free to act as she wished, not within limits imposed on her by her father, her mother, and everyone else. And not following conventions meant running considerable risks. What fascinated me about her, what made me want to know her better, was her nerve, her willingness to shatter the preconceptions held by Philippe, by the courtiers, by everybody. Because of her actions, she ended up alone, condemned to an impotent clarity. Her quest for independence backfired on her, and Philippe, who was better at dealing with people than she, was able to isolate her right from the start, cementing loyalty—even from the Spanish—with gifts and promises.

Juana used her body as a weapon time and time again. Perhaps so many pregnancies had been a means to assert her power, to display the love Philippe held for her. A pregnant woman was a symbol of female sexuality. A pregnant woman did not conjure up images of a Madonna, but of a real woman, in bed, making love. I found pregnant women enchanting to watch. I loved the lumbering sweetness that floated around them like a halo of life. I hadn't told anyone, but I hadn't gotten my period that month and I was distraught and anxious, especially when I thought about my recent conversation with Mother Luisa Magdalena. That weekend, when I was lying naked beside Manuel, he held one of my breasts as if he were weighing the evidence, and told me that they'd grown. He said making love was maturing my body. Surely that was it. It wasn't the first time I'd skipped a period. When I was fifteen, the nuns had even taken me to a gynecologist to see what the problem might have been, and the doctor had told them it was normal, especially at first, when hormones and cycles were still adjusting. My periods eventually became regular. Perhaps this was just another phase, maybe my body was entering maturity. After all, Manuel and I had been very careful. Especially him. So I shouldn't worry too much about it. I had to take my emotional state into account and assume my fears would prove to be unfounded.

I walked out of the metro into the chill of the street, and stopped off at the bakery to buy croissants. The girl behind the counter wrapped my package in Christmas paper and tied it up with red and green ribbons. Águeda had told me that she would very much like to have me stay with them over Christmas vacation. The nuns had already agreed. My grandmother, at my request, wrote to the mother superior to say that I was mature enough to make that sort of decision on my own. It was a huge relief to know I had been spared from going to Málaga, where the foreign boarders spent cheerless vacations.

I walked down the street back toward school thinking about Juana and her confinement. During the coming week I wouldn't see the streets, or cars, or the hustle and bustle of the city. The gray walls would swallow me up. I crossed the somber, tiled front hall and pushed the door open. I heard it close behind me. The echo of the wood hitting the frame followed me all the way to my room. The idea of having to spend six more months there made it seem an eternity. I imagined the sense of liberation I'd feel when this unchanging routine finally ended. I wondered what would become of me and the other girls in a few years' time. Where would we end up? Huge differences separated us: they had parents; I didn't. They were virgins; I had a lover. They dismissed the prejudices that stood like obstacles in our path. I imagined those prejudices aligned against us like an army. They'd shoot at our legs to prevent us from going very far without help. Perhaps not being a virgin would make things more difficult for me when it came to marriage. We all had to be on the lookout for those who would just as soon turn us into caretakers: nurses, secretaries, second-rate citizens.

I missed not having parents to guide me. My father had been a successful banker, a lawyer by profession, but I had no interest in studying law. My plan, before Manuel arrived on the scene, had been to finish high school and then move to New York and study humanities; Isis could help me figure out exactly what to do and how. History maybe, I thought now. I liked reliving better than living. Maybe that's why I felt so comfortable evoking Juana, her history, her life story, delving into her past. Or maybe it was just that the future seemed so uncertain. When the year ended, I'd be done with school: no more convent, no more nuns. And no matter how boring I thought boarding school was, no matter how badly I wanted to get out of there, I had no idea what would become of me afterward. I couldn't imagine how my relationship with Manuel would change my plans or what would happen between us once Juana's story came to an end.

CHAPTER 17

On the morning of January 7, 1506, I watched the port of Flushing fade into the distance from the deck of the *Julienne*, a Genovese carrack. A year and a half had passed since my mother's death, and Philippe and I were finally on our way to Spain. I sent for a chair and intended to sit for a good long while, stewing over the latest affront to my pride. To protect myself from the cold, made worse by the brackish sea breeze, I wrapped up tightly in my fur hood. My husband would probably be drinking wine with his chamberlains in the captain's cabins right now, ranting about me. I didn't care. I even smiled, recalling the expression on his face when I forced him to disembark the ladies whom—without my consent—he proposed to bring as passengers, attempting to pass them off as female escorts for me. I threatened not to board myself unless he heeded my request. I had prepared for this journey carefully, and he was not going to ruin it by stirring up my jealousy with those women.

I closed my eyes and breathed in deeply, trying to match my heartbeat to the rhythm of the waves. Behind us lay Flanders and the year 1505, *annus horribilis*, which had announced itself late in 1504 with my mother's death.

I had been expecting the news for months, and yet I was unprepared for how powerfully it affected me when it finally came. I received the messenger with Philippe at my side. He began to believe his own fabrications, fearing that I would act like the madwoman they have made me out to be. Juana the Mad. (I know that my detractors already call me that. How unfair that the same passion that in men gives cause for admiration, in women is seen as a sign of instability. I do not know how to behave any other way than that which my emotions dictate. Perhaps I was not born for the court, which is the same as saying that I was not born for hypocrisy.) I didn't shout. A vile sticky darkness, a black liquid filled my veins, as if all my life's sorrow had been turned into a sea of ink. I felt I was drowning, I felt all the colors around me fade to black. I was overcome by panic, and I don't know if it was life or death that I feared. Philippe must have been scared, because suddenly he stopped being the other. He hugged me. He stroked my hair and whispered sweet nothings to me, as if he were comforting a baby. My sobs quieted slowly with his tenderness, and gradually the black liquid stopped constricting my throat. It was early December and cold seeped from the walls of Coudenberg Palace. Philippe sent for firewood; he sent for furs to wrap around me; and he got into bed with me and sang like a minstrel. We spent an entire week in bed, he and I. He was trying to relieve my look of despair. Never had my eyes grown so dim, he said. Perhaps my mother's spirit floated above us before she died. Mary was conceived during that week of love in which Philippe seemed to glow while he slept like a naked god beside me. We talked. He asked me to understand that he had only dismissed my servants because he had found out they had been conspiring among themselves to take Charles to Spain, leaving us without a son. I did not contradict him; I did not dare. I feared the other Philippe would return.

But it was just a question of time. I should have known. At the royal exequy for my mother in Saint Gudule on January 14 and 15, he alone received the sword of justice and proudly displayed his new coat of arms, which now included the insignias of Castile, León, and Granada, as if they were just a few more possessions in his kingdom. Two hundred copies of his brand new coat of arms adorned the cathedral in Brussels, and thousands had the insignia emblazoned on their torches. Given that he was the consort and I the queen, it should have been me who was honored, but before his subjects, he decided to change the order of things without so much as consulting me, not caring a whit about casting me aside. As he was being acclaimed, he exchanged his mourning hood for a regal one, lined with ermine and embroidered with the new coat of arms, and then he proclaimed himself king. Indignant, I was forced to sit several steps below him, to the right of the altar, with my mourning clothes and my veil, dark and nearly invisible beside his dazzling vanity. I felt sorry for his stupidity, his ambition. Several days later, when the news arrived that my father—using Martín de Moxica's testimony—had convinced the Cortes in Toledo that due to my incapacity to rule he should be named regent, I didn't become furious. I was more overjoyed at the humiliation inflicted on Philippe than I was surprised at my father's shrewd maneuver. I imagined that he wanted to avoid the possibility of Philippe usurping the throne from me. And I accepted his judgment, reasoning that if I had to pick between an Aragonese and a Fleming to rule over my kingdoms, I would take the Aragonese. At least he spoke the language!

To legitimize the situation, my father sent me a dispatch, asking for authorization to rule on my behalf. He was perfectly aware of the fact that I was not incapacitated, which was precisely why he sought my mandate to rule. I signed right away, but my valet, Miguel de Herrera—curse him—took the dispatch straight to Philippe, who, neither dim-witted nor idle, trampled my authority once again. Not only did he rip up the parchment, he also tortured the poor emissary—my father's secretary, Lope de Conchillos—leaving him crippled and disfigured. And even if he had placed Conchillos on the rack and imprisoned him, I didn't fare much better. Philippe forbade any Spaniard from speaking to me or coming near me and locked me in my rooms yet again, this time with a dozen archers stationed in my first chamber to ensure I could not escape.

With me incommunicado, Philippe and Gómez de Fuensalida forged my signature and composed a missive in which I swore loyalty to my husband and defended his right to succession.

At some point during all these machinations with which—one could easily think—both husband and father were attempting to usurp my power, someone informed the king that I was locked up. He, in turn, flew into a rage and used the information as a justification for not recognizing my supposed vows of loyalty to Philippe, threatening to make public the affronts I was suffering if he did not immediately set me free and treat me with the respect due the Queen of Castile.

But rather than fear my father's warnings, what Philippe truly feared was his own father's censure, and it was during that time that—alarmed at the news of our disputes—Emperor Maximilian arrived at the palace. Finally, my door was unbolted.

Filthy and disheveled, my long hair hanging loose and dirty, dressed in a gray robe that showed my taught, round belly on the verge of releasing Mary, I strode past my jailors, through the first chamber where the archers stood, and ran into the garden, desperate to cast off the murky shadows of weeks of darkness. It was August. The sun, air, and trees were bursting with their bounty; blue bellflower vines overflowed with blooms; ants marched busily, transporting food to their nests. After so many days of dimly lit imprisonment, my eyes teared up and I saw everything filtered through their gauzy humidity. From the balconies and corridors, courtiers watched the show. I let the sounds of their murmurs be carried off by the wind rustling the garden's leaves, so that my happiness should not be spoiled by their curiosity.

Despite my relief at being freed, I must also say that I had begun to realize that each time I was locked up, I became more skilled at carving out my own private world, extending its horizons, and triumphing over my loneliness. Were that not the case, I might well have lost my mind. And yet at the same time, I knew that this ability to inhabit my own world made the outside one fade away until the people around me were just blurred outlines in the distance. Still, it was painful to live without the silent, generous bounty of nature. This banishment filled me with a physical longing, a yearning for green, for towering canopies and open sky, that slowly turned into a vegetative burning in my fingertips, just like what I imagined flowers feel as they die of thirst. I sat beneath a birch tree, my arms and legs stretched out, my forehead to the sky, and I began to sing, to hum softly, bathing in the sun and the breeze.

I cannot say how long I lay there, happily, before some Flemish ladies came to take me away. I let myself be led to the baths. They would be discussing the scene in the garden as if it were another fit of madness, but I didn't care.

Mary was born, healthy as all of my children. This time a physician and a midwife accompanied me. My father-in-law arrived and agreed to hold her over the baptismal font. It seemed that peace reigned once more in my palace. I attended jousts and banquets, despite the looks of fear and mistrust from my courtiers, and the cold watchfulness of Gómez de Fuensalida and the other Philippe.

And now I am finally on my way back to Spain. I have hardly even seen my children over these past months. They will stay in Coudenberg during our absence. I weaned Mary in Middleburg, where I oversaw preparations for our journey and gave her to the wet nurse. I feel sorry for my children. They will all be kings and queens. Perhaps unhappy ones. I cannot give them happy childhoods when I suffer, as I do, from so little love and so much imprisonment. Perhaps I do not love them; perhaps I have not been allowed to love them. They never looked at me with the same eyes after I returned from Spain. They have probably been told that their mother is mad. And rather than see the look of fear in their eyes, I prefer to see them seldom, almost never.

"MANUEL, I DIDN'T GET MY PERIOD THIS MONTH."

He stared at me. Silent.

"It could just be hormones. This happened to me before, two years ago, it sort of came and went, but I thought it was better to tell you."

"Wait, Lucía. Don't get distracted. Let's keep going," was all he said. But I could tell he was worried by that way he had of pondering several things at once.

"I FORGOT TO MENTION THAT THE ARMADA THAT ACCOMPANIED Philippe and Juana comprised forty ships, carrying not only their luggage and their retinues but also two thousand German soldiers. Though the Spanish nobles had offered to support Philippe and Juana and battle Fernando's aspirations, the archduke thought it would be best if they were prepared to wrench the crown from him by force, if necessary. So he contracted *lansquenets* as a sort of private army. Always concerned with gaining the favor of his servants, Philippe not only ignored Juana's wishes and embarked the ladies whom Juana had ordered off the ships, but he also snuck on a rather large group of prostitutes. Close your eyes and don't get distracted, because the ship neared Calais during the windy, stormy season, and your fleet sailed right into a tempest. You had a premonition about it."

✳ I WAS WATCHING THE WATER, THINKING THAT JONAH'S WHALE made an accurate metaphor for where I hid when life tried to sink me in its depths, when I sensed the sea's uneasiness. It had gone very still, as if its soul had left it. More than afloat, the *Julienne* seemed suspended on the water's surface, her topsails limp and lifeless. The dense air was thick, almost viscous. The sky—leaden and opaque, impassive since our departure from Flushing—now flashed threateningly as if someone were behind the canopy of heaven, pouring down liquid silver. Though it was quite beautiful, I thought of an assassin putting on satin gloves. "There's a storm coming," I whispered. An old sailor halfheartedly tightening the tackle nearby looked up at the sky and nodded, grunting. "And a bad one," he said.

At three o'clock, the sun vanished. The sea and sky began their ritual battle. The wind came out of hiding and began to howl like a lonely wolf. The waves raised their arms in protest against the darkness that had surrounded us. I went down to my cabin, crossed myself, and commended my soul to God, now free from the anxiety of the premonition and the waiting. My only duty now was to ride out the storm. No king or queen, as far as I knew, had ever died in a shipwreck and we were not going to be the first. But just as I was beyond fear, the others were entirely in its clutches. Philippe arrived, pale as a lily, and dragged me off to the common room, where ladies, gentlemen, and nobles were crammed in together, looking like a pack of rats surrounded by ravenous cats.

I sat before them at the captain's table. My tranquility must have appeared to them like disdain. The boat rocked from side to side, emptying the courtiers' delicate stomachs of their bitter contents. I, on the other hand, felt hungry and so took the bowl of nuts from the captain's table and began to nibble away. The rain hammered down as if the sea had been relocated to the sky and was trying to return home. Thrust by the wind, the water whipped against the ship's sides and hatches. Seeing everyone's panic, I tried to calm them by explaining that no king or queen had ever died in a shipwreck. But they just stared at me, mouths agape, as if I were stark raving mad, so I shrugged and returned to nibbling the nuts. There in the captain's chamber, books slipped from their shelves, objects rolled off of tables, maps fell, spyglasses, liquor, and furniture came crashing to the floor. Weeping ladies found nothing to hold on to; some grabbed curtains to cover their faces and vomit into. Thrown to the floor, dukes and counts, thus degraded, no longer bothered to lift their heads before vomiting and just lay there in their own spew.

Philippe shouted for us all to commend ourselves to God; Gómez de Fuensalida wept openly without bothering to wipe the snot running down his beard. Lightning was striking as one endless bolt. And the thunder was so close it rattled our bones. Keeping calm at times like these makes one wise and meditative. I began to ponder the importance of remembering—particularly for those who were suffering so—that in the face of nature, man is insignificant, his power risible, incapable of unleashing a storm or making the wind howl. We were nothing on that sea, with our petty sorrows and our worries. In minutes, the tempest had taken us straight back to the terror of childhood, or of nothingness.

At some point, the roar of a tree crashing down exploded above our heads. We heard the captain's voice shouting to his crew, announcing that the mast had snapped. Philippe ran after him and returned with a wineskin tied to his body. I can only assume he thought it would keep him afloat should we be shipwrecked. I had never seen him so pale, or so solicitous. I believe he even approached me to beg my forgiveness for locking me up and treating me poorly. Fortunately, it was not the time for conversations. I knew how quickly he would forget those words once the sea had calmed.

But the storm showed no signs of abating. The captain came belowdeck with increasing frequency to inform us of one mishap after another. We had lost the mast and there was no sign of the other ships. On one occasion he asked for permission to throw part of the cargo overboard. Gómez de Fuensalida agreed, and I heard him order the crew to throw the prostitutes who were down with the horses overboard as well, since surely this storm was Divine retribution.

Seeing these men behave like cowards, willing to commit such a crime, was more than I could tolerate. I stood and told the captain that on pain of death, which I personally would ensure was meted out the moment we reached dry land, I prohibited him from committing such an atrocity. "You will not throw one single woman overboard unless accompanied by those who so disgracefully brought them *onto* the ship, to our great misfortune, beginning with the king, my lord, who is no doubt responsible for this arrangement."

The captain thanked me with his eyes and took his leave; neither Fuensalida nor Philippe dared contradict me. Among the sailors, I gained respect for being the only passenger not to vomit and whimper and lose all self-control. They were stunned at my composure.

On the third day of sailing off course and feeling the ship heave to and fro as if it were being carried by a herd of stampeding elephants, the storm finally died down. We could make out other ships in our party, but few were in any condition to carry on. After improvising sails and making what minimal repairs he could, the captain decided to chart a course for the English coast, where we could seek help.

On reaching Portsmouth we found we had lost seven ships. I saw the women I had ordered off the ship in Flushing totter ashore, their faces still distorted by fear. Watching them disembark was mortifying. I locked myself in my cabin without speaking to anyone. I no longer knew how to react in the face of so many humiliations. I had to fulfill my role as a queen, but Philippe toyed with me. He laid traps at every opportunity, belittling me in front of the entourage that accompanied us. Faced with his behavior, I reacted with the desperation I felt at being so unloved. How could I believe his words of contrition, his affections, his declarations of love offered amid the lashing storm? It took so little for my heart to burst with joy and hope, only to deflate soon after, spent, inert, and airless. I hated myself for being so naive, for wanting willfully to believe him, for forgiving his insults and affronts time and again, for letting him put me through such torment. I could not comprehend why I was so disposed to believe that things between us would go back to being the way they once were. I refused to consider his offenses in the same light I did the tiniest sign of love. A simple gesture was enough for my hopes to embark gleefully and set sail on the high seas as if favorable winds were everlasting. In a flash, I forgot the affronts that, hours earlier, seemed a sequence of horrors that could never be forgiven.

The ship's captain made sure, during those days, that I was comfortable and well served. I suspect he might have even fallen in love with me. He looked at me with great tenderness and admiration. And I was well aware that, as a seaman, he valued my bravery in the storm over the gossip and rumors that the royal escorts might have wanted him to believe. And so he faithfully fulfilled my wish, communicating to Philippe my intention to remain at the port while he and the others traveled to Windsor in the carriages that Henry VII had sent for us, once he heard that misfortune had led to our fleet docking on his shores.

I would have been happy to remain on board, enjoying the company of the captain, who was a cultured man with whom I had many agreeable conversations, had not my sister Catalina—whom the English called Katherine—come personally to find me. Seeing her after nearly ten years of separation was a great joy. Poor Catalina. She looked awful: thin and bleak, her face permanently marked by sadness and displeasure. The widow of Arthur of Wales, she was now engaged to the future Henry VIII, but she was dreadfully unhappy at the prospect of this marriage. "Why can we not end up with sweet men like that captain, so gentle and simple and handsome?" she lamented. The princes in our destinies are cause for nothing but tears and sorrows. She was shocked that I was still beautiful. After five children, I still had a girlish figure and my face was as yet unwrinkled and free of that scowl that seemed glued to her face like a permanent mask. We cried together for our mother. And it was a great consolation to me, despite all the years gone by, to be with someone I knew would not betray me and with whom I could confide.

When we said good-bye, Catalina remarked that her father-in-law, the king, had been very impressed with me. One of his ladies overheard him say that he was astonished anyone could accuse me of being mad when he had judged me to be so sensible, so self-possessed. If only *he* could have a queen like me in his palace. "You must be careful," my sister warned. "They accuse *you* of being mad, but our father seems to be showing more signs of lunacy, marrying Germaine de Foix, a woman younger than either of us, just to engender an heir so that he—instead of you—can occupy the throne of Aragon." Catalina was sure that Ferdinand, being a good Aragonese, would have no qualms about allying himself with Philippe against me in order to control the crown of Castile. I, on the other hand, confessed that I trusted he would protect me from Philippe's ambitions. If he did, I would be happy to rule with him, as our mother had. I was not prepared to allow Philippe to rule in Spain at my expense. Catalina feared the cunning of the pair of them. In struggles for power, women were always the ones who lost. Not even our mother had succeeded in keeping Ferdinand from meddling in my realm.

Catalina and I had precious little time together. All too quickly, her father-in-law called for her return to London, after the banquets and ceremonies at Windsor Castle. During those days, the king had been negotiating her dowry with my father and surely would not wish for me, as the next queen of Castile, to intervene on my sister's behalf. Before leaving, she arranged for me to go from Windsor to Arundel, in the English countryside. Her friends, the Dukes of Exeter, graciously lent me their castle so that I could rest and recover from my turbulent journey. After a week of idyllic repose among courteous, obliging people who treated me with all the respect a queen deserved, I felt much better. I was in a good mood when Philippe arrived to meet me. I forgave him, as I had so many times before. He was passionate and genteel, as if the English air had somehow filled him with sweetness and chivalry. I had no idea that this was to be our final happy, peaceful time together. It was then that we conceived my last daughter, whom I would name Catalina, my fellow prisoner, the posthumous daughter of my beloved Philippe the Handsome.

IT WAS NEARLY FIVE O'CLOCK WHEN MANUEL BROUGHT ME BACK TO the twentieth century, telling me it was time for me to get changed and go back to school. When I pulled Juana's dress over my head and stood in front of the fireplace, he took my hands in his to pull me close. He gazed at my naked body in the firelight. His brows knit, he stared intently and took one of my breasts in his hand. Slowly, he rubbed the other hand over my belly, his index finger tracing the path of fine, dark hair that had grown from my stomach down to my pubic hair in a mysterious straight line.

"So you say you haven't gotten your period. How late are you?"

"Ten days," I said. I insisted he shouldn't worry. It was probably just hormones; maybe my cycle wasn't fully in sync yet, so there were irregularities.

He ran his hand over my stomach and looked at my breasts again.

"Look how dark your nipples are. Good God, Lucía, what have I done to you?" Suddenly he was anguished, full of nervous energy. He lit a cigarette and paced in front of the fireplace, running his hands through his hair over and over again.

"Come on, Manuel. Don't be like that. It's probably nothing, I already told you. . . ."

"I studied medicine for two years, Lucía," he interrupted, turning toward me with an intent look." And I think I can safely say that you're pregnant. You're showing all the signs: amenorrhea, swollen breasts, darkened nipples, and that dark line on your stomach." He dropped onto the sofa and cradled his head in his hands. "This is insane. It's unforgivable. I will never forgive myself for this. Ever."

"It can't be," I said, less sure now. "We took so many precautions. You were so careful."

"Well, Lucía, it seems you're like Juana in more ways than one. You couldn't be more fertile if you tried. And look how much you resemble her." His eyes shone strangely as he gazed at me; it was a look that bore through me and into the past. "I'm sure you'll have no trouble giving birth, either, just like her. But we'll take care of everything, Lucía, don't you worry. Águeda and I will take care of everything. You'll have everything you need."

"But hold on, Manuel. Slow down for a moment. Don't jump so quickly to such serious conclusions. Let's wait a few days."

"We can wait if you want," he said, standing as he glanced at the clock that marked the time for me to be back at school, "but I'm right, you'll see. You won't get your period, you can bet on it. Come on, get dressed and I'll drive you back to school."

I dressed hurriedly, perturbed and confused. Then I went to say good-bye to his aunt Águeda, who was in the kitchen polishing a collection of silver objects she'd laid out on the dining room table.

"I'm so glad you're going to spend Christmas with us, sweetheart," she said. "I haven't made Christmas Eve dinner for years! Your friend Manuel is very disinclined to engage in any kind of religious celebrations, and I don't tend to have the energy to put up a fight. But with you around, things will be different. We can cook together! We'll have a grand old time, you'll see."

I nodded with a rote smile, unable to stop thinking about how all our lives would be turned upside down if Manuel's instincts were correct. I could not possibly imagine what might happen. I refused to entertain the possibility.

CHAPTER 18

My period never came. I began to doubt myself; Manuel's certainty had become contagious. I was experiencing new symptoms: nausea, tender breasts. If I squeezed my nipples, a whitish liquid oozed from the aureole. The cold of winter had seeped into my bones. My teeth chattered constantly and I could hardly concentrate on my exams. The nausea would come and go with no rhyme or reason. I avoided Mother Luisa Magdalena's every perceptive look. I thought of Juana. Manuel's words haunted me: I not only looked like her, but I was as fertile as she was. Again and again I wondered what to do. I was obsessed with avoiding the embarrassment of the nuns finding out I had gone astray. The only person in the world I could share this information with was Isis. I wondered if instead of spending Christmas with the Denias, I should go to New York. Isis would look after me. And she wouldn't tell my grandparents. She and I could come up with a story. But Manuel was the father. I couldn't just pretend he had nothing to do with it. I fell into a kind of trance, an absent presence. I wandered around pretending that neither my body nor my womb belonged to me. At night, I'd close my eyes tight and concentrate, hoping to return to my life as a student before I met Manuel, before that male Scheherazade had seduced me, made me feel I was soaring on the wings of a naive romanticism. I refused to entertain any alluring fantasies, telling myself that a man as old as Manuel would never be the father of any child of mine. Children?

Me? During the boarders' mass, I would pray with all my soul for God to remove that child from inside me. "Father, take this cup from me." And then immediately, I would repent. I felt vile and despicable for wanting to destroy a creature that deserved nothing but love. In my head, I ran though all the scenarios—during class, in the lunchroom, at recess. I'd never graduate. And with just a few months to go. I thought of stories about girls my age who bandaged their stomachs so no one could tell and kept going to class. The idea of not graduating—of quitting school—mortified me. And the only place I could imagine living with a baby was in New York, someplace where I could be anonymous and live like a character out of a Charles Dickens novel: a life of tragedy, misery, and shame.

Not being able to express my anguish to anyone was almost unbearable. I couldn't wait for classes to end on Friday so I could see Manuel and find out what he had in mind. He was a responsible adult, an experienced man. Surely he'd know what to do.

Mother Luisa Magdalena was very attentive to me those days. Her nun's intuition kept her in tune to the moods and needs of all the students, and she must have sensed that I was going through some sort of crisis. Still she of course would never have guessed that it was anything of the order that—had anyone at school found out—would have caused as much outrage as earthquakes did in my country, where in seconds entire cities were demolished, the landscape altered forever. I could see the rumor spreading through school like wildfire, the faces of the nuns and students reacting in horror. It was as if I could hear the chorus of parents' voices, at home, as they asked over and over, in hushed tones, how something like this could have happened in our exclusive, respectable young ladies' school.

I wasn't ashamed to cry like a baby in front of Mother Luisa Magdalena. My tears flowed so profusely that they reminded me of my hometown during torrential rains. The approach of Christmas always affected the girls who were far from home, and I was telling the truth when I bawled, saying that I just couldn't get used to the fact that my mother wouldn't be there for any of the major occasions of my life. She wouldn't be there for my graduation, or when I got married, or for the birth of my first child. Mother Luisa Magdalena wasn't suspicious of my grief, although she did admit to being surprised that it had come on so suddenly.

"Tell me, child, what's brought this on all of a sudden? It's understandable, of course, but has something happened to make your sorrow surface now?"

I blamed it on the Christmas smells of pine needles and cinnamon, and the end of the semester, which made me think that the year would soon be over, and I'd have to leave behind the school that had been a sort of womb for me, a refuge. She consoled me as best she could, but she wasn't excessively concerned about my tears. It was her opinion that I was finally coming to terms with the tragedy of my having become an orphan. She saw my grief as a sign that I was at last facing up to my pain and therefore on the road to recovery. She even thought that my relationship with the Denias—feeling the warmth of a family—might have penetrated my defenses and brought my emotions to the surface.

On Saturday Manuel was waiting for me as I walked out of school. He looked pale and had bags under his eyes. He started walking beside me without a word, after giving me an awkward hug. At seventeen, I could not conceive of how a man of his age could possibly be more upset than me. And yet confusion and uncertainty were plainly inscribed on his face and in his silence. It was cold, but we didn't take the metro to his apartment or to Águeda's house. We got out at the station by Puerta de Alcalá and walked.

When he finally spoke, it was to tell me what I could already plainly see. That he couldn't sleep, and did nothing but think about *that problem* (that was how we'd christened my pregnancy). He was so sorry to have been so stupid as to believe his method would work. His previous relationships had been with older women who had taken care of those things themselves. Contraceptives had just come into use, but the drugs were new, and neither their effectiveness nor their side effects had been proven; afraid of harming my young body, he hadn't wanted to buy them for me. I should know that there were only two alternatives: I could interrupt the pregnancy by having an abortion, or I could have the baby. Abortion was illegal in Spain, but he could take me to London the very next day if that was what I decided. As far as he knew, it was a simple procedure. On Tuesday or Wednesday I'd be back in class as if nothing had happened.

Instinctively, my hands flew to my belly. The mere thought of an abortion had made my muscles contract. He noticed and said nothing. We'd sat down on a park bench. He rested his elbows on his knees and put his face in his hands.

"Or would you rather we get married? That's the other option," he said. "You leave school, we get married and live with Aunt Águeda."

"I don't want any scandals breaking out at school. My biggest worry is that the nuns will find out. I don't want to get married. Not like this."

"You'll be on vacation next week. You'll come to our house and we'll think it over better there. We'll have more time."

I wanted the earth to swallow me up, to disappear and not have to explain anything to anyone, not have to go through the unbelievable shame of it all. If no one found out, it would be as if it hadn't happened, and I'd have more time to get used to the idea, to consider whether or not I actually wanted to marry Manuel. If the idea of telling my grandparents or even Isis was troubling, having to tell Mother Luisa Magdalena seemed unbearable. Completely unbearable.

"You don't have to marry me, Manuel. You just have to help me."

I realized I sounded like an actress trying to stick to her lines. I was trying to imagine what my mother would have done, what my grandparents would have said. Rather than actually think about the consequences of my pregnancy, I was more worried about the present, as if once the child was born all the problems would be miraculously solved.

"Let's deal with the problem in stages," I said. "The first one is to make sure no one finds out. Later we can deal with the rest."

"The 'rest,' as you call it, is the most important thing," Manuel said, smiling sarcastically. "Your grandparents, Isis, and the nuns finding out is the least of our concerns. . . ."

"Maybe for you; not for me."

THE WEEK BEFORE CHRISTMAS, ÁGUEDA SHOWED UP AT SCHOOL, having volunteered to help set up for the yuletide festivities. The second

I saw her at the door, staring at me, I knew that Manuel had told her what was happening. She treated me like a member of the family—with affection and resolve, but especially with a sense of propriety. The nuns would be more comfortable with the idea of me spending the Christmas vacation with them if they knew her better, she said. I was surprised to see her chatting so naturally with the groups of mothers planning the Christmas party.

The day of the party, she showed up with cookies, cakes, and table-cloths for the tables where we'd be selling our baked goods. The idea was to raise money to buy presents for children in the slums where the nuns did their charity work. For the first time since I'd been there, I mingled with my classmates' families, accompanied by adults who were taking care of me: my adoptive "aunt and uncle." Their presence freed me, albeit temporarily, from the stigma of feeling like a lonely orphan, an object of pity; that was what had always made me the saddest in previous years, feeling like that amid the revelry of all those happy families.

When the party was over, aunt and uncle lingered in the doorway with the other parents, all the conversations and good-byes filling the entrance hall, as Mother Luisa Magdalena thanked them effusively for offering me their hospitality. It would do me a world of good, she joked, to spend a Christmas without being surrounded by purple habits and nuns for once. Finally, she turned me over to their care, happy and at ease.

I hugged Mother Luisa Magdalena tight when we said good-bye. I'd put all my clothes into my suitcase, leaving just a few things behind so as not to arouse suspicion. Unless the pregnancy was a false alarm, I wouldn't be coming back, I wouldn't see Mother Luisa Magdalena again. I never imagined how distressed I'd feel, walking out of that tiled corridor for the last time. I thought about Margarita, who had left early that year to spend Christmas with her family in Guatemala. I thought of Piluca and Marina and that portion of my innocent and troubled life that would linger on there, floating above the garden beside the silent pine tree, the still fountain, and that lovingly stern nun.

We were almost silent on the way to calle Cid. Manuel wouldn't let me carry anything. He took the books from my arms, and my toiletries bag, and pulled my suitcase across the tiled garden.

Almost the moment we walked in, Águeda asked us to sit down at the kitchen table, before I went up to unpack. I hadn't been expecting this.

"I'm probably a strange old lady, Lucía. Perhaps I should be dismayed and reproach you both for having gone off the rails as you did. I've already told Manuel that I find *his* conduct, more than yours, reprehensible. Quite clearly, it is not fitting behavior. But what's done is done, so what can I say? I'm touched at the news. I don't know why, but ever since you first walked in the door, I knew you'd come to stay. I could feel it. And now you'll be one of us. And Manuel, whom I thought would be the last in our line, will have someone to carry on his name. With any luck it'll be a boy, another Marquis of Denia. You're probably frightened, but you've got nothing to worry about. Manuel and I will take good care of you; we'll make sure you're comfortable, that you have everything you need."

"I can't go back to school," I said, staring down at the floor. My cheeks must have been red because I could feel my face burning.

"Of course not; imagine the scandal," she replied.

"I don't know what I'm going to do." I couldn't figure out what to do with my hands. Having this conversation with Águeda conferred a sense of reality to the matter I wasn't ready to accept, at least not with the certainty of my hosts. I sat sliding my mother's pearl ring on and off my finger.

"I've thought about this," Manuel said gravely, methodically, his elbows on the table as he pressed his fingertips together. "When Christmas vacation is over, you'll stay on here. When the nuns call us to ask why you haven't returned to school, we'll say that we put you in a taxi back to the convent and that's the last we saw of you."

"But what about my grandparents, and Isis, and Mother Luisa? They'll come looking for me. They'll investigate. They'll call the police." I wanted to say it was a harebrained idea, but I contained myself.

"Wait, let me finish. You'll write a letter to your grandparents, to the nuns, to Isis. You decide. We have time to think about its phrasing.

You'll say you're safe and sound, that's the main point. Then you can say whatever occurs to you: that you fell in love with a boy and you're eloping, that you don't want to go back to school. It happens all the time. It's not that far-fetched. They won't like it, they won't agree, but at least they'll know you're safe. They'll interpret it as the recklessness of youth. After all, you're not a baby anymore. My mother left home at your age."

"That's right," said Águeda. "And nobody looked for her."

"We can get married if you prefer. I've already told you that," Manuel murmured.

"No," I said. "I wouldn't like to get married under these circumstances."

Every time Manuel brought up marriage it gave me a start, a surge of adrenaline. I said no almost automatically, reflexively. I was sure I didn't want to get married. I had no doubt about that.

Águeda interrupted.

"There's no need to rush your decisions. I can be modern about this sort of thing. I don't need formalities to legitimize the family's offspring."

"For the time being, I'm most worried about the scandal," I said. "I don't want anyone to find out. I'd die of shame. I like Manuel's idea. It might work." I told myself I'd think about it later, when I was alone. The story they were proposing I use as an alibi didn't fit my character. But maybe it wasn't so far-fetched. Those kinds of things did happen.

"Eventually you'll show up with your baby and you'll see how powerful a child's smile can be," Águeda said philosophically, perhaps recalling when Manuel first appeared in her life.

I couldn't picture myself with a baby. Maybe there'd be no baby. It seemed to me that Manuel and his aunt were getting a little ahead of themselves.

Águeda got up. I was surprised to see her take a bottle of champagne from the refrigerator. We should toast, she said. A child was a blessing. And we toasted. I still felt as if I were in a fog, dismayed at seeing myself catapulted into some strange world. I didn't know if Manuel's plan would work, but there was still time to think about it. We'd see. Besides, there was still a chance that I'd get my period any day now. Maybe the whole pregnancy thing was just a false alarm. I, for one, still could not accept it.

Manuel walked me up to my room. He said that the next day he'd walk me through the house so I could choose some more furniture for my room, given that this time I'd be staying much longer.

"I want you to feel completely comfortable and at ease. Like a princess." He smiled, his old carefree expression returning for a moment. I smiled too incredulous that his obsession seemed perfectly intact, even at a time like this. I followed my train of thought as he walked over to the window and looked out at the garden, pensive. I'd look beautiful pregnant, he said out of the blue. I'd look majestic. And I'd understand Juana even better.

"Let's keep going with Juana's story after dinner. It'll do us good," he added.

Águeda made me a special lunch with quail and wild rice. At one point, she began to speak of her religious convictions. She said that the mystery of conception, regardless of its circumstances, was something to be celebrated. How many young girls, scared of what they had done, went to London for abortions, tarnishing their souls with a crime that would stay with them the rest of their days, she decreed. That was why it was important for me to know that they would protect me and not let anything bad happen, either to me or my baby. It was inevitable that she felt partially responsible, for not having realized that our relationship was carnal as well as platonic, but given that it was too late, there was nothing else to be done. She repeated that as far as she was concerned, any descendant of the Denia line would be received not only with love, but with joy. After all, the child was innocent and had no reason to suffer for his parents' sins.

"You will go to confession, Lucía, won't you?" she asked, serving me more rice.

I nodded so as not to contradict her. There was no sense telling her about what had happened last time I went to confession.

Manuel and I exchanged complicit glances. Then Águeda said, quite demurely, that she was a little embarrassed to ask, but that as long as

Manuel and I were not married and were living under the same roof, she'd like us to humor her and keep sleeping in separate bedrooms.

"Oh, Auntie, come on."

"I'm old-fashioned, what can I say? I know it's silly. But when it comes to important matters, I can put my beliefs aside. I'm not a prude."

"You're right, Águeda. Don't worry," I said, feeling my face burn with shame.

"And there's one last thing. You might think it's excessive, but I think it's essential: you mustn't leave the house. Your body will start changing soon and the shop girls will all notice, all the women in the neighborhood will notice, they don't miss a trick. It's best if they don't even know you're here, so they can't identify you now or—more importantly—later on."

"Do you agree, Manuel? I mean, I'm not even showing at all yet."

"Aunt Águeda is right. For this plan to work we need discipline and discretion. Lots of discretion. You have to be invisible. Trust us, Lucía."

"Now, let's not talk anymore about this. Look at this dessert! Go on, enjoy it. It's caramel custard," Águeda said.

After dinner we retired to the library and, as if nothing had changed in the slightest, I put on my Juana dress and Manuel took up where we'd left off with her story.

CHAPTER 19

The constant ebb and flow of our love, the sudden way in which we went from harmony to sworn enemity, unsettled me no end. Inside my mind and body, reason and illusion battled it out, leaving me listless, exhausted, moored to such deep sadness within I thought I'd never find release. When we reached port at La Coruña on April 27, 1506, I still had no idea that Catalina had been conceived. Our original plan had been to land farther south, in Seville. There Philippe would meet with the Duke of Medina Sidonia and other nobles to advance toward Toledo for a meeting with my father, backed up not only by his German army but also by forces supplied by the Castilian nobles themselves. But the gales conspired against this plan. We were on the verge of being shipwrecked. Four days our captain sailed off course, and we were forced to change plans and disembark in La Coruña. As soon as people realized the identity of the passengers traveling on the ships that so unexpectedly docked on their coast they rushed to prepare a fitting reception, proud to be honored by their new monarchs' first visit to Spanish terra firma.

While Philippe was excited at the idea of parading through the streets on the beautiful Arabian sorrels we'd brought, dressing up so as to inspire the admiration of his new subjects, I wondered how to handle the delicate situation. I did not want to risk casting doubt on my father's authority by having our triumphal entry be interpreted as an attempt to displace him. As per the agreement signed in Salamanca on November 24, 1505 (after my astute progenitor married Germaine de Foix, thereby destroying the alliance Philippe and my father-in-law had made with the French), my husband had no choice but to accept that he and I would reign together, but with my father as governor and rights to half the kingdom's income. But this agreement, like so many others those two men signed, was not worth the paper it was written on. Neither was willing to cede. And they were constantly stalling for time in order to take stock of their forces and their plots. I was the wild card, decisive for both of their hands, and my plan was to side with my father to keep Philippe and especially his counselors from ousting me with their trickery, leaving the Flemish to usurp Spain's power. I had to act carefully, showing restraint and intelligence, so as not to send mixed signals. So I decided not to exercise my royal authority until I had met with my father and we had determined how we would share our power. Our hosts, surprised that I did not accept the keys to the city nor confirm their privileges, thought they might have somehow offended me. I tried my best to calm their fears and took lodgings with Philippe in a Franciscan convent they offered us out of hospitality. At the bidding of his counselors—particularly Gómez de Fuensalida—Philippe sent word of our arrival to the leading nobles in the kingdom. Over the next days, they began to arrive with their considerable retinues, and I saw, to my dismay, how most of them opted to side with Philippe; he, meanwhile, didn't miss a chance to throw in my face what he saw as the stupidity of my decision to wait for my father rather than taking what was rightfully ours, once and for all. Ferdinand would simply have to accept his disadvantage and pull out of Castile, he said. If I'd been planning to rule with my father, I could forget about it. The nobility was sick and tired of his iron will, and what was more, of the taxes he made them pay.

As in Flanders—although this time without locking my doors—Philippe subjected me to a campaign of isolation in my own country. He alone received the nobles as they arrived. The confessor at the convent, a good man with a gravelly voice, told me in the darkness of the chapel that there were rumors that my consort had taken me prisoner. I neither confirmed nor denied this, hoping that the situation would be resolved sooner rather than later.

I suppose it was in order to silence rumors, that Philippe allowed me to receive the Marquis of Villena when he arrived to pay his respects. The great doors of the reception chamber were opened so that other nobles milling around could also catch a glimpse of me. My compatriots' glances were sharp as arrows, attempting to penetrate my brain and ascertain for themselves whether I was in my right mind. The Marquis of Villena brought very affectionate letters for Philippe, from my father. The more challenging my husband's stance became, the more humble and kind my father's response. I wondered what he was up to.

A few weeks after we arrived, the arrogance and impenetrability of Philippe's Flemish court had become a brick wall against which Spanish ambitions were shattered, as nobles saw their hopes of receiving privileges, incomes, and appointments dashed. Tensions were mounting in the convent, and wide-ranging dissatisfaction was so great that even *I* heard the complaints aired in the chambers about the long waits and humiliations that Philippe and his men forced proud, impatient Spaniards to endure as they attempted to exchange their loyalty for privileges.

One fine day, Philippe burst into the modest room where I was reading and attempting to escape the heat to inform me that he'd had news that my father, the Duke of Alba, and other supporters were advancing with the alleged intention of halting our progress inland. We'd be leaving La Coruña as soon as possible.

Watching Philippe hatch plans and behave like a consecrated king—all the while hardly able to conceal his fear that I might wield my power against him—filled me with a strange mixture of outrage and pity. I was his captive, but being my jailer did not free him from the judgment in my eyes, nor the hidden shame he must feel at treating me this way. After all, despite my jealousy, I was the mother of his children and the woman whose love I knew had given him more pleasure and passion than any other. Whenever we made up, he himself acknowledged his remorse. He clung to me desperately, alternating love with the resentment he felt for knowing himself under my spell. He called me a witch, a bitch, and a whore, but we were two halves of the same whole and we fit together as perfectly as water fits inside the jug that holds it. In his heart of hearts he admired my stubborn defiance. The fact that I rebelled, my love of what was mine, reminded him of his grandfather Charles the Bold, the person he most worshipped and respected in all his family. As for me, I knew my majesty was indissoluble. It was rooted in a notion of personal freedom and independence that his incarcerations could never take away. When I compared my strength to his weaknesses I felt a sense of perverse delight. Along these twisted emotions our confrontations fed the very passion that destroyed us even as it bound us together in a malignant embrace from which neither one of us could escape.

We departed La Coruña and traveled changing direction time and again, despite the enormous army accompanying us—two thousand German pikemen and nearly one thousand knights from the nobles' own retinues—because my father had spread rumors of ambush and attacks along almost every road. Finally, Philippe received word that Ferdinand awaited him in a small, old chapel in the outskirts of Villafáfila. I was not informed of this meeting. Philippe wanted to keep me from joining up with my progenitor at any cost.

My hosts, the Marquis of Villena and the Count of Benavente, tried to divert me so that I would remain unaware of the preparations being carried out for my husband's meeting with my father. Alas, I would have had to be dead and buried not to notice Philippe's tumultuous exit, given that he headed a party of one thousand armed horsemen. Concealing my anxiety at what I took to be perhaps the first step in a war between my father and his son-in-law, I personally went to look for the marquis and demanded an explanation. He assured me that there was no need for me to torment myself with speculations. It was just a march, a drill intended to combat the complacency and lack of discipline rife in the German ranks. I pretended to accept his word, but I became convinced, after talking to him, that he was lying. My father was probably close by, and he and the others were simply following Philippe's instructions to deceive me and keep me from seeing him.

Although I was convulsed with rage and gripped by anguish, I had to remain clearheaded, for if I did not act with the appropriate urgency I would miss my chance to meet with Ferdinand. That he had not requested a meeting with me himself seemed suspect and ominous to me, but I preferred to blame it on Philippe and his ruses.

I used a pair of emerald earrings to bribe one of the cooks in the small palace. Through him I found out what everyone in the palace knew already. Ferdinand and Philippe were meeting in Villafáfila that day to sign a treaty that would give Philippe regency of Castile and stipulate that my father would retire to Aragon. As I later found out, unlike Philippe who arrived with his multitudinous and well-armed escorts, Ferdinand showed up with only two hundred knights, all smiles and affability. The treaty they signed curtailed my power and prevented me from governing, alluding to impaired mental faculties, which could endanger the sacred interests of the kingdom. Besides, my father also agreed to leave Castile, which he did after conversing alone with his son-in-law for two hours, without so much as requesting to see me. Just as Catalina had feared, the two men were making alliances, casting me aside. But things were not to remain so. Before the day's end my father would turn against Philippe, and I got ready to follow suit. As soon as I discovered that a meeting between them was taking place, I began scheming and finally managed to be allowed to go for a ride with the Count of Benavente and the Marquis of Villena.

My stratagem not was based on any calm, rational decision, but in my desperation it was the only alternative I could see. It was June 27. The day was hot, but lightly breezy. Wildflowers lined the trails where our horses trotted. The moment we reached wide open fields, I rearranged myself on the saddle and spurred my horse on, taking off at a gallop. What joy I felt, at that wild, unbridled ride! My face, my breasts, my arms cleaved the wind like billowing sails. The countryside, and the scent of oak and pine, were the very essence of life, whipping my lungs, so thirsty for open spaces. Soon the trampling hooves of my companions' horses died away as they gave up their frustrated pursuit while I rode on at a steady gallop among the trees, searching for my objective: the meeting place. My heart pounded, boring a hole in my chest.

But clearly, I was too late. It had all ended hours ago. The chapel in the woods was deserted. Trampled grass showed signs of the many horses that had passed. I circled the place, shouted my father's name—more to vent my anger than for any practical purpose—and finally, after I regained my composure, I contemplated the consequences of my escape: the punishment Philippe would impose on me for my audacity. I was riding at a canter when I passed through a small village and, without stopping to think, I dismounted, tethered my horse to a fence, and knocked on a door. The woman who opened it was a simple, friendly peasant with a gaunt face and strong hands. She told me she was a baker. I am your queen, Queen Juana, I said in turn. Kindly let me in, give me a glass of water to drink, a chair to sit on, and shelter. Taken by surprise, she looked at me but silently did all I asked of her and sat with me, neither believing my words nor daring to contradict me. She had hardly begun the tale of her woeful existence when we heard the thundering of horse guards and Philippe himself stepped into the shack, his cheeks flushed, astounded. Probably because he was still savoring his triumph against Ferdinand, he chose to address me ironically, trusting that his tone would humiliate me more than a violent tirade.

He gave me a succint version of the terms of the treaty by which he and my father had decided to split the regency of the kingdom. He said they both agreed that it should be they and not I who dealt with matters of State. Even Cardinal Cisneros, he added, had expressed his assent and offered his loyalty, because after my inappropriate behavior in Alcalá de Henares and Medina del Campo, he was convinced that I was a threat to the interests of the crown. Seeing my chagrin at his words, Philippe put a hand on my shoulder and asked me to accompany him. I shook him off in rejection. If he wanted me to return to the palace, he'd need to send for my father. I was not leaving otherwise.

I kept insisting to myself that Philippe had deceived my father into signing the treaty. If he could see me, I thought, he would realize I was not mad. I ordered Philippe to remove the soldiers from the baker's house. Out of respect to my hostess, no one but Philippe or my father would be allowed to enter her home, I commanded.

Poverty, no doubt, has a calming effect. Too many colors, too much luxury, affect one's sobriety and incite pride. It might have been the atmosphere that brought a change in Philippe's demeanor, for he began to speak to me as if he were the tender father of an unruly child. Please, Juana, why take refuge in these games, these extremes, when everything can be resolved without discord? The woman stared at us, eyes like a pendulum, moving back and forth between the two of us, understanding everything. But my ears were already deaf to Philippe's endearments, and though he spoke at length, nothing he said convinced me.

That week, the shack where I stayed with Soledad—that was my unwilling hostess's name—became a queen's refuge. The lowly village fed me pigeon and rabbit and other dishes. After a few days, news arrived that while Philippe was busy announcing his victory with great fanfare to all and sundry, my incorrigible, shrewd father had disauthorized the treaty the moment he reached the border of Aragon, proclaiming throughout all of Castile that Philippe had forced him to sign under duress, with the presence of his army. His statement declared that he would never consent to limit my freedom nor would he deny the rights that were lawfully mine.

The court broke camp and left Benavente Castle. Realizing that there was no longer any point in waiting, I said good-bye to Soledad and mounted my horse to go and join the cavalcade on its way to Valladolid.

As soon as Philippe discovered I had joined the march, he rode back to find me and talk to me. We rode together for a while. It did not cease to amaze me how free he felt to ill treat me and impose his will. He behaved as if I were a wild mare he had been asked to break. He informed me that we'd stop in the small town of Mucientes, since my most recent escapade had convinced him that there was no reason to wait any longer before having the Cortes declare me unfit to rule and grant *him* authority to issue commands meant to bring stability throughout the kingdom. For my own good, his and our children, I should accept that this was the course most advantageous to all. The following day, the procurators from all the Castilian towns would arrive in Mucientes and convene the Cortes, he said. I must promise him that I would maintain my composure and not do anything that might once again shame either him or

235

me. Looking contrite, he spoke of the anguish I caused him when I behaved without good sense and sound judgment. Of course he knew, he conceded, that when I was well, no woman in the land was as charming or as clever, but governing a kingdom was men's work. I should not be led to believe that cases like my mother's were anything but exceptional, and what was more, even a great woman such as herself always had a strong man by her side. So why should I, who had not one but two men to govern, not gladly relinquish my power and allow them to see to matters of State? The way I saw it, I told him, neither he nor my father was capable of seeing eye to eye. What was more, as the dutiful wife and daughter that I was, I would be willing to accept their joint rule, but I could not simply sit back and allow them to declare me mad and unfit to rule and treat me as a witless fool in order to achieve whatever they wanted. Besides, he should know, I continued, that I was now carrying his sixth child. I could not but be saddened knowing that he was so petty with the very person whose good labors had provided him with descendants. He looked remorseful for a brief moment, but then turned back to me and repeated his order that I behave sensibly and not get in his way.

That said, he spurred his horse and trotted back up to where Fuensalida rode.

As I watched him ride off, bottling up my spite, I thought that indeed I *would* act sensibly, even if we both understood this to mean different things.

At the church in Mucientes everything was readied for the meeting of the Cortes the day after our arrival. I had only one lady at my service, Doña María de Ulloa. She was a woman of few words, and was getting on in years. But despite my initial misgivings, her considerate opinions, soft demeanor, and perseverance managed to wear down the hostility I felt for the attendants Philippe assigned to me.

For my appearance before the Cortes, Doña María helped me slip into one of the magnificent lace-and-brocade gowns from the queen's trousseau that I had brought to Castile, and she braided my long black hair and then tied it up around my head with a diamond-and-pearl diadem. Looking majestic was important, given my intentions, and when I saw myself in the mirror, I was satisfied at the regality and elegance of my appearance.

I made my entrance into the salon on Philippe's arm. As I walked, I was reminded of the way my mother carried herself and of Beatriz Galindo's advice: princesses must always carry themselves tall, their backs straight. The procurators rose in unison. As I walked to take my place, I was pleased to see among them the Admiral of Castile, my old friend Fadrique Enríquez, and my mother's loyal knight, Pedro López de Padilla.

The session opened with salutations, followed by much hemming and hawing during which, finally, the terms of the Villafáfila Treaty were raised. Philippe and his advisor De Vere addressed the audience to convey to them how both my father and my husband had come to the conclusion that it was in the kingdom's greatest interest for me to delegate the governing of Castile to my husband, given that my unstable health and lack of interest in matters of State would seriously jeopardize my duties and occupations as queen. It was then that the office of the court was to accept Philippe as proprietary king, instead of king consort, so that the swearing in ceremony could take place in Valladolid.

I listened to the arguments exchanged between one side and the other regarding my aptitudes to rule and the convenience of the proposal.

It infuriated me to see so many men in that room sitting around, deciding my fate, as if some natural order had invested them with more wisdom than mine or that of my own mother when she elected to name me her heir. I think they would have yielded to Philippe's plan had I not become so incensed listening to them that I lost my patience and decided to put an end to their convoluted debate. Rising amid their stunned expressions and the sounds of their perplexity I made my way to the center of the chamber and stared at the faces around the room. Then I raised my voice and asked them whether or not they knew me to be Juana, the legitimate daughter of Queen Isabella the Catholic. Look at me well, I demanded. Was I not the the very woman whom the great Isabella had invested as her sole heir?

They reacted as if they had been suddenly jolted out of their sleep.

"Yes, we do know who you are, we recognize you, Your Majesty," the president of the Cortes said, bowing.

"Well, given that you do recognize me," I said, "I am ordering you to move the Cortes to Toledo. There you will swear your loyalty to this queen of Castile and I will swear to defend your laws and your rights. Are you, perchance, unaware that my father disaffirmed the treaty of Villafáfila that his lord the archduke refers to?"

A frenzied debate broke out, with people shouting from one side of the hall to the other. Some said that since I had avowed my desire to be recognized, they were obliged to lend me their ears and discover the truth about what they had been told of my state of mind. Others took Philippe's side, and still others sided with me, recalling that my father had not only refrained from ratifying the treaty of Villafáfila but had actually renounced it, given that it was signed under duress. Finally, they requested a private audience with me, and I accepted immediately. I announced that I would await them in the monastery cloister.

Having said that, I withdrew. I felt Philippe's eyes glower furiously at my back.

A few hours later, the procurators arrived before me, very humble and respectful. Some of their questions were logical and indispensable. For instance, would I govern alone or assign some special role to my husband? Others were absurd, uttered out of who knows what sense of vanity, such as whether I was prepared to dress in the Spanish manner and employ more ladies in my household. I laughed at those concerns, calming their fears about the style of my gowns, and telling them that the number of ladies in my waiting and who they were was a matter for me to decide and bore no relation to the council. I stressed my desire to have my father and not Philippe govern with me until my son Charles had reached the age of majority.

They left apparently satisfied, but Philippe and Cardinal Cisneros went on the offensive the next day, insisting on my incapacity, telling them that the full moon had upset me, that little could they know of my mental state in such a short time. And thus the Cortes designated the admiral of Castile to hold a long interview with me to asess the well-being of my mind.

Ten hours I spent with Don Fadrique. Ten very pleasant hours, I must say, during which he behaved as a father and listened with a pained face to my recounting of the affronts I had been subjected to. He would do everything in his power, he said, but I had to realize that I was swimming in shark-infested waters, and that they would gnaw me with their teeth if I did not advance carefully every step of the way.

Before the others, Don Fadrique dismissed the notion of my inability to rule. He said it was a fallacy to affirm that I was not in my right mind.

I relinquished my demand that the Cortes be moved to Toledo, and finally, the procurators decided to proceed with the coronation ceremony in Valladolid.

I had gotten them to agree to proclaim me their queen.

Philippe and I paraded down the streets of the city on horseback while the crowds gathered everywhere to cheer us. The royal standard of Castile and Leon flew before me, just me: Juana of Castile.

And once again I was magnanimous, or a vassal to my unremitting love: during the ceremony in which they anointed us monarchs, I agreed to share my title as proprietary ruler with Philippe, as the "legitimate husband of the legitimate queen." And thus he escaped the fate of my father, whose mandate had come from his wife's authority.

Despite this, Philippe still made constant efforts to displace me. He named Cardinal Cisneros—who was convinced that I was an obstacle in the way of Spain's glory—as his chief advisor. Not a day went by without Cisneros and Gómez de Fuensalida conspiring to entangle me in their nets and leave me out of their game. They intercepted a letter I wrote my father, requesting his presence beside me. They held meetings with Don Pedro López de Padilla, inciting him to withdraw his support. Then they pressured Philippe to convince me we needed to go to Segovia, since the Marquise of Moya had taken the Alcazar and refused to surrender it to anyone but me. They were desperate. The nobles whose loyalty they needed were daily threatening to switch camps and join my side.

The trip to Segovia was motivated by Philippe's and his advisors' desire to take me to the Alcazar—a fortress—and confine me there so I could no longer thwart their plans. Those were terrible days for me. My authority was accepted or rejected at will. I was the apple of discord, full of worms, surrounded by hostile faces, fearing for my freedom, for my life, not knowing which friends might suddenly turn coat and become my enemies. Depending on his mood, Philippe treated me either as a helpless, deranged child, or a sworn enemy.

Doña María was my only solace, though I was afraid to trust even her completely. At night I could scarcely sleep, for fear of waking to find myself under lock and key. During our rushed journey to Segovia I managed to sleep only a few hours, when we were camped out under the stars.

In the town of Cogeces del Monte, which we reached one afternoon, appropriate measures were taken so that we might be housed in the monastery of La Armedilla. But something in Philippe's demeanor, in the obsequious yet uptight manner in which he praised the preparations under way to ensure my comfort at the Jerónimos convent, led me to suspect that, like a cat, he was preparing to pounce. I would have to be taken for a madwoman again, I thought, but no one was going to make me spend the night within those walls. I smiled beatifically, saying that while the court and soldiers settled in, I would go for a short ride on my horse. A bit of exercise would suit my nerves.

The steppelike landscape surrounding the town was broken here and there by monumental rock formations. Pine forests grew in ravines alongside small streams. Philippe assigned one of his German soldiers to escort me. He was a fierce, toothless man who looked like a barbarian, but beneath his harsh appearance lay a discrete gentleman who kept a courteous distance while I rode undisturbed along paths leading up to the rocky promontories. I knew just how trying and long the night would be, and after galloping for a while, I stopped by the brook that brought water to the village and, still on my saddle, watched the sunset. As it began to grow dark, the soldier said that we should return to the monastery, but I told him to go back on his own, because I planned to spend the night there. That disconcerted him. We were far enough for him not to dare to leave me alone while he went to give notice. They would send a search party for us, I said, he need not worry. It saddened me to see his rude face transformed into that of a frightened child. Because I spoke his language he bonded with me and showed me respect. I engaged him in conversation and he told me about his wife and his fields of barley in Bavaria, stopping himself every so often to beg me to return with him to the monastery.

As I had guessed, the sound of galloping hooves was soon upon us, and Philippe's messengers arrived shortly to order us back to La Armedilla. Instead, I got off my horse, tethered it to a tree, and sat down on a fallen trunk to watch the stars while my soldier paced nervously, not knowing how to react.

It was a repeat of the situation with the baker in Villafáfila, except this time in the open air. I did not know how many nights I would have to refuse to enter the monastery, but it was summertime and the cool pine forest was pleasant.

However, fortune looked kindly upon me this time. Early that morning, news arrived from Segovia that Gómez de Fuensalida had managed to gain entry to the Alcazar, canceling the motive for our trip there. Philippe sent word that we would continue on toward Burgos, to the palace of the constable of Castile, married to Juana of Aragon, my father's stepdaughter. I went back and joined the march.

As a consequence of the night I spent outdoors, I fell ill. We were forced to stop in Tudela del Duero to wait my recovery, as everyone feared my pregnancy might be at risk were we to continue the trip.

We reached Juana of Aragon's palace two months later, in September. I was looking forward to staying with my half-sister Juana in her beautiful palace—designed by Simon of Cologne—where my mother had once received Admiral Christopher Columbus. But mean-spirited Philippe accepted to lodge there on the condition that she and her husband, Don Bernardino Fernández de Velasco, move elsewhere during our stay. He feared the idea of a couple loyal to my father taking care of me and encouraging my rebellion. I didn't know what Gómez de Fuensalida and the constable of Castile had negotiated over the palace that Philippe so inconsiderately usurped. But I later found out that the good constable agreed to cede his home in exchange for the promise that I would not be denied my freedom. Philippe's capricious demands so upset me that I felt as if my heart had emptied itself from the love that for so many years had alternately made me soar up high and dragged me so low. I was overcome by despondency, and the only energy I felt came from the sparks bursting out of the rage forging in my chest. I found myself invoking the power of God and the devil against Philippe. The sound of his voice was enough to send the hatred coursing through my body like a raging river where I sometimes feared the child I carried would drown.

Once they became masters of the house, Philippe and his counselors decided to liven up the nobility who favored them and the troops by offering several days of continuous festivities, banquets, jousts, and hunts. They wanted to ease the tensions around us, since the people and courts, who all over the kingdom had been extremely generous with their favors, were growing tired of lodging us and being charged heftily to feed, clothe, and pay the salaries of so many foreigners. As if that were not enough, the plague had reappeared, and there were rumors that peasants and animals were dying in neighboring towns.

Despite the hatred that clouded my vision, I remember how beautiful and euphoric Philippe was on the third day of revels, when he came into my rooms to announce defiantly that he would think of me when his lance pierced the boar he was going to hunt that afternoon. Arrogant, proud, wearing a coat of mail, baggy breeches and a green tunic over his dark hose and high leather gaiters, he stopped beside the window and looked down at me, full of spite. "Look what your countrymen have turned you into," he scoffed, "a bleak queen who dresses in black, just like her mother."

"The color suits me," I replied. "You killed the scarlet of my gowns and my spirit."

That afternoon a tattered Philippe was brought back to me. He had collapsed on the hunt, after a dizzy spell. If just a few hours before he had been the defiant picture of health now he was shaking, wracked by fever and sweating like an oarsman. It happened so suddenly. To see him suffer, cling to my hands and my eyes, desperately ill and anguished, made me feel I would lose my mind. I felt guilty, wretched, and vile for the intense way I had wished his misfortune. I ordered for him to be lain out on my bed, and for damp cloths to be brought. Needless to say, no one pretended I was mad while I was doing what was required to restore his good health. Both physicians and advisors obeyed me willingly. Philippe seemed calmer on seeing me take charge of the situation. For five days that man, *my* man, surrendered himself to me the way a young boy surrenders himself to his mother's arms. I held him, I sang to him, I wiped the pus from his festering wounds, and night after night I wet his lips again and again, cracked and parched as they were from the fevers. My poor Philippe. His eyes, which had once wrought havoc on my heart, lit up with love when I drew near to him. He whispered tender words, he begged my forgiveness for his tantrums and his ambition, he spoke of the love he had for our children and for my fertile womb. I swore I would let nothing bad happen to him. He had to be strong, I said, he couldn't let the plague devour the body that I loved so. We were young, we could put our lives back together, our love, reign in peace and harmony. I begged him not to torment himself with remorse, thinking of what could have been. "I have never loved anyone like you, Juana, no one has ever taken your place in my heart, no woman's arms have encircled me like yours do, no woman has your neck, the soft curve of your hair as it falls down the beautiful arc of your back, no one trembles beneath my kisses the way you do, no one has been so present nor put up with my stupidity, my vanity, the way you have."

Alas, I thought, if only we could be as lucid in life as we are in death! Beside the decrepit body of the man whose children were borne from me, who burrowed into me like a man digging a tunnel to let go of the sea that drowns him, I watched scenes of our agreements and disagreements parade by like ghosts reflected in a foggy mirror. I clung to his life, refusing to accept that it could be extinguished like the thousands of candles that burned out, one after the other, in the darkened room. Despising my parents' God, who listened to my prayers so selectively, I prayed desperately to other, more compassionate gods that I invented in imaginary Olympias. All to no avail. On the fifth day of fever, Philippe died in my arms.

It was September 25, 1506. Philippe was just thirty years old.

CHAPTER 20

n the library beside Manuel, who so desperately wanted to feel Juana through me, I cried over Philippe's death.

"It's not him that I feel for, it's *her*," I explained, trying to make light of my sentimentality. "She was so full of love, she created a Philippe worthy of her feelings. From broken pieces and shards, over and over, she made him into what she dreamed him to be so that the reality of who he was and his pettiness would not demean the tremendous love that made every sacrifice of hers worthwhile. I can identify with her. You find excuses for the people you love because if you condemn them, you're condemning yourself. I mean, even knowing what I know about my father, I can't curse him. I feel like it wouldn't hurt him; it would hurt me, because my love for him is part of who I am. "Does that make sense?"

"Philippe dying so young, and so suddenly," I continued, thinking aloud, "must have contributed to Juana's adoration of the 'other' Philippe, the idealized figure that she so desperately wanted to believe in. Nostalgia probably diluted her hatred, taking the sting out of her bad memories." I hadn't been alive that long, but I knew how crafty the mind could be at smoothing out one's memories until they became a soft wrap one could cuddle with. Manuel smoked with his glistening eyes fixed on me. He seemed to be moved by my display of emotions. For a minute I even thought he was going to start crying too. Instead, he took off my gown and made love to me next to the fireplace, as if he were trying to offer a different ending to the same story. Tenderness took hold of us, as if our exposed, bare, vulnerable bodies and the frailty of our own uncertain, unforeseen situation were a reflection of that sad moment in our characters' lives.

Gently, sweetly, he licked away my tears. He cradled my head against his chest and answered my sobbing with a plaintive, hoarse sound that rose up from the bottom of his lungs. He spoke of the paradox of loneliness being the emotion most deeply shared by human beings. Anyone could understand what it was like to experience it. It was hard to hate Philippe as he lay dying, as he went through that solitary transition, the most solitary of all. One could identify with him in that circumstance and feel compassion. Every time one imagined someone else's death, it was like rehearsing one's own. His theory was, he said, that the moment of transit from life to nothingness, the moment one consciously realized everything would be lost, *that* was hell; a hell where all sins were purged, an inferno no one could escape.

"And yet, Miss Lucía," he said, getting up to pour himself a glass of cognac as I got dressed, "life is such an ephemeral deceit. Only through knowledge can we achieve a certain degree of self-realization, because knowledge is the sum of all other lives, and that multiplicity is the only thing that gives our infinitesimal existence the illusion of permanence and purpose."

"Sex is another one of those eternal continuums," he said. "If the solitude of death is hell, then copulation is heaven." He smiled maliciously, raising his glass to me and making me laugh at his obscure philosophies. His affection made me feel much better. I went to bed calm. I didn't think about anything. I slept a deep sleep on that first night of what I imagined would be a long stay at the Denias' house.

When I woke up the next day and went down to breakfast, Águeda told me that Manuel had gone out.

"Don't let it bother you that he goes out. He likes to be alone. He goes to his apartment, but he'll be back. He always comes back, and now that you're here he's got all the more reason. Why don't I walk you through the house? You've never seen the whole thing."

I accepted, curious. Deep down I felt an almost canine sense of gratitude toward Águeda. Another woman in her place would not have agreed to be an accomplice and would have told the nuns or my grandparents. So I was willing to do whatever she asked of me. Águeda opened a small wooden box that hung on the wall and took out a large ring of keys. I had already realized that she was methodical and orderly. Her routines probably helped her pass the time. And now I was going to see how she spent her days. Weekends she'd hardly interfered in our comings and goings, because that was when she went to church and to have her hair done.

I followed her upstairs. Though I was still hoping that my pregnancy would fade away with the appearance of a big red stain on my underwear, the possibility that another member of that family could be taking shape within me made itself felt in the way I saw the house now. It had a square foundation and a high, coffered ceiling made of beautiful wood. The spiral staircase was off to one side and led up to the second- and third-floor hallways, with the bedrooms leading off of it. The top floor, as Águeda explained, had been rebuilt, which was why it looked more French, with rounded corners and cornices.

"Because this is a very Castilian house. Have I already told you this? It was built by Juan Gómez de Mora, the same architect that designed the Plaza Mayor in Madrid. It dates back to 1606. Francisco Gómez de Sandoval, Marquis of Denia, was the first man to live here when he moved to Madrid at the behest of Philippe III, as his premier. I disagree with Manuel's view of our ancestors, but I must admit that he was quite a schemer. There's no doubt that he increased the power his family held, but he wasn't completely honest in his methods. Ask Manuel about it. He knows all of the Denias' black legends." She smiled ironically. "Poor thing. I think denigrating the family is his way of reconciling himself to what they did to his mother. Well, anyway . . ."

We were walking through the wing that I hadn't seen yet. The solid double doors all had modern security locks on them, in addition to the original ones. Águeda opened door after door. Despite the semidarkness, I could see that the closed windows were all spotlessly clean and in excellent condition, the furniture covered with gray and white slipcovers. "Aunt" Águeda led me through the music room, the sewing room, and a tiny chapel that she still used, with a beautiful sculpture of Christ, burning votive candles, and a wooden prie-dieu. The floors and ceilings of each room were antique wood marvels, solid and gleaming, and beautiful tapestries hung on the walls. It was hard to keep the paintings and tapestries in their original state, she said, which was why the rooms had such thick curtains and dehumidifiers in the corners. Every month, Águeda explained, a professional cleaning company came to polish the floors and do a thorough job of cleaning everything. She had no patience for cleaning ladies, and besides, she didn't trust them with all the fragile objects. She preferred to dust and polish them herself. It helped her pass the time. We reached a room smaller than the others, and she pulled a dustcover off of a beautifully shaped rolltop desk with a whole series of tiny drawers under its lid. It might be useful to me, she said, given that there was no writing table in my room. "And you'll be writing a lot of letters," she added, with a touch of irony that I didn't find funny. We walked out and crossed a hallway with several closed doors on the third floor.

"Our most valuable possessions are in there. Many of them date back to Doña Juana's days. They used to be scattered all over the house, but I moved them into what used to be father's study, so I could clean them and take care of them better. I'll show you some other day."

"How did your ancestors end up being involved with Doña Juana?" I asked. "Manuel hasn't really told me much about it. He clouds over when I ask him about it."

"It was on March 15, 1518. Emperor Charles I of Spain and V of Germany named Don Bernardo de Sandoval y Rojas as governor of his mother Juana's household, and of the town of Tordesillas. Don Bernardo had been first governor to Juana's father, King Ferdinand the Catholic, since 1504. He was with him until his death, and his final act was to take the king's body to Granada and place it beside his wife, Queen Isabella. They were cousins, you see. Ferdinand and Don Bernardo were cousins. That's why King Charles trusted him. They were a very illustrious bunch. Grandees of Spain. Only twenty-five families in the whole kingdom had that distinction. Plus, Don Bernardo was married to Doña Francisca Enríquez, who was related to Don Fadrique Enríquez."

"The one who took Juana to Flanders, the admiral of Castile?"

"The very same. And Spain was in a state of turmoil then. The Denias took their obligation to protect the crown very seriously. Perhaps they were overzealous. But Juana's madness—or instability, if you prefer—was a risk. There was no lack of opportunists who tried to use the mother's lack of wits as a means of robbing the son of his power. But the Marquises of Denia were utterly loyal to Charles, who was the legitimate king, given that his mother couldn't rule."

"But that's just it," I said, "she *could* rule."

"Oh, it doesn't matter who's right anymore, child. Neither she, nor them can contest what history has judged to be true, nor can they argue with increasingly fickle historians. I don't want to talk about it anymore. Come, I want to show you something before we go back downstairs. Manuel will be back soon."

I followed her to the end of the hall. She opened a door and we walked into what must have been a child's room.

"This is where Manuel spent his childhood," she said. "I'd come up here to tell him bedtime stories."

It was tiny and narrow, like a cell. The furniture was dark, wooden, and somber, and I could see models piled up on all the bookshelves. Clearly, assembling them had been Manuel's favorite pursuit since he was a boy. I pictured him as a pale, serious, ten-year-old boy, lying in bed, reading beneath the crucifix on the wall. I felt sorry for him. It was a sad room. Just one tiny window, high up on the wall, like an attic. Now it was just a storeroom for things no one used anymore. In one corner stood a crib with carved rails, the hook for a mosquito net carved into the chubby face of a wooden cherub.

"This looks like my room at boarding school," I said.

"My parents were fervent believers in Castilian austerity. They said it built character. But the crib is lovely, don't you think? And what's more, it's the family crib. This is where your son will sleep once he's born," she said without looking at me, gliding over it lightly with the feather duster hanging from her waist.

"Or my daughter," I replied.

"Oh, it'll be a boy, you'll see," she said with an expression that left no room for debate.

I wanted her to be wrong. I didn't want to give the world any more Marquises of Denia. I didn't like the cold, severe faces of the ancestors whose paintings hung on walls all around the house.

After we went back downstairs and Águeda began to make phone calls, I wandered around the rooms, sensing the presence of history in the air, staring at the Persian rugs, the tapestries, the grand piano in the corner of the salon. Aside from the ancient oil paintings, and unlike the house where I grew up, here there wasn't a single photograph of the modern-day Denias.

Manuel came back at lunchtime. He asked me how I felt.

"Fine," I said. "Your aunt showed me around the house. She told me a little about your family history."

"Her version," he said.

"And she showed me your old room."

"Ah!" he said wryly. "If those walls could talk."

"Let's go to the library," I suggested. "I want to know what Juana did after Philippe died, what happened next. And you'll have to tell me about the Denias."

"All in good time." He smiled, pensive.

CHAPTER 21

I've already told you that Juana's behavior after Philippe's death has been interpreted in a variety of ways. In general, historians to this day have barely stopped to consider what it must have meant for a woman of her age, pregnant, in love, and besieged by intrigues of State, to have to face the sudden, unexpected death of her husband. Paraphrasing a poet, Juana and Philippe were an "ill-adjusted but tightly embraced couple." That she got depressed would be considered nowadays a natural reaction, given the chain of events. Machismo might be the reason why, in her case, history has chosen to omit those considerations when judging her. Now, personally, I think Juana immersed herself so totally in last rites and funeral processions to avoid making decisions and allow Ferdinand time to return from Italy. Though her faith in her father had dwindled, she preferred this alternative rather than run the risk of the nobility casting her aside to set up her father-in-law Maximilian as regent until young Charles came of age. I think she realized she wouldn't be able to take Philippe's body all the way to Granada. She knew her time to give birth was fast approaching.

BEFORE THE EMBALMERS TOOK PHILIPPE'S BODY AWAY, I ASKED TO be left alone with him and sat down by his side. I took his hands and stroked them, lifting each of his fingers in turn. Using the fingernail of my index finger, I cleaned under his nails, which were still dirty from his last game of pelota. He didn't move. I stroked his forehead, straightened his hair. The submissiveness of his body was a new experience for me. I leaned over and tried to open his eyelids, so I could look into his eyes once more. For an instant I saw death stare at me in the total absence of light: the pupils dilated, fixed, opaque, like a door forever shut. I pulled my hand away in fear. Philippe, I whispered. Philippe, can you hear me? He made no reply. I was suddenly struck. With a clarity that left me breathless I realized that Philippe would never answer me again. I believe it was then that I became aware that ever since I saw Philippe for the first time, I had never imagined my life without him. And as I tried to visualize the future, I was filled with panic: I could only see myself keeping vigil over his cadaver.

Cadaver, I murmured, cavern, calamity, calvary, corpse, catafalque. What an awful word. The very sound of it was rigid, cold, putrid. That and nothing else was my husband now, the father of my children. After just four months in Spain he'd gone from the throne to the catafalque. I cried, imagining my children's faces when they heard the news, but my tears were short-lived downpours, like sorrows that wouldn't condense. I could hardly weep because I could hardly think. Ideas appeared in my mind, but they came crashing down with the weight of pebbles dropping into a void. I thought that if I stayed with the body, eventually I would have to convince myself of the reality of what had happened, but Philibert de Veyre—Philippe's ambassador in Spain—and Archbishop Cisneros appeared a short while later and compelled me to leave him. I gave in. I let him go with them. That night, a Burgundian-style wake was held. Philippe was laid out on a dais in the Casa del Cordón, dressed in his best clothes and surrounded by beautiful tapestries. The following day, doctors embalmed his body, and on the third day we held a procession that went from the constable's house to the Carthusian Monastery of Miraflores. I took part in the funeral services. The fluttering of life in my belly was the only thing that kept me from feeling as dead as Philippe.

When at last I was able to lock myself in my rooms, alone, I suddenly felt clearheaded and I plotted, coldly, exactly what I would have to do. My mother, who died in Medina del Campo, had been taken to

Granada. Philippe, as the anointed king he was, should lie beside her. He himself had made that clear in his last will and testament and repeated it to me on his deathbed. Carrying out his portentous request would give me the opportunity to travel to Andalusia, surround myself with supporters, and, once I had backing, assume my responsibilities as queen. I thought that under those circumstances, going to Granada would give me a chance to renew alliances, rid myself of Flemish courtiers, and guarantee that my son Charles's succession was assured beyond any shadow of a doubt.

My isolation at court, and the suspicions and fears all around me, turned out to be formidable obstacles that hindered my plans to take charge of the kingdom. I was informed then that while I was attending to Philippe on his deathbed, Archbishop Francisco Jiménez de Cisneros had managed to get appointed regent of Castile and had forced all the grandees in Spain to swear that not a single one of them would attempt to make use of my power or approach me to have it vested on them.

But Cisneros's regency wasn't to everyone's liking. After a few days, camps had divided into those who advocated my father's return and those who thought my father-in-law, Emperor Maximilian, should rule until Charles reached the age of majority.

Not a single one of the nobles—not even my good friend the admiral of Castile, Don Fadrique Enríquez—deigned to consider that I might be capable of taking charge. They must have felt it was more in their interest to obtain the favor of Ferdinand or Maximilian than that of a woman—a lonely, very pregnant widow. And as for me, I had not even the money required to buy the unconditional loyalty of soldiers and servants. The Andalusian nobles were the only ones willing to defend me, and they were several days' journey away. Maybe the people who did recognize me as queen would have opposed an attempt to cast me aside, but while I was seeing to the funeral rites, Archbishop Cisneros issued a number of edicts promising exrtemely harsh punishment to whoever dared rise up in arms. That way he made sure there would be no popular uprising in my favor.

With Philippe dead, I reorganized my household, employing ladies I considered loyal, but they slowly proved themselves to be subservient to my father. His influence over the court was so great that, faced with the facts, even Cisneros chose to surrender and wrote him a letter requesting that he return from Italy: despite his repeated demands, I refused to sign this request, given that it could be read as an indication that I declined my right to rule.

When he received Cisneros's letter on his way to Naples, Ferdinand replied, recognizing my authority and my right to the throne, and affirming that Cisneros's regency was baseless. But as isolated as I was, my only means of disavowing the prelate's authority was to refuse to sign documents he presented me with, so that for several weeks the country was rudder-less, while at the same time my poor subjects were being decimated by the plague. The nobles—each more ambitious than the last—tried to turn things to their advantage by using their armies and privileges in order to sow chaos and settle old scores in an attempt to acquire influence they might keep once the situation had settled down.

In the solitude of my nights, I pondered my true duty, and yet my strength or desire to act could not surmount the apathy I had fallen into despite my best intentions. I suffered from a constant headache since Philippe's death. My only company was the child in my womb, who I dreamed was a boy that I would call Philippe. I pictured him as handsome as his father. I imagined that Philippe's spirit would live on in him and that somehow, mysteriously, his father's life would alight next to me once again when he was born, this time without causing me pain. Twice during that time I visited the Cartuja of Miraflores, where my husband's coffin lay. Both times, I had it opened to ascertain that his body was still there. I knew that the Flemish had taken his heart in a gold urn to bury it beside his ancestors, and I feared they had made off with his body too, given that they had no qualms about taking every possession Philippe had brought to Spain. They carted out tapestries, furniture, armor, jewels, horses, paintings, and more, as payment for services that I had no other means of reimbursing. I did nothing to stop them because at the time nothing mattered to me, but I did want to make sure they had not robbed me of his bones.

The second time I had the coffin opened was before I left for Torquemada on December 20 (I planned to stay there until I gave birth, far from the intrigues and pressures of the nobles who surrounded me at Casa de la Vega. I had stayed there since Philippe's death, for I had no wish to ever go back to the house where he had died.) So opposed were the clerics to delivering Philippe's catafalque to me that I suspected his body was no longer inside. They opened the wooden box and then the lead one, and just like the first time, I saw him lying there, immobile, swathed in bandages and lime. The ambassadors and prelates were horrified that I could approach him and even touch him, but anyone who has loved as much as I would understand that seeing his corpse was no shock to me. In any case, there was nothing to see except the bandages covering his shape. For me what mattered, given my general distrust, was to corraborate with my own eyes what I had been told and free myself from the torment of speculation.

Finally, after praying before the coffin at the charterhouse altar that day, I made some decisions aimed at restoring order and royal patrimony.

My first act was to revoke all of the favors Philippe had conceded to nobles, since many of the legal disputes that had arisen were the result of my husband's munificence when it came to taking my father's supporters' possessions and distributing them among his own followers. I got rid of the members of the Royal Council that had been named by Gómez de Fuensalida, and held an audience with the procurators of the council. I ordered all things to revert back to the way they had been during my mother's life, and the government to be run in the same manner as when she was alive. Echoing Cisneros's wishes, they proposed that I invite my father to return from Naples to take over the matters of State. I neither agreed nor disagreed. I expressed affection for my father but signed no letter. Instead I reaffirmed my desire that they follow through what I, their queen, had commanded.

For me to assume my royal authority seemed to disconcert them, but I let them be disconcerted and ordered my entourage to depart for Torquemada with Philippe's coffin in tow.

NEITHER I NOR ANYONE WHO ACCOMPANIED ME NOR THE PEOPLE who watched our procession go by would ever forget the images of that night. It was the source of endless stories and legends, since after all of the setbacks we did not leave that day until an hour after sunset, amid a dense fog that seemed more like an eerie sea whose waves swelled and broke on terra firma. In order to light the way through the white clouds that enshrouded us, I ordered a great number of torches to be lit. Through the mist, my caravan advanced, led by the four horses that carried the coffin—covered in black-and-gold cloth—and Flemish cantors. We followed behind, the court and the clerics intoning funeral services. It must have looked like death itself was parading through the night, decked out in ghostly gauzes and ashen curtains.

I walked for quite a distance. I can recall the women who lined the roads to see me pass, and the way they gazed at me. They showed the veneration befitting a sacred personage, but in their eyes too was boundless understanding. As women, they knew the most hidden sorrows of my heart, and silently they showed me the support and compassion due to a widow about to give birth.

My travels over the course of those days gave me a little peace. The wide open country, pine trees clustered beside streams, red earth covered in olive groves, flocks of sheep and their tiny shepherds, and the blue sky after days of intrigues and imprisonment in Casa de la Vega did more for my spirits than all the incense and prayers for the dead. I was twenty-seven years old and life was coursing through my veins. The music of my Flemish cantors—the most precious thing I had held on to from my rule in Flanders—brought me great solace when we stopped to rest. During those days, Philippe's spirit, young and enamored, returned to me. Without him there, it was easy for me to invent a tale of the indescribable happiness that, despite our rough patches, we had shared. Sorrow and nostalgia erased all of the bad memories, and before my eyes danced only pleasant recollections of the man I had loved so dearly, whose love I could now hold and cherish without the disappointments of life.

I would have liked to carry on after a few days in Torquemada, but my body finally reminded me of the obligations my mind tried to forget and avoid. The moon waned, and with it, the baby in my womb announced its arrival.

At the home of the Cortes representative, who so hospitably housed me, my waters broke. I was so fatigued I thought I would not survive childbirth. The women accompanying me must have thought the same, for never before had I sensed such anxiety around me when I delivered. At times I have thought that Catalina bore herself, because all I remember is the urgency with which she pushed her way through my entrails. I simply relented. Without will, I abandoned myself to my body's labor, neither clinging to life, nor longing for death, but submitting to a destiny whose power was greater than me or my desire to challenge it. And when I was finally hollow and heard my baby cry, I closed my eyes and was happy to still be alive. Right after I saw her tiny face, a heavy torpor came over me. It was a girl, and she resembled me more than Philippe. Her eyes had a wise look from that very beginning. I had a feeling that more than a daughter, I had given birth to someone who would watch over me.

Further on, I often thought that Philippe's repentance moved my daughter's spirit, turning her into both my companion and my solace. Her love sustained me during so many long years.

CHAPTER 22

I awaited the outcome of Juana's story as if time went by only for her inside that house. I ran to the bathroom to check my underwear constantly. The slightest dampness made me jump up, and I'd rush to look between my legs, like someone expecting to see ice melt in red-hot flames. A few days before Christmas the gray weather and dry cold of a Madrid winter made me gravitate toward the library with a book in my hands. I watched the Denias going about their daily routines. In the afternoons, Águeda phoned her friends in the Captives' Club, as Manuel had dubbed them. But the phone hardly ever rang. Occasionally there were calls for Manuel. Students, he said, or his friend Genaro. After so many years of spending my vacations in student residences or in hotel rooms with my grandparents, the quiet family life was an unexpected gift. Laying on the sofa with my feet up, a blanket warming my legs, reading *Jane Eyre,* I was happy. Only at times when the book resting on my belly weighed on me, I would startle myself. Someone else was living beneath, I'd tell myself. I imagined the life of that concealed creature, swimming around like a fish in a dark aquarium. I'd run my hands over my skirt, measuring the space left between my clothes and my waist, with a fascination that sometimes turned to horror and incredulity.

"Manuel, isn't there some way of finding out for sure if I'm pregnant or not?" I asked that afternoon.

"I have no doubt whatsoever," he said, glancing up from his book.

"But I do, and I'd like some proof."

He stared at me. It was a question of taking a urine sample to the lab and giving a fake name.

"I've been trying not to leave any incriminating evidence, in case the nuns or your grandparents decide to go to the police, or hire a detective."

"Oh, I hadn't thought of that," I said, reassured that his excuse seemed rational. "Let's wait till after Christmas."

I started pacing around the library. He stared at me from the sofa.

"Juana must have been just like you. You know, I've often wondered if when we die, our conscience returns to its source enriched by new experiences, and then goes and fills other vessels, other bodies. That would explain the theory of the collective unconscious, the idea that when we're born we already possess the knowledge of those who lived before us."

I THOUGHT OF THE MONTHS THAT MANUEL HAD SPENT TURNING MY body into a shell from which to listen to a sea that had existed before him or me.

I looked at him and wondered if my little girl would have his blue eyes.

That night he came to my room with the antique dress over his arm. It would be better for me to get changed there and come down wearing the dress, he said. That way I wouldn't get cold. I asked what his aunt would think. She might be surprised, he said, but she would end up considering it was more than appropiate that another Juana wandered around that house.

"She'll think you're Juana's ghost." He smiled. "But she won't mind walking into that ghost."

I got changed, pulled my hair up into a bun, and then went downstairs to find Manuel.

At the bottom of the stairs I crossed paths with the aunt, who was just coming out of the kitchen. I tried to explain to her that my disguise had been her nephew's idea, but rather than surprised she seemed fascinated. Lifting a finger to her lips to silence me, she left me bewildered when she curtsied and walked ahead to open the door of the library for me. I smiled and, keeping in character, I walked by her as if I were a queen.

Manuel was waiting for me beside the fire.

"Let's continue," he said.

He was dressed in black. Dark clothing made him look taller and thinner, accentuating his angular features. I thought he seemed somber, almost sad, which was unusual for him; he always seemed so in control of his emotions.

GIVING BIRTH TO CATALINA WHEN I HAD SO BONDED WITH DEATH was a supreme effort that consumed all of my energy and left me physically and mentally weak at the worst possible time. The first year of my widowhood was inaugurated by the cries of my daughter, born on January 14, 1507; it was a year marked by long sleepless nights. I was afraid to sleep. In my dreams, Philippe appeared before me and begged me to come to him, for he was so lonely and so cold. His appeals were so vehement that I felt the icy cold of his leaden coffin in my bones, and my teeth chattered. In seven months, I spent thousands of maravedis from my meager savings to have wax candles burning around him at all times. I paid for services to be held every evening and maintained the salaries of the Flemish cantors, thinking that their melodies would sweeten my husband's sorrow at having died so far from his beloved Brussels. I was sure that Philippe had still not managed to cross the threshold of his new existence. I harbored the notion that he would only die for good when he was put to rest next to my mother, because she would forcefully pull him inside the marble of her catafalque in Granada. To explain this to anyone was a useless endeavor. Yes, I admit it: Philippe's death seduced me with a passion as acute as the one he had inspired in me during his life. My certainty that inexplicably he continued to exist flanking my life had led me to try to shield other women from his charms. I had refused to spend the night in convents fearing he would wander among the cells at night, cosseted in his incorporeality, stroking the impure fantasies of the nuns, slipping beneath the vapor of their foul-smelling habits. Other times I had imagined he could take over soldiers' bodies and take solace in the barred sexuality hiding in the nuns' nocturnal cells. I refused to accept a simple end for my Philippe, perhaps because well disguised beneath my bereavement there was the joyous feeling that I was at last free from his cruel machinations and his ambition, and I was afraid he might discover that darkest secret of my heart and avenge himself.

Daily I was beseiged by nobles and priests who tried to confound my reasoning so that I would betray one group or another. Cisneros moved his army to Torquemada, claiming that it was to protect me. To free myself of his pernicious meddling and his spies, I recommenced my progress to Granada, but not before I confirmed the orders I had issued to revoke the favors Philippe had granted. I also held a hearing with council members to insist they continue to govern in the same manner as when my mother was alive.

Any sign of my reason or authority was enough to fill the prelates and nobles with apprehension. On the one hand, they lamented my alleged madness, and on the other, nothing upset them more than the evidence of my good senses and the possibility that I might decide to claim my royal rights. Gradually it was becoming more and more clear that I was up against many odds. That I would reign didn't enter into anybody's plans. For them, the question at hand was who would rule in my name and who might I nominate to do so. Alone, with no armies, no money, my position was precarious. I realized that my only way out was to form an alliance with my father and establish a form of government similar to the one he had shared with my mother. I knew that he had left Naples and was on his way to Spain. I didn't want to appear to be the one calling him to my side, so I used evasive tactics to avoid signing a letter that Mosen Luis Ferrer—his emissary—insisted I send to request his presence. I could not, however, refuse his petition that I order rogations throughout the country for my father's s safe journey home. In the end, I could not avoid appearing to have encouraged his return.

Our encounter took place in Tórtoles on August 29. I traveled there from Hornillos, a tiny village where I spent four months after leaving Torquemada, and where my retinue caused considerable damage for which I had to compensate the inhabitants. Even their church was destroyed by the fire caused by the candles that burned beside Philippe's coffin. His very body was nearly incinerated by the carelessness of those charged with watching over him.

Located in the province of Burgos, Tórtoles was—by virtue of its size—more suited to receive the king of Aragon. He was not the kind who could settle anywhere, like I did.

More than four years had gone by since I had last seen my father. I confess that when we met, I was stunned not so much by the filial affection that overpowered me but by the blow of seeing how readily the nobles who had pledged their loyalty to me rushed to join his entourage. In the end, I was forced to appear before him surrounded by only those few ladies who were still in my service. What could I do but admit my disadvantage? I would have liked to appear distant and inscrutable, so that he would realize that although I was his daughter, I was now a queen and thus his equal. Fool that I was! I had forgotten his uncanny ability to ease my suffering with nothing but a glance. I approached him and raised my black widow's veil. The moment I met his eyes, his attempt to bend his knee and kiss my hand seemed incongruous to me. I dropped down to embrace him, overwhelmed with a feeling of love and relief. Right then and there, as he held me in his arms, I settled my contradictions. I closed my eyes as a line from the Pater Noster crossed my mind: "Thy will be done on Earth as it is in Heaven." Let my father's will be done. At last, I would rest.

With the understanding that I remained queen and that I would have the last word, I granted him the regency and administration of the kingdom. I stayed a short time in the village of Santa María del Campo, and then I decided to reside at the Villa de Arcos, three leagues from Burgos. My father would have liked me to move there, but I had no desire to return to the city where Philippe had died.

The Episcopal Palace in Villa de Arcos, where I set up my residence, was a simple yet beautiful stone building that shared its cloister with the parish church, which meant that I could see the church's nave and watch over Philippe's coffin without leaving the premises. There were three other large residences in the area, enough to house the small entourage that would be attending Catalina, Ferdinand, and I.

Little Ferdinand had come back to me after the death of his father. He arrived in Simancas accompanied by the kind Pedro Núñez de Guzmán, who had been charged with his upbringing. I was moved by how faithfully he had kept the memory of me, despite all the time that had passed. My little four-year-old man not only identified me as his mother, he clung to me, so hungry for my cuddles and kisses, that he made me feel needed and loved. When I suckled Catalina, he wanted me to nurse him as well, which I would have done willingly if the sorrows and fatigue of the last months had not taken its toll on the amount of milk that flowed from my breasts. Those days, nothing made me happier than hearing Ferdinand's carefully vocalized words, so unusual for a child his age. He spoke with astonishing fluency, and he loved when I recited the epic song of "El Cid" for him. At night, snuggled up in bed with Catalina and Ferdinand, no nightmares visited my dreams. I, who had never much played or spent time with my children, found in Ferdinand's innocence, in his spontaneous and generous love as well as in Catalina's tiny warm body, a safe harbor to love and be loved, a saving grace. I promised myself I would become a true mother for them and that I would never again let them be apart from me.

Eighteen months I spent in Villa de Arcos, shepherding my sorrows until slowly they allowed me to rein them in. I sensed I was emerging step by step from a rocky valley blanketed in fog, at whose end I would find the crossroads where Philippe and I would go our separate ways: he toward death and I back to life.

Although I didn't take it seriously, I was flattered to hear the rumor that King Henry VII of England—the same one who had gone down to Portsmouth incognito to catch a glimpse of me all those years ago—had asked for my hand in marriage. I began to laugh aloud with my ladies again. I was slowly recovering the spirit that once inhabited my skin: strong, daring, and avid for music, dance, and beauty.

But after the winter of 1508, as the promise of warm days announced itself with the arrival of summer and I began to long for leisure and lengthy walks in the Castilian countryside, my calm was shattered into a million splinters. My father decided to travel to Córdoba to punish the Andalusian nobles who still refused to submit to his authority, and to take little Ferdinand with him. He feared that, in his absence, the nobles could take the throne away from Charles—who was still in Flanders—and name Ferdinand, who all of them considered more Spanish than his brother. Rather than protect Charles's rights, my father was just worried that this maneuver would strip him from the regency of Castile, something the nobility had already tried to do shortly after Philippe's death.

I didn't want to be separated from my son. I dreaded the idea of him growing up to be a pawn of others' power struggles. But everything I did—begging first, screaming after that, trying to impose my queen's authority, and even locking myself with him in my room like any mother determined to protect her child—was futile. Forcefully they snatched him from my arms, oblivious to the boy's cries and to my own.

My father's cavalcade left Arcos, and I closed myself up in my rooms desolate, bitter, and enraged. I refused to eat or bathe. Again I expressed my resistance using my weapon of last resort: my body.

"LOOK, LUCÍA. HERE'S WHAT THE BISHOP OF MÁLAGA WROTE TO Ferdinand the Catholic:

'After Your Highness left, the queen was peaceful, both in word and deed, so she has not hurt anyone nor spoken slander. Let me also add that since that time she has not changed her shirt, or her headdress or washed her face. She sleeps on the floor and eats from plates set in front of her in the same place, refusing table or cloth. And many days she won't attend mass.'"

"I can imagine what she must have felt. I can feel her fury like a bitter taste in my mouth," I whispered. "Poor Juana."

"When Ferdinand returned from Andalusia, he commanded that Juana be moved from Villa de Arcos to Tordesillas whether by 'patience, entreaties, or threats.' He personally supervised the operation, which included moving Philippe's body and little Catalina along with Juana. In this day and age, we would call that a coup d'état."

"But why did he feel the need to do that?" I asked. "Juana was quite obedient."

"She was obedient but not docile. And Ferdinand had many enemies among the Castilian nobles. He was afraid that if they had free access to the queen, they might take advantage of the quarrels between father and daughter to convince her to act against him. He was afraid that Juana, furious at having been separated from little Ferdinand, might retaliate. He was afraid she might name Emperor Maximilian regent until Charles was old enough to rule. He felt that if Juana continued to be free, she might put his interests in jeopardy. Knowing that no one would object if he pulled her out of the game, Ferdinand preferred not to run those risks. He felt he could do anything if he used her "madness" as a justification. After all, Philippe had already paved the way."

"You have to admit, though, that Juana's behavior was somewhat unrestrained: her love for Philippe, her subservience to her father, the ways in which she chose to rebel that left her open to people's scorn."

Manuel gaped at me, his brow furrowed, as if he couldn't believe what he'd just heard. To see him there, comfortably reclined on the sofa by the fireplace, pressing the tips of his long fingers together, made me think of the day I first met him at the Hotel Palace.

"*Love, that strange word.* Juana had no one on her side, and her father was very powerful. It happens to this day. Just look at our own family histories: my mother died alone in a hotel room. You mother died for love too, even if she took your father with her." Manuel stood up and began pacing in front of the fireplace. "My grandparents were incredibly cruel to my mother because she fell in love with a nobody. In a way, they drove her to what she did, to kill herself. In this world we usually receive the worst blows from the people we love the most. Therefore the crimes of passion, the madness of love. Lovers give each other a bunch of arrows and then hang a bull's-eye on their chests. In theory, both agree not to attack, but if the pact is broken . . . a bloodbath ensues."

"How is it that you know so much about all this?" I asked sarcastically.

"I'm a historian," he said with a wry smile. "Just look at Ferdinand, fifty-three years old, and he marries Germaine de Foix, the niece of the king of France, who was only seventeen. He tried everything to have a son with her, and in the end, the concoctions Germaine gave him to try to arouse his virility were what killed him. Love, the loss of love. From Troy to the Anglican Church, what other abstract concept has had so much influence on the course of history? And as far as Juana's methods go, back then, no one understood them. She was very modern in that sense; she believed in her own, individual strength. In the end, the very thing that, according to some people, caused her downfall enabled her to survive as long as she did in Tordesillas."

CHAPTER 23

Manuel's classes had been dismissed for Christmas vacation. It was snowing in Madrid, which was unusual. Through the kitchen window, the yard was a beautiful, ghostly white. I was coming to the end of *Jane Eyre* and drinking chamomile tea in the library. There was nothing more befitting that silent mansion full of secrets than sitting around reading Brontë. The fictional world that Manuel and his Aunt Águeda inhabited was not without its charms. And in that world, I was Juana. As enamored of and possessed by the queen's ghost as they were.

Browsing through the packed bookshelves in the library, I found several genealogical references to the Denias, some of which were quite amusing. They hailed from Valencia. One of the first Sandovals, Sando Cuervo, had met his death saving King Pelayo's life as the king crossed over a gorge on a beam of wood. Another ancestor had accidentally killed King Enrique I with a tile. The Denia coat of arms showed Don Pelayo's black beam of wood. Later, five stars were added when the family became related to the Rojases by marriage. I also found facsimiles of Charles V and the Marquis of Denia's letters regarding the care of Doña Juana. There were full of polite expressions, but it didn't take much to see the degree of complicity between the Denias and the emperor when it came to the web of falsehoods in which they kept Juana, denying her information about what was going on beyond the four walls of Tordesillas Palace. Using the excuse that the presence of other ladies "disquieted" her, Denia surrounded Juana with women in his own family who were part of the conspiracy to keep her isolated. So that she could never escape vigilance, the marquis ordered that there always be one woman inside her rooms, while another kept watch at her door. Juana had absolutely no privacy. Her every move was monitored by the household staff.

What stunned me the most as I read through the correspondence was to corroborate that her own son Charles had no qualms about putting her away, nor about doing everything he could to keep her from receiving news or getting in touch with the outside world. In his letters to Denia, he even approved the use of physical force in "extreme cases," leaving it to the marquis to judge which of the queen's actions might be worthy of that label.

THE DAY BEFORE CHRISTMAS, MANUEL WALKED INTO THE KITCHEN and up to his Aunt Águeda. He snuck up unexpectedly and took the key hanging from the key chain at her waist—the one that opened the wooden box where she kept all the keys to the rooms on the upper floors. Sitting there drinking coffee, I could see her stiffen at his playful affection when he grabbed her waist as she was laying silverware out on the kitchen table.

"I think I remember where the nativity scene is," he said. "I'll go bring it down so we can have a little Christmas spirit around here."

"I'll go with you," she said, turning toward the door. "You don't know where things are. You haven't been up there in so long."

"Oh, Auntie, don't worry. If I can't find it, I'll call you, but I don't want you to come with me. I want you to let Lucía and I go up there alone." He spoke with authority, as if to a child. I couldn't see either of their expressions, just Manuel's back, but I gathered this wasn't the first time they'd had this discussion.

"All right, all right, but don't touch anything. Leave everything the way it is."

She went back to her silverware, her back bent over the table. I saw a look of sulking distrust come over the face framed by the blond, impeccably coiffed hairdo. She looked like a cat forced to remain in place, claws at the ready. Manuel had me go upstairs ahead of him. The third floor smelled of wax and cleanliness. From there one could get a view of the floor below the staircase, the circular foyer inlaid with the precious stones arranged in a circle, like a solar system full of multicolored planets. Manuel stopped in the hallway by two heavy, modern doors with several locks on them. He opened the one on the left, unlocking it with several keys, one of which I remember was very long.

Since the room was very dark, I couldn't make out anything until Manuel turned on the wrought iron lamps hanging from the ceiling and opened the curtains. I found myself in a sort of overcrowded but impeccably clean museum, with tall, glass-encased bookshelves lining the walls and an assortment of Castilian-style furniture arranged in groups by type: armchairs with bronze appliqués, platforms, footstools, tray tables, bureaus, braziers, objects whose names I learned that afternoon as Manuel pointed them out. Judging by the doors on the hallway, the large rectangular salon at some point must have been several contiguous rooms. Behind the glass doors of the shelves lined against the wall there were antique books, crucifixes, ciboria, large vessels such as the ones used in religious ceremonies, small daggers, glasses, combs, board games, rings, brooches, silver candlesticks, mirrors, objects that sparkled even in the dim light from the lamps above. In one corner stood a tall wooden container, filled with tapestries and rugs, all neatly rolled up and labeled with little white tags. Besides them, the only discordant element in the tidy organization of the room was a series of old boxes and trunks stacked one on top of the other.

"Doña Juana's riches were lost along the way. Some of them were lost on the ships that sank on her first voyage to Flanders and her two voyages back to Spain. The Flemish carted off some of her things when Philippe died. Then her children, Charles, Catalina, and Leonor, plundered the bulk of her jewels even when she was still alive. What we have here is just a minuscule sample of what remained in my family. I haven't been able to determine exactly everything they kept, but look, for example, this is the solid gold crucifix that Juana gave her son Ferdinand"— he pointed—"and there are eight missals with priceless miniatures, tapestries, altarpieces. Did you know that back then they calculated what altarpieces were worth not by the painter's skill but by how much gold they contained?"

Manuel went up to a long, low piece of furniture with vertical dividers and pulled out paintings depicting religious scenes: the Nativity, the Annunciation, the Adoration of the Magi. He said they'd been painted by Flemish masters: Van der Weyden, Memling. Priceless.

I wandered back and forth, incredulous, drinking up everything with my eyes, fascinated. To be amid the objects that at one time had been a part of Juana's daily life was like seeing the scattered pieces of a loved one's existence after her painful, tragic death. I imagined her hands handling these utensils, the pressure of her fingers around a glass or a crucifix, the sweat of her palms. It was as if memories became condensed, giving me a feel for visions I had only partially imagined, making them present, palpable.

I'd say that lingering among Juana's belongings, I felt my identification with her reach a level that even to me bordered on hallucination. I felt as if I was her returned to life, revisiting her lost past. My body got chilled and I shivered, apprehensive, looking at Manuel, wondering whether he carried with him his family's cruel streak.

He had no idea of my frame of mind. He was rummaging around in drawers, looking for the nativity scene, I guess. Suddenly he pulled out a photo album.

"Look what we have here!! Family pictures. Let's take them down to the library. Let me show them to you." He handed me the leather-bound album and kept fumbling around, moving things back and forth.

I think I grabbed onto the picture album in the hopes that looking at more modern family members would allow me to break the inexplicable, powerful spell that had me confused between reality and imagination. I sat on a leather armchair that was flanked by different kinds of tables and opened the album. It was filled with Denia family pictures. I recognized them by their coloring. Thin, well-dressed men and women, the women wearing coquettish feathered hats, from the early twentieth century, or perhaps the end of the nineteenth. It was hard to know for sure. I wondered if there would be a picture of Manuel's mother. I flicked through the pages and came to a series of pictures of the house. There was one of the third floor, of the very same room we were in. Águeda had said it was her father's study. I guessed he must be the man with the eye patch sitting behind the desk, wearing a suit and bow tie. The study with its tall wood panneling looked very classy. My mind, with no particular intent, began to supersimpose the previous layout of the room to the current one, trying to place where this or that would have been. I noticed the absence of two windows that, in the photograph, could be seen behind Manuel's grandfather. It was puzzling. Those windows were nonexistent in the present-day room, there wasn't even a trace, as is usually the case when windows are sealed over. Surely you'd be able to see some sign of them on the wall, I thought. Instead, the room seemed smaller, as if it had been shrunk by a feat of magic.

"This room used to be bigger when your grandfather was alive, wasn't it?"

"I don't think so. Why do you ask?"

"Because of this picture. It seems there were two more windows in this room."

"It seems we found the nativity scene," he exclaimed. I got up, photo album in hand, and walked over to him.

He was taking the little figurines out of their protective straw packing and showing me the sixteenth-century Castilian-style, polychrome religious images. I put the photo album down on a table and sat down to admire them one by one. They were gorgeous. Fine, angelic faces, sweet, pious expressions in their glass eyes, rich satin and velvet gowns embroidered with gold thread. There was the Virgin Mary, St. Joseph, baby Jesus, the mule, the ox, and the manger. Afterward, I helped him repack everything back in the box, since he said it would be easier to carry it downstairs.

Finally we turned out the light, Manuel locked the door, and we took the box down with us, along with the photo album.

For Christmas Eve dinner, his Aunt Águeda announced that she'd prepare roast leg of lamb, trout mousse, and the traditional Christmas almond *turrón* for dessert. She and Manuel would go shopping so that we could also have some champagne along with caviar, Serrano ham, Manchego cheese, and I don't know what else before dinner. I'd stay home to set the table, complete with tablecloth, candles, and the silverware that Águeda had polished. Excited at the prospect, I said good-bye and planned to get down to work. I don't remember exactly what I was doing when I heard the alarm system that locked the house at night start up. It was a sound that always scared the daylights out of me, the sound of all those antiques being sealed, lock, stock, and barrel, in an airtight vault. I jumped, as I always did, and then realized that they had left, and I was locked up with their treasures. I ran to the kitchen door and tried to open it. It wouldn't budge. Nor would any of the windows or other doors I tried. Breaking into a sweat, I told myself to calm down and not lose my cool, that Manuel and his aunt wouldn't be gone long. Getting hysterical wouldn't do me any good. But I couldn't calm down. I was panting, and I knew I'd hyperventilate if I took in more oxygen than my lungs could process, but I couldn't stop. I remembered there was a girl who fainted a lot at school, and Mother Luisa used to put a paper bag over her mouth. So I got a paper bag and started breathing into it. I couldn't understand why they had thought it was necessary to leave me shut up under lock and key inside that big old house. What if something happened to them and they couldn't come back? What if a short circuit started a fire while they were gone? The electric wiring in that house was ancient and dysfunctional. In the kitchen, you couldn't use the toaster if someone was running hot water. The circuits were always getting overloaded. Even my hair dryer was a problem. When I used it at night, it made the lights flicker. "Old houses have their ticks, child," the aunt would say, undisturbed.

I looked out the window. The winter garden was laid bare, lifeless, full of withered, dry leaves. On the ground, the shadow of the naked trunk of the chestnut tree with its branches spread out looked like a deformed monster lurching toward the house. It was a sunny day, at least, and that consoled me somewhat. Suddenly, my willing confinement was forcefully imposed on me. They'll be right back, they'll be right back, I kept thinking. Better to convince myself nothing dramatic was about to take place. The Denias were going to return in a few hours. There wasn't going to be a fire. I had to calm down. I went to the kitchen and drank a glass of wine. It did me good, warmed me up. My cheeks were burning.

Slightly more composed, I was suddenly possessed by the ridiculous fear that I might bump into Philippe the Handsome's ghost wandering about the house. You can't be such a fool! I told myself repeatedly. Philippe is in Granada! And I recalled my trip to the mausoleum and the glib tour guide who explained the sculptor Domenico Fancelli's intention in making the head of Philippe's effigy—in contrast to Juana's—barely make an indent on the marble pillow where both their heads lay. "As you can see, he was an airhead!" he had exclaimed when someone commented on it. I decided to go into the library, but when I was halfway there, my feet took me to Manuel's room instead. I started humming to block out the silence. I didn't want to think about Juana, or about the fact that I had just been locked up by her jailers' descendants. The house in *Jane Eyre*, Thornfield, with the crazy lady in the attic, was also creeping into my fears. What if I suddenly heard someone cackle? What if there was another girl like me locked up in the room that I suspected lay at the top of the stairs? I thought how easy it was to go crazy, how narrow the margin between sanity and insanity. I felt my eyes widen, bulging out of their sockets, barely blinking, my mouth parched, dry. I don't know what I was expecting to find in Manuel's room. His bed was made. Books were piled on his nightstand. One was a medical book, with a scrap of paper marking the place where his reading had stopped. Then there was Homer, and Dante's *Purgatory*. I opened his dresser drawers. Socks, underwear, sweaters his Aunt Águeda had knitted. Lots of them. Way too many. Instinctively, I smelled them. Clean smelling. His shirts were hanging in the armoire. I went into the bathroom and opened the medicine cabinet. Cologne, shaving cream. I went back to the bed and sat down. I was trying to find something, anything, to fix my attention on. I picked up the medical book and opened to the page that was marked. It was a gynecological section. There was a part underlined in pencil, with a little asterisk beside a word in bold. *Pseudocyesis.* I read:

> *False or imaginary pregnancy, usually associated with a strong desire to procreate. Though conception has not taken place, menstrual periods cease, the abdomen becomes enlarged, breasts swell and secrete milk, simulating a genuine pregnancy. The uterus and*

cervix may also show characteristic signs and urine tests may give a false-positive. In some cases, women report feeling fetal movements. Those suffering from pseudocyesis may be so convinced of their pregnancy that they fall into a deep depression on realizing no birth will take place. It has been suggested that depression can sometimes alter the activity of the pituitary gland to such an extent that it causes hormonal changes that mimic those occurring during genuine pregnancies. Both Mary Tudor and Isabel de Valois, the second and third wives of Philippe II of Spain, suffered from the condition.

I reread the paragraph countless times. Then I closed the book and left Manuel's room. I didn't want to touch my belly, but I did. I felt the slight bulge that I had taken to stroking, because it promised an end to my orphanage, one achieved by my own means, because in the end that was how I'd resolved the issue of whether to let it live or free myself from it. My choice not to have an abortion, more than fear or guilt, was based on a feeling of complicity with that tiny creature that—still in its larval state and more aquatic than mammalian—was a biological tie to another human being, my only family. But just reading a simple paragraph in a medical textbook was enough for my bubble to burst. Was Manuel afraid this might be my case, or did he think that was all it was?

I hadn't fully recovered when I heard them return. I heard the voices along with the sound of the locks being released.

I WENT TO THEM AND TOLD THEM I NEVER AGAIN WANTED TO BE left locked up in there. Never, never again, I repeated. I had never been so scared in my whole life.

"But it was for your own safety, child. Did you think we were going to leave you here alone with no protection? How could that scare you, after all those years in a convent?" asked Águeda.

"I hope you didn't think we were imprisoning you, like Juana," Manuel said, smiling.

Nothing more was said. I helped them unpack the food. The aunt pulled out Christmas puddings, candy, chocolates, chatting away about how much she was looking forward to preparing a proper Christmas Eve supper, one that would make me forget all those Christmases I had spent alone in Málaga. Although my irritation slowly wore off, I was left with an empty feeling down inside. And yet, if it was true, if my pregnancy was false, imaginary, pseudocyesis or whatever it was called, everything could revert to the way it had been. I would regain my freedom, even if it meant I would go back to being alone.

Manuel suggested that for Christmas Eve dinner I wear Juana's red velvet gown with the black front panel, and even managed to get Águeda to agree to lend him the gold crucifix locked up with all the treasures upstairs. When I saw myself in the mirror—my hair pulled back, wearing a gold-trimmed headdress—I was astounded at how much I resembled Juana's portraits. Dressing up like that was a concession to my hosts' obsession, but that night I didn't care. I preferred to feel like a princess or a queen rather than an orphan. I preferred Juana's ghost over the many other ghosts that stalked me, determined to prove, perhaps even through what was going on in my womb, how deceptive reality could be.

During dinner, as Águeda and Manuel chatted away, reminiscing and stirring up innocuous or pleasant memories, I debated whether Manuel's refusal to take a urine sample to the lab reflected his suspicion that I might be suffering from a false pregnancy. But then, why bother to claim he was so certain I was pregnant as to dismiss the need to confirm it with a scientific test? It didn't make any sense, the logic was beyond me. I shouldn't have champagne, they said, it would be best if I had fruit juice at dinner, given my state, but I insisted on having a glass of champagne. I didn't finish it, though, plagued by new doubts. What if Manuel had just come across that description while he was reading up on pregnancy? The asterisk might just have been his way of acknowledging his surprise. Maybe he wasn't aware cases like that even existed. It didn't mean he thought it was my case. At some point, watching the two of them eat and laugh, I felt ashamed at having felt they could be so mean as to want to imprison me, and I was relieved they had no way of ever discovering my private conjectures. Dread gave way to my urgency to love them with that youthful energy that constantly tries to make reality match wishful thinking.

When it was time to say good night and go to bed, I hugged Águeda. Manuel got into my bed that night, and when I told him again how frightened I'd been when I heard the locks click into place that morning, he looked at me flirtatiously, imitating my little-girl pout very seductively. Now, you're not identifying a little *too* strongly with Juana, are you? he wanted to know. I ended up laughing at myself. I was going to ask him about the book in his room, but then I decided not to. After all, I couldn't just say that I'd been in there, rummaging through his drawers, looking for proof that I was his only star pupil. We made love languidly, almost lazily, taking our time to cuddle each other like a pair of vulnerable children that quickly evolve into felines grabbing and going at each other in a passionate contest. My waist was hardly wider, although it was losing its definition slowly but surely. My breasts, on the other hand, were undeniably bigger. And my nipples darker, like eclipsing suns. On the bed, next to Manuel's light skin, mine looked like brown sugar. I told him I wanted to go ahead with the urine test right after Christmas.

Manuel went to his room to get cigarettes and a snifter of cognac. He came back barefoot, wearing sweatpants, and laid on the divan. I stayed in bed, curled up under the blanket. He had been thinking about the picture of the room on the third floor, he said. He blew the smoke from his cigarrette, making rings in the air. It was intriguing, he admitted.

"Do you realize that nobody outside of our family has ever been up there? You're the only one. That's precisely why I find your observation bewildering. You know, once you get used to your surroundings you don't even notice the obvious. Remember how I told you about Juana's trunk, the one that disappeared without a trace? My mother, who I met furtively a few times when I was a teenager, told me that there was evidence that proved that Juana had not been mad, but that our family hid it, fearing it would discredit them—not so much because of what had taken place in the distant past but for preventing the information from becoming public domain. It tends to happen with lies and secrets. Keeping a secret can end up becoming a worse shame than the secret itself. My mother used to draw a parallel between that secret and the one related to my birth, but the relationship between the two always escaped me. Both were family secrets, I guess. Because until I turned thirteen, I was led to believe that Águeda had adopted me from an underprivileged family. Only when my grandfather died did she come clean and reveal to me that my mother was her sister." Manuel took a sip of cognac.

I was befuddled. I didn't know what to say. I felt sorry for Manuel.

"A strange family you have. Maybe all families are strange, full of secrets."

"The trunk I was telling you about disappeared eight days before Juana died. There was such an uproar when they found out it was missing. A papal nuncio went as far as writing a bull of excommunication for whoever had dared to take or destroy it, a thing I find rather odd. For all I know, once Juana died my ancestors might have feared the wrath of God. Maybe I'm just speculating and the trunk no longer exists, but it is a sort of archaeologist's dream for me. I picture myself discovering it, opening it, reading all the documents inside."

"What kind of documents do you imagine?"

"Diaries, letters, accounts. I sometimes imagine that my intimate understanding of Juana comes from knowing that if I were to read all those papers, they would resemble the reality you and I have been weaving together. It is as if I had already read them. I imagine this story is the same Juana would have written, the same that has been kept hidden, waiting for someone to come along and discover it, so that justice can be done to the kingdom of her memory."

WHEN I WOKE UP AND WENT DOWN TO THE KITCHEN FOR BREAKFAST, all I found were Manuel and Águeda's coffee cups in the sink. It was late, almost eleven o'clock. I got scared for a minute, thinking they might have locked me in again. But when I tried the door to the garden, it opened right away, much to my relief. The neighbors could see into the backyard from their windows, but it was sunny, and the fresh air was too tempting for me to resist. Wearing my slippers, clutching my flannel robe tightly across my chest, I went down the two or three steps between me and the gravel path that led to the fountain under the chestnut tree. It was cold, but the blue sky was dotted here and there by white, puffy, clouds. It was a beautiful, luminous day. I rushed out to the fountain and back, like an inmate escaping into the prison yard. When I got back, just as I closed the door, I felt Manuel behind me. He took my hands. "You're going to catch cold," he said, obviously annoyed. Nothing would come of it, I said. It had been just a brisk outing to get a breath of fresh air.

"This isn't child's play, Lucía. You and I have to be careful, or we could put my aunt in a very awkward position. I don't think that's how she deserves to be repaid for all the hospitality she's shown you."

I didn't answer. I thought he was being overzealous, but I also felt guilty. I filled the teakettle with water and put it on to boil.

"I'm sorry, Manuel. It won't happen again."

"Come to the library after you change your dress."

Manuel knew exactly how to make me feel silly and small. Changing the tone of his voice and his gestures, he could, in an instant, establish a distance between us, and I could not rest easy until I felt I was back in his grace—which could happen in the same inexplicable manner: all of a sudden he would be affectionate and gentle again. Occasionally he remained distant for long stretches, leaving me to wonder whether he was silently cursing the day he met me. Back at school I had already noticed these sudden changes, but now that we saw each other every day, I became aware that this behavior pattern for some strange reason made me docile, submissive.

I took a bath, got dressed, and rushed down to the library. Then I became Juana again, this time imprisoned in Tordesillas.

CHAPTER 24

On February 14, 1509, three hours before dawn, my father stormed into my room in Arcos, shouting. Imperious and harsh—as he was in my worst childhood memories—he made me scurry out of bed and forced me to depart for Tordesillas.

Clearly, he'd counted on taking me by surprise. How could I be anything but surprised by that peremptory order that shook me from a deep, predawn slumber and forced me to be on my way? I assumed the plague was at our doorstep or that a rebellion had broken out and our lives were in danger. Thinking of Catalina's safety, hoodwinked by the joy of seeing little Ferdinand arrive with his grandfather, I agreed to proceed to the move, caught up in the urgency of those scampering around me, packing and rushing off with furniture, tapestries, and curtains.

By the time I reached the patio, the horse-drawn carriage was already there, waiting with Philippe's coffin, the torchbearers, and the clerics from my retinue. Doña María de Ulloa, still wiping the sleep from her eyes, carried Catalina, who was frightened and crying. I took my daughter in my arms and sat her on my horse, Galán, with me. And then, under my father's personal vigilance, our long procession hauled out. The villagers came out to wave me off, many still wearing nightshirts beneath their jackets. We made slow progress through the rugged Castilian plains, dotted here and there with dark pinelands where we stopped to rest. Flocks of birds would suddenly take flight above us, flying to and from the Duero River, whose rushing song began to be heard in the distance. I can distinctly recall the silhouette of the Convent of Santa Clara, to the right of the stone bridge we crossed as we entered Tordesillas. Before it housed the cloistered nuns, the convent had been a beautiful palace, built by Alfonso XI to commemorate the battle of Salado. Pedro the Cruel had lived there his romance with María de Padilla. When she died, the king ordered his daughter Beatriz to bequeath it to the Santa Clara nuns. Philippe and I had visited it on our first trip to Spain. We'd sat beneath the Mudejar chapel's gold-plated ceiling, and even Philippe had to admit that no church in all of Flanders boasted such magnificent coffering. Neither he nor I could have know then that his body would lay beneath it for sixteen years.

To the left of the village, behind the walls, I saw the Church of San Antolín and the exterior corridor linking it to the palace, with the charming, conical-roofed tower at the end of it. From there most certainly one would be able to see the wide river, slithering like a green snake among the tall reeds on the banks. Storks rested atop other towers in the distance; their nests looked like gray balls of yarn balanced precariously on the tall domes and roofs of the village.

Finally we reached the palace, followed by the watchful eyes of the villagers who came out to get a look of the strange procession that, in more ways than one, would alter their lives. I waved left and right, fully awake now, and frightened. I was beginning to realize that I could expect nothing good from such a hurried relocation. The Palace of Tordesillas was medium size. When it was first built by Enrique III, it must have been comfortable and majestic, but since that time it had fallen into disuse and was almost entirely unfurnished. The night Philippe and I spent there it had seemed sad and neglected to me: salons and ballrooms surrendered to age and decrepitude. It never occurred to me that this place would be my final destination. I thought it was just another move. I remembered my father mentioning that the tiny village of Arcos, where I had lived for eighteen months, could no longer accommodate the court.

Our procession went first to the Convent of Santa Clara to deposit Philippe's body in the chapel. The sisters had obviously been informed of our arrival, because the prioress was waiting for us and the cloistered nuns could be seen behind the trellis where they heard mass. Once inside the central nave of the church, I ordered that every candle be lit and stayed there for quite some time, keeping vigil over my loved one. Catalina and Ferdinand dozed beside me, sprawled out on the chapel benches. "Wait here," my father said, leaving me in the care of Doña María de Ulloa. A deep fatigue had taken hold of my bones. I figured that having Ferdinand back had released me of the anguish and rage I had carried within for so many months. My body needed to rest. With no strength left, I submitted to whatever was to come. As long as I had my children by my side, anyplace would do. Maybe Tordesillas, near Valladolid, was actually a good place to set up residence. While prayers for the dead were being said for Philippe, while the nuns sang the Dies Irae, I drifted off to sleep. I foresaw long, monotonous days in Tordesillas, unaware that this would be my final resting place, the last stop in my pilgrimage both through Spain and through life.

My father departed, leaving me settled down in the palace. It wasn't long before I realized I was being held prisoner. At first I had been occupied furnishing the palace to make it more inviting, hanging tapestries on the walls to make it warmer. I don't recall exactly when it was that I noticed that my maids, Anastasia, María, and Cornelia, were restless, talking among themselves in whispers and exchanging sorry looks. I called them over to inquire the reason for their distress. Teary eyed, Cornelia confided that she had overheard a conversation between two members of the Espinosa Royal Mounted guards, who according to her, were commenting that they had received orders from Mosen Luis Ferrer—the palace governor designated by my father—to prevent me by any means from going out of the palace. If I wanted to go to church, I should use the palace corridor that led to San Antolín; if I chose to visit Philippe's body, they were to accompany me and form a human wall around me so that no one could see or approach me. Because, he had told them: "The queen is mad and no one must know about it." Cornelia finished, weeping and distraught at having to bring me such news.

I ordered my maidens and Doña María to get me ready and prepare themselves to go out for a stroll in the village. But then, that small man, Mosen Luis Ferrer, came before me. He was short, his chest puffed up with the effort of keeping himself erect, hoping, I guess, to compensate with his posture what he lacked in stature. His round head was nearly bald, but he had a small, well-cared-for beard, many rings on his fingers, and impeccable clothes. Though I had seen him often, I had rarely addressed him. His beady eyes sparkled defiantly when he told me that under express orders of King Ferdinand, my father, I was not to leave the palace, as the plague was spreading through neighboring villages.

"And how is it that no one but yourself has mentioned the plague?"

"Your Majesty, your illustrious father thought it wise not to divulge the information so that you might not worry and panic not spread through court, but I tell you that the palace is surrounded by the plague like an island by water. For your own good, you must stay within its walls."

I suspected it was simply a stratagem to keep me isolated. And indeed it was. The plague came around every time I attempted to get out. At times I thought I had no option but to come to terms with that confinement: I read, meditated, took care of my children. Other times I would be seized by despair and lash out like a caged animal, pouncing against everybody, including myself. I would throw myself on the floor and refuse to eat, to bathe. My utter impotence would keep me crying day and night and the hatred for my father overwhelmed me, obscuring my reason and gnawing my entrails.

But it wasn't just my freedom they disposed of. My son Ferdinand was taken from me too, soon after that. I had no way of knowing to what extremes their hostility and desire to silence me would take them. Like a cave, the palace was populated by equivocal shadows. A new, childlike fear swept over me, keeping me constantly on edge. I arranged for Catalina to sleep in a room that could only be reached by crossing mine. Nights found me closed up in my quarters with her, fearing she would also be snatched away from me.

"WHILE IN TORDESILLAS, JUANA WAS BEING THRUST INTO A WEB OF deceits aimed at making her accept a false reality, King Ferdinand unencumbered and holding the reins of both Castile and Aragon applied himself to the conquest of Europe," said Manuel, bringing me out of my reverie. I threw my head back against the sofa and listened to him, staring at the afternoon light, unable to tear myself away from the image of Juana embracing Catalina, besieged on all sides.

"A square patch of blue can contain the entire sky" a mad poet from my country once wrote from a cell that had just one small window.

"After two years of plotting and forging alliances, Ferdinand had consolidated his power in Naples and Castile. His troops marched into Navarre and finally separated it from France, giving him control over the Pyrenees pass."

"And he didn't even go back and visit his daughter?"

"In 1509, Fernando signed a pact with Maximilian that named him legitimate guardian and governor of Juana's 'goods and her person.' Although the document recognized her as queen, it stripped her of her royal authority by claiming she was unqualified to exercise it. Once his position was guaranteed, Ferdinand came to visit in 1510, accompanied by the constable and admiral of Castile, the Dukes of Medina-Sidonia and of Alba, the Marquis of Denia, archbishop Santiago, and Emperor Maximilian's guests. He snuck into her chambers because Mosen Luis Ferrer had told him that Juana was going through one of her rebellious stages, refusing to eat, change clothes, or leave her rooms. He wanted everyone to see her in that state, to justify his position as regent. Juana was outraged when she realized what he'd done and insisted that the visitors stay long enough for them to see her behave as the queen she was. She sent for her royal gowns, got changed, and appeared before them again, but the damage was already done. The nobles and ambassadors had seen her 'weak and disheveled.' It would be nearly impossible for them to see that her lack of personal hygiene was a form of protest, a way of acting out against the manner in which Ferrer dealt with her. It's quite well known that he went so far as to punish her physically—what they called 'giving the lash'—under the pretext that it was the only way to make her eat and thus save her life."

"Didn't Juana have any way to tell someone what was happening?"

"The whole purpose of her incarceration was to keep her from being able to contact anyone. Four of her ladies-in-waiting, Francisca, Isabel, Violante, and Margarita, were relatives of Ferrer. The rest of her household was loyal to Ferdinand and his governor. They were, that is, until Ferdinand died. It's quite revealing that her father would go to such lengths just to isolate a 'madwoman,' don't you think? That he felt the need to constantly restate her incapacity to rule. But the constraints did result in her isolation, which was quite effective. Mosen Luis Ferrer, and later the Marquis of Denia, even refused to allow her to go to the church using the high corridor outside of the palace that led to San Antolín. They feared she might shout from there down to the people going by. Tell me, how would you have broken through such a degree of isolation?"

"I would write, perhaps; I would keep a record of everything that was happening to me in the hopes of delivering it to someone who would make it public or would use it to set me free. I would remember that under Philippe's orders, Martín de Moxica wrote a log that my father later used to get the Cortes to cede him rule of the kingdom. I certainly wouldn't resign myself and do nothing. It was not in Juana's character to silently tolerate abuse."

"You see? I was right," Manuel cried triumphantly, grinning and looking smug. "You are like her. You and Juana, two young women, centuries apart, are very much alike."

AH! THE COUNTLESS HUMILIATIONS I SUFFERED AT THE PALACE IN Tordesillas from the time of my arrival in 1509! It was rage that provided me the strength not to submit. I learned to be alone with myself, to speak only to Catalina and Augustina, my washerwoman. When Mosen Luis Ferrer's rudeness and cruelty became intolerable, I would infuriate him by refusing to eat. I knew that my father needed me alive to carry out his plans. If I died, his regency was over. The Flemish would seize Castile and Aragon from him, because Germaine's youth had not granted her the fertility she so envied of me. Ferdinand had not been able to produce the heir he so longed for. The baby born in May lived only a few hours. He even brought his new wife to Tordesillas once, hoping I would reveal to her the secret of my fecundity. I was kind to her, for she was just a child, but I made sure she knew that nothing other than the ardor and zeal of my love had made my womb bear fruit. And what fiery passion could she know, when she was forced to lie with an old man who wheezed and snored? Find yourself a lover, I was tempted to say. Which she did later on. I found out. She had a daughter, Isabel, from my son, Charles.

Desperate at seeing that my strength did not wane, one fine day Mosen Luis Ferrer dared to do the unthinkable. Six soldiers came and took me from my rooms to the palace cellars, dragging me along like a lunatic. I fought them all the way, kicking and screaming, but finally they ripped off my shift. A hooded man lashed me with a whip. I did not cry as the leather tore through my flesh. I slipped away in my mind, as I often did, recalling the music in my life, the birth of my children, my love for Philippe. My back crackled. I felt as if a pack of wildcats were ripping me to shreds. But I made not a sound. Once I was alone, though, oh how I wept! The image of my mother flashed before me, and I saw her, sobbing also in her queen's eternity, separated from her children. Not even she, hard as she was, would have wished this upon me. Wretched destiny of ours: strong women feared by men! They had to imprison us, humiliate us, beat us, to mask the terror we inspired in them and feel like kings!

Those were years of constant rebellion. Years I held on, recording my hardships, years I harbored vengeful dreams that belied my Christian upbringing. At least my rooms overlooked the Duero, and the sight of those waters flowing out to sea soothed my soul. They talked of moving me to another wing of the palace, allegedly to protect me from the cold and the elements, but it was from men, not the forces of nature from which I needed protection. Neither rain, lightning, nor blizzard caused me the sufferings they did. Catalina and I went about in rags. Dressed like the most destitute of my vassals, my little girl ran around in a leather doublet while I wore what looked like a nun's habit made of coarse wool. But my daughter and I had our own secret world. I told her tales of my life as if it had been what I had wanted it to be. These fantasies amused her. She'd beg me to tell the same stories over and over. I even described the New World for her as if I'd seen it. I spoke of great jungles full of strange foreign trees, populated by flocks of brightly colored birds. I described the bare-breasted Indians and their glittering gold. Mosen Luis Ferrer could never guess how free we were in the confines of my room! A window overlooking the river was enough for us to sail the open seas and to discover worlds that only Catalina and I would ever know.

My father died on January 23, 1516. I had been in Tordesillas for seven years without seeing a calendar, or counting the weeks or months, because seeing all that time mount up was too distressing. But I recall that day perfectly. I woke to a great ruckus, the whole town congregated in the little plaza beneath my window, clamoring for Mosen Luis Ferrer to be dismissed and punished. Doña Juana, Doña Juana! Anastasia exclaimed joyfully. They're running him off! I ran to the tower of San Antolín, and there I saw him being led off by a scornful crowd. Someone said that my father had died, but then someone else denied it. I presumed it had to be something serious for people to have dared to go after Ferrer, considering the rumors everybody had heard of how dreadfully he treated Catalina and me, but my confessor assured me that although my father was ill, he was still alive. Four years would go by before I finally found out the truth. That day, I closed my eyes for a moment, suddenly blinded by a surge of tears at the thought that it could be true. Oh, Juana, how easily you cry! I said to myself. I didn't cry anymore. I felt sheltered by the commoners who had come out in my defense.

Cisneros, who despised me, was kind enough to name Don Hernán, the Duke of Estrada, as head of my household. He was a handsome older man, Don Hernán, and from the moment he laid eyes on me he never once doubted neither my strength of character, nor the clarity of my thoughts. I could have easily made him my lover. I knew that my eyes, my voice got under his skin. The two of us spoke as I had never before spoken to any man or woman. For two years, we were like Abelard and Héloïse, and my wrath and outrage subsided. But my passion was never rekindled. Strange, how one could come to this, to become a stranger to the pleasures of the body. Now only my mind brought me joy. Neither baths, nor perfumes, nor the feel of satin and velvet could arouse my flesh. My fire had been extinguished, and the carbon of my ashes had hardened into diamond. Sometimes I was saddened to recall the sensations my sex and my breasts had given me, but the clarity of my mind made up for my lack of desire. Seen from my barren outlook the world was like amber in which vestiges of my previous life were frozen. It was a prism allowing me to see the spikes, the multiplicity of human existence, the complexity of the stories we tell one another.

Don Hernán took pity on my little Catalina and ordered a large window to be opened in her small room. My daughter throws coins down to the children of Tordesillas, who play in the plaza below, so that she can watch them when they return every day. From here, every afternoon, I can hear her arbitrate their games and races and I marvel at the boundless fantasies of her childhood. Of course, Don Hernán could actually let her go out to play, but he's a man. He fears the others. He is kind, but his kindness doesn't go that far.

CHAPTER 25

A few days after Christmas, Manuel took my urine sample to the lab in a little cup, and a few days after that he came back and told me that the results were positive, just as he'd suspected. I was absolutely overjoyed for one fleeting moment, and then almost immediately wracked by new doubts. My mind surged back and forth, rising into high tides of maternal emotion and then ebbing into a melancholic state, resigned, with no illusions.

The week between Christmas and New Year's, I started to hear noises upstairs. The sound of Águeda setting the security system, locks clicking into place, was scary enough, but these new sounds—creaking and footsteps—kept me awake at night. My guess was that Manuel was either looking for the windows that appeared in the photo of his grandfather's study or else in search of Juana's trunk. In the mornings he'd get up late, bags under his eyes; plus he'd stopped coming into my room at night after his aunt went to bed. Just seeing his expression when he came down to breakfast was enough to tell me that his hunt was not proving fruitful. I would have liked to go with him, but I chose to feign ignorance. I couldn't force him to include me. To unveil that mystery was his prerogative.

The air in the Denia house was as thick and heavy with tension as it is before a tropical storm. Águeda flitted around the rooms with nervous energy. From the library I could hear her cleaning doggedly, busying herself here and there with her ever-present feather duster. She went up to the third floor a lot, muttering to herself as she wandered from one room to another, a trail of unintelligible sounds in her wake. I suspected she was troubled because her nephew was on the trail of secrets she'd rather not stir up. Their obsession with history, the house, and everything in it bordered on the pathological, but I realized that even I felt an incomprehensible degree of fascination. I was intrigued by the mystery and electrified at the idea of unraveling it. I pictured myself taking part in a historic discovery that would be all over the headlines as soon as word got out. I pictured what it would be like to clear the hazy aura of madness that enshrouded Juana's image, to show her to the world as I could see her, now that I had grown so close to her and could fathom what she must have felt. Given that I never went out, and only breathed the entranced air of the house and its possessions, I had no reality to curb my imagination. On the stairs and in the halls, I imagined that I heard a little girl's footsteps following me. I imagined little Catalina, dressed in a coarse woolen sack dress, looking for someone to play with her in the gray rooms of that cold, lonely house on dark afternoons.

On New Year's Eve we ate dinner early. The Denias weren't in the habit of waiting up for midnight with the traditional twelve grapes and revelry. Manuel did make one concession to festivity, though, bringing out an almond tart. He was serving it when Águeda, in an unexpectedly sharp tone, asked when I was supposed to go back to school. Her demeanor and her cold stare startled me. The dry tart got stuck in my throat.

"January 7."

"Well, that's right around the corner. We'll have to decide what we're going to tell the nuns when they come looking for you."

"Auntie," Manuel said parsimoniously, "we'll say that she left here to go back to the convent, that we put her in a taxi and haven't heard back from her."

"Easier said than done. They'll investigate. We'll be the chief suspects in her 'disappearance.' I hope you've thought well and hard about this."

"Well, I thought we were all on the same page so far."

"Yes, I was. But the more I think about it, the more complicated it gets. I don't know if it's such a good idea for her to write those letters."

"I'm a little worried about that part too," I admitted. "The other option is for me to go to New York. That's where Isis lives. You know, my mother's friend; I've told you about her."

"You're not going anywhere," Manuel said, suddenly stern. "And that's the end of this conversation. Águeda, you and I will discuss this later."

Nothing else was said. Águeda looked down and jabbed a fork violently into her crust. Manuel seemed to possess some sort of bizarre psychological ability to dominate her. All he had to do was raise his voice or get his feathers ruffled and look like he was ready for a cockfight and she—that self-confident, secure woman—would suddenly shrivel up, reduced to a powerless, frail old lady. Her wrath was visible only in her eyes. It scared me to see her looking at Manuel that way. Her pupils sparkled with a caustic, purple, pained glimmer.

I couldn't eat any more. I felt the apple of good and evil stuck in my throat. I stayed down in the library while Manuel went upstairs to talk to his Aunt Águeda.

In the old Denia palace, with its austere, quadrangular Castilian architecture, it was impossible to overhear their argument. I caught snatches of random words and the angry tone. I covered my ears with a sofa cushion. I thought that Águeda must finally be showing what she'd felt all along. It hadn't made any sense for her to be so calm and blasé about everything, given what had happened. To a certain point, I was relieved to see her behaving like a normal aunt. But then, her discomfort also made me face up to the precarious reality I had been avoiding by spending all my time with Juana and her ghosts. I felt a painful, empty feeling in my stomach.

The argument ended suddenly, and at almost the same instant Manuel walked into the library, looking flustered. He strode over to the table where he kept the cognac and poured himself a glass, downing it in one gulp.

"Manuel, Águeda's right. It would be better if I went to New York before they start searching for me. The other plan is really starting to seem ludicrous."

"I said no. You're not going anywhere," he declared categorically, pouring himself another glass.

"But—"

"But nothing. Let me handle this. I know what I'm doing. Águeda will get over it. Believe me, I know what I am saying. She's jealous, that's all. She's always resented having to share me with other women. Not even my mother escaped her. But she'll get over it. Relax. I'll tell you about the Denias. This is a good time for it. Go get changed, and put on the black dress."

✳ IT PAINS ME TO SAY IT, BUT THE PROCESS THAT TURNED MY CON-finement into a persistant, inconsolable torment began when my son charles and Daughter Leonor came to Tordesillas, on November 4, 1517. I'd been there nine years. The last few had been quite peaceful, thanks to Don Hernán. On November 6—my birthday—I awoke just like any other day. I was informed that Guillaume de Croy, Seignior de Chièvres, whom I remembered from Flanders, was here to see me. Not knowing what it was about, I welcomed him without much ceremony. He appeared before me, gushing and reverential, spoke of Charles and Leonor, and asked me if I had any desire to see them. I said of course, there was no need even to ask such a question.

I had no idea they were so close. They'd arrived two days earlier, though I had been told nothing of it. De Chièvres walked over to the door and opened it. Two youths stood before me. The last time I saw Charles and Leonor, he was five and she was seven. Twelve years had passed. Now he was seventeen and she was nineteen. I could see the specter of Philippe in their faces, mixed in with the lost beauty of my younger portraits. I recognized the children who'd been born of our love. They bowed before me. I closed my eyes. Living in a state of delusion, deceived and lied to by everyone, I could not trust my eyes. Are you really my children? I was stupefied, overcome, I devoured them with my eyes. My son had Philippe's face without Philippe's beauty; the face of a tired, lusterless young man. Leonor, on the other hand, looked majestic and had my mother's light skin and blond hair. We sat down to talk. They behaved like the Burgundian prince and princess that they were, both in manner and language, as they hardly spoke a word of Spanish. I spoke to them in French, which surprised them. Every question I asked seemed to leave them aghast, as if they could not quite work out my ability to hold a conversation and were more confused by my sanity than they would have been at finding a deranged madwoman. Leonor laughed easily at several things I said, but Charles showed the same distrust I remembered so well from when I returned from my first trip to Spain and he came with his father to meet me at Blankenburg. Since then, he had never acknowledged me. It saddened me to see him so uncomfortable, so distant. Visiting me was clearly a formality for him, and he made no attempt to hide it. Overcome by the devastating pain of having lost them irrevocably so long ago, I insisted they should go to bed early and rest.

And then I was alone with de Chièvres, Charles's first chamberlain and trusted advisor. He set about very kindly informing me of all the prince's wonderful qualities. It must be a comfort to me, he said, to have a son like him to further the interests of the kingdom. He was of the opinion that I should hurry and abdicate in his favor so that, while I was still alive, he could learn all he needed to know to be a good sovereign. If I gave my royal consent, the Cortes would authorize him to rule with me. I would not oppose it, I said. I presumed my father had agreed, which was reason to rejoice. All I demanded was the respect owed to me as queen: recognition for my royal stature and that he would rule in my name and with me, like my father should have done.

The Cortes imposed eighty-eight conditions before allowing Charles to be king. Three of them were in regard to the governing of my household and the dignity with which I was to be treated, as proprietary queen. Another specified that if God saw fit to return my good health, Charles would step down and allow me to rule. It was this clause that turned him into my enemy.

After Charles, avowed by me, began his rule, his attention turned to his sister Catalina. Everyone around me knew how I loved her. Catalina was my stability, my anchor, she was what kept me afloat. Charles, who'd had a very pampered upbringing with Marguerite of Austria in Malines, was horrified by her modest dress, her games at the window. So he and his advisors hatched a plan to steal her away, to take her from me. And because there was no way to reach her room without crossing mine, they dug a tunnel through the wall and covered it with a tapestry, and then one night they forced Catalina through it, lowering her down onto the street. I reacted as anyone could have expected: I begged for death. I began a radical fast and abandoned myself to the most terrible and inconsolable despair. My servants and Don Hernán must have told Charles about my state. For once, my prayers were answered and my rebellion had a positive result. Three days later, I had Catalina back. She ran to my arms. We both wept. Juana Cuevas, my servant, told me later that the princess had warned her brother, saying that if I became distressed, nothing would stop her from coming back to me.

Catalina returned, but that episode was just the beginning of what was to come.

Just three months after his first visit, Charles withdrew kind Don Hernán, the Duke of Estrada, from my service. In his place, on March 15, 1518, he sent Don Bernardo de Sandoval y Rojas and his wife, Doña Francisca Enríquez, the Marquises of Denia. My peace of mind and body ended the moment Don Hernán walked out the door. When we said our good-byes, I lamented the fact that no one had consulted me. "We are both servants of others, Doña Juana," said the gentle man who, through it all, had attempted to be my friend and had, within the confined space of my captivity, managed to make me feel I was still a woman.

The Denias built a wall of faces, hands, and eyes around me. They forged a barrier of silence and oblivion to cloister me and conceal whatever evidence of my reason could threaten those who would stop at nothing to usurp my reign. Circles of hell, was how I referred to the nooses they used to strangle my voice. And there were three: in the first circle, two women kept guard, one inside and one outside my rooms, day and night, denying me the relief of privacy, the solace I could get from my own unemcumbered self. In the second circle were the twelve women allegedly charged with my care. And beyond them, in the third circle, were the twenty-four *monteros*, elite armed guards, who surrounded me. I was forbidden to go to San Antolín. I was forbidden to attend mass at Santa Clara. The Marquis of Denia, pale, gray-haired, his eyes cold and blue, was the very picture of courteousness. But with every bow, he stabbed me in the back and still expected me to ignore it. Just like Mosen Luis Ferrer, he used the plague or my father's authority to justify my internment.

Why had I gotten it into my head that my father was dead? he once inquired when I expressed my doubts. He was ill, true, but he was laid up at a monastery, spending his days praying to our Lord. I should write to him. He would be so happy to have news from his daughter Juana.

"You write to him, Marquis," I said. "You are his cousin; you write to him. You may give him my regards."

The Denias were despots to my few loyal servants but went to church to display before wooden statuettes the devotion they didn't feel for their fellow human beings. I always considered religious ceremonies to be just public rituals that did little or nothing to ennoble the spirit. Even back in Flanders I was not particularly devoted. But the marquises worried about my soul, and so they arranged for masses to be said inside the palace so that they could force me to worship God and dispense with my need to go out under the sun. I categorically refused to attend these services and I only went to church when they allowed me to walk along the palace's exterior corridor to San Antolín. Once at the tower there, I would go down the spiral staircase to the Aldarete Chapel. I did this more to look at the view than to pay my respects to a God who had forsaken me.

I waged an all-out war against the Denias, using the few arms at my disposal. I lay in wait constantly, so that no one could take me by surprise. But I knew nothing of what went on outside the palace walls, and that was one weapon my jailers could always count on. While I was locked up, rotting away, Spain was being plundered. The riches from America were shipped off to Flanders. Foreigners were appointed to the highest positions of power. A seventeen-year-old boy was named cardinal of Toledo, and Adrian of Utrecht became governor of Castile.

When my son Charles left to be crowned Emperor of the Holy Roman Empire, on May 20, 1520, the people rose up in arms, having wearied of the constant abuse by the Flemish.

Juan de Padilla, a native of Toledo and the son of Don Pedro, one of my most faithful defenders, was the leader of the rebellion. The Santa Junta de las Comunidades, or Holy Assembly of Communities, as the rebels called themselves, said they were rising up "in service to the queen, Doña Juana."

I often sought Denia out to ask him about my children, and the state of my realms. He would become flustered and look uncomfortable. On one occasion I held him six hours, refusing to let him go until he gave me a report, but the man was a liar. To explain why my son was to be crowned emperor he tried to make me believe that my father-in-law Maximilian had abdicated in Charles's favor, as if I could not guess that he had died.

Just two days after this conversation, I found out Denia had ordered that the corridor I used to walk to San Antonlín be sealed off. I ran to berate him and order him to have it reopened. We were quarreling when Bishop Rojas, president of the Council of the Kingdom of Castile, arrived, asking me to sign a decree condemning the Comuneros who had risen in arms.

Denia could not keep me from meeting with the bishop. And it was he, pale and sweaty, fearful of the chaos that had spread like wildfire, who told me that my father had died four years ago. From his lips too I learned that indeed Maximilian had died, and judging by what he said, I gathered that the rebels were up in arms, protesting at the way my son had left Spain's rule in the care of foreigners. The uprising was gaining strength, he said. Unhappy peasants discontent with their lot had joined the rebels.

"Believe me, Bishop," I said, "everything you have said is news to my ears and hard to discern from a dream. No one has told me the truth for sixteen years; I am mistreated by all, and the marquis here is not the first to deceive me."

The bishop looked at the marquis. For the first time in all those years, he was frightened; I saw it on his face and felt overcome with joy, especially when I listened to his contrite attempts to justify himself, claiming he had been forced to lie to me to "cure me of my passions."

✳ I REFUSED TO SIGN THE DECREE THE BISHOP HAD BROUGHT UNTIL I could verify what I'd been told. On August 29, I received the Comunero leaders, Juan de Padilla, Juan Bravo, and Francisco Maldonado. I heard out their grievances and their grounds, and I entrusted them to do what they felt most benefited the interests of the kingdom. It was all so sudden and so overwhelming that I panicked at my own ignorance. My life was so full of falsehood that I doubted my ability to distinguish truth from lies.

In mid-September, an authority from the Santa Junta and the Cortes expelled the Denias and the ladies who kept me locked up. I went out onto the balcony to greet the crowds packed into the plaza in front of the palace. The leaders of the rebellion, and the people themselves, urged me to defy Charles and govern the kingdom on my own, expelling the Flemish and impeding the flow of riches and tithes from Spain.

It was marvelous to feel so much affection coming from people who had never even seen me. But if freedom made me feel light on my feet with joy, doubts weighed me down and paralyzed me. So many years of confinement had turned me into a fearful woman. And what did I know about government anyway? I had spent my whole life defying and despising authority. Who was to say that these men would not imprison me too were I to do what I thought right and not what they wanted me to? I never had any great desire to be queen. I said so more than once. And if it meant warring against my children, I had none at all. I couldn't forget that those who were offering to serve me hated Charles and needed my support to oust him. I needed time, time to think, to discern the truth. Suddenly, an enormous responsibility had been thrown on my lap, one that I had not chosen. I decided to take my time and meanwhile refused to commit and didn't seal or sign anything.

Yet again, nobody understood me. I had scarcely salvaged my desire to dress in a way befitting my rank, the authority to appoint my own household, the freedom to venture outside the walls of the palace, when the Comuneros lost their patience and tried to force me to sign their decrees. They even threatened to starve Catalina and me if I continued stubbornly to wait. Perhaps in the end my fears damned me and I lost the only opportunity I had to change my fate, but I told them again and again that I needed time to heal, time for my mind to clear the fog caused by so many lies and so many tears.

The nobles struck back with renewed vigor and put down the rebellion. A traitor paved the way: Pedro Girón, who took over from loyal Juan de Padilla as commander of the Comunero army. Girón let them through so they could retake Tordesillas. The rebellion lasted only seventy-five days. Between December 5 and 6, Tordesillas surrendered to the royalists.

I awaited the grandees on the palace courtyard, holding Catalina's hand.

One signature of mine would have sufficed to put an end to Charles's power in Spain, but instead of showing me his gratitude, my son didn't even have the courtesy of granting me the quiet freedom I deserved. On the contrary, Charles reinstated the Denias and left them to ride roughshod over me. Vicious and arrogant, fully endorsed by Charles, the Denias came back to run my household. And I did not free myself from them until the day I died.

✳ "UNTIL THE DAY SHE DIED?" I ASKED.

"April 12, 1555. It was Good Friday. Juana was seventy-six years old. She'd been imprisoned in Tordesillas since 1509, when she was twenty-nine. The first Marquis of Denia died. His son, Luis, came after him. But Juana was told that the old man had fallen ill. They never told her the truth. The Denias kept her forever entangled in a web of falsehoods, they forced her to live in an upended world; a world of darkened rooms without windows, populated by hostile faces that mocked her and tormented her mercilessly. She died covered in sores, with gangrene, a rebel to the end, refusing the treatments they offered her, refusing mass and religious ceremonies almost right up until her last day. When she died, the Denias and her children plundered what remained of her treasures. Remember the golden cross you wore on Christmas Eve? Juana always had it with her. It was a gift from her son Ferdinand—probably the only unselfish gift she ever received in Tordesillas—and she loved it dearly. And what did Charles do, knowing how his mother detested the Denias? He gave it to them when she died. Juana must have turned over in her grave."

"What about the trunk?" I asked. "How big was it? Are there any descriptions?"

"When Doña Juana arrived in Tordesillas in 1509, they took a very careful inventory of all her belongings. Eight days before she died, the Denias took another one. During the forty-six years Juana spent there, her treasures dwindled considerably. Her father led the way, robbing her of huge quantities of gold and silver. My ancestors got in on the act too, of course, helping themselves generously. Then her son Charles finished off, absconding with all that was left under the pretext that it was for Catalina's trousseau, since she was to wed the king of Portugal. Just picture it, Lucía: Charles ordered the trunks to be taken from his mother's room while she slept. And then, so she wouldn't realize what he'd done, he had them filled with bricks. But Juana figured out what had happened. She made them open one of the trunks and saw the bricks. And rather than accuse her servants, she realized who had really robbed her and said that she hoped her children would enjoy themselves. Juana's classy response shamed Charles. Embarrassed, he ordered that nothing else be touched, and he kept his word for a year. But after that, he started raiding Juana's things from Tordesillas again. Every time he visited his mother—which was not very often—he left with everything he could get his hands on that seemed valuable, or anything his wife Isabel wanted. But the trunk in question disappeared eight days before she died. It was made in Flanders, small and rectangular with a gold lock and rose-colored engravings. There are statements from Juana's washerwoman Catalina Redonda, her two sisters, Marina, Doña Francisca de Alba, and other servants, all insisting that she always kept it carefully hidden in a place that only she had access to. They said that whenever the queen got it out, she'd make her ladies and servants turn their backs so they couldn't see what it held."

"She must have been afraid they'd steal the few jewels she had left," I said. "What makes you think it held documents she'd written?"

Manuel smiled and smoothed his hair, staring at me with eyes that betrayed how enthused he was about his own theories.

"There's a reference in one of García del Campo's documents—he was the quartermaster of her chamber—that mentions a document holder containing 'all of Her Majesty's writing.' Think about it. 'All of Her Majesty's writings.' The way he calls them 'writings' shows he didn't know how to qualify what Juana had written, and 'all' means there were a lot of them, so I think Juana wrote quite a bit. We knew she could, after all. She'd studied with Beatriz Galindo. Her written Latin was as good as her Spanish. And what would Juana write, Lucía? She wasn't religious. One of the grounds for calling her mad was her lack of devotion. Since her early days in Flanders, she hardly went to services, to mass. She had intelligent friends. Erasmus of Rotterdam, for one. I've always thought that his *The Praise of Folly*, though it's dedicated to Sir Thomas More, was a sort of homage to Juana, a vindication of her. It was one of the books she had on her nightstand when she died. It's not unreasonable to think that she might have taken solace in writing."

"You're right," I said, admiring the queen. "Take me to the room upstairs," I begged. "Please? I was always good at working out puzzles. If you'd just let me help you. Two minds are better than one."

"You think you're the heroine in a novel, that you're going to find the hidden treasure, don't you? Keep in mind that writers who write thrillers build their imaginary plots very carefully. I've seen it done. They assemble them as if it were a mathematical equation: first x happens, resulting in y, and so on. It's all tied together so that cause and effect follow one another in an orderly fashion, but real life doesn't work that way."

"But I was the one who noticed the difference between your grandfather's study and the way the room is now. You didn't pick up on that."

"You had me obsessing over that clue like a fool. And you were right. There's no obvious logic or reason to explain why they made the room smaller. There's a dividing wall. I found a way through it, and it leads to a narrow space, but there's no trunk in it. Just a bunch of old junk, broken objects that no one's bothered to throw away. But you win. I've already lost the game. Maybe you can see what I missed."

He produced a key from his pocket and held it up. It was a copy of Águeda's. She saw herself as the only guardian of the Denia treasures, but he had as much right as she did. We'd wait for her to go to bed. His aunt had always taken sleeping pills, he said. That's why she hadn't heard his nighttime expeditions. She would never have allowed them, he added.

"After having lived alone with all those things for so long, she feels like they're an extension of herself. And she's never liked to be touched."

We crept up after midnight. Manuel took a flashlight and some candles from one of the kitchen drawers. The third floor was warmer than the rest of the house. On the first two floors, the heating barely made a difference in the January cold that sneaked in through the cracks in the windows. It was very dark. The humming of the dehumidifiers was hardly audible, but I found it comforting. I didn't like the idea of going into the room at that time of night. But we went in. Manuel flicked the switch and locked the door from the inside. The ceiling lamp cast a dim light. We crossed the room and went over to the far wall. It all looked the same to me, but Manuel walked over to one of the glass-front cases. Inside was a beautiful image of the Virgin's Immaculate Conception and other gold and silver liturgical objects inlaid with precious stones. I helped him pull the case back from the wall. I couldn't see anything different behind there; just the same wood panels that bordered the room, each one topped with a rounded molding.

"This is it," he said. "This is where you go through."

Manuel took a chisel from the floor and slipped it beneath the molding, then started to pry at it gently.

"It's not exactly a door. It took me ages to figure out that the molding in this panel isn't just decoration, like the others. It can be pried open, and the panel comes all the way off. Not as sophisticated as a secret door, but you can imagine that when it gave and I saw that it could be removed, I couldn't contain myself. I was convinced I had found the secret hiding place." He was still levering away with the chisel, and soon the molding, which seemed to have a pressure fit gave way with a crack, and the wood panel came all the way off.

Manuel lifted it off and put it on one side. I felt a gust of stale air, and dust hit my nose and eyes. I coughed.

Hoisting up a leg, he slipped through the opening and then helped me through. Rather than a room, it was more like a false-bottom suitcase, a narrow space, no wider than the two little vaulted windows covered over with black paper, the windows from the picture. Broken chairs, latticework, doors, and curtain rods were all pushed up against the back wall, which was covered in a layer of grime. A pile of cardboard boxes sat in front of the windows, with a series of iron fittings leaning up against them, and a small, round table where Manuel sat the candles. The collection of useless, broken objects lined the room in a disorderly fashion, amid dust and cobwebs. A frayed tapestry hung on the wall. The darkness, cramped space, and stale air made me feel breathless and claustrophobic. Wanting to run out of there as fast as possible, I covered my nose. Dust billowed up in clouds the second we touched anything. I stepped very carefully. Curiosity forced my body to move against its will, to overcome my discomfort. I walked the short length of the room and went over to Manuel, who was poking around by some leather suitcases that must have belonged to his grandparents.

"We should open all the boxes," I said. "And the suitcases."

"I already have. There's nothing here. I went over everything you see inch by inch. What do you think I've been doing these past few nights? I'm telling you, there's nothing here," he whispered, as if anyone could hear us.

"But don't you think that's odd? Why would they go to the trouble of dividing the room? Who needs an attic when the house is so big? It stinks in here," I added. "Old clothes."

"There are a few overcoats in one of the boxes. And a rat's nest. I think that's what smells so bad."

"Yuck!" I felt a shiver run through me. It wasn't an unbearable smell, but it was bitter and unrelenting, and if I thought about it I knew I wouldn't be able to breathe.

In the semidarkness, Manuel swung the flashlight back and forth. The tapestry was a Virgin of the Annunciation. I could just make it out in the flashlight's dim beam. A woman's face with a fixed stare. I lit a candle.

"Careful," Manuel said, turning around. "What are you doing?"

"I want to look at the tapestry. That flashlight is not bright enough."

Manuel glanced down at his flashlight and then back at me, offended. It was old, aluminum, and very weak.

"I've had this since I was a kid," he said, shining it on the wall. "Anyway, what about the tapestry? It's all frayed and faded. I'm surprised they haven't thrown it out."

"Exactly," I replied. "And it's nailed to the wall."

"Probably harder to get it down than just leave it where it was."

I drew all the way up to it with my candle.

"And look," I said, "it's a Virgin of the Annunciation with dark hair and eyes. I've never seen one like that. They're always blond."

"The tapestry," Manuel whispered behind me, finally taking my hint, then getting more excited. "The hole they took Catalina out by was covered by a tapestry. That's why Juana didn't know about the tunnel they'd dug. But, of course, I kept wanting to see a trunk, Lucía. Like an idiot, I expected to see the trunk. But wait. Let me think a minute." He lit a cigarette and inhaled desperately, as if it were oxygen. The smell of tobacco was comforting there. "It's so obvious, really, isn't it? The hiding place behind the tapestry. Ages ago, I looked behind every single one in the house, behind every painting too. And then what happens? I get this far and then it doesn't even occur to me here. Just like it didn't occur to me that they'd built this wall to hide the obvious."

He'd gone into a state of rapture, contemplating the wall.

The tapestry was nailed to a wooden frame that was attached to the wall. Manuel felt all the way around it. He'd have to use the chisel to get the nails out, he said. He handed me the flashlight. It flickered on and off, petering out slightly.

"Shit," he said. "I didn't think to change the batteries."

His hands were shaking slightly. His cigarette dangled from the corner of his lips. It upset me to see him so worked up. I was nervous too, and my hands were cold. I felt like an archaeologist on the verge of a great discovery, but his excitement seemed to border on anguish. He yanked at the tapestry urgently, as if he were clawing desperately from inside a coffin, having been buried alive. What would happen if, rather than an exorcism, the find resulted in a reiteration of the curse that had plagued his family for so long? To come face-to-face with Juana's condemnation would be daunting, despite the centuries gone by, despite the fact that his blood held almost no trace of the Denias who'd imprisoned her. I was scared that this obsession would haunt us all: me, because of the child I was carrying, Manuel and Águeda because of the power they ascribed to the past. The nails were coming out. Dust tickled my nose. Suddenly, the flashlight went out altogether.

"Damn it!" Manuel shouted. "Hang on."

I passed him a candle, which he lit with his lighter. Then we lit two more and dripped candle wax onto one of the old tables to hold them down. Finally, all of the nails on one side were out. Manuel held up a candle so we could see into the space behind it. I could hear his surprise, his breath.

"What can you see, Manuel?"

"There's a door!" he cried. "A door," he repeated.

He was panting.

"A door!" I couldn't believe it.

We had to take the tapestry all the way off the wall. His impatience was contagious. We were both sweating. Hot wax was dripping onto my fingers and burning my skin. I don't know how much time passed before I helped him yank the tapestry off the wall and heave it over to one side. A narrow door stood in front of us. Manuel pushed it. It opened into a short, nearly circular space that seemed to have been hollowed out of one corner of the house and ended at a few steps that led down. We must have been in a really ancient part of the house. The walls were rough and uneven. Manuel was talking to himself, something about when the third floor was remodeled. His grandfather must have known about this, he whispered. We crept toward the stairs. Manuel had one candle. I had another one. I was leaning my hand into the darkness looking for support when I touched what felt like a wood engraving.

"Manuel," I said.

He stopped. We both saw the niche in the wall at the same time; it had a wood cover carved with Mudejar patterns. Crisscrossed over it were two narrow cords and a wax seal stamped in red: a coat of arms: five stars and a wood beam, the Denia coat of arms. Manuel held the candle up to the wax seal and touched it, incredulous. Beads of sweat were forming on his white skin. I was shivering. He handed me his candle and yanked on the cords. I closed my eyes. When I opened them, I saw that the cover to the niche was open, and there, inside it, was the trunk.

It was more like a small chest, covered in dark, almost black leather, with three lighter, vertical bands all the way around it. It was as if it had come from the dead, rather than just the past, like a strange replica of Juana's coffin in the monarch's crypt in Granada, resting beneath the sculpted tombstone of her parents, the king and queen. I clapped my hand over my mouth, trying to contain my irrational fears.

"Don't touch it, Manuel," I said. He looked at me like I was mad. "We know where it is now. Let's just leave it, some things are better left unknown."

He pushed me aside and then handed me his candle. Wax trickled down, burning me.

"Put that down and go get a few more," he commanded.

I dripped wax on the floor and stuck the candle into it, then ran to get the two or three that we'd left on the table. Manuel shouldn't open that trunk, I thought, thinking of curses and spells in horror stories, archaeologists who died after discovering secrets in Egyptian tombs. I felt ridiculous, superstitious. I came back with the candles, and he handed me his lighter, telling me to light them and prop them up on the floor. Manuel's face had transformed. He was concentrating intently, but he also had a smile that seemed to have come from his childhood. He gazed at the trunk lovingly as he slid it toward him, carefully, delicately, as if he were holding a hand that had been reaching out to him for centuries, a hand, I thought, that could just as easily yank him back into the past forever.

Once the trunk was on the floor, I held the candle while he rushed to open the tiny gold-and-rose-colored locks. He was babbling to himself, unintelligible sounds that only he could understand. I felt like a voyeur, witnessing his unbridled love for Juana; if it wasn't madness, it certainly resembled it. He loved her the way Juana loved Philippe, a love beyond death. A love of death, maybe. Manuel wished I were Juana, but in reality he was the one who resembled her. Not the Juana he wanted me to embody, but Juana the Mad who'd been imprisoned by her ancestors.

Manuel pulled two folders from the trunk, one looked modern and one ancient. He sat down on the floor in that cramped space, and I followed suit. Like him, I couldn't take my eyes off the folders. The passageway, the stairs, my curiosity to know where they led, would have to wait. Paler than normal even, Manuel looked like a man possessed. I don't think he was even aware of my presence. Beside him, silent, expectant, terrified, I trembled for other reasons too. After flipping through the newer folder that held who knows what documents, he opened the older one. I saw several sheets of parchment and got the chills. I recognized that distinctive medieval calligraphy, slightly faded, the words scrunched together with no spaces, no punctuation.

While he was absorbed in the text, I leaned against the cold wall and rubbed my eyes. I felt a deep, sweeping sadness pressing down on my brain.

"Manuel, I'm here. Read it to me too. Read it out loud."

"All right," he said. "Close your eyes."

I T'S JANUARY. 1525. A COLD WIND RISES THROUGH THE BATTLE- ments making the bells of San Antolín toll lightly. Night has fallen over the Duero. The frost-covered water glimmers in the moonlight. Catalina has left to marry the king of Portugal. The ambassadors took her away, sobbing. My daughter, that flesh of mine living outside my flesh, without which I am no longer Juana nor anyone who wishes to live, has taken her memories of this prison to the royal court where she will soon learn the deceits of liberty. We were free here, she and I, amid these towers. Locked up behind these walls and belfries that are home to storks, we lifted up our hearts, Sursum Corda, and saw with no eyes, heard with no ears, ate with no mouths, wakeful while the world slept. But she will do well, my Catalina. I do not deceive myself into thinking that this slow death is life. Meanwhile, I will start my journey, the journey that will end on the other side of the Styx in the land of the dead where my parents live, where I will find Phillipe, my brother Juan, my sister Isabel. Nobody there will attempt to strip me of my sanity because power disputes will be done forever.

I know I shall live a long time. Life clings to me as one of its own. It recognizes me, like a cloud does water. Further on, my granchildren perhaps will take pity on me, the sons and daughters of Ferdinand, María, Isabel, Leonor, and Catalina, my offspring. I will take whatever they might wish to grant me and continue to rebel against the Denias who, despite being closest to the beating sounds of my heart and my words, refuse to see me for who I am and choose to view me in the dark light of their own fantasies.

Mine has not been a placid existence. I came into this world with too much impetus, with my chest laid bare. My thirst for air and space confounded those who live ganged up in pens and stables occupied with fattening their flesh or their pockets. I dread the long lonely days that await me, the battles I will still have to fight against confessors and priests who will try to tame my soul, since they were unable to tame my body. I am aware of the clerics that already have snuck into my room to practice exorcisms while I sleep. Because they are incapable and cannot understand me, they presume Satan inhabits me, that he lays with me at night, that it is he with whom I quench the legendary passions of my flesh. Little can I do to straighten out their tangled thoughts. It pains me though to imagine the dim echoes of the bells that will toll on the day of my death. Oblivion has already begun to grow around me like ivy covering ancient ruins. Juana the Mad, they'll say. That deranged queen, the one who went mad for love. They won't even acknowledge me for the queens and kings that issued forth from my womb: Charles I of Spain and V of Germany; Leonor, queen of France; Isabel, queen of Denmark; María, queen of Hungary; Catalina, queen of Portugal; and my little Ferdinand, emperor of Germany. A long, spiraling lineage coming out of me will leave its imprint in Europe and the vast lands of the New World. But all of that will be of no consequence to those who will hear the funeral bells or or see the sad, little cortege that will escort my remains. It is of no consequence here in in my tiny, dark room in Tordesillas, with the woman who embroiders by the door and the one who sits outside, tallying up each one of my sighs. They have gone through such lengths in order to keep me deaf and dumb; they fear that I might escape, wander through the village and speak to the villagers, that the court might remember I exist! Strange that they can be so afraid of a madwoman and choose to guard her so! They have chosen to bury me alive! As for me, I have no choice but to leave this imprecation for the centuries, these scrolls that I will hide, that I will keep writing, this ink that will be my blood speaking to the future.

Perhaps I am mad. I have no doubt they will convince me of it one day, that I will end up hallucinating, seeing cats. One can end up believing in lies if the lies are repeated incessantly, especially if they are all one hears. Mad was, no doubt, my passion for Philippe. It was certainly madness to love him like I did. But love does not choose its object according to reason or convenience. Love beseeches love, that is what love does. Fire burns, but so does ice, and I chose the flame. I am neither the first nor the last woman who loves without measure, who bangs her fists against a door that won't open, who pounces on a chest whose breath she needs to breathe. And I won't be the last who sets down her heart like a pennant in the ground she has carefully seeded and watered, and who keeps vigil from the highest tower, arms and steeds at the ready, so that the enemy armies shall think twice before flaunting their blond manes in the wind, or unsheathing the smiles they hide behind iridescent fans. I fought every one of my battles. I waged war for all those whom I loved. It was for me that I did not fight for, and now I shall struggle to find liberty within my silence, within the vast fields of my indefatigable imagination, which will take me away from here to places where neither the Denias nor their descendants will ever manage to capture me. Perhaps I will lose myself as I wander through meadows and reedbeds, through the wide-open terrain of my imagination. So much have I lost that I no longer care. Yet I have one last endeavor: to win myself for myself. And I will prevail, even if no herald announces it, even if the centuries come crashing down on me like rumbling crumbling walls. Who will dare? I shall dare.

uana went back to her silence. I opened my eyes brimming with tears. Manuel exhaled deeply and lit another cigarette.

"My God, our intuition barely caught up with her," I said.

He turned back to the folders. I saw him pick up the newer one. Suddenly, I was doubtful.

"Manuel, what you just read is what Juana wrote?"

He didn't answer. He was holding a legal-size sheet of typewritten paper. He looked at it and raised his hand to his forehead, again and again.

"What's the matter, Manuel? What's wrong?"

He stared at me, wide-eyed. In the candlelight he looked transparent, his lips blue.

"This really is a night of surprises, Lucía. Do you want me to keep reading? Do you want me to read out this certificate that states that Águeda is actually my *mother*?"

"Águeda? What do you mean?"

"Come on," he said. "Come with me. I have a feeling I know where this staircase leads." He snatched my hand frantically. He wasn't letting go. I followed him down the short hallway to the dark stairs, which we felt our way down, me asking all the while, What's wrong? Where are we going? I was afraid of his urgency, of his words. We reached the last step.

We must have been on the second floor. Another door. He pushed it. It didn't budge. He kicked it. And suddenly, we stood in the semidarkness of Águeda's room. She was sitting up in bed, an expression of sheer horror on her face, covering her mouth, having been shaken so suddenly from the deep sleep she drugged herself into each night.

Manuel let go of me. Águeda was staring at us. I stood up against the wall in the darkness, aghast, trying to make sense of what I saw before me: adorning the walls of Águeda's bedroom, like decor in an actress's dressing room, were dresses that looked like they were from Juana's time. Three, four, five, maybe more.

Manuel, meanwhile, rushed to her bed and threw the stack of papers on her lap.

"Would you care to explain this? You *have to* explain it," he shouted, and then snatched up the papers again, pointing at her. "It says here that you're my mother. This certificate says that you gave birth to a child the very day of my birthday. What does that mean?" he repeated, pacing back and forth before her. "More deceit? What is it, some sort of genetic defect? Good *God*! How many lies will I have to unravel in this family? Why, Águeda, why has it become such a pattern?" His voice was deep, hoarse, almost howling. "My God, you can't be my mother! You have been so many things to me, but please, you cannot possibly be my mother!"

Águeda was whimpering, her face taut, totally distorted.

"Damn your curiosity, Manuel. Damn it!"

Manuel was livid. Calmer, but at the same time more enraged. I didn't even know what was being hinted at, but I felt nauseated. I had to get out of there, I thought, had to breathe.

Águeda spoke. I didn't move a muscle.

"Let me stand up," she said, getting out of bed, pulling on her dressing gown, her slippers, smoothing her hair, turning on the bedside lamp. "Maybe we're all wicked people, but the woman you thought was your mother—Aurora—admitted it. She had the bad blood of the Denias in her veins, she deceived people without scruples, she lived a dissolute life, intent on making the most of every day, every minute, saying that for her there was no past and no future. It took a long time before I understood her, and by then it was too late, she was gone. I couldn't see that I was no better than her. But back then, when I was young, your *Aunt Águeda*," she said sarcastically, "was the good girl, the introvert, the studious one, the obedient one. Like you, Lucía," she said, looking at me. "I was the apple of my father's eye, the one who straightened up his study, his papers, the one who discussed history with him, and then one day grew up and got pregnant. It happens. As you know. And to salvage the family's honor, my parents decided that, since Aurora was already a lost cause, she would be blamed for it. They hid me away until the child was born, and then, Manuel, they passed you off as *her* son. What difference did it make, they said, if I was going to be the one to raise you anyhow? They spread a rumor about Aurora's fall from grace, and they themselves took it so seriously that they disowned her and abandoned her to her fate. And you know how she ended up."

Engrossed in her story, paralyzed by it, I leaned up against the wall. It was trembling. I'm imagining things, I thought, it must be my body that's trembling.

"Tell me who my father was," Manuel commanded his aunt. They were staring at each other.

"No, Manuel. I can't do that," she replied. Her face was a mask of horror.

"Tell me."

Águeda ran from the room.

Manuel ran after her, and I followed suit. The second we were out in the hallway I realized what the vibration I'd felt was. The house was on fire. The third floor had gone up in flames. The walls were making a terrible groaning sound. I couldn't believe how fast it was happening, how quickly the fire was spreading. The burning smell was unbearable. Chunks of blazing wood were beginning to fall. The house was filling with smoke. The roof was on fire, it was going up like a torch.

"Manuel, my God, the manuscripts!"

I was going in circles, not knowing what to do. Manuel too had stopped short. It was as if he couldn't react. Suddenly, he turned around and ran back toward Águeda's room. A second later, I heard the locks being deactivated.

"Go, Lucía, run," he said, absurdly calm and determined. "Go. I'm going to find Águeda. I can't leave her in here. I'll see if I can save the manuscripts." And he pushed me, shoved me, toward the back door.

"No, Manuel. Come with me."

"I'll be right there. Now go, run," and he gave me one final shove. I thought the house would keep standing until the firemen arrived. I ran toward Recoletos, the main avenue, but stayed on the sidewalk, as close to the house as possible.

The flames kept spreading. The crashing sounds were deafening. Beams fell, walls crumbled like paper. The house roared like an animal. In the distance, I heard the sirens approaching. I prayed, implored the firemen to hurry up. Flames were shooting up everywhere and Manuel was not coming out. He wasn't coming out. There was no sign of Manuel. Nothing. No sign of Manuel. Or his mother.

CHAPTER 27

I've seen pictures of the fire. It went down in Madrid history as a tragedy in which fabulous works of art were lost forever. When the sun came up, the house was still on fire and onlookers crowded around to see the damage firsthand. Dressed in my long, red, square-necked velvet gown, wearing Juana's cross on my chest, I was in a state of shock. All I could do was replay the scenes from that night in my mind, a kaleidoscope of choppy images dancing before my eyes. I stood motionless, glued to the sidewalk, trembling from both cold and fear. I told one of the firemen I was a friend of the marquess and her nephew, and he handed me a blanket. Around six in the morning, they brought Águeda and Manuel out in black body bags. I wondered if any part of Manuel had been saved from incineration, if, like my father, a hand or an arm had remained intact. I pictured him chasing Águeda through the huge house, her trying to save things from the fire, him maybe running back for Juana's manuscripts. Had Águeda revealed his father's identity? Was that what had killed them both? Was Manuel's grandfather also his father, did that explain the passageway from his office and her bedroom? What had happened between Manuel and his aunt? Why could he not accept that she was his mother, why was he so horrified at the thought of it?

I wandered down Recoletos for ages. Every possible explanation I came up with seemed more horrifying than the last. I had been saved.

Maybe from a fate worse than death. But the fire haunted me. I couldn't get rid of it, couldn't stop seeing it, stop smelling it. My eyes were still burning. Even in the fresh dawn air, I couldn't get free of the soot, the smoke. One blaze had left me an orphan, now another left me as the sole custodian of the last, innocent Denia descendant. I wondered if the baby now growing in my womb would somehow, without seeing, without hearing, sense the strange universe it came from: a father obsessed by a love as mad as that of the woman he was obsessed with, in love with ghosts, both of them. And grandmother Águeda, a captive in the prison of her undisclosed offense, unable to claim her son as hers. Such dreadful ancestry, steeped in lies, silence, and captivity.

WITHOUT KNOWING WHERE I WAS GOING, I ENDED UP AT THE FOUNtain of Neptune and then in the lobby of the Hotel Palace. I took advantage of my privileges, my grandfather's name. I asked them to call him, to authorize payment for a room. The concierge could not help staring at my outfit. I am an actress, I finally managed to tell him. I have been playing Queen Juana's role in a play. Juana the Mad? he asked. No, I said, Juana of Castile.

When I was sure that my pregnancy was not one of Manuel's fabrications, I debated as to whether or not to end it. After what I'd been through, I thought it might be best if I put an end to the Denia line. I suffered over Manuel, but I also feared the traces of his ancestors feeding off my blood. In the end, it was Mother Luisa Magdalena, who came to the hotel when I called her, who made me see the baby as a vindication of Juana. After all, the baby's father had died because of his obsession, trying to right the wrongs of history. His daughter would be a clean slate, a new page, she would have another outlook: the one I'd provide for her, the history that Juana's brave, unrelenting spirit had revealed to me, the voice that Manuel had brought to life from within me.

"It's as if you were pregnant with Juana," the nun told me. "Think of it that way. A Juana who will be loved, who will never be locked up."

I said we didn't know that it was a girl. It is, it is, she said. You'll see.

A few days later, Mother Luisa Magdalena said good-bye to me at the airport.

My daughter was born in New York.

❋ I HAVE BROUGHT MY DAUGHTER JUANA HERE TO TORDESILLAS TO show her the place where the queen lived, the same queen her mother so often talks about, the one her father loved. This is where she was held prisoner, I tell her. She flaps her arms. She wants to chase the birds on the balcony. She stares at me with her blue eyes. The wind lifts her skirt and she giggles. Look, I say, you can see the storks' nests on the roofs, look at their long legs, see that one flying off, spreading her wings over the river.

While she plays on the balcony at the top of the church's spiral staircase, I sit on the little stone bench in San Antolín's tower, the same one Juana must have sat on to let her soul follow the wind out the window.

Now I will be the one to gather the memories of her reign. The schoolgirl who used to write letters at study hall in a neat, round hand, the one who was captivated by the bridges that her words built and the way they took her out of that tiny, constricted space, will collect the threads, exorcize her demons, and write another story, another truth to defy the lies.

She is the one who still owns the red velvet dress. And who wears it some nights, the nights when she remembers Manuel, and Philippe.

Santa Monica—Managua, January 2005

The many contradictory accounts of Juana of Castile's mental health and lucidity that are found in firsthand historical references have allowed historians—males for the most part—ample freedom to interpret the queen's behavior according to their own subjective perception and—why not say it?—prejudices. That is what prompted me—as a twenty-first-century woman armed with a different understanding of the motives and reasons that lead us, women, to act one way or another—to try to imagine Juana's inner life from a female perspective and to draw the conclusions this novel suggests.

In the process of researching this book, I found that many analyses of the illness that might have afflicted the queen concluded she was schizophrenic. Nevertheless, none of the psychiatrists I consulted agreed with this diagnosis. Schizophrenia does not improve or worsen depending on whether a patient is or is not in a pleasant environment. The data that is available on Juana shows that, when she was treated well, the queen went through long periods "with no episodes of madness." This does not fit with a schizophrenic diagnosis. Juana's crises— when she refused to eat, bathe, etc.—always corresponded to times when she was forced to accept others' decisions or restrictions, or was separated from her children. They happen to coincide, curiously enough, with her rebellions. This is not standard schizophrenic behavior. According to those who so generously offered me their medical interpretations, Juana might have been bipolar, suffering from a manic-depressive condition, or she might simply have suffered from chronic depression, which would be no wonder, given her circumstances.

Personally, I think that any woman with a strong sense of self, confronted by the abuse and the arbitrary injustices she had to withstand, forced to accept her powerlessness in the face of an authoritarian system, would become depressed. We all have our own ways of showing depression, and it is easy to see how Juana's lack of inhibition when it came to expressing dissatisfaction and unhappiness would be interpreted as madness, especially at a time when repression was the norm.

And then too, as I have already mentioned, it's important to consider the standpoint of those who were doing the interpreting. My reading of the documents, essays, and books on Juana points to the existence—even among male historians—of an unresolved controversy as to whether her behavior was pathological or simply the result of the tangled web of intricate conspiracies she was forcibly embroiled in. For the majority of scholars to lean toward the madness theory is not surprising, given the light in which female historical figures have been seen for such a long time.

It's obvious that Juana did not have the wisdom, political savvy, or willpower that her mother did. It's also true, however, that her circumstances could not have been more unfavorable. Like Juana *la Beltraneja,* who ended up cast off in a convent despite her legitimate claim to the throne of Castile, Juana of Castile fell victim to interests of State and the ambitions of those conspiring against her.

At least, as she was being cast off, she kicked and screamed enough so that, centuries later, we can now make sense of her unrelenting rebellion.

ALTHOUGH THE PLOT OF THIS NOVEL IS FICTITIOUS, JUANA'S HIStory is not. The facts have been reconstructed based on existing historical data, taken from original sources and from the ample bibliography provided by scholars to whom I am very much in debt.

The information I found in one or another account often showed discrepancies in the dates and the names of places. I chose the dates and places that seemed best supported by documents from the time. I also took a few liberties by simplifying the retelling of events whose details were unnecessary to the story's aims. For reasons of literary convenience, I also decided to locate Francisco Pradilla's painting, *Juana la Loca at Her Husband's Coffin,* in the Prado Museum, when in fact it is at the Casón del Buen Retiro.

ADDITIONAL SOURCES

Following are additional texts that are held at the Simancas Archive, which may be of interest to the reader. One is the speech Juana gave the Comuneros on September 24, 1520, the only long speech the queen is on record as ever having given, at her first hearing with the Comuneros' Council during their rebellion against Charles I of Spain and V of Germany, when they attempted to put her on the throne and end the imprisonment she had been enduring since 1509.

The other is an excerpt from Catalina Redonda, Juana's washerwoman, in her account of the hiding place and contents of the trunk (that Lucía and Manuel find in the novel) whose disappearance—in line with the plot—I attribute to the Denias.

Santa Monica, January 2005

❊ JUANA'S SPEECH TO THE COMUNEROS

After God saw fit to take my lady—the Catholic Queen—to Heaven, I always heeded and obeyed my lord, the King, my father, husband of the Queen; and with him I was without care, because I knew that no one would dare undertake evil deeds. And after I found out that God had taken him, I was very sorry indeed and wished not to have learned the news, and wished he were still alive, and that wherever he was, he lived, because his life was more important than mine. But since I had to learn this news, I wish I had learned of it earlier, that I might have remedied everything that I.*

I have a great love for all people and any harm or injustice they might suffer weighs heavily upon me. And for so long I have been surrounded by evil men and women who have told me lies and falsehoods and dealt me only trickery when I would have wished to take part in all that affected me, but since the King, my lord, chose to put me here, perhaps because of she who came to take the place of the Queen, my lady, or perhaps due to other considerations of which His Highness is aware, I have been unable to do so. And when I learned of the foreigners who had arrived and were in Castile, I was greatly aggrieved, and thought that they had come to see to certain matters for my children, but it was not so. And I am full of admiration that you have not taken revenge against those who have wronged you, as anyone would, because all things good please me and all things nefarious weigh upon me. If I did not act, it was to ensure my children not be harmed, neither here nor there, and I cannot believe that they have departed, though I am told with all certainty that they have departed. You must watch out for them, although I believe none would undertake any evil, given that I am a lady and second or third proprietary [queen], and thus did not deserve to be treated as I have been, for I am daughter of a King and Queen. And I rejoice to hear of your attempts to remedy wrongs that have been committed, for if you did not, it would weigh upon your conscience. Thus I entrust you to act upon it. As for me, I will endeavor to act, wherever I am able. And if I cannot, it shall only be because I must one day soothe my heart and overcome the death of the King, my lord; though as long as I am able, I will endeavor to do so. And so that not everyone pays call at once, I ask those of you who are here now to name among yourselves four who know the most about these matters to come and meet with me, to tell me everything, and I will listen, and I will address you, and I will hear out your case, whenever necessary, and I will do all that I can.

* It appears that the scribe failed to make note of the end of the sentence ("that I *can*").

What is known is that in a room in Her Highness's quarters was a trunk like that described in the declaration, in an Anzeo case, and Her Highness ordered this witness to bring out said trunk when she wished to open it because Her Highness had the key, and in this witness's opinion said trunk was quite heavy, and as Her Highness required that I turn my back when she opened it, this witness could never see what it contained, but could only see that it was filled to the brim with bundles tied with white cloth, and this witness knows not what said bundles contained and saw only one stone which seemed to this witness to be a diamond set in gold, as big as a thumbnail, with a handle enameled in gold to hold it by, and the last time Her Highness asked [sic] *this witness to bring out the trunk was around the day of San Miguel in September of 1554, eight days before or after* [. . .] *and that when the inventory of said declaration was taken, and eight days before Her Highness passed away this witness could not find said trunk and said so to those who were undertaking the inventory* [. . .] *and this witness knows that no one went into the place where said trunk was kept without Her Highness's permission nor could anyone enter without Her Highness seeing. . . .*